D1499049

THE DAY BEFORE

THE DAY BEFORE

THE DAY BEFORE

LIANA BROOKS

This is a work of fiction. Names, characters, places, and incidents are the product of the author's imagination or are used fictitiously, and are not to be construed as real. Any resemblance to actual events, locales, organizations, or persons, living or dead, is entirely coincidental.

[illegible faded text block]

HA   CASS COUNTY PUBLIC LIBRARY
      400 E. MECHANIC
      HARRISONVILLE, MO 64701

HARPER
VOYAGER
IMPULSE

An imprint of HarperCollins Publishers

0 0022 0523130 7

This is a work of fiction. Names, characters, places, and incidents are products of the author's imagination or are used fictitiously and are not to be construed as real. Any resemblance to actual events, locales, organizations, or persons, living or dead, is entirely coincidental.

THE DAY BEFORE. Copyright © 2015 by Liana Brooks. All rights reserved under International and Pan-American Copyright Conventions. By payment of the required fees, you have been granted the nonexclusive, nontransferable right to access and read the text of this e-book on screen. No part of this text may be reproduced, transmitted, decompiled, reverse-engineered, or stored in or introduced into any information storage and retrieval system, in any form or by any means, whether electronic or mechanical, now known or hereafter invented, without the express written permission of HarperCollins e-books.

EPub Edition APRIL 2015 ISBN: 9780062407658
Print Edition ISBN: 9780062407672

10 9 8 7 6 5 4 3 2 1

To the painted-on pants.
Thanks for the memories.

CHAPTER 1

The late Dr. Everett's Many-World interpretation of
quantum mechanics is notable for two reasons. One,
it is laughably simple. Two, it is almost correct. Had
Dr. Everett recalled that there is no particle without
a wave, our research would now be an exercise in
tedium. Alas, it is the failing of generations past that
they did not consider the wave form and thus antici-
pate the eventual collapse of iterations not held stable
by Pointer States, or einselection nodes.

~ **Excerpt from Lectures on the Movement
of Time by Dr. Abdul Emir I1–20740413**

*Friday May 17, 2069
Alabama District 3
Commonwealth of North America*

With an asthmatic wheeze, the engine died. It figured. Stuck in a man's craw, it did. This truck had been
his daddy's and his pappy's, and before the Commonwealth government forced him to replace the diesel
engine with the newfangled water doohickey, he was
certain he'd pass the truck on to his son.

He'd been playing under the hood of trucks since he was six, and now he was stranded. Embarrassing, that's what it was. He climbed out of the cab to check the engine out of habit. The ice-blue block of modern fuel efficiency stared back. Three hundred bucks it'd cost him, straight from his pocket.

Oh, there was a government subsidy, all right. A priority list. Major population centers, they said. Unite the countries of the Commonwealth on a timeline, they said. And what did all that mean?

It meant the damn Yankees got upgraded cities and free cars before the ink was dry on the Constitution, and what about the little man? Nobody thought about the working class. No one cared about a man covered in oil and grease anymore.

He thumbed his cell phone on. No reception. Figured.

So much for the era of new prosperity. He'd hoof it. There was a little town about five miles down the road, where he could call Ricky to bring a tow truck. It would have been cheaper to pay the diesel fines than get all this fixed.

Off schedule. Over budget. Son of a—

He stared at the distant trees. Well, it wasn't going to get any cooler.

He grabbed his wallet and keys from the cab of his truck. The tree line looked like a good spot to answer a call from nature, then he'd see if there was a short-cut through to town. A meadowlark sang. Not a bad day for a hike. Would've been better if it weren't so dammed hot, but at least the humidity was low. He

THE DAY BEFORE 3

wouldn't like to walk in a summer monsoon, not at his age, with arthritis playing up.

Under a sprawling oak, he unzipped his pants. As an afterthought, he glanced down to make sure he wouldn't stir up a hill of fire ants.

A hand lay next to his boots.

He blinked, zipped his pants slowly, and turned around. "Hello?"

Cicadas chirped in answer.

"Are you drunk?" The quiet field that looked so peaceful only moments before was now eerily sinister. He nudged the hand with his foot. It was swollen and pale and crusted with blood, just like a prop out of a horror movie.

Maybe it was a good idea to *run* to the next town.

They say a coward dies a thousand deaths, a brave man only one. Where underpaid, overstressed probationary agents fell in that spectrum, Sam wasn't sure, but she'd bet her last dollar she was headed down the slippery slope of a thousand cowardly deaths. Any sensible person wouldn't have picked up their work phone after eight on a Friday night, or at least would have the spine to tell their boss they weren't going to work on the weekend.

Which was exactly what Senior Agent Marrins wanted Sam to do.

On a curving old road between two towns untouched by a century of change, in a place where streetlights were still considered new technology, some broke-down trucker had found a body. Three miles west, and it would have been someone else's problem. In any other district, it would have been the senior agent's problem, and she would have tagged along to get the work experience needed for promotion.

Sam didn't work in any other district, though. She worked in Senior Agent Marrins's. Which was why she was driving out to this rural stretch of road.

The wash of the Milky Way glittering overhead was beautiful if you were into that sort of thing. Sam would have preferred the gaudy show of lights in any major city in any major first-world country. "Saint Jude, pray for me who am so miserable," she whispered as the crime scene came into view. Three police cars, an eighteen-wheeler, and an ambulance . . . not your typical Friday night in Alabama District 3.

An unfamiliar police officer knocked on the window and made a circular motion. "Ma'am, this is a crime scene. I'm going to ask you to keep moving."

"Officer, I'm Agent Samantha Rose from the Commonwealth Bureau of Investigation, and I'm going to ask you who the hell you think would drive out this far from civilization at this time of night."

He blinked at her.

"Precisely. Would you please step away from my car and call the officer in charge? Thanks." Men. They weren't all idiots, but she'd seen little evidence that these illiterate hicks could prove it.

"Rose?"

Sam closed her car door and looked around. "Detective Altin?" A man who towered a full foot over her should not have been able to hide.

"Behind you."

She spun and almost tripped into the older man. "I thought you were going to the movies with your wife."

"She took the kids instead. Twenty-five years married to the force, she'll forgive me." Altin's teeth flashed as he grinned. "You just won me a bet. The sergeant from Cherokee County was certain Marrins would come out himself."

"Has the sergeant *met* Agent Marrins?" Sam asked. "The only time that man hustles is when there's a fresh box of donuts at the secretary's desk. I live on this side of the district. Marrins wrote this off as effective delegation of resources."

"I thought Marrins would at least try to get this on his resume. The last time we had a homicide where there were actual questions was that horror-house case that hit all the national news stations, and that was over a decade ago. Isn't that how the bureau promotes?" Altin's grin widened.

Sam rolled her eyes. "Yeah, but a dumped clone isn't a homicide investigation. It's littering."

"Who said it was a clone?"

"Agent Marrins."

"He's psychic now?" The detective raised a skeptical eyebrow.

"He said the police called him about a dumped clone, and I needed to sort it out."

Altin shook his head. "I wouldn't jump to conclusions. People might be eager to dump their clones before the Caye Law goes into effect, and they have to pay a tax on them. But there are organ-donation stations that take the clones for free. No one's going to drive all the way out here to chop up a clone and dump it. Too much work."

"There are still reasons why someone might skip the legal methods of disposal." Like having an illegal clone. Her first case fresh out of the academy in Langley had been busting an illegal-clone ring using stolen DNA to sell fetish slaves to stalkers. Rows of growth-accelerated children who went from infant to adolescent in under a week, half-starved and chained to the walls of the California mansion's attic. Their vacant stares still haunted her dreams.

She crossed herself out of habit, then pulled on her forensic gloves. "Okay—let's go meet Jane Doe."

CHAPTER 2

The greatest threat to our national security is perversely the foundation of our national stability. Any weapon we use to maintain our freedom can be used against us.

~ Quote from a confidential source within the Ministry of Defense I1–2074

Monday May 20, 2069
Alabama District 3
Commonwealth of North America

Jane Doe: age undetermined, hair black, eyes brown, race possibly Hispanic, age somewhere between twenty-five and forty, cause of death . . . Sam sighed. The description fit 80 percent of Commonwealth citizens living between the Panama Canal and the Arctic Circle, and the firsthand account of a middle-aged trucker didn't help.

There were a couple of dozen missing persons in a five-hundred-mile radius who fit Jane's description, but the cranial damage hadn't left enough of her face to try a visual or retinal match.

Sam growled at the computer. In the academy, she'd learned protocol, that you followed the steps to the right conclusion every time. In the eight weeks she'd had at her first assignment, the agents she'd mentored with seemed to solve their cases by magic. Granted, they all knew the area well, and all the homicides were related to either drugs, gangs, or clones, but it was still done so intuitively that she feared she'd never close a case herself. Moving to District 3 after the debacle with her father hadn't offered her much opportunity to develop those skills.

And now Agent Marrins wanted a report by lunch-time, and no one down in the coroner's office had even fingerprinted the Jane yet. At least that was something she could follow up on herself. The county coroner's office was in the building next door, and no one would notice her missing for a few minutes.

The phone rang.

"Agent Rose," she answered, "how may I help you sir or ma'am?"

"Agent Rose, this is Agent Anan, senior agent over in Birmingham. I heard you found a clone."

"That's the rumor. No confirmation yet."

He sighed. "We've got a major clone-ring case I'm trying to close up here. The guy in charge took all the clones out and burned the bodies before we could get proof-positive tests on them. I know for a fact one of the clones got away. She's four, but age-advanced to look twentysomething, and Hispanic."

"That matches my Jane. I'll get the coroner to test for the clone markers first thing."

"Can you get it to me by Wednesday? I need something solid to push for a court date, and that clone would really lock this up for me."

"Can I get my name on the report?" If she wanted the job in D.C., she needed another good case under her belt to look competitive.

"Done."

"You'll have the test results by Wednesday." Sam looked out her window to the county mortuary next door. It was an easy stroll if you didn't mind walking four meters feeling like you'd gone for a swim. Apparently, an air-conditioned hall hadn't fit in the district's expenditure forecast. No surprise there, nothing fit in the bureau budget unless you greased it down and squeezed.

The secretary nodded as Sam hurried past. She hit the door, but ducked back out of habit, scanning the lawn. The sprinklers had a habit of turning on without warning. Today, no black sprinkler heads popped up to soak her. She took a deep breath, counted to ten to be sure, and stepped out into the baking, sticky heat of the Alabama summer.

"Wait!"

Hot, rotten-egg water shot up at her.

The maintenance man peeked around the corner of the building. His grin turned to a leer. "Sorry, we're still working on getting the system right."

Sam plucked at the white shirt that clung to her like a bad boyfriend. "Of course you are. It's not like you would wait to turn the water on as I stepped outside.

That would be silly." Of course he'd done it on purpose. Going back in to file a complaint would mean letting Marrins see her soaking wet, going home meant losing time, going to the morgue meant letting another woman see her bra. The complaint paperwork could wait until her shirt had at least dried.

"Uh . . . right. Silly."

"Good morning to you." Her heels clicked a satisfying rebuke as she crossed the damp sidewalk to the morgue. *Monday, you loathsome bastard, what else do you have in store for me?* The morgue door was warm but not hot enough to burn flesh just yet, so her escape wasn't hampered further. Next time she took the side door, she'd ditch her heels and run for it.

Sam pulled her bedraggled hair back, spun it around, and tied it in a bun as she kicked the door shut. It was a test, of course. All of it: the case, of course, but her current situation as a whole. The bureau wanted to see if she was really committed. She'd taken emergency family leave less than eight weeks into her rookie assignment, so they'd retaliated and assigned her to the worst district in the Commonwealth to prove she wouldn't flake out again. They were going to learn that nothing could scare her.

She glanced at the paperwork to double-check the coroner's, Harley's, office number . . . MACKENZIE.

Who on Earth was Linsey MacKenzie?

She'd never seen her at the biweekly staff meetings. Even the interns managed to stop by and grab donuts, but nowhere in her memory could she find a MacKenzie.

Room b593 . . . down in the basement. Whoever designed the morgue thought narrow halls, poor lighting, and mazes added ambience. Even the stairwell was designed for maximum moodiness. A single bare bulb swayed over a dark shaft of concrete stairs, and a metal railing with peeling paint led the way down.

It's all a test . . .

The door creaked on its hinges, opening into a dark hall lined with battered hospital lockers. "Dr. MacKenzie?" The words bounced, echoed, and mutated into something sinister.

Budget cuts were all well and good, but how much did a lightbulb cost? No one should have to walk down a dark hall on a sunny day. Especially not people who still slept with a night-light.

Which she didn't want to think about at the moment.

Muted shafts of light cut across the side hall from windows in the offices. At the very far end, a less natural light illuminated a window. She slid her ID across the reader and stepped inside. "MacKenzie?"

A gangly ectomorph in blue scrubs covered in red up to the elbows hovered over an opened body dripping blood onto the cement floor.

Sam gagged, covered her mouth, and backed out of the room to lean against the cold wall, shivering in her wet clothes. She thought about flowers, daffodils, and jonquils, and dandelions. Anything other than corpses.

The man in scrubs followed her out into the hall.

With a hard swallow, she forced her stomach to settle. "Is Miss MacKenzie here?"

"M-miss?" The voice was strangled.

"Records said Linsey MacKenzie. Does she go by Doctor?"

"No. I'm . . . I'm Linsey. Just-just give me a minute," the man stuttered. He stared at her chest.

Sam glanced down: white shirt, black bra, back arched . . . Way to make an impression. *Saint Samantha, protect your namesake from her own stupidity.* "I'm Agent Rose. If you can pull yourself away from the massacre in there, I need the results from all the tests you've run and your signature ASAP. Birmingham has an illegal-clone case, and we're going to hand Jane off to them as evidence."

He stripped gore-covered gloves off and rubbed his hands on his scrubs in a nervous gesture. "Can't. I'm operating on a clone. It's already prepped with the transplant and anticlotting proteins. I need to . . . to harvest the organs." He took a deep breath. "The owner wants the organs frozen."

Sam raised an eyebrow. "This is a county morgue, and you're an agent with the bureau. What are you doing freelancing as a chop-shop doc?"

"It's evidence," he whispered. "Police have a . . . a case." MacKenzie slumped back, leaning his shoulder on the wall. His vacant gaze wandered to the ceiling. After a minute, he said, "I need to go back." He wiped a hand across his mask and blinked at Sam as if he had forgotten she was standing there. "I'm sorry. Can . . . can this wait?"

She stared. She knew there were bad agents in the

bureau—her training officer at the academy had loved toting out the old "crazy agent" stories—but she'd never expected to see one. *Have to love District 3. . .*

She grimaced, and went on, "Look, I just need the Jane Doe report. Tell me where the test results are, and I can get your signature before you go home."

He looked at her, hazel eyes swimming in his pale face. "Test results?"

"Standard procedure for a case like this: you find the body, you run all the general blood tests, and you check the little box on page three that says clone marker found. Then we call the case closed and all move on with our lives." She gave him an encouraging nod.

"It . . ." He swallowed, "it wasn't—" He shook his head, eyes down. He was doing a very good impression of a drunk about to lose his dinner. "She was dismembered. Abused."

"And I find that sickening, but a clone isn't a person. If it has a clone marker, the killer might need professional therapy, but it won't be funded by the prison system."

"She . . . she . . ." MacKenzie shook his head.

"She what?"

"No test results!" he shouted, his voice echoing through the drafty corridors.

Sam rocked back on her heels. Marrins should be the one dealing with this, but if she ran to him, he'd use it as an excuse to end her career. If she couldn't handle one crazed coworker, what kind of agent was she? Sam forced herself to smile politely . . . and not punch MacKenzie right in the face. Wouldn't mother be proud? "Agent MacKenzie, it takes less than a minute to run a basic gene scan for the clone marker. Don't we have interns to do that sort of thing?"

The medical examiner took a deep breath. His fist started tapping the wall behind him in an uneven rhythm. "The specimen is o-over twenty. Too old for the rapid clone test. I need to check for Verville traces." He squeezed his eyes tight and lifted his head so he was at least facing Sam, even if he wasn't looking at her. "She might be a person. Someone . . . Someone might love her."

"Right." Sam dumped a body's worth of doubt into the word. They listened to the sigh of the air conditioner. "I for one would *love* for *someone* to run those tests on her," she finally said.

He managed a feeble, defiant glare.

"Have you ever tried sorting through all of the missing persons reports in the Commonwealth when all you have is the description 'female, dark hair, age fifteen-plus'?" Sam asked. "It's not fun. While you're in there playing police intern, I'm trying to sort through over three thousand possible Janes. Until you do your job, I'm spinning my wheels and getting nowhere. I need those test results. Or fingerprints at least. Can we get someone down here to fingerprint her? I understand weekend delays, but Senior Agent Marrins expects timely results."

MacKenzie's jaw locked, jutting out.

Apparently, invoking a higher power didn't have the desired result.

Sam tapped the folder on her thigh and raised his pout with a full-on glare.

Hazel eyes narrowed. "I need time. Three days. Maybe four."

"Three days?" She shook her head. "Why can't you do it today?" He shivered and held up a shaking hand. "Okay, fine, you need some downtime. Why can't you do it tomorrow?"

"Blood . . . blood work takes time."

"Not *that* long." She pursed her lips in disapproval but realized there wasn't much she could do to make him finish the tests any quicker. "Fine. When you're done playing Dr. Grim, I need this case to be top priority. Can you make that happen?"

He nodded slowly.

"Great. I'll follow up on Wednesday." There, parameters and expectations defined. Deadline set. Textbook leadership.

Let Marrins put that in her evaluation.

Sam's shirt was just beginning to dry when Marrins yelled her name down the hall. One day, she'd have an office with a door and a minion to turn away all the people who thought they needed to talk to her. Today was not that day.

"Sir?" She pulled her jacket on. It didn't pay to look sloppy. "Yes, sir?"

"Detective Altin has a robbery he wants a bureau assist on. Go chase stolen barrettes across the district lines with him." Marrins slid an efile across his desk.

"Thank you, sir." She tried to sound like she meant it.

"You wanted something more than clones. Altin is good for that. Can't find his pants without a map and permission written in triplicate, but that's what you get from his sort of people. Take care of it."

She wasn't sure if Marrins meant people of color, people who worked hard for justice, or people who had more than two brain cells to rub together. Whatever the senior agent meant, it put her firmly on Altin's side of the line and well outside her comfort zone.

She skimmed through the notes. "Sir, do you have any further information? This report is . . ." a scrawl— *Altin wants bureau asst.*—" . . . not complete."

"Theresa downstairs took the call. She might have something more. Do you have Jane's paperwork yet?"

Her smile froze. "Not yet, sir. I'm waiting on blood tests and the fingerprints. I should have it to you in the next few days. Agent Anan from Birmingham thinks Jane might be tied to a case he's working, so I'm trying to make sure everything is court ready."

Marrins grunted, whether in approval or disgust she couldn't tell. "Fine. But anything you send to Anan needs to get cleared through me first. I'm not letting some rookie embarrass me."

"Yes, sir. I'll send a report on the robbery as soon as I've talked to Altin, sir."

He waved a hand, and she slunk out of sight. A year

ago, she'd been the office hotshot, the girl with the high-speed career. Now she was the embarrassment of an old man who'd never risen in the ranks past senior agent of a backwater nowhere. She shook her head, gathered her things, and made her way to Marrins's secretary.

Theresa scowled at her through pink cat's-eye glasses as Sam crossed the polished lobby floor to stop at the secretary's great round fortress in the lobby.

"Stolen hair clips? Marrins says you have all the details." Sam smiled winningly.

The secretary rolled her eyes with the grace of someone who had put up with the antics of rookies for decades. "Novikov-Veltman Nova Laboratory is a private physics and astronomy lab on the south end of the district. They had a break-in over the weekend. Detective Altin sent a call for assistance because one of the scientists is demanding bureau involvement. Technically, since some of the research is government-funded, we could call it our jurisdiction, but it's just property damage. There's broken glass in the atrium, but none of the labs were touched."

"Sounds like a thrill ride," Sam said. The address was on "her" side of the district, which meant she could stop to change before going to the lab. And let the dog out.

At least this won't be a complete waste, then. Any chance to spend some time with my "roommate."

She headed for her car, unplugged it from the charger, and turned the key. The water engine bubbled to life.

Once upon a time, in some fairy utopia that existed before she was born, there was no such thing as a bedroom tax. Now, having more than one room per person resulted in a luxury tax, and, legally, a single person could only rent a single-bedroom apartment. She got around that by listing her landlady's mastiff as her animal companion. At 180 pounds, Hoss more than qualified for his own room. It meant she got to live in a beautiful old house where there was no risk of having a meth lab next door, but it also meant getting home in time to let the dog out because her landlady wouldn't walk over after dark.

Driving down the country road, she sighed.

When she'd decided to join the bureau for a paycheck that wasn't considered a living wage, it had been in a fit of pique and the belief that she'd be promoted quickly. The bureau was her escape from her life as an ambassador's daughter and the threats of marriage to one of her mother's cronies. A meritocracy where she would be rewarded for her brains and talent while she helped build a new nation.

So far, the meritocracy she'd signed up for was her mother's world of glittering favoritism done on a budget.

A faun-colored dog lay in the crabgrass wagging its nub of a tail as Sam parked on the lawn outside a stately white house with a wraparound porch shaded by oak trees. A withered old woman with skin the color of roast chestnuts and a Smith & Wesson rifle stood in the doorway.

"Hello, Miss Azalea. Hello, Hoss!" Sam waved as she stepped out of the car. Hoss leapt to his feet. A foot-long trail of saliva dragged behind the dog like the tail of a comet as he bounded toward her.

"Hoss!" the woman shouted. The dog sat, skidding on the remnants of a gravel driveway until he bumped into Sam's knee and looked up with unabashed adoration. His giant head nudged her hip, looking for a treat. Black eyes lost in a black mask of fur watched her expectantly.

Sam patted him affectionately. "You're hungry, aren't you?"

"He's always hungry." Miss Azalea eyed her, and Sam knew the woman was weighing her against the Southern standard for beauty as she walked up to the house. "Jus' looking at you makes me want to eat fried chicken. Child, you need to put some meat on those bones. What are you doing home this time o' day?"

"Changing my shirt and going to see Detective Altin about something." Hoss's nails clicked on the wooden floor as he followed her inside. "I have some lemonade in the fridge if you'd like some."

Miss Azalea waved her hand. "I jus' come up to water the plants in the nursery, hon. Let Hoss run for a few minutes. Can't imagine how he stands it in this heat. Jus' looking outside gots me sweatin' like a sinner at a prayer meetin'. I'm fixin' to melt." The door snapped shut behind her.

Sam left her landlady in the empty living room, hurrying to change into dry clothes. When she got back downstairs, Miss Azalea and Hoss were both in the kitchen at the big wooden table that didn't fit in Miss Azalea's little house by the creek. "I made us sandwiches. You want me to bring up some supper for you?"

Baloney sandwiches on white bread. Nothing special, but a chance for Miss Azalea to spend some time with her. Sam didn't really have the time, and besides, Sam ate hers in three bites anyway. But she liked her landlady and appreciated the food. "I can't do dinner with you tonight, I'm sorry. I'm meeting Brileigh at the gym, and she'll holler if I'm not there to spot her."

Miss Azalea nodded. "I'll come up tomorrow to let Hoss out. Leave some fried chicken in the fridge for you. You'll have the rent check? I'm fixin' to leave for Florida by Friday. Gotta see my grandbabies."

"I'll leave it on the fridge," Sam promised. Hoss stole some crumbs off her plate. "Poor baby, you're going to be stuck in the house all day all alone. I wonder if I could smuggle him into work." Hoss's nubbin of a tail wagged hopefully, and she almost felt bad for bringing it up. "I don't think he'd even fit in my office."

"Honey, he wouldn't fit in your car!" Miss Azalea laughed. "I'd take him with me, but my boy has two dogs. Little things. They'd be snacks."

"It won't be a problem. I can come home during lunch."

Hoss licked her face. He wouldn't care what happened as long as he got cookies out of the deal.

"**A**gent Rose, we've got to stop meeting like this," Detective Altin said, as she got out of her car. He was a trim, older man with wiry, steel-gray hair who often had the thankless task of smoothing out wrinkles when the police chief and Marrins butted heads. "People are going to start talking."

"Hardy-har-har. You should try stand-up comedy, Detective, you're a natural," Sam said, as they walked toward the nondescript building. "What's all the fuss about?"

"Oh, just your standard weekend vandalism with a side order of fried electronics. The local hooligans decided we were getting too much experience raiding drug labs, so they added breaking and entering to their repertoire. Now I get to teach a class about tracking down stolen property to all our new recruits."

"What was stolen?"

"Nothing that we know of yet. I have Officer Holt leading the team checking the inventory lists, but a refresher course never hurt anyone."

"Lovely." As they stepped inside, the lab's glass atrium was a cool respite from the rising heat and humidity. A large black desk stood guard at the far end of the space, looking over a sea of gray marble and white-barked beeches and gardenias planted in raised beds, reaching for the skylights. "I like the yellow police tape. It adds a touch of roguish punkery."

"Good use of taxpayer dollars. To the left we have the government-sponsored labs run by a Dr. Esther

Vergeet. To the right of the guard desk you have the workshop where the team keeps older research displays, abandoned ideas, and Dr. Abdul Emir's modern projects lab." Yellow police tape hung over the second door, which had been warped and crumpled into a mass of rippled metal.

"Walk me through this. I see two main entrances. The front door"—Sam pointed behind her to the door she'd come in—"and the doors over there." She nodded to an identical set of wide glass doors that looked out over a courtyard with picnic tables. "The labs are to the left, with six cameras I can see, a security desk, and ID locks. Over to the right is?" Sam looked at the double doors leading to the brick addition.

"The green door on the right leads to the lecture and conference hall. Next door is a multimedia room for greeting the press and holding high-school career fairs and such."

"So the thief came in through a back door? Fire escape? Down through the roof maybe?" Sam guessed.

"That, we don't know." Detective Altin led her to door number two. "On Sunday nights, two human guards man the desks. Robotic security with heat sensors patrols the back rooms. The lab is closed at noon Sunday and doesn't open to general staff until ten Monday morning. Weekends, the lab is open only to staff with level-four security clearance or higher, plus the designated security guards, who never go past the atrium. Dr. Vergeet came in at five this morning to this mess. There were no phone calls, nothing from security, and all the electronics in the building are fried. She isn't happy."

Sam nodded and started taking notes. "I wouldn't be happy either. Cameras in all the halls and standard perimeter security?"

"The latest and greatest, before the incident. Sunday night, one of the security guards logged out early, claimed he was sick. His name is Mordicai Robbins."

"Where's he now?"

"Unknown. He's a weekend-only guy. Records from HR say he's single. The morning security guard says Robbins likes to take off at random—fishing trips, that sort of thing. We're trying to reach him, but he's got his phone turned off.

"The logs for security that night show both Mr. Robbins and"—he consulted his notes—"Melody Chimes worked Sunday night. We have the phone record of Mr. Robbins calling in to the main office asking permission to leave. Miss Chimes is on the recording, too, confirming that she would contact the on-call backup officer, Leandra Kinsley. We sent an officer out to talk to Kinsley, who says she went to bed at eleven Sunday night. She reported to her day job in Edmond at eight the next morning, and didn't hear a thing about the break-in until the police called at three."

"Chimes?" Sam looked at Altin, expecting a laugh. "Melody Chimes? Really?"

"It's legal."

"Some parents are cruel," she said with a shake of her head. "Where is Miss Chimes?"

Altin frowned. "Also missing."

"Miss Chimes called a friend and broke into the lab? Is that the theory?"

"That's *a* theory."

"I hear a 'but' coming."

Altin nodded as he said, "Miss Chimes is a nineteen-year-old college student working on an art and marketing degree. She hired on as a part-time night-shift employee with the Wannervan Security Firm last fall to earn some money on the side. Good family, no financial problems, she's passed every drug test. There's nothing in her profile that's a red flag for a destructive crime like this."

Sam nodded. "So work it the other way: what's missing and who would want it?"

"Nothing obvious is missing," Altin said with a tired sigh. "We did a check of the high-end, easy-to-move stuff first. Computers, monitors, the break-room television, that's all here. All the data is here, all the lab reports are here. All we have is the fried electronics and the broken windows. Dr. Vergeet called as soon as she pulled up and has her teams going over the computers to see if anything was uploaded or downloaded. So far, there isn't a keystroke out of place." He spread his hands in defeat. "It looks like careless vandalism, maybe a crime of opportunity although I want to find Robbins and Chimes before I write it all off. Also, there's this." Altin handed her a set of forensic gloves. "Check this door out."

Sam ducked under the police tape and inspected the broken hinges. "That took a lot of force."

"These are steel fire doors. Each one weighs over a hundred pounds, and the hinges are supposed to support over four hundred pounds each."

"You did your research."

"I got bored waiting for you to show up," Altin said. "Dr. Vergeet is ready to file a vandalism claim with the insurance and be done with it, and the rest of the mess fits. But this doesn't. You'd need a battering ram to bend the door like this, and to get it at this angle, I think you'd have to be standing inside the guarded portion of the lab. I mean, I need to run some computer scenarios to prove it, but to me it looks like the door was pushed out, not in."

Sam frowned at the beige walls and black flooring of the rear hallway. Electric hookups for security bots hung in small alcoves every three meters waiting for their sentries to return. There were cameras, smoke detectors, sprinklers—everything a high-security building needed to handle a small war. "Did the lab lose power at any time Sunday night?"

"Not a flicker," Altin said, as they walked slowly down the hall. "The cameras are out, the computers are down, but the electricity is still running to everything. It doesn't look like a power surge."

"I see the stations for the robotic-security patrols. Did you confiscate the bots, or were they stolen?" The black market for security tech was growing, but there could only be a few buyers in the area.

"We took 'em. I sent half to the district tech lab, one to the local PD techgeeks, and the rest to the bureau tech lab in Atlanta."

"Too bad," she said. "Stolen security bots would make life interesting."

Sam studied the scene, trying to glean some sense from what she was seeing. Every door down the hall hung off its hinges. Black security glass littered the floor on both sides of the windows. "Does this look like an explosion to you, or is that just me?"

"No residue from a blast although the impact fractures on the wall support the theory. Dr. Vergeet assured me there is nothing in these labs that could cause an explosion. They don't even have a flammables locker."

Sam shook her head. "What about residue from your missing security guards? Did you get anything there?"

"Not a single hair. There are no signs of physical violence, and both cars are gone. We have an APB out for them, but anyone with half an ounce of sense stripped those cars down and left them in Atlanta, with the keys in the ignition. They're gone and sold for parts by now."

She moved down her checklist. Security, fried electronics, and the actual target . . . "You said this part of the lab belonged to Dr. Emir? Where is he?" Maybe the intended victim would have some insight into the whys and wherefores of the crime.

"Right this way although you may regret asking," Altin warned. "He's the one who demanded the bureau be called in. If Dr. Vergeet had her way, the cleaning crew would already be fixing this up." Altin led her into a small workspace in front of a bank of broken windows. The windows looked over a curved black lecture hall with stadium-style seating focused around a teaching space at the bottom of the dell. A spotlight illuminated a single heavy table and a small box perched on top.

A thin man with a white beard and thick glasses fussed around the box, looking like Santa Claus after he discovered dieting and exercise. He blinked at Detective Altin with a scowl. "Yes, Detective? Have you found another way to ask the same question? What are we on, the third or fourth round?"

Altin went poker-faced. "Dr. Emir, this is Agent Samantha Rose of CBI. She's here to take your complaint."

Santa gave her a dismayed look. "You are the best the bureau has to offer?"

"Yes, sir." Sam squared her shoulders and tried to look smart.

"Are you familiar with the work of Echeverria, Klinkhammer, and Thorne?" Emir asked, lifting his chin so he could glare down his nose at her.

"No."

"Ah." Emir pushed his spectacles up. "I see. I suppose it is too much to hope you read up on the work of our namesakes before traipsing out here to do your dancing-bear act?"

Altin covered his mouth to hide a smile. Sam grimaced and turned to the doctor. "The bureau's understanding was that you wanted a trained agent on-site as soon as possible, not that you wanted to hire a new intern. Rather than insulting my intelligence, why don't you fill me in on what I need to know?"

Emir's eyes went wide. He turned, shouting in a language Sam didn't understand, and went off to yell at the younger men still hovering around the box.

One of the younger men broke from the group and walked toward her and Altin, arms spread wide. "I'm so sorry about that, Agent Rose. I'm Henry Troom, one of the doctor's assistants. You have to understand, Dr. Emir is very upset. Please don't judge him by this . . . outburst." The young man shook his head and smiled. "Would you let me help you?"

Sam held out her hand. "Dr. Troom—"

"Henry—I'm still working on my doctorate." He shook her hand, smiling with obvious pride in his approaching title despite his attempt at modesty.

She gave him a curt smile. "Of course. Mr. Troom: why was I called out here?"

"Dr. Emir is worried the lab was broken into so that the perpetrator could steal a copy of his work. Only the doors on our side of the facility were damaged, and the doctor's research is easily transportable although not easily replicable. Still, if someone made a copy, the consequences could be devastating."

Right, earth-shattering. He'd probably lose a grant

or something. "What is Dr. Emir studying?" Sam asked as she pulled out her notebook again.

"Uh." The man ran his hand through his shaggy dark hair. "How familiar are you with theta waves and Minkowski metrics?"

"Never heard of them."

The intern winced. "Right. Well, in that case . . . what Dr. Emir is designing is a communication form that would exploit hypothetical systems of computation involving Novikov's self-consistency principle." He frowned in concentration; Sam frowned in confusion. "It's all fundamental work to test Dr. Emir's theories at this point. If we can build an operable machine, it will be the first step to ultimately improving the entire cloning industry. In theory." He dropped his gaze to avoid direct eye contact.

It sounded dodgy. Sam looked at Altin for help. The detective shook his head. "You lost me," she said to Troom. "Back up—Dr. Emir is creating an improved mode of communication? With a long-term benefit to the cloning industry?" She kept the distaste out of her voice with effort.

"Yes, in the particulate sense. Consistency theory and antimatter proofs show that one thing cannot exist in two places. If you—"

"Stop!" Dr. Emir bellowed, marching toward them. *Yes*, she thought, *stop*. If Troom was hoping to become a teacher, he wasn't doing a very good job at it. Apparently, though, that wasn't Dr. Emir's problem. "This man is not cleared for this information!" he shouted, stabbing a finger at Altin. "This is why I required someone from the bureau. Someone with clearance must be the one to look into this matter." He put a hand on Sam's shoulder and steered her away from Altin. "You must understand, Agent Rose, this is government research. I cannot trust a country cop"—he spat the words out like a profanity—"to understand the delicate nature of what I do. Nor do I trust them to keep their mouths shut."

With a snap, Sam shut her notebook. The last thing she needed in her life was another bigoted old man. "Dr. Emir, the detective is here to help. Two security guards are missing, and you believe your research is threatened. I need to understand what is going on before I can move forward with this case. Who would want your notes badly enough to break into the lab?"

The doctor glared at her, looked over his shoulder at the machine, and turned back. "Everyone. My research could rewrite human history."

"I'm sure it could."

"No," Emir said, ignoring her sarcasm. "You aren't. You think I'm a raving madman. I'm paranoid, but not without reason."

She gave him a cold, flat stare she'd learned at her first duty station.

Emir blinked. "In the past, I had research that was equally controversial. Adaptations of cloning techniques. Gene-therapy work that worried people with an overdeveloped sense of ethics. I have survived assassination attempts. I am no stranger to duplicitous individuals using badges and titles to steal my work before betraying me."

Sam nodded. It wasn't bigotry keeping Emir from trusting Altin, it was fear. Not uncommon in citizens from the old United States. "I understand, and I will do everything in my power to protect you. But I trust Detective Altin. He is going to serve as the main investigator for this case. I'll be there for backup in case sensitive research is threatened."

The doctor looked grim, but nodded. "You will be the one interviewing me?"

"Yes." She nodded to Altin. "Can I speak to you a moment?"

They stepped outside and away from the oppressive atmosphere of the lab. It wasn't until they were out of sight of the lab that Sam felt comfortable talking. "I really want to find the missing security guards. Can the PD make it a priority?"

"Sure, I'll list them as persons of interest and hunt 'em down. No problem. What are you going to do with Emir?"

"Interview him. He says he's received threats in the past. Who knows, I might get lucky, and this will be something unrelated to the work here at the lab. But I'm thinking if someone came to the lab looking for information, that means the person knew it existed to start with. In a tight-lipped academic community, that's a pretty small suspect pool."

Altin's eyebrows crept up. "Inside job?"

"A textbook case."

CHAPTER 3

> It is not the nature of man to kill. Men are born in
> fear. They strive for popularity and power to stave
> off the inevitable day when death will woo them
> to her silent domain. To kill, a man must shed his
> innate humanity and embrace the worship of the
> only true deity—Death.

> ~ Excerpt from *The Heart of Fear*
> by Liedjie Slaan I1–2071

Wednesday May 22, 2069
Alabama District 3
Commonwealth of North America

Bright light stabbed through the high window, burning Mac's eyes as the world swam into bleary focus.
Softer light from the computer screen illuminated
drifts of paper. He picked one up for closer inspection:
a diagram of the bones of the hand printed on flimsy,
recycled paper. Why had he printed bone diagrams?
The reason escaped him.

Foggy memories begged for his attention. Something about . . . about . . . He rubbed his face with his

hands and tried to figure out why his ears were ringing. Where was his coffee? He vaguely recalled asking one of the interns to bring him coffee.

Pushing aside papers, he groped for his cup of sanity. Papers crashed to the floor, knocking his phone as it rang. He grabbed the red coffee mug like a drowning man before picking up the phone. "H-hello?" He tipped the coffee into his mouth. Nothing.

"Agent MacKenzie?" The woman's voice on the other end of the line had an angry edge to it.

Another memory pushed its way through the fog, the memory of long, tan legs, a black-lace bra, and deep red lips. Her. Heaven bless the erratic sprinkler system that had caught the agent off guard.

"Agent MacKenzie?"

"Uh, yeah, Agent . . ." *Lips? Red? Something about red . . .* "Rose?" He shook his coffee mug upside down. The wispy remains of a dead beetle floated to the ground.

"How's Jane?" Agent Rose asked.

"Who?" Tipping the mug toward the sunlight, he peered into the depths at sludge and something fuzzy. Penicillin was a mold. That made fuzzy healthy. Mac looked around for a spoon.

"Jane Doe." Agent Rose sighed in exasperation. "The Jane you've had rotting in your morgue since last Friday. The one I've patiently waited for a report on. That Jane. Do you have the autopsy and test results yet?"

"Um . . ." He frowned at the computer screen. That could be Jane Doe's autopsy file, maybe. "Sure?"

"Great. We're shifting Jane's files to Birmingham this afternoon. See you in twenty." The phone clicked off.

Twenty? He blinked in confusion. Did she mean she was coming down in twenty minutes? He swore and pulled open the desk drawer. There had to be a packet of instant coffee in there. His fingers slipped around the familiar shape of the pill bottle. The pills tempted him, offering a way out of the coming pain and humiliation. Escape in an orange bottle.

He shoved them in his lab-coat pocket and fumbled for the last packet of instant coffee.

The Deep South never fit in. Maybe it was the checkered penal-colony past, or the lingering hostilities from the Civil War that fractured the United States in the 1860s, or maybe it was simply that every country needs a place for the malcontents to gather. Pushed from the cities, beaten back by the glowing lights of progress, they turned to the overgrown cotton fields for solace.

Bureau agents in California called it the war zone. This was the last battlefield of national unity, the place where no one had voted in favor of the new Commonwealth but instead had it thrust upon them. This is where agents came to die.

Somehow, Senior Agent Robert Marrins had managed to survive. A former Texas Ranger with no family, he'd not only managed to fill a vacancy in Alabama District 3 but hold the place and keep the peace. But instead of being the living legend Sam imagined when she had first heard about him, she found an avuncular old man with a red nose and sagging belly who didn't so much keep the peace as hide in his office and avoid anything that looked like work. He just happened to be in a district in which nothing seemed to happen. *Lucky for him; sucks for me.* He got to sit in his creaking, oversized office chair, and his junior agents did whatever happened to come across his desk.

So it was a little bit frightening when Marrins showed up for work on time that morning to harangue her about what he called, "That damn clone case."

"This is going too slow," Marrins said, the smell of antiseptics and coffee wafting around them as he continued his rant. "The regional director wants murders wrapped neat and tight with a seventy-two-hour turnaround. The government's made promises. No more three to six months waiting for trials. No more twenty-year-old cold cases. People need closure."

"I know, sir, but Agent Anan was very specific. It needs to hold up in court. I need more than a weekend to get everything done." The handle of the heavy morgue door burned Sam's hand as she held it open for Marrins.

"You take orders from me, not Anan. It isn't hard, Rose. Three pages of paperwork and two signatures. You've got to know how to handle people like MacKenzie. Lean a little. He doesn't have the balls or the backbone to stand up to you, even if you are a girl." Rubicund jowls vibrated with anger. Marrins shoved the next door toward her as they walked into the cold autopsy room.

Sam caught it with a grimace. "Leaning on Agent MacKenzie won't guarantee accurate results, sir. There's still a chance that Jane Doe isn't a clone."

"Bull pucky!" Marrins growled with his thick Texas drawl that came out when he was angry. "You've seen the statistics for this kind of crime. How often has a case like this not turned into a clone in our district? Come on, Rose, how many?"

She pulled a lab jacket off the coat tree and shoved her arms in. "None, sir," she admitted.

"You're chasing shadows," Marrins said. "Do you know when the last violent crime was in District 3?"

"The Horror House case six years ago." It was the only bit of interesting crime history in recent memory, and the lurid details of the case had been accompanied by graphic images that still made her ill when she thought about them.

"And that was a set of clones, too," Marrins said.

"Statistics prove that people who abuse clones or animals move on to human victims in 80 percent of cases. It's not a huge jump between a clone and a human, sir. One genetic marker's worth of difference, and you have a psycho moving from legal disposal of a clone to the illegal torture and murder of a human being. It's happened before, and we're going to see more cases like it when the Caye Law gets passed."

Marrins buttoned up an extralarge lab coat with a heavy sigh. "You're as dense as you look sometimes. If you want that promotion, let this go. I'm getting pressure from my superiors, and the buck stops with you.

Get Jane Doe off my desk and out of my district by Friday, or kiss your promotion and transfer good-bye."

Sam bit back an angry response.

"If MacKenzie gives you trouble, threaten to turn that *gez* in for abuse."

Sam frowned at the profanity.

Marrins ignored her. "Everyone knows he's here because of drug problems. Another report of behavior unbecoming, and we'll put him in medical-therapy retirement. Best thing for him. Then we can get a decent corpse-flicker."

There was the inevitable clearing of a throat behind them.

Sam snapped her jacket shut and turned with a tight smile to MacKenzie. "Where's Jane?"

The ME closed his red-rimmed eyes. "Over . . . over here."

"See what I mean?" Marrins hissed in her ear.

She watched the medical examiner freeze half a second before opening his eyes and stiffly walking away. Ignoring the senior agent, she turned to MacKenzie. "Well?"

With a jerky nod, the ME led them over to a viewing console.

"No body?" Marrins sniffed. "Back in the day, they showed you an actual body, not a mock-up."

"This is a body," MacKenzie snarled.

Sam cleared her throat. One thing she'd learned to do very fast in the academy was get between all the bloated male egos. "Sir, the body stays in cold storage unless there is a question with the scans. Even then, we would need your signature to cut into a body. The only exceptions are clones when the owner has requested organ harvesting."

Which a senior agent should know. . .

Marrins grunted. He glared at the scans as he hooked his thumbs in his pockets.

The ME gave her a grateful look as images of the corpse appeared on the screen in 3D. "The victim was between thirty and thirty-five, Latino descent. Her pelvic saddle has no marking from childbirth." Images of bone structure flashed past. The screen zoomed in on the skull, then muscle layered over the bones. Finally, skin appeared. "That's the computer's best guess at what Jane Doe might have looked like."

A basic Hispanic face, nothing out of the ordinary, but disconcerting in its similarity to what Sam saw in the mirror every morning. She grimaced as the computer added wavy black hair and a dark skin tint. Sam surreptitiously glanced at the ME to see if he was smirking. Both the men stared at her face on the screen without recognition.

"Wetback?" Marrins harrumphed. "Looks like a friend of yours, Rose. You know her?"

"I was born in Toronto, sir, and not all people who look Hispanic actually know each other."

"She looks familiar," Marrins said. "Think I saw a whore with that face back in Texas once."

"Not all Hispanics look alike, sir, but it's an easy mistake to make. All white people looked the same to me until I took the bureau's sensitivity course about racial differences in the workplace." Her commentary sailed over Marrins's bald head with room to spare.

"Go on, MacKenzie."

The ME cleared his throat. "The victim . . ." His lips worked around the words. "Tortured," he spat out. "The body shows evidence of torture."

Marrins made a circular, hurry-up motion.

"Evidence of electric shock, mutilation, and legs skinned over a period of days. There are bedsores on the back and right hip. She . . . she didn't die quickly."

"Are you sure none of that was postmortem?" Sam asked, taking notes. "Vultures could have skinned her while she was lying in the field."

MacKenzie shook his head and shut down the screenful of gruesome images. "Not the way it was done. She was alive, but . . . that wasn't the cause of death. Jane Doe was severely malnourished. There are early signs of desiccation. Atlanta is testing for toxins. I-I don't have cause of death yet." He gulped, grimaced, and looked at the floor. "I don't have time of death yet. There were inconsistencies. Her body temperature was near zero, but she showed no signs of cyanosis around the fingers or lips. The body went into rigor mortis forty minutes after the original call came in." He shook his head.

"So, Jane was freshly dead when she was discovered."

MacKenzie tilted his head from side to side. "Rigor mortis sets in usually within an hour or two of death.

Postmortem lividity, the blood pooling, hadn't occurred when she was found, but her body temperature should have been close to normal. It's was eighty-nine degrees outside when she was found."

Sam frowned. "You said she showed signs of prolonged confinement. Could she have been kept in a climate-controlled area? Moved in a refrigerated truck? Extreme temperatures are often used as a torture device."

"Possibly," MacKenzie conceded.

"Doesn't really matter," Marrins said. "Let's get the signatures and send it up to Agent Anan in Birmingham."

Sam hesitated, far more interested in the nature of Jane's death than Marrins seemed to be, before nodding. "The blood work came back clone positive?" She felt the sting of regret. The bureau wouldn't waste time or money on a clone. But oh how she wanted to sink her teeth into this one and get some answers. Voicing that desire would only be another black mark on her record. Clone sympathizer wasn't a title the bureau approved of.

MacKenzie stared with bulging eyes. "Um . . . it did?"

Sam glared. "You don't have the test results yet?"

"Atlanta," MacKenzie said. "I'm sending samples to Atlanta."

"Fine," Marrins drawled. "Rose, if you want D.C., wrap up this case. Suicide or clone, whatever you want, but I want that paperwork by Friday." He tapped the diagnostic screen for emphasis, then nodded to MacKenzie and walked out, whistling.

Sam waited until the autopsy-room door thumped shut before turning on the ME, who was slumped against the wall. "What was that? You said you were ready, that the autopsy was done. This isn't done. No test results, no cause of death, you can't even give me an accurate age!" She pointed at his emaciated frame. "Do you want a medboard out? Is that it? You looking for an excuse for the bureau to drop you?"

He shook his head.

"Did you even run the fingerprints yet?"

"The interns did. She's not in the system as a runaway, missing person, or on the open-access registry."

Saint Jude, give me patience. "Did you check the clone registry and the secured registry? Anyone with the money can pay to have their fingerprints put in the secure levels, and they're the ones most likely to have clones."

"The . . . the interns don't have clearance. I . . . I was . . ."

"Busy," Sam finished for him. "Do it as soon as you can or send me the files so I can check it."

"Suicide doesn't fit the . . . the evidence. We can't . . . You can't . . ."

"I don't want to list Jane as a suicide, but I will if we can't find anything else." She took a deep breath. "I need to close this case. Understand? I need a promotion in the next six months if I want a career with the bureau. Right now, all I have is the original statement from the trucker who found her. Give me more. Give me test results. Give me fingerprints. Give me something to work with, or I won't be able to do anything other than close the case Friday as a suicide . . . and recommend you be dismissed."

Sam left the morgue with a sour taste in her mouth. If Agent MacKenzie was right about Jane Doe's age, there was a serious problem. The first clones produced in the early thirties had died within a decade. They'd been early experiments, the result of scientific hubris and curiosity rather than something the world needed. Second-wave clones lasted longer but had a tendency to . . . melt was how Sam always thought of it. The cells lysed rapidly, resulting in catastrophic organ failure.

No one had cared. Cellular printers were available in every hospital to grow new organs if a replacement was ever needed. It was expensive, but quick and virtually risk free. Until the Yellow Plague swept across the globe, cloning was simply a curiosity and a McGuffin in a legion of spy thrillers. Then, almost overnight, cloning went from underfunded oddity to a mainstream necessity.

Because the plague shut down the hospitals.

They'd started as quarantines for the fast-killing virus, and by the time the research team at the Centers for Disease Control discovered that the virus had a twenty-seven-day incubation period, it was too late. The hospitals were sealed with their dead, mausole-

THE DAY BEFORE 43

ums with the names of plague victims etched in stone memorials outside.

As humanity rebuilt, the survivors realized they no longer had an easy way to replace organs, and the fear of a second plague outbreak kept people away from new hospitals. The superstition that the organ printers had caused the plague hadn't helped. Cloning took off, a safe, private way to ensure that any damage done to your body could be repaired. In 2048, the Clone Stabilization Gene, CSG, gave clones life expectancies that matched those of their human counterparts. When the Caye Law preventing the breeding of new clones and the indentured service of unwanted ones went into effect in January 2070, though, cloning would end. A strange footnote to the history of the reconstruction of society.

Sam could only hope the old Central American Territories' tracking program had a list of missing women born in that narrow window of time between when the first stable clones were created and when the CSG markers became a legal requirement.

The CAT list was a nightmare of overlapping files, missing data, and six languages. The updated, translated files headquarters had promised in January had yet to appear.

Pulling up the file, she saw a date stamp with an update made two minutes before. At least MacKenzie was sharing his test results. The autopsy notes were there along with a copy of the fingerprints and the eerie computer simulation of Jane's face. Sam dumped all the new data and set search parameters for women living in a three-hundred-mile radius born between 2040 and 2048. Hopefully, Jane was a girl who had stayed close to home.

Her phone buzzed. "Agent Rose, how can I help you, sir or ma'am?"

"Agent Rose? You must come at once. At once! I am in terrible danger. Things are quite violent. Quite violent."

Her heart rate picked up as adrenaline surged. "Please stay calm, sir. First, may I ask who I am speaking to, and where you would like me to go?" she asked in a carefully practiced, neutral tone.

"Don't you know me?" the man demanded.

"Not by voice alone, sir, no." The number didn't match any of the bureau phones from nearby districts, and it didn't sound like any from Altin's department.

"This is Dr. Emir. I've spoken to you about my work."

She relaxed a bit. She had a hard time thinking Santa from the lab was in that much trouble. "Yes, I remember you now. Is this about Detective Altin's case, Doctor?"

"No. Yes. Possibly. My work is . . ." Emir trailed off. "I am in danger. My work is threatened."

She perked up again. "Can you describe the threat, Doctor?"

"The history of the world is in danger."

She relaxed . . . again. Repressing a sigh, she asked, "Could you possibly be a little more specific?"

"Someone is attempting to steal my research."

"Yes, we discussed that on Monday. Have you found any evidence that your computer was tampered with? Mr. Troom was doing a keystroke check on the computer when I left."

"Henry found nothing."

"I see. So this isn't about your research, it's about the vandalism?"

"I suppose."

"And, you're aware Detective Altin is handling your case? It's out of my jurisdiction unless we find evidence there was a violent crime committed or national security is at risk."

"Yes."

"Did you call Detective Altin?" She drew a few stars on her notepad.

"I did."

A few more stars appeared while she counted to ten. "Did Detective Altin say anything about the threat?"

"He said he would look into the matter."

"I see. Has he?"

"No!" Dr. Emir said triumphantly. "I have waited patiently, yet nothing has been done."

She glanced at the time on the large city clock. "Tell you what, Doctor—Detective Altin should be back from lunch by now. Why don't I call the precinct and have a chat with him?"

"You must tell him how important this is. Impress upon him the vital nature of my work."

"I will talk to him about it," Sam promised as she

hung up. With a sigh—this time very audible—she dialed Altin's number. This would make his day.

"Agent Rose? Is this urgent?" Altin made it sound like anything less than a definitive yes wouldn't be worth the interruption.

"Dr. Emir just called."

"He called me twenty minutes ago," Altin said, sounding annoyed.

"He's the type who wants things done yesterday."

Altin mumbled something under his breath.

"Is there anything I need to know right now?" Sam asked.

Altin sucked air in with a hiss. "Yeah. I was going to call you in an hour or so. We can't find Mordicai Robbins."

"He's the security guard who left early, isn't he?" Sam pulled out the case notes to confirm.

"That's him." Altin paused, then added, "A fisherman reported a sunken truck in the water this morning up past the dam."

"Mr. Robbins was in it?" Sam guessed.

"Not that we can see yet, but it's the same make and model as his truck. I was waiting for them to finish hauling it up so we could check the plate numbers. If Mr. Robbins is in there, I'll let you know, but I have a nasty hunch we're going to have a truck sans driver."

"What about the girl, Melody Chimes? Have you found her yet?"

Altin chuckled. "That one, Lord above, no. Her primary address is the campus dorm, but they're on summer break, and she's not enrolled for class. None of the people in the dorm admit to being her roommate."

Sam raised an eyebrow. "Accomplices maybe?"

"That would be the place to get them, and one of them has a rap sheet—underage alcohol consumption, speeding tickets, busted with a fake ID—nothing major but enough that we'd pull her in for a second questioning if we found a connection."

"A cheesy fake driver's license to vandalism of government property is a big jump. Unless she's with part of a radical antigovernment organization, I doubt she's involved."

"It's tenuous. I'll have someone look into it more, but I'm not sure that's the angle."

Sam bit her lip, thinking. "Have you tried catching Melody at work?"

"Miss Chimes put in for a week's worth of leave two days before the break-in. She won't be back until Monday."

"Next of kin?"

"Way ahead of you there," Altin said. "Miss Chimes didn't list anyone on her work record or insurance. I had my lieutenant do some digging, and we found a number for her last known address before she left for college. The property is owned by her parents, but the phone number goes straight to an answering service, and no one is calling us back."

"Where do you see this going?"

"It's anyone's guess right now. I half expect to see

her body in the truck, but it doesn't fit. Robbins and Chimes worked together, but they only worked the same shift a few times in the past three months. The ages and backgrounds don't make them a natural partnership. I just—"

There was an incoherent shout from Altin's end of the line.

"Rose? I'll call you back. We have the truck out. The crew's hosing it down now. Give me an hour to get a body count and figure out who's still missing." He hung up abruptly.

Grumbling under her breath, Sam called Dr. Emir back. The phone rang twice before switching over to voice mail. She left a succinct message telling the doctor that everything was being done and that he could request extra police drive-bys if he felt they were warranted. Then, in preparation for Altin's return call, she pulled the files on Mordicai Robbins and Melody Chimes. The missing person report was easy enough although she left a few slots blank until Altin could fill in the details. Then she pulled out the report on Jane Doe.

Minutes ticked by as she stared at the forms. For a fragile moment, everything hung in the balance— justice, her career, truth—Jane deserved more than to be buried in a pauper's grave under political red tape.

In class exercises, there was always a right answer. There was always *something*. You didn't find bodies with no ID and no evidence. Jane Doe was a statistical anomaly turning into a major roadblock. She felt bitter defeat rising in her. Shaking it off, Sam started to fill in

THE DAY BEFORE 49

the forms to close the case. On the question about type of death, she hesitated.

Homicide was the correct answer, but a homicide case couldn't close until the killer was prosecuted and found guilty. Her pen hovered over the right answer. Just underneath, taunting her, was Class Five Suicide—a suicide with questions. Something she could close now and reopen whenever she wanted. Feeling guilty, Sam put the paper at the back of the pile. The cause-of-death pages were enough to keep her busy while Atlanta finished the blood tests.

She was finishing the report when Altin called her back.

"The truck belongs to Mordicai Robbins," he reported, "but there's no body. Somebody dropped a block of concrete on the accelerator to make the car run. I want a missing person investigation opened by the bureau. That truck's a classic, beautiful detailing work. It's not the kind of thing a man abandons of his own free will."

"Not what I wanted to hear," Sam said, "but I have the paperwork filled in. I'll send a copy to your office so you can fill in the details on the truck. I'll run a public database search for his bank activities and online activity, see if I can build a timeline of what happened when he left the lab."

"Thank you."

"What about Melody Chimes?" Her hand hovered over the button to submit the report she'd already prepared.

Altin muttered a curse. "Hold off. Technically, she's not missing. I want to talk to her, but it can wait until she comes to work on Monday. Unless Mordicai shows up dead, I'd rather let her have her vacation in peace, ya know?"

"Are you sure about that?"

"No." Altin cursed again. "But I'm having trouble pinning this on her. She had a good reputation with the company, good grades at school, no criminal record. At the most, I think she skived off work to go on vacation early. Maybe she meant to call the replacement guard and forgot. Maybe she dialed the wrong number. I just can't see her being our girl."

"But you think she's safe?" Sam asked.

"We have some broken glass but no blood. If I weren't looking at Robbins's truck, I'd say this was nothing."

"Robbins's case could be unrelated. Coincidence *does* happen."

"But with crime, it rarely does."

"Don't I know it," Sam said, frustrated. "Call me when you have an update on Miss Chimes, please. I'll let you know if we turn up anything on Robbins."

On her way out the door, Sam dropped the report about the lab break-in and Mordicai Robbins on Marrins's desk. Like a cherry on a sundae, she left her promotion packet right on top.

CHAPTER 4

> MWI presupposes that all things that could
> happen will happen. Childish thinking. Rough
> nonsense. Consider the quantum particle, it can
> be in two places at once, yes? Yes. But not three.
> There is a finite number of possibilities reachable
> from any STTL incursion into space-time.
>
> ~ Student notes from the class
> Physics and Space-Time I1–2071

Thursday May 23, 2069
Alabama District 3
Commonwealth of North America

Sam read the report Altin had handed over to the
bureau along with a waterlogged truck that was sitting
in the city impound. Mr. Robbins had an old man's fear
of government. In the year prior to the States' joining
the Commonwealth, he'd pulled all his money out of
the banks, moved to an off-grid solar system for power,
and put in a well. Even his salary from Wannervan was
paid in cash. Which made tracking him nearly impossible.

Down the hall, she could hear Marrins talking on the phone. Time to sneak out. She locked her desk and hurried toward the stairs. It didn't help. Marrins was lurking outside his door with his arms folded.

"You think you can quit working just because you requested the transfer?"

"No, sir."

Marrins held out a file folder. "We need background checks done on all the lab personnel. Two hundred and eleven people have access to the labs. Wannervan Security has thirty guards cleared for lab duty—they're sending those files over tomorrow. Altin thinks someone with access to the lab headed the break-in. It's probably a lot of fuss over some drunk college kids, but you're the bureau go-to girl."

"But . . ." Sam stared at him in disbelief. "I need to talk to people. Find the body, or the person, or—" She shook her head. "This is my big case. My chance to build a career. Can't Altin have someone handle this? I told you Robbins was off the grid. Finding him is going to take me at least a week of knocking on doors unless I catch a lucky break, and I still need to finalize everything for Jane Doe."

"Altin's people don't have the clearance levels to do background checks, you do. Guess what I think is more important at this point? Let the police do the legwork."

"Altin's legwork isn't getting anywhere!" she protested. "He can't even send people outside the city limits to Robbins's address. At least let me go knock on the guy's door."

"The police found Robbins's truck," Marrins said. "That's more than I expected them to do."

Sam dropped the efile in her purse and followed Marrins to his office. "Sir, we both know the bureau badge is going to open more doors than anything the district PD can throw around. I want to be on the ground for this. "

Marrins sat in his overpadded chair with an oomph. "Robbins has a standing prescription for antidepressants that hadn't been filled in a week. Did you know that? No, because you were going down some schoolroom checklist instead of thinking for ten seconds straight. But I knew. Wannervan Security's health insurance is only accepted one place in town. I called their pharmacist to see what medical support Robbins needs."

"I didn't know you had a warrant for that, sir."

"Didn't need it. That's the advantage of living in one place for so long. People know you. They trust you. You want a promotion, that's the sort of thing you need to do. Play nice with people. Follow orders. Get those background checks done."

Her shoulders dropped.

Marrins's swivel chair whined as he twisted comfortably. Booted feet clunked on his desktop. "Why are you still here?"

She shook herself awake with a sigh. "I'll drop this in my office safe and make it a priority in the morning."

"Good." Marrins smiled, pushing layers of flub into a creeptastic leer.

"Did you approve my D.C. papers yet?" Sam asked. "I know the JD case isn't much, but it meets quota for a junior district agent. I have everything I need to become a full agent and transfer to another district."

"Everything but balls," Marrins agreed. "I'll make it a priority when the Jane case is officially closed. Even put in a good word for ya. You aren't a brilliant agent—no spine or creativity—but you work well enough for a woman. What D.C. will do with you, I can't guess, but they need secretaries more than I need deadweight."

"Thank you, sir."

"Get on home." Marrins waved his hand. "It's late."

She dropped the files in her safe and walked out as Marrins answered another late-night call, door slamming shut behind him.

A feeling of deep contentment filled Sam as, sweaty from a run, she walked into the quiet Southern house. Hoss wagged his nubbin of a tail in unfeigned adoration as she found him a piece of bacon while she made dinner. Ever so slowly, she was chasing away the smell of dust and neglect with good meals cooked in the large kitchen.

Sam showered as blueberry muffins baked, then snagged one from the oven and danced through the empty living room and up the stairs to her refuge. Her new bedroom had received the bulk of her interest when she moved in two months ago, and now it was the perfect place to read or relax.

Knowing that she wouldn't be here that much longer probably added to the allure.

An alarm buzzer sounded as she flopped on her bed. Sam dumped her purse on the white quilt, and three manila folders fell from her bag. The Jane Doe file was glowing red. A private addendum, added in chicken-scratch handwriting under the classified notes section: "Jane Doe is probably not a clone–L.M."

Sam pulled out her phone and dialed MacKenzie's work number, audio only. It rang for a long time, then there was a grunt that might have been a rudimentary attempt at communication. "Agent MacKenzie?" Another grunt. "This is Agent Rose. What do you mean Jane isn't a clone?"

"Um, Verville?"

She quietly beat her head against her pillow. "Agent MacKenzie, full sentences, if you please."

"The, ah, the blood work. Atlanta. No Verville traces."

"None?" The Verville list was the holy book of cloning. Every company that legally produced and sold clones on the international market was required to keep their code sequence on the Verville list. "Is Atlanta double-checking its work?"

"Mmmhmm."

"That does support Marrins's black-market-clone hypothesis." She chewed her lip in consideration. "Jane didn't have a tattoo, did she? Some of the rape houses that use black-market clones brand their merchandise." Clones were a luxury item, but there was always someone willing to rent

"Nothing. I . . . I don't think we're looking at a clone."

A shiver ran up her back. "Murder victims with no identity . . . you just . . . no. That doesn't happen in the real world. Everyone is on the grid, you can't get off it, not legally. Next you're going to suggest Jane was some anti-Commonwealth terrorist or something outrageous. There *has* to be an explanation as to who she is."

There was a noncommittal grunt from the other end of the line. "The body . . ." MacKenzie choked on the other end of the line, then coughed.

"Are you okay?"

"Mmm. The body doesn't make sense."

For a brief moment, Sam pictured MacKenzie trying to talk to a corpse. The image was surprisingly easy to piece together—disturbing, but not far-fetched. "What doesn't make sense?"

"The . . . the injuries don't match the evidence." He coughed again. "I w-want to see the kill field."

"The dump site?" Sam frowned in confusion as she checked the time. "Fine. First thing tomorrow morning work for you? I'm supposed to have the report on Marrins's desk by five tomorrow, and if you're sure Jane isn't a clone, that complicates matters. You are sure, aren't you?"

"Pretty sure. I . . . I sent a second blood sample to Atlanta."

"Good thinking. I'll double-check the missing persons list. Are you sure about the age?"

"There was . . . was a lot of, um, bone trauma. She was very active. Maybe military or something like that. Maybe . . . maybe knock off a few years?"

"I'll widen the search. It won't be the first time someone misestimated a victim's age. See you in the morning." Her eyes lingered on the computer-generated image of Jane Doe, her face. *My face.*

Not that it didn't happen. Weren't people always saying how they ran into someone who looked just like them? Of course, if life were like her mother's favorite telenova, Jane would turn out to be her long-lost twin sister, or her secret clone made by a stalker ex-boyfriend, and everything would be wrapped up neatly in under an hour when the detective found a fingerprint left behind by the killer.

If only it worked like that in real life.

She closed the files and set the alarm. Tomorrow, Jane had one more chance to tell her story.

CHAPTER 5

> What is "I"? Who is "Me"? These are abstract concepts with no meaning beyond the limited definitions society grants them. The belief in "Self" is as dangerous to the welfare of the Collective as the belief in gods.
>
> ~ Excerpt from *The Oneness of Being* by Oaza Moun I1–2072

Friday May 24, 2069
Alabama District 3
Commonwealth of North America

Sam pulled into the bureau parking lot and stopped in front of the morgue, where Agent MacKenzie sat on the curb. "Get in," she said through the rolled-down window. "I want to get out of here before Marrins notices that I'm missing. I'm supposed to be doing background checks today."

The perpetual *eau de morgue* that hung around MacKenzie like swamp gas climbed into the car with him.

"I was thinking about the Verville traces last night. Isn't the absence of the Verville a good argument for a black-market clone?"

He rubbed a shaking hand through shaggy brown hair—probably dislodging a whole colony of lice—and sighed. "Jane is . . . was . . . in her thirties."

The car switched on with a soft hum and swish of liquid cells coming to life. Cold air seeped between the seats as she pulled out of the parking lot. "You keep saying that like it means something."

"Jane would have been about ten when the clone-marker law of 2048 was passed. When she was born . . ." MacKenzie stared off into space for a moment. He shook himself. "When Jane was born, the United States wasn't . . . wasn't even a signer of the United Charter. The United dollar wasn't the basis for currency in the western hemisphere, and cloning was in its infancy. People weren't cloning shadows for possible organ transplant in forty years, they were cloning . . . replacements."

Sam turned off the main highway. "So, she was an expensive clone?"

"Replacements. Children lost t-to tragedy, kidnapping." MacKenzie shrugged in a forlorn way. "People don't . . . didn't talk about them."

"Kid goes missing, mom and dad go traveling, kid comes back," Sam filled in. "I've heard about it, but she could still be a clone. The same laws apply. Even if she predates the clone marker, something will show up on the Verville traces. That was part of the law, too: every cloning technique tried, used, or hypothesized needed a test on file."

MacKenzie shook his head. "Early clones were . . . th-they didn't last long. Twenty years, twenty-five. The first clones are already . . . dead."

"I checked that. There are clones that predate 2048."

"Not black-market clones. They cut corners. Do things so the clones age faster. It . . . it makes finding the Verville traces hard."

She glanced at him, trying to keep her anger in check. Nothing was ever easy. But they all had jobs to do, and *his* was to find those markers.

The car chimed, and a red phone light blinked. "Ambassador Pinuela-Rose," the car announced as it slowed automatically to compensate for driver distraction. A little yellow light blinked on the outer rim of the side-door mirrors to indicate that the driver had taken a call and was distracted. It was one of those little safety features that Sam could have lived without if law allowed.

"Rose here," Sam said in her best I'm-working-keep-it-quick voice.

"Samantha." Her mother's voice filled the car. "You haven't called me in over a week."

In the seat next to her, Agent MacKenzie turned to the window, doing his best impression of a rock. It was almost as convincing as his impression of a human.

"Work problems," she said, keeping it vague. MacKenzie gave her a strange look; he probably thought he was her work problem. *He's not too far off the mark.* Sam turned the phone volume down and the AC up, so it blasted his head. *Subtle-hints-r-us.*

"It's Friday, I expect you'll be at Mass tonight?"

"That's my plan," she lied, snapping a quick glare at MacKenzie to keep him quiet. "Mom, this isn't a good time for me. Can we talk later?" She put as much emphasis on the word later as she could.

Her mother tutted. "I'm traveling this weekend. Embassy receptions and a new general to meet. I'll call again on Monday to straighten your schedule out. There's a D.C. visit coming up in my schedule if no one cancels again, and I want you to be there."

"Washington, D.C., isn't really driving distance from Alabama. The Commonwealth is a little bit bigger than Europe."

"Samantha, darling, that wasn't a request. I will send my itinerary to you on Monday when everything is finalized. Be good. Go to Mass and confession."

"Yes, Mother. Good-bye, Mother." Sam hung up and rolled her eyes. "Sorry."

MacKenzie didn't acknowledge her.

"All mothers are nags, right?" she tried again.

"Don't know. I haven't talked to mine in five years."

Sam felt a twinge of guilt. "Oh. I'm sorry. I didn't realize she was dead."

"She's not."

They drove the rest of the way in silence. She parked the car next to the open field. The sad, sun-bleached evidence flags waved in the faint breeze, marking where pieces of Jane had been found. "Here we are, Jane's penultimate resting place."

MacKenzie climbed out of the car and scanned the field with a frown. "Here?" He pointed at the open field in confusion.

"Yes, here." Sam stepped into the field, ready to do the tour. They walked the perimeter. The ground was hard from weeks without rain and showed no evidence of recent activity. No tire tracks. No footprints. For all the world, it looked like Jane Doe had dropped from the open sky.

"This . . . this doesn't fit," MacKenzie said with a shake of his head.

While the ME stumbled around, Sam knelt to get a ground view of the scenery: bare field, pine trees, oak, and scrub on the hazy edges, wildflowers wilting and going to seed in the heat, a glint of metal on the ground. She reached under a spiky weed for the glint. Just in time, Sam remembered she was at a crime scene. "There's something here. Go get my evidence kit from the backseat."

MacKenzie fetched her bag from the car and handed it over. Using a green flag to mark the spot, Sam picked up a silver ring with her tweezers and dropped it into the evidence bag. It was delicate and pretty, something a woman would wear.

The silver ring shone in the sunlight. "Did Jane wear a ring?" Sam peered closer, she'd had a ring like it years ago. She'd lost it in one of the moves after college.

MacKenzie frowned at her. "Um . . . ?"

"Was there a tan line on her fingers? Is there any reason to think this is hers, or is this something we should be trying to pin on a suspect?"

He turned away, dodging the bag. "I-I have to check." He looked around the field in confusion. "Jane was frozen after death. She . . . when she showed up at the lab, the decomposition was slowed, but still fairly advanced." He frowned at the field as if personally offended by the Alabama sawgrass.

She tucked the evidence bag in her kit with her gloves and shrugged. "So they brought her to the dump site in a refrigerated truck?"

"Yeah . . . probably." Now he was staring at the cloudless sky.

Sam craned her neck to look up. Maybe he was looking for aliens, you never knew with his type. "Missing something?"

"Trees. Jane's face. Her head was crushed postmortem, like she'd run into a wall or been thrown into something. I'm still doing reconstruction." He sighed. "Jane Doe was tortured, over days. Strangled by ropes, and hands. Killed, I don't know how. Frozen. Crushed. Arm torn off."

"She had to fall somewhere. Her face was crushed by an impact of some kind." She studied the empty sky with renewed interest. "There are some trees near the stream over there where the truck driver found her arm and hand." She pointed out the copse of pines to MacKenzie. "The rest of the body was in the middle of the field, but we didn't find rope or anything."

"Plane?" he guessed.

"That's what I thought originally. The only case I've seen with that kind of facial trauma was a parachute accident we looked at in the academy, but the nearest airport is over forty miles away. It's a major metro airport, high-security, no baggage allowed. Strictly commuters to Atlanta and Birmingham."

"Crop duster?"

"No crops in this area, this whole place is marked for natural renewal through 2107. No planting, farming, gardening, or harvesting of biological materials allowed." Sam raised an eyebrow at his impressed expression. "What? I did do my homework after I read the full autopsy."

"Sport diving?"

"Skydiving?" Sam shook her head. "I haven't heard about anything like that out here, but I can check to see if there are any companies that use this area."

They walked through the field twice more in search of more clues, but their hopes were in vain. Discouraged, they retreated from the baking heat to the cooler confines of the car.

"I see three possibilities," Sam said as she turned the car on and started driving back to town. "The most likely is that Jane Doe was killed by someone she knew, they dumped her, and they are the only ones who would have reported her so, no missing person file. Domestic dispute is the top of my list. There may have been elements of bondage play."

MacKenzie stared out the window. "No."

"It's a possibility."

"No evidence of rape."

"Maybe her husband was a psycho killer. It's happened before. The second variation there, which you keep trying to rule out, is that Jane is a clone. Her owner didn't want her, and she was dumped. Or maybe we're looking at a case of heavy self-aggression: if you can't commit suicide, you can kill your clone. The ultimate-sacrifice style of thing."

"Killing a clone is not the ultimate sacrifice," MacKenzie cut in vehemently.

Sam looked over at him. His face was white, and his jaw clenched. *Message received: no-fly zone.* "Right. Sorry. Moving on." She waited to see if he would relax. Mackenzie did, a tiny bit, and she nodded. "Scenario three, Jane isn't listed as a missing person because no one knows she's missing yet but her killer. Maybe she was the artistic type who liked to hike through the hinterlands, and her family wasn't expecting her back for a few weeks."

"Doesn't fit the timeline," MacKenzie said with a shake of his head.

"What was the time of death?"

The ME shifted in his seat. "Hard to determine. She was a . . . a prisoner for over a month."

"Over a month? How much over a month?"

"From the rate of healing and the sores? Maybe . . . maybe three months? Maybe a little less."

"So Jane went missing in February?"

Agent MacKenzie nodded.

Sam crossed herself. "Missing for three months changes things a little. I suppose Jane could have moved, then gone missing during or just after the relocation. Her old friends wouldn't be looking, and there would be no one locally to sound an alarm."

MacKenzie shrugged.

"There were no hits on her dental records?"

"Not in the public files."

"You have third-degree clearance—check the private citizens, government workers, and run a check on missing-presumed-dead from around when Jane was born. I'd hate for this to turn into another Torture House case, but it's looking like we can't rule it out." She chewed on that for a minute. "Marrins will start salivating. He'd love a big case like that."

And he'd scoop it from me in a heartbeat, leaving me a case shy of getting out of here.

"There's . . . there's another option," MacKenzie said in a quiet voice.

"Mmm?"

"Jane could have been replaced. She was muscular, real . . . real fit. A soldier, maybe. Or . . . or law enforcement. The muscles were"—he moved his hands as if trying to twist something—"were right. The wear on her bones was right." He stopped, and Sam waited for his brain to catch up with his tongue. "She could have been killed and replaced with a clone."

Sam made a face. "That's just disgusting. Wouldn't someone notice?"

"A well-trained shadow? No. No . . . Jane could be . . . be the woman we have in the morgue and h- have a shadow running around as . . . as her."

She arched an eyebrow. "Really? I think you've been reading too many science-fiction books."

"It's happened." He rubbed a hand across his face. "There was the Elendorf Securities case back in '64, and at least two intelligence agents targeted . . ." Mac faltered as he looked up at her. "What?"

"How do you know this?"

"The Elendorf thing was all over the news. It sounded like a soap opera, 'CEO's son replaced him with clone to keep stepmother number four from getting near his trust fund.' Someone threatened to make a movie about it. How did you not hear about it? "

"I meant, how did you know about the intelligence agents?"

Mac shrugged. "I talk to people."

"It's still sounds far-fetched."

He shrugged. "We tried to match Jane to a missing person, and we couldn't. If a shadow stole her identity, we're searching in the wrong pool for our fish."

"Fine, let's rule out the shadow theory. Run Jane's profile through the census database. If she's still alive, I'll convince the judge to keep the case open and get a warrant for a DNA sample. And MacKenzie," she said, as they pulled up in front of the morgue, "get off the pills."

He started guiltily and nodded.

Sam turned the ring, still in the bag, so it caught the light, and she could read the inscription again. *"Soyez fidèle à les petite choses, parce-qu'il est dans lui que ta force restais."* Be faithful in small things because it is in them that your strength lies. A quote from Saint Mother Teresa of Calcutta.

She had the same ring with the inscription in English once upon a time. It had been a gift from her mother when she'd graduated from St. Catherine's, probably the only gift her mother had bought for Sam herself. All her other birthday presents were bought by her mother's personal secretary. There was a little Catholic bookstore across the street from St. Catherine's imposing main gate where you could buy a ring like this with the quote in English, French, or Spanish. On their way to the graduation ceremony, they'd stopped to purchase a chapel veil to replace the one her mother had forgotten at home, and her mother had bought the ring at the same time. It was a trinket, really, but it meant her mother had thought of her.

Sam clicked through the images on her computer screen. There was nothing about the ring that made it stand out from the millions of other rings that were the staple of the Christian retail market. Still, part of her wanted to say this was a St. Catherine's ring.

"Rose?" Marrins knocked on her doorframe as he walked in. "Just got off the line with Birmingham. Where's their Jane?"

"Sir? I put a copy of the blood work report on your

desk this morning before I pulled the data from Agent Anan's case. Atlanta confirmed that Jane Doe is not a clone."

Marrins sighed and collapsed into one of the rickety aluminum chairs meant for visitors. The chair creaked under his weight. "No hits on the public database?"

"No, sir. MacKenzie is accessing the public-census database, and I sent a request to the regional headquarters for permission to check the private database. I can't access that information at my pay grade."

"And they bounced it back to me." Marrins shook his head. "I've checked. This Jane doesn't match anyone. Trust an old man's instincts on this: she's a clone. I've seen a hundred cases just like this."

"But there were no Verville traces."

He waved her into silence. "Lab error. Atlanta will rerun the test and find the traces."

"And we have already started that test, so we should have confirmation soon. But, sir, we have the ring—"

"A ring that fell off her hand." Marrins exhaled noisily. "I saw your note, Rose. It's nothing." He sat up a bit straighter. A bit.

Hard to sit straight when you're so round. . .

Sam looked at Marrins guiltily, unsure if she'd said it aloud. But the senior agent continued, saying "I need you to refocus on the lab case. Altin is turning up nothing, and I need suspects. Start working the phones, call the tech people who have the cameras. *Do the background checks I asked you for.* I want to know what they saw. I'm tired of loose ends all over the place."

"Yes, sir," Sam mumbled, as Marrins rose and lumbered back out the door.

A ring. A body. Nothing more. No suspects. No witnesses. Not even a name on the corpse.

Her phone rang, and she picked it up with a weary sigh. "Agent Rose speaking, how can I help you, sir or ma'am?"

"I've . . . I've got a problem," Agent MacKenzie stuttered over the line.

"Yes, you do," Sam agreed. She heard Marrins's door slam down the hall.

"Are you at your computer?" MacKenzie asked.

Ice crawled up her spine, and she had to glance over her shoulder to make sure he wasn't staring in her second-floor window. "What do you need?"

"I'm"—there was a click on the other end—"sending a file. I need help."

A black-and-white picture of circles appeared on her screen. "What is this, MacKenzie?"

"Bone fragments. Patterns on bone."

She zoomed out of the picture to see the whole of Jane's skeleton. "The bone looks like it's rippled. Can bone ripple?" she asked.

"I don't know," he said.

Sam snarled in exasperation. "MacKenzie, you're the one with a medical background. I took two years of basic biology in uni. They didn't cover melted bones. What caused this?"

"I . . . I think it's what killed Jane. The murder weapon."

She raised an eyebrow. "Like the shatter around the entry point of a bullet? Or are you saying she had a genetic defect that left her like this, and she died of natural causes after being tortured?"

"Like the bullet," he said. "I . . . I think I've seen it before," he added in a whisper.

"Way too much hesitation, MacKenzie."

"I've seen this before," he said, still quiet but firm.

Sam tapped her finger on her desk. "Are you sober?" There was a splutter of protest from the other end of the line. "I've got to know if you're reliable. Are you sober? Right now?"

"I'm trying. The pills . . . I need them. I need them to sleep."

"Well, then, you're no help to me—I'm being ordered to wrap this up now." She took a deep breath. "Look, I'm going to call this a Class Five for now, which means we can always follow up on it later. In the meantime, try taking a hot shower and reading a book," Sam said. "Call me back when you're sober, and your pickled brain remembers what caused this." She hung up, putting the receiver down a bit harder than she needed to.

Growling under her breath, Sam started to fill in the forms to close the case. Jane deserved so much more. A name on her gravestone, the promise of her killer brought to justice. No one deserved an anonymous grave to be buried and forgotten. Sam marked Class Five, suicide with questions.

Saint Peter have mercy, Jane didn't die like that. Surely God and the saints would understand. *As soon as I have more information, I'll give Jane back her name.* She'd tell the Father at confession and say a few extra Hail Marys. At least Marrins would be satisfied, and her transfer paperwork could finally get processed.

CHAPTER 6

> When I close my eyes for the last time, I pray to the un-
> feeling gods that my last thought is not one of regret.
> Let me live while I live, so that I might die in peace.
>
> ~ Excerpt from *The Heart of Fear*
> by Liedjie Slaan I1

Monday May 27, 2069
Alabama District 3
Commonwealth of North America

Sam deleted the itinerary from her mother and took a bite of her blueberry muffin and perused the list of possible matches for Jane Doe. Still nothing. Searching by estimated height, weight, and age wasn't connecting Jane to any person missing or dead in the public database. Sam tried to dismiss the feeling she was missing something. All the flags were there for a black-market-clone case . . . except for the known clone markers. Agent Anan in Birmingham was still holding out hope that Atlanta would find Verville traces, but that only made the decision to close Jane's case worse.

"Agent Rose." The receptionist's voice over the intercom stopped Sam mid–internal rant.

She hit the REPLY button. "In my office."

"You have a visitor, Agent Rose. The lady identifies herself as Miss Chimes. Should I have her come back another time?"

"Show her up, please." Sam brushed the crumbs off her desk and slipped out the pair of handcuffs issued to her for emergencies. She dropped them into her lap as she heard voices in the hall.

"This way," the secretary said. "Last office on the left."

"Thank you," was the demure reply. A woman stepped into Sam's office, dark skin, green eyes, wiry curls with a tint of red. Atlantic Islander Irish with a mocha-latte baby resting on her hip. She didn't look like a college student working her way through school.

"Miss Chimes?" Sam motioned to the free chair. "Won't you have a seat?"

Miss Chimes took the seat with athletic grace. "It's Chimes-Martin now," she said with the crisp accent only an expensive private education could buy.

Sam quickly reassessed her guest. "You aren't Melody?"

Mrs. Chimes-Martin gave her a bland look. "I'm Dulcet, Melody's older sister. Detective Altin said you were handling Melody's disappearance?"

"If the police determine she is missing, yes, I'd take over. I'm the bureau liaison for the case."

"If she is?" Dulcet Chimes-Martin said in a tight voice. "What do you mean, *if she is*? My sister isn't answering her phone. How much more evidence could you possibly need?"

"There is no evidence your sister is missing, only that she left work. The summer course she's enrolled in starts in two weeks so she hasn't missed any classes yet. She hasn't missed work. She hasn't been reported missing by her family—unless that's what you're here to do. According to her work file, she was going on vacation and planned to spend the week with her parents. The bureau is not in the habit of chasing down people on vacation when all their paperwork is in order."

Mrs. Chimes-Martin set her baby on the floor, then leaned forward. "I know the protocol for situations like this. Under the circumstances, I feel I have been exceptionally patient. Melody's name has been all over the news as a suspect, but no one has contacted my family. Why did no one knock on my door? Why weren't my parents notified?"

Irritated, Sam turned back to her computer and opened the file. "Melody had no next of kin on record. Her listed addresses for the past three years were Dorm C, rooms 102, 312, and 314 respectively. Detective Altin sent a patrol officer out to interview the roommates, but everyone denied knowing her. Detective Altin also tried her mobile number, and the listed number for your parents. Both went to answering services." Sam sent the file to her handheld and pushed the small screen to across her desk.

Dulcet Chimes-Martin's expertly applied makeup creased in a frown. "I don't understand."

Sam took a deep breath and tried again. "Some people like to go on vacation and disconnect."

She let that sink in, then continued, "Nothing at the lab suggested anyone was injured. There's some broken glass and a few fried cleaning bots, but no signs of bodily violence. If anything, your sister is guilty of negligence and will probably lose her job for leaving work early. The police would like to speak with her, but she isn't a suspect, no matter what the media are saying. We've pursued her with due diligence and come up with nothing. Can you look at her information? Maybe there was a typo, or she used an old phone number? Any help you can offer would be appreciated."

Reluctantly, Mrs. Chimes-Martin took the data pad. She frowned at it, then shook her head. "I don't understand this address. This is wrong.". She handed the pad back. "My sister never lived in the dorms. Our parents bought her a house next to the school."

"I'm sorry, that's what we have on record."

"Melody's files must have been mixed with another employee's." There was a note of desperate pleading in the woman's voice.

Sam pulled up her work for Melody's missing person report. "Mrs. Chimes-Martin, at this time, would you like to officially state that your sister is missing?"

The woman looked at her in bewilderment. "What?"

"I need an official report to get the bureau involved. As her sister, do you want to report Melody Chimes as a missing person?"

"Yes!"

Sam nodded. "When was the last time you saw Melody?"

Mrs. Chimes-Martin scooped her baby up and held her close. "Um, two weeks ago, I guess. She comes over every other Sunday after choir practice. Usually, she calls home once or twice a week, but she didn't call this week."

"Is it possible she's with your parents?" Sam asked as she filled in details.

"My parents? No, they're at their summer home on the Riviera. Melody doesn't like it there. She was planning to work all summer. She's saving for a trip to Ireland next fall. My parents are making her pay for half of the expenses."

"Why would she ask for vacation time to visit her parents if she wasn't going?" Sam countered.

Dulcet Chimes-Martin shook her head angrily. "You must have someone else's file."

"That's doubtful. All files at the lab are genetically coded. This is the file linked to your sister. For whatever reason, she chose not to list anyone as next of kin, and she lied about where she was going on vacation. Apparently, she lied about her address, too. Do you know if she had a boyfriend? Could she have left town with friends?"

The baby started to cry. Mrs. Chimes-Martin hugged her child and stood. "I don't like what you're insinuating. My sister is a loving, caring, honest girl. She wouldn't run off without talking to me first." She bit her lip as if afraid to say too much. "My sister is missing, Agent Rose. I'm saying that officially. She is missing. I want a report filed. I want her found."

Marrins is going to love this.

The graveyard on the outskirts of town had a white stone fence, two lion statues in bronze at the entrance, and an old-world feel of elegance at odds with the modern memorials lining the main thoroughfare. Sky-blue pillars of light crowded the walkway with faces and laughter. Electronic ghosts, the latest way to make your loved one live for eternity.

Sam's car phone played the first few bars of a dirge. "Averton Place Memorial Park, who are you visiting with today?"

"I am here for the Jane Doe service, public space 88-751."

"Our condolences on the loss of Jane Doe, public space 88-751." The blue ghosts flickered, and the console map illuminated a path to Jane's grave.

Nothing like an automated message to bring the sentiment home. . .

Blue-light projections of the dead flitted around the car as Sam drove through the memorial arch to an open field. Jane's grave was here under the bright blue Alabama sky, cast adrift with the other flotsam of society.

Her heels sunk into the freshly watered grass. Marrins stood talking with the funeral director in a quiet voice, not sparing her a glance. Public-service drones—freed clones released from their owner's service for one reason or another—carried the flimsy pine box up the hill. A third vehicle pulled in on the gravel driveway. Agent MacKenzie unfolded from his truck, blinking against the bright sun.

Detached, Sam watched the clones lower Jane into the red-clay earth. The funeral director murmured a few words of memorial before tossing a handful of religious trinkets in after the casket.

Sam crossed herself, said a brief prayer to Saint Anthony of Padua, patron saint of lost things. Jane lost not just her life but her name as well. Perhaps the saints and angels would get it back.

Plus, she could honestly tell her mother she'd prayed this week. That should earn her a few brownie points.

Agent MacKenzie's accusing glare stopped her as she walked to her car. "You stopped looking." His harsh whisper came out full of anger and hurt. "Why'd you close the case?" He was shaking again, but the stutter was gone.

She waited in silence until Marrins left. "I saved both our careers. Marrins wanted Jane laid to rest, I made that happen. Like I told you, if we find something, I can reopen the case." She hesitated as his eyes narrowed. "I promise, if we find proof Jane was human, I will find her killer. But right now, I've got to focus on a girl who might still be alive."

He stalked away, anger and exhaustion seeming to flow off him in competing waves.

I know exactly how you feel, MacKenzie.

CHAPTER 7

> A weapon in the hand of a civilian is like fire in
> the hand of a child: the end result will be a world
> in flames.
>
> ~ Minister of Defense on the antiweapons
> amendment to the Collective Constitution I1–2070

Tuesday May 28, 2069
Alabama District 3
Commonwealth of North America

Empty pill bottle in hand, Mac stumbled back to his room, mouth tasting of mint toothpaste and vomit. It was dark, he was tired—there was a connection there, but he couldn't name it. Weak yellow light from the parking lot cut through bent plastic blinds and fell on his rumpled, sweat-stained sheets. He leaned on the door, trying to decide what he wanted more: a pounding headache or nightmares.

The headache won.

He kicked a pile of clothes near the bed, dislodging a long-legged something that skittered away in silence.

With no regard to his personal well-being, Mac thrust a hand into the pile of discards, pulling out a shirt. It didn't look familiar, but nothing did these days. The pills turned the past into a mist of colors and scents that no thought could penetrate. Little details slipped away, names, when he had a shower last, when he ate last, but it didn't matter. He could work, and the rent got paid.

But now the pills were gone. He'd cut the prescription dose in half, trying to stretch his supply until his refill came. Little good it did, leaving him in a limbo of fuzzy memories and disturbing dreams. The half dose meant other, stronger, memories crept back in. Memories that woke him screaming in terror.

Mac rubbed his arm, not entirely sure what he'd dreamt about. There had been blood, and the smell of burning human flesh, and screams. Something about a baby. His hand twitched, grabbing air where a gun once sat in his holster.

His memory was playing tricks on him again, reality and nightmare becoming a muddle of incoherent thoughts. He was still able to recall the face of the female agent who'd walked into the morgue soaking wet. Well, if not her face, enough detail that he could identify her again. And he remembered bones.

Bones with circles.

Mac stared at the peeling paint of the wall, trying to remember why the circles were important. He pulled on the shirt that didn't smell any better than the rest of the room and trudged out the door. The morgue was three blocks away, and since it was a nice night, he'd walk and see if someone would try to mug him. It would be a welcome change.

Mac only fumbled the lock once. The morgue door opened with a groaning protest, and cold air washed over him. An antiseptic floor bot blinked a green light at him, but it wasn't programmed to do anything more than scrub floors. He shut the door to keep the bot from scrubbing the sidewalks and trudged down to his office. A narrow, rectangular window ran along the upper quarter of the wall, giving him a view of grass and the parking lot during the day. It wasn't much, but the streetlight in the bureau parking lot next to the gentler light of the moon was more than enough to illuminate his mostly subterranean office.

Closing the door, he stared at the stack of papers on his L-shaped desk. He knocked them to the floor to reveal the hidden diagnostic screen. Piling anatomy texts three deep on top of the screen probably voided the warranty, but if the manufacturer hadn't intended for the screen to be used as a desk, it shouldn't have designed it to look like one. Mac found the ON button after two guesses and watched with curiosity as the machine started to warm up. Eighteen months in the hot purgatory of Alabama, and he'd never needed to do anything like this.

This was work, the kind that required an actual functional brain.

Mac pulled up the image of Jane Doe's body lying akimbo in a field of wilted grass. Her right arm had been found several feet from the body, torn off but torn straight. Jane's head had rolled to the side, attached with no teeth marks, which ruled out animals scavenging off the body before it was found. There were pieces of flesh strewn throughout the field, with slivers of metal and glass in them.

Manipulating the image, Mac pulled Jane back together. Assuming everything had moved in a straight line . . . Her attached arm was up, her head turned, one leg was twisted up at an unnatural angle, and she was on her back. It wasn't the position he expected a body to land when it was thrown out of a car, which was currently the best guess as to how Jane Doe found herself in the field.

In a situation like this, he expected the body to land face-first. Grab the arms and legs and toss, but that took two people. One person would drag the body. Mac stood, twisting his torso as he mimed carrying someone. A fireman's carry would work. Jane's head hanging over the killer's back, then the killer hunched forward before throwing the body down. Jane would flop. And the leg? Maybe the killer kicked her.

Pulling a notepad out of his desk, Mac started writing. If the body flopped, Jane was freshly dead. There was no sign of either rigor mortis or livor mortis. The body came in fairly clean, no bloating or smell, no insect growth. Mac scratched his head.

That couldn't be right, could it? The insects in Alabama were notorious for the rapid destruction of decaying bodies. That far from civilization, ants and vultures should have reduced the body to bone in a matter of days. Insect growth would have started within the first hour.

Making a note to check for recent bruises, Mac pulled up his original file on the case and the notes from the police department.

He skimmed over the data: found date, height, clothing . . . There. The pictures of the crime scene again showed Jane had been lying less than three feet from a large ant nest. Body showed no signs of insect infestation and was cold to the touch. The police department's report had a question mark next to that.

Jane died somewhere after being tortured, then she was tossed into a refrigerated truck that rapidly cooled her postmortem and dumped on the side of the road. Within an hour, the body was discovered. That sounded awfully convenient to him. But the man who found the body had a pickup truck with broken air-conditioning, hardly the vehicle needed to move Jane.

With a frown, Mac peeled back the layer of skin electronically, so he could look at surface wounds. The computer displayed a nightmarish bruise of purple and blue with slashes of white. The white areas were recent, unhealed, injuries. All the injuries faded to purple, then black the older they got. Jane was a mess of injuries. Mostly on her feet. A white handprint circled her right forearm, and her back was one giant smear of white. Just looking at that, he guessed she'd been hit from behind. Or thrown. He could see multiple scenarios. In one, someone tried to pull her to safety, bruising her arm. In the other, someone grabbed Jane and slammed her back against something hard.

So what had Jane hit?

Doing some basic math, he tried to figure out the force needed to throw someone, while holding their wrist, to sever their arm from the body. The answer eluded him, but a human amped up on drugs probably couldn't do it alone.

Frowning, he peeled back the layers. The muscles looked good, strong and tight without much excess fat. Jane had been healthy when alive, up until the end, at least. There were early signs of malnutrition and muscle loss, but a month of torture would explain that. The bones told a different story than the skin. There was a fracture on the left ankle, maybe five years old and fully healed. Both shinbones showed signs of abuse, like Jane had been a runner. But the broken trauma he expected from the impact with something hard wasn't there. The head was damaged, part of the skull collapsed, but the spine and the rest were fine.

Mac rotated the image to focus on the spine and neck. A snapped spine would have twisted the body, but no. Impact on the left jawbone that shattered the side of her face, and nothing more. He zoomed in closer. Hairline fractures radiated out.

He pulled back the focus and tried to trace the fracture. Once again, it seemed to confirm his initial thoughts: it looked like the bone had rippled.

He shivered.

Sunlight poured through the window as Mac massaged the knots out of his hunched shoulders. If he could just get the computer to spit out a list of possible matches. Something, anything—no one went from birth to adulthood without leaving a trace. Dental work, bone fractures, somewhere in the system was Jane Doe. Someone knew her name. Someone knew why she was dead.

He stared at the computer screen, willing the answer to appear. Searching the database by age range, gender, possible jobs . . . none of it worked. He deleted all the parameters. Start over. Try it another way.

Try smashing my fist into the computer and see if that interfaces.

Maybe not.

Mac pulled up Jane's file again. There it was, everything he had on her from DNA to fingerprints. He dumped it all into the search system. No parameters. Every single person, living, dead, or cloned would be checked against Jane's record.

The computer screen turned green. A little search box popped up in the corner: SEARCHING—estimated time 216 hours.

Fine.

He turned off the screen and picked up the papers his boss, Harley, had dropped in his box when he strolled in this morning. There was one regional autopsy to review vids of because the case was being contested, and one house to be swept by a bureau agent.

Why? When did the ME become the de facto crime-scene tech? Oh, the joys of being a bureau agent. Mac packed his bag, shuffled through the drowning Alabama heat to his apartment, and drove across town to a brick house with pale green shutters, a hummingbird feeder hanging from the front porch, and a familiar gray Alexian Virgo he knew from the office parking lot outside.

"**A**gent Rose?" Mac knocked on the open door as he stepped inside the house. The house was decorated with pictures of a cheerful family at various events from graduations to weddings, a Disharmonic Blitz poster with a ballerina in blood red, and Agent Rose, frowning at the contents of the fridge.

She looked up at him. Quick elevator eyes, a downturn of the lips, and Agent Perfect slammed the fridge. "Rotted meat still in the marinade. Half a gallon of milk gone sour. There's a note on the calendar about a date with someone named Lim next week, but otherwise no sign of Miss Chimes."

Mac looked around at the tidy house with just the finest layer of dust over every surface. "What am I looking for?"

"A body?" Agent Rose said with a tight smile.

"Where?" The house smelled clean.

Agent Rose shrugged. "If I knew that, I wouldn't be here to follow up the police walk-through. Detective Altin is sending someone over in about an hour to clean up the fridge and do a walk-through again with the girl's sister. Sister dearest, a Mrs. Chimes-Martin, showed up in my office yesterday, ranting and raving about bureau incompetence. She did file a missing person report, though, so at least I'm free to investigate."

He looked around the empty house again. "Is this a crime scene?"

"Not officially, Melody Chimes was last seen at N-V Nova Labs. Making this a possible crime scene."

"Foul play?"

"You tell me. She works weekends as security at N-V Nova Labs. Someone broke the windows, both the guards went missing. One was on record as leaving sick; Altin found his truck in the lake Friday. The other, our Miss Chimes, vanished without a trace. Supposedly on vacation with her family but apparently not." She made a circling motion with her hand. "Go. Look around. See if you see anything I missed."

It took thirty minutes to tour the house with limited-touch-gloves-only rules. Wet clothes were starting to mildew in the washer, pajamas lay carelessly on the bed, the radio still hummed in the study. "It looks . . ." Mac frowned. "It looks like she meant to come back."

"That's what I think, too." Agent Rose scowled like she had a personal vendetta against the house. "I just don't see anything that suggests violence."

Mac made a noise of agreement as he studied one of the pictures; Melody Chimes in a green graduation robe and hat. "I . . . know her." He blinked at the picture, a pretty girl in a shimmering green shirt twisting to smile at the camera as she ate dinner with a group of friends. He'd seen the face somewhere. A paper. What paper? Newspaper . . . No, not there. It wasn't on the nets. It wasn't . . .

The memory of a similar picture on his computer nudged him. The same face, but beaten, smashed at high speed. "She's dead. Impact trauma."

Agent Rose laughed. "What, you're psychic now?"

"No." He shook his head. "I've seen her file in the Jane Doe case when I first got to District 3. We buried her a year ago."

More laughter. "Right. That's great. Don't try the jokes in front of the family."

"I'm serious!"

Dark, cold eyes sobered him. "Agent MacKenzie, you need help. This is your first, last, and only warning. Get off the pills, and clean yourself up. I don't give a bear's tit what you do on your own time, but on bureau time, you stay sober."

"I am!" He stabbed a shaking finger at the picture. "That's the JD that was here when I arrived. I'm . . . I'm almost sure." Surety withered and died under Agent Rose's hard stare. "Pretty sure."

"You need help." Agent Rose walked to the far end of the small living room, apparently intent on studying pictures of a wedding.

"I might be right."

The Look.

"I . . . I want to check."

"You're seriously suggesting that the JD you buried fourteen months ago is Melody Chimes?"

Possibilities spun through his head. If he could just get it all sorted. Mac grasped at the obvious. "The search wouldn't," *wouldn't work*, "wouldn't show a minor. We looked for a woman age eighteen to twenty-five."

"Melody Chimes isn't twenty yet." Agent Rose bit her lip, seesawing into believing him.

"Standard search wouldn't pull her up."

"A clone?"

Mac looked back at the wall of photos. "Money."

"A shadow." She moved again, not quite pacing. Just . . . wandering, looking at the photos in a thought-filled silence. "Melody listed a dorm as her home address. This was the address her sister gave us."

"Maybe she didn't want to be found."

"Kill your owner, take their life?"

"It's possible." He licked his lips. "If it was a clone, the lab has . . . had serious problems."

"Problems? A clone in a lab with government research is a security nightmare. It's so illegal, you can get arrested for *saying* things like that." She tugged on her ponytail in frustration.

"It fits."

Barely . . . Hopefully she sees what I'm seeing.

"That's the problem." Agent Rose sighed as she studied the pictures. "What sort of person can beat to death someone with their own face?"

He took a shaky breath. "Two Jane Does," he whispered more to himself than her. Two unidentified women beaten to death. A memory fizzed at the edge of recall, similarities between the bone fractures, the placement of the facial impacts. Circles on the bone. "Can . . . can you authorize a reevaluation for the old case?" Agent Rose raised an eyebrow but dipped her chin in acknowledgment.

A battered white car pulled in front of a bright pink Montero Sunlit. Mac let out a whistle of appreciation in spite of himself. A Sunlit. Those things cost more than the national debt of most wartime nations. Bells, whistles, AI, private highway usage—people who could afford that could easily afford a clone or three for their kid.

"That's Mrs. Chimes-Martin and the PD," said Agent Rose. "Keep your mouth shut. Contact me when you've looked at the paperwork. If you can find anything that links the old Jane Doe with Miss Chimes, I'll file for reevaluation."

"Yes, ma'am." Mac tried not to look like he was running for the door.

"MacKenzie?"

He froze in the doorway.

"Don't even think of touching the pills. If this goes to court, you need to be stone-cold sober."

"I am . . ."

The Look, again.

"Roger that."

CHAPTER 8

> Picture a wave, it crests and collapses without
> losing anything. There is energy. So much energy!
> Time is much the same, choice creates energy, the
> energy crests into a wave of possibility, a thousand
> iterations rising, but in the end, the water returns
> to the ocean. The prime iteration is stable. In the
> end, all possibilities lead to our reality.
>
> ~ Student notes from the class
> Physics and Space-Time I1–2071

Wednesday May 29, 2069
Alabama District 3
Commonwealth of North America

A lime-green Sista' Twista' slid over the wet tabletop.
"All the taste, none of the toxins," Brileigh said as she
slid into the chair beside Sam. She sipped her drink,
eyes closed, and groaned. "See, right now I'm in a trop-
ical paradise while the cabana man named Juan rubs
my feet."

The club music poured over them, hot and tribal.

"Come on, Sammie, give. Why so mopey?"

Sam tasted the Twista', all tight citrus notes with a hit of heat at the end. "Work. It's stressing me out."

"Why do you think we're here? It's girls' night! We're out getting drinks and dancing instead of sweating like hogs at the gym. This is fun!" Brileigh punched her arm, not a light tap either. Her weight-lifting partner had a mean right hook.

Sam tried to shrug it off. Melody Chimes was missing, and she was at the bar with her best friend acting like she didn't have a care in the world. Guilt gnawed on her insides, making her question every action.

"Drink your Twista'," Brileigh ordered. "You need some steps tonight."

Her phone vibrated. Brileigh snatched it away before she could answer. "Hello? Nope. This is Brileigh. I said no!" *Your Mom,* she mouthed.

"Brileigh!" Sam hissed. "Gimme the phone!"

"Mom says she loves you!" Brileigh sang out. "Oh, she loves you, too," she said back into the phone. "Of course, she said that. Right after she got her tongue out of the mouth of . . ." Brileigh laughed. "I'm joking! Aren't you all overprotective?"

"Brileigh, give me my phone back."

"Sorry, I couldn't hear you over the wild party in the background." Brileigh stuck a finger in her free ear.

"Brileigh." Sam looked around for a distraction. Bri's neon-pink Tumble Me Now sat half-empty on the table. "Bri, I'll finish your Tumble Me."

That earned her a look of outraged shock. Sam reached for the drink.

"She loves you, too," Brileigh said again. "She'll call you tomorrow. Yup. Busy. Loves! Bye." Brileigh clicked the phone off and tossed it to Sam as she reached for her drink. "Your mom says she misses you. Why didn't you call? What's going on?" Brileigh sipped her Tumble Me.

"I've been busy. With two cases open, it's hard to find hours to call home. She's trying to catch up on the fourteen years of boarding school when she never called once. You'd think someone so career-oriented would understand."

Brileigh wrinkled her nose in distaste. "Really?

Sam rolled her eyes. "She's dedicated to her country and international peace. She sent letters. Every Tuesday, like clockwork I'd get a letter written in Spanish telling me what she'd done during the week. My dad sent some, too, not as regular. His were all in French."

Bri drummed her nails on the table. "And nothing about that situation strikes you as odd?"

"Everything about it does! Does anything about my life strike you as normal? I had to rent an apartment when I went back to Toronto to take care of my dad because I don't know where my parents' house is. My mother was too busy to talk, and my dad . . ." She let the sentence drop. "I don't do normal relationships."

"You don't do relationships at all," Bri argued.

"I dated Joseph!"

"While working with him on a case . . . and then you dumped him."

Sam rolled her eyes. "He was cheating on me."

"Which is a good reason for dumping him, I agree. But it isn't the same as dating multiple people."

"Yeah, well, I dated one guy, and it ended badly. I have every right to be gun-shy."

Bri shrugged. "I'm just saying, it wouldn't hurt to give the males of the world a second chance. It's okay to live a little first." She eyed the crop of locals. "Maybe not these ones . . ."

"Yeah." Sam finished her drink and eyed the dance floor.

"One more drink?" Brileigh asked.

"One more, then we salsa." One little salsa before she left wouldn't hurt.

Dinner was cheese sticks with pepperoni as she tried to get the laundry under control. Images of the day kept replaying in her head. Images of images, even; Melody Chimes—a younger version of her older sister—in the graduation gown, in a bridesmaid dress, out at dinner with her friends.

Hoss whined, and she let him out as her work folder beeped. Sam flipped the folder open, scrolling down to look at the new notes. MacKenzie had tagged a photo to the bottom of the file: Jane Doe 756584347183, found February 11, 2068, a dark-skinned young woman wearing a silvery sage-green shirt with black slacks. Part of a broken pencil with the letters A-U-B was found in her hair.

Saints and angels. . .

Except for the evidence of a brutal beating, Jane Doe-183 was a physical match for Melody Chimes. She wrote a note back to MacKenzie. "Report acknowledged. Prep JD-183 case files. Argue to exhume body and open case for reevaluation in the morning."

She salsa-ed tonight. Tomorrow, she tangoed with a year-old corpse.

CHAPTER 9

> It takes a very strong person to see a parallel world
> for what it is: an illusion. The average person can't
> walk into a false reality, remove the einselected
> Nodes, and step out again unchanged. We are not
> looking for the average person.

> ~ From Colonel Aina's speech to incoming cadets
> at the Ministry of Defense War College I1–2072

Thursday May 30, 2069
Alabama District 3
Commonwealth of North America

Mac trudged from the morgue to the main bureau building through the sweltering morning heat. The summer warmth didn't seep to the bone. Even with the temperature pushing triple digits, all he could feel was the cold. His head spun a little; the lack of sleep was catching up with him. But sleep meant pills, and pills meant another chewing out from Agent Perfect.

It really was a shame the army had downsized after unification. That woman was born to be a drill sergeant. Somewhere, a very lucky private first class was missing out on a whole set of erotic fantasies featuring Agent Rose. And here he was taking medications that impacted libido.

Maybe going off the pills won't be such a bad thing. I could use a fantasy or two.

Showing his ID to the frowning secretary—*I wonder if she frowns at everyone, or just people who look like they've woken up in a Dumpster*—Mac took the stairs at a slow pace. A wave of vertigo made the building tilt out from under him. He leaned against the wall with his eyes closed.

From around the corner he heard Marrins shout, "I don't care what you think, this needs to get done. Emir, do I care about that? No. I'm doing everything I can on my end." The senior agent's door slammed shut.

Shuddering, Mac pushed himself off the wall and shuffled to the conference room. Agent Perfect was there, apparently fresh from a photo shoot for the next recruiting poster: black hair pinned neatly back, ruby lips, pressed white blouse, navy skirt he guaranteed landed a regulation two-and-a-quarter inches above her patella. She probably checked the length with a ruler before leaving her house every morning.

He collapsed into a chair and swallowed bile while her pen drummed on the table. The quiet hum of the air-conditioning wove a dangerous lullaby, inviting him to rest his head on the table and sleep.

She stopped tapping. "MacKenzie, do you need to go to sick call?"

The tabletop was cool and smooth. If he closed his eyes, he could pretend it was nap time.

"Earth to MacKenzie," Rose persisted. "Are you dead, dying, or just drugged?"

A heavy hand fell across his back, knocking the wind out of him.

"How's it going, Rose?" a man asked. There was a beat of silence. Mac was willing to bet the newcomer and Rose were sharing looks of disgust aimed at him. "What's wrong with him?"

"I work for the bureau, Detective Altin, not the Vatican. I don't do miracles or mind reading," Rose said.

Mac opened an eye and caught sight of the dour detective taking a seat by the door.

Altin held out the papers he'd brought. "I got your report on the Jane Doe from '68. The chief was ready to bite through her desk when she saw that."

The conversation swirled around him.

Rose took the papers. "Did you talk to the family?"

"Mr. and Missus Chimes, the parents, are still out of country. Mrs. Chimes-Martin was able to answer some of the questions. Turns out both she and her sister have shadows. One each, as far as she knows." Altin tapped the paper. "The shadow house is out of state."

"What's out of state?" Marrins demanded as he walked into the room. He plopped down in the chair opposite Altin with a jiggle and a scowl.

"The Chimeses kept shadows for their daughters." Altin gave Marrins a copy of the report. "It's out of my jurisdiction. I called the bureau's senior agent over there and asked him to send someone over to confirm that the Shadow has a clone marker.

Marrins read through the interview with a frown in place. "We need to exhume Jane Doe-183: Melody Doe. Good work, this is more than I expected from you, Rose."

Maybe she's not so perfect after all.

CHAPTER 10

> We are inebriated by the concept of Self, by the
> idea of the individual mind. We want Self to exist
> to such a degree that we have built an entire cul-
> ture around the worship of Self and the need for
> such inanities as Personal Growth.
>
> ~ Excerpt from *The Oneness of
> Being* by Oaza Moun II–2070

*Friday June 7, 2069
Alabama District 3
Commonwealth of North America*

If the saints were listening, and inclined to grant
miracles, then the phone would have exploded
twelve minutes ago when Detective Altin put Dr.
Emir on speaker to rant. Friday was a day without
miracles. The phone worked fine, and for a quarter
of an hour, Sam listened to the blistering rage of the
aging physicist. "My research is threatened!" Emir
yelled again.

Sam pushed the phone a little farther across the

desk. Maybe the phone would fall and accidentally hang up on the good doctor.

"These men would turn my work into nothing more than a stage for hate and fear! I won't stand for it."

Marrins knocked on the wood frame outside Sam's office.

She sighed, grabbing the phone while motioning her boss in. "Neither will we. I assure you that the bureau is doing everything in its power to pursue this"—she fumbled for a word—"injustice to the fullest extent. We are doing everything in our power to safeguard your work. Detective Altin is a fine, upstanding law-enforcement officer, and if you have any complaints about his behavior—"

The dial tone sang in her ear.

"Good-bye." Sam clicked the phone to its OFF position and docked it beside her computer. "The wonderful paranoia of Dr. Emir," she told Marrins with an apologetic smile. "Three shows daily."

He snorted. "What's he want this time?"

"Assurance that no one working the case is going to steal his data, or force him to misuse his device, or something. Honestly, I don't understand half of what he says."

Marrins's beefy hand landed hard on her shoulder in a brutal pat of camaraderie. "I heard you spent the night with corpses."

Sam winced. "It was a mess from start to finish. Trying to find a particular body in a hole full of bodies is hard enough to begin with. But then someone drove by last night, the PD didn't have their lights on, and the guy digging was in plain clothes, so of course there was a ruckus. After that documentary on grave-robbing and cemetery vandalism ran on the news last month, people have been calling in weekly to report suspicious activity, and a concerned citizen held up the dig for almost an hour." She rubbed sleep from her eyes. "Add to that—again—that mass grave is a disaster. Harley has everyone on the morgue staff working overtime, but we still haven't found our Jane yet. If she's not in there . . ." Sam shook her head. "Just to be on the safe side, I sent MacKenzie to pull all the old files he could find in the system. If anyone down there followed protocol, we'll have her autopsy on record."

"Good thought." Marrins sat on the desk, making it groan in protest. His lips smacked together. "Why don't you close up shop? We're not going to find anything in the next forty-eight hours that's going to change the world. You need a vacation. And I need you out of my district."

The smile dropped from her face. "Sir?"

"Just got off the horn with an old friend of mine, thought it might interest you. Senior Agent Barsol in D.C. is looking for a field agent fluent in Spanish."

"I'm fluent in Spanish and French," Sam said cautiously, heart fluttering with hope.

"He's scrapping the bottom of the barrel if you ask me, but he's desperate. I owe him a favor, so I tweaked a few things and gave you the leave time you need. You've got a flight out of Atlanta this afternoon. Take the rest of the weekend to enjoy yourself. By the time you get back, all this will be taken care of, and you'll be on target to go to D.C. I promise."

"Thank you!" Sam had to force herself not to jump up and hug the surly old agent. The stodgy old misogynist had finally come around and seen the value in her work. "This is wonderful."

"Pack up. Lock up. Enjoy your weekend." Marrins thumped her back again.

Sam waited until she heard Marrins settle at his desk before she reached for her phone. Down the hall, Marrins's phone rang, and he started talking. She dialed Bri.

"Sammie! How's life?" Brileigh asked with her customary enthusiasm.

"Great! I have an interview for a job in D.C."

"Fantastic!" Bri said. There was a muffled scream in the background, then Bri yelled, "Knock it off, or I'll duct tape you to the hood of the car!" A wave of whining rose at the edge of hearing, then Brileigh was back. "So, D.C.?"

"Yes, a full field-agent position. The bureau even bought my plane ticket!" Sam laughed, turning her chair.

Agent MacKenzie stood at the edge of her office, hand raised to knock. She held up a finger to let him know she needed a minute.

"About time they promoted you," Bri said. There was a muffled scream in the background, and Bri yelled, "So help me, I will use you for catfish bait!" In a more normal voice, she said to Sam, "Other than a good-bye party and help packing, what do you need from me?"

"Can you watch Hoss? I can drop him at your place, or you could go pick him up."

"What?" Bri yelled something unintelligible away from the phone. "Sammie? What was that?"

Sam held up a finger to keep MacKenzie from interrupting. "Hoss, the dog? You said you'd watch him if I ever got a weekend free?"

"Oh, right. Can't. Sorry. Jake scheduled a weekend at the cabin for us. Fishing on the lake, kids trying to drown each other. Family time. You know how it is."

"Not really."

"Whatever. Look, I'm already three hours out of town. Can the landlady watch him until Sunday? I could pick him up Sunday night."

"She's down in Florida visiting her grandkids."

Bri hummed. "How about a neighbor?"

"Don't worry. I can call a kennel or something. Maybe take him with me." She pulled up the Web page for Hartsfield-Jackson International Airport in Atlanta to see if there was a kennel on-site.

"I'm sorry, Sammie! Really, if I'd known you were going, we would have taken the dog."

"It's not your fault. It caught me by surprise, too." Sam winced as Bri yelled something at her kids again. "I'll call you later. Bye, Bri."

"Bye!"

No kennel at the airport, and mastiffs were listed

as a restricted breed that couldn't fly. She snarled at the computer and turned to MacKenzie. "Hi. Can I help you?"

MacKenzie looked clean for a change. Almost sober. His eyes still looked like he hadn't slept in days, though, but she knew after last night, she couldn't really talk. "We identified five more bodies, two of them clones." He hesitated, then stepped into her office. "I pulled the files from the Melody Doe autopsy I did when I first arrived."

"Anything interesting that you missed?"

He tossed a file on her desk. "You're not going to like it."

"There's very little I like after two hours of sleep and a long day," Sam said. "Hit me."

MacKenzie took a seat in the chair opposite her and leaned forward to turn the file on. "Jane Doe-183—the one we're calling Melody Doe—was found in the same dump site as the Jane Doe we brought in a few weeks ago. Over the past five years, seven clones have been dumped there, not a big deal. But . . ." He scrolled through images and pulled up a close-up of Melody Doe's femur. "Circular ripple patterns on the bone. Not as pronounced as on Jane, but they're there."

Sam pulled the file closer. "What did you classify this as when you did the original autopsy?"

He rubbed his neck. "Scanner error. It was old, only worked half the time."

"You do good work when you're off the pills."

He looked out the window. "I just needed sleep."

"You—"

"I didn't say that!" Marrins angry yell cut off her reply. There was the sound of a phone slamming down. "Someone get me the number for District 2!" Marrins hollered down the hall.

Sam rolled her eyes and said a silent prayer that Senior Agent Barsol would like what he saw when she arrived. Forgetting what she was going to say, she looked back at MacKenzie and said, "It looks good. Let Harley's people handle everything this weekend. Sleep, if that's what you need. If something comes up that needs your classification level, I'll call."

MacKenzie cleared his throat. "I, ah, I thought you were leaving town this weekend." His gaze stayed firmly on the floor.

"Were you listening to my phone call?"

"I'm . . . I'm sorry. You told me to wait . . ."

She shook her head—it wasn't that big a deal. "If I can find a place to leave my dog in the next thirty minutes, yes. Otherwise, it's going to be a phone interview."

"Do you want me . . . ?" He coughed, face bright red. "I mean, I could watch a dog."

She raised an eyebrow. *Was not expecting that.* She thought about it for a second, then asked, "You promise not to kill my dog?"

MacKenzie nodded quickly.

"All right, the security password for the house is 'Sam said I could.' Hoss's food is in the bin in the laundry room, and don't worry about his size, he's a big softie, really." The twinge of pity kicked her. "There's some steak in the chest freezer. Go ahead and help yourself to a few, as a thank-you." She scribbled down her address. "Seriously, don't kill my dog. No pills. No dead dogs. I'm attached to my puppy."

He smirked and looked up at her from under long lashes. In the right light, he had killer eyes.

Didn't expect that, either.

"The dog will be alive on Monday. Promise."

D.C. smelled of rain and city, the air vibrant with the sound of traffic and chatter. After the silence of the Alabama house, it was heaven to her ears.

Leaving straight from the office for the Atlanta airport, she'd waved her ID and grabbed the last government-reserve standby seat on the two o'clock flight. Ninety minutes wasn't long enough to read everything about the D.C. agent's career, but she picked up the highlights. Reading about successful convictions was a pleasant distraction from the tractionless case at home. It gave her hope that one day she'd close some cases of her own.

After the plane landed, she took a taxi downtown, fiddling nervously with the latch on her carry-on through the whole, silent drive.

Senior Agent Barsol's office was in a nondescript gray building with the familiar aging receptionist glaring at newcomers. Sam presented her credentials and was guided through a labyrinth of cubicles. It wasn't as laid-back as the office in San Diego where she'd worked fresh out of the academy, nor as slovenly as the neglected offices in Alabama District 3. Agent Barsol was a bald man with deep frown lines around his mouth, gold-rimmed glasses, and a diamond earring. He gave Sam a smile as she stepped into his bare office. "Sorry for the decor—or lack thereof; the conference room is being renovated, so everyone is using my office for team meetings. I'm Mike Barsol."

Sam shook his hand. "Samantha Rose, thank you for inviting me to come, sir."

"Thank you for coming up. Agent Marrins said your lot is in the middle of some big case."

"We're following up on an old Jane Doe case," Sam said modestly. "It won't be big until we find what we're looking for."

"Well said." Agent Barsol thumbed through her folder. "So, you speak English, French, and Spanish fluently. Former Canadian citizen, still a minor when the Commonwealth was formed, top marks at the academy, wonderful reviews from the senior agent in California. Why are you in Alabama?"

Sam took a steadying breath. It was inevitable that the question would come up. "I took emergency family leave shortly after joining the bureau. My father was ill and needed me. When he was stable, I'd already been replaced in my previous posting. I didn't have the time in service for most of the postings available and couldn't extend my leave to wait for the next assignment cycle. One of the agents in Toronto called Senior

Agent Marrins and asked him to reopen his junior agent slot. The senior agent felt he could justify having a third agent in his district, especially since Agent MacKenzie spends more time working for the county coroner's office than the bureau. So I moved there and was grateful for the post." Although she was less grateful when she found out her ex had gotten her the job by telling Marrins she was an easy lay. She'd cleared that up with a cold dismissal of the senior agent and a heated rant session with Bri.

"Good, it's best to be up-front with these things. Do you expect your father to suffer a relapse, or do you have any other reason you might need to leave the bureau in the near future?"

"No, sir." She'd made it clear when she left Toronto that her father was on his own. His struggle with prescription pain medication was real, but he wasn't willing to quit, and she wasn't willing to spend the rest of her life patting him down for contraband.

Agent Barsol nodded. He ran her through a few scenarios, let her read a file on a closed case, and asked questions—standard bureau hiring procedures. But at the end of the interview, he was frowning. "Rose, you seem like the ideal candidate, but I'm looking for a field agent. Someone who can follow directions and work with a team."

"I can do that, sir." Desperation choked her. The job was slipping out of her fingers.

"Would you be happy?"

"I'm very social, sir. I enjoy working with a team."

Barsol sighed. "Let me rephrase that: would you be happier working as a field agent with a team, or working as a senior agent with your own command."

"Everyone wants a command, sir, but I don't have the time in service."

"Over two years with the bureau," Barsol said. "Not enough to take my job, but an office in a smaller district? You could handle that."

A new fear bloomed in her chest. "I'd rather not stay in Alabama District 3."

Uncertainty crossed Barsol's face, then he raised an eyebrow and laughed. "Is it really that bad?"

"Humid, hot, isolated. It's a swamp when it rains and a red dust bowl the rest of the time. There's only one restaurant open after nine, and it's a dive. I'm desperate to escape Alabama. I'll go anywhere. The Arctic Circle. Panama Canal. Nothing fazes me as long as there's a city in easy driving distance."

Which was all true—no need to go into the stultifying professional climate when the actual climate was such crap.

Agent Barsol chuckled. "Noted. We'll see if D.C. can find a desk for you, but keep your eye open for other opportunities. A smaller district would be lucky to have you."

A few more dismissive pleasantries, and Sam walked downstairs to hail a cab. At first, she couldn't help but be pleased by his confidence in her ability to lead. But by the time she got into the taxi, cold certainty settled over her. She hadn't gotten the job.

"**G**ood horse . . . ah, Hoss. Good, Hoss." Mac held up his hands as a giant tan monster bounded toward him. Light from a gibbous moon fell across the dry lawn, washing the dog and Rose's house in velvety shadow.

The monster bumped a huge head against Mac's hip. He patted it tentatively. "Good boy?" What was Rose thinking? The beast had to weigh more than her. Probably more than him. When she said "puppy," he'd expected something more United Standard, like a golden retriever. Or a Chihuahua.

"Good, Hoss. That's a good massive. Er, mastiff." He pushed open the front door to the house. "Uh, Sam said I could?" His voice echoed through the empty house as the security system turned lights on. Hoss stepped in, and he followed, letting the door snap shut behind him. So far, the dog wasn't chewing . . .

Something wet and cold smeared his leg. Mac looked down, prepared to see blood and bone, but there was no pain. Hoss looked up at him, head connected to Mac's leg by a trailing gob of bubbling drool.

"Fantastic." Mac shook the slime trail loose. "Let's get your food." His feet slid on the polished wood floor. Agent Perfect might be a hotshot in the dress department, but she seriously needed to consider hiring a decorator. Buy a couch at the very least.

A morgue-like smell filled the house. The heavy, familiar smell of death. Mac hesitated by the stairs, hand running along the smooth end cap of the balustrade.

He'd seen Rose a few hours ago. All right, eight hours. She was fine.

The scent of decay pulled him up the stairs.

She had to be fine.

The steps creaked under his weight, the soft song of well-used stairs worn under the loving tread of living people. This house had history, weight. Nothing prefabbed or postdated. Real wood on the floor. Real stone in the foundation. Real trees outside instead of gen-engineered pollution eaters.

How the hell does she afford this? But the smell was his primary concern.

The first door he pushed opened into a south-facing room with a wide window and plants. Neat rows of soil sat beside the glass, inviting him to play in the dirt. Hoss knocked him aside and walked into the room. Nubbin of a tail wagging madly, the dog sniffed the pots and sneezed. "No marking," Mac warned. He dipped a finger into the nearest pot, still moist, recently watered. "Let's go."

There was a blue-and-white bathroom with an elegant white towel that smelled of lavender laundry soap. A gold-framed black-and-white print of a couple dancing in Paris hung over a sunken tub. Pure luxury. Probably sixty years old, maybe eighty. He flicked the tub and heard the semiporcelain thunk. Not biodegradable at all.

There was a spacious empty room at the end of the house, filled with dust and memories, a lazy ceiling fan turning in an unfelt breeze. A linen closet stood opposite the bathroom. That left one door. The dog lifted his head and whined.

Maybe he'd hallucinated the smell. "Mind if I peek?" Mac asked.

Hoss's nubbin thrummed with delight.

The door swung inward. Wooden floors, polish worn down by bare feet. A large lilac shag carpet beneath a brass bed, lilac-and-white quilt, a computer, a wooden hope chest pushed under the window that had white-lace curtains blocking a view of the trees in the drive.

Agent Rose's perfume lingered in the air, drowning out the smell he'd followed upstairs. A pair of navy-blue heels were tossed thoughtlessly in the corner, a little scuff mark on the wall where they'd hit after a long night. He touched the computer: cold.

The closet was filled with sensible business suits, a few workout uniforms, and a winter jacket Agent Rose didn't need in June. Everything was well used, a few years old, and normal. Perfectly normal for an agent on her way up. She'd probably built her wardrobe out of the first few paychecks. The winter jacket might be a holdover from her college days.

A picture by the computer caught his eye. An older couple with thirties haircuts—her parents maybe, smiling and happy. The room couldn't be more perfect if it were staged by a Hollywood director.

He went downstairs, grinding his teeth. Would it kill her to have one skeleton in the closet? Just one thing that made her semihuman? Mac kicked the door to the kitchen open and stepped back, gagging at the smell of putrefaction.

The smell of rotting flesh brought memories: heat, blood, screaming until his throat was dust dry. His left hand convulsed over a knife handle that wasn't there. No more knife. No more gun. Not even a Kevlar helmet and flak jacket to hide behind.

Overhead, the ceiling fan hummed.

That didn't fit with the memories. Hell didn't have ceiling fans, or the faint smell of jasmine. Mac closed his eyes.

Focusing on the smell of flowers helped. Agent Rose wasn't in the next room. He'd seen her leave from the office for the Atlanta airport. Ignoring a treacherous voice that whispered facts about decomposition rates of a body in this heat wave, he steadied himself.

Whatever was dead in the kitchen, he could handle it. For a few minutes, he could handle it.

"Skeleton in the closet. I wanted a skeleton, not the whole bloody body." Mac glared at the ceiling. "God, not funny. Just in case you're still listening." Probably not. He and God had quit talking years ago.

Hoss whimpered behind him as he pressed against Mac's legs. Mac dropped his hand to pet the dog. "Yeah. Me too." There was prayer and a cowering two-hundred-pound dog. Neither inspired real confidence. He took out his cell.

Phone in hand, he tried the door again. Hoss trailed behind him. The back door swung on broken hinges like a lazy drunk. The kitchen was clean, but the chest freezer with Agent Rose's steak was propped open. Mac almost sobbed in relief.

She must have left it open before work. Maybe she pulled dinner out and forgot to slam it shut. No dead bodies or skeletons, just a waste of prime-grade steaks. A weak chuckle escaped him as he edged toward the freezer.

A lock of black hair curled out from under the lid, escaping with the oversweet smell of decay.

Switching the phone to his right hand and clutching it like a teddy bear, he lifted the freezer lid with his elbow. "Um . . ."

Hoss lay down and whimpered.

Mac leaned against a tree, eyes watering as his stomach dry heaved. Hoss leaned against his leg, pushing him sideways. With quivering hands, he dialed Agent Rose.

Two rings later, she answered with a sharp, "Yes?"

"Um . . ." Mac swallowed bile and terror, watching the back door. As long as the body inside didn't walk out, he felt he could stop dry heaving for a few minutes. "Uh. Hi?"

"Agent MacKenzie?"

"Yes?"

"Why are you calling in the middle of the night?"

"I . . . I . . . found Robbins."

"Call Altin. Bring him in for questioning." There was a muffled sniffle, then she was back sounding a little more normal. "Where did you find him?"

"Your house." Silence. "Agent Rose?" More silence. Somewhere behind Agent Rose, he heard the filtered sounds of the city. A car horn blared. Someone screamed.

"Is this a joke?" she finally asked, her tone making it clear that if it was a joke, she might kill him for it. Considering the dead body in her freezer, he wasn't so sure she wouldn't kill him anyway.

"I wish."

"What do you mean my house? Is he prowling around? Is he sitting there? Give me details."

"He's dead. In your freezer. He is dead and decomposing in your freezer." Mac took a shaky breath.

Agent Rose took a moment to digest that. "Dead?"

"Yes, ma'am."

"You're certain?"

Mac closed his eyes. "There's obvious trauma to the neck, maybe an entry wound for a bullet or a jagged-edged weapon. Something tore open his throat, and it isn't neat." He looked at the house in resignation. She was going to ask him to go back inside. "Before you ask, yes, I'm sober." He wished he weren't.

"Mother Mary, God give me strength, I didn't think today could get worse." Rose sighed. "MacKenzie, call Altin and Marrins. Get a forensic team there. I want them going over that house with a fine-tooth comb." She took another ragged breath. "Is Hoss okay?"

"Yeah, he was sitting out front when I got here."

"Out front? I locked him in the kitchen this morning."

"The back door is busted, it's swinging from the doorframe like a drunk at Mardi Gras."

Agent Rose muttered something away from the phone. "Look, call the team. I'll get the first flight I can home. Can you handle this?"

What a loaded question. "Um . . ."

"Stop starting your sentences with 'Um!' You're a bureau agent. For the love of all that's holy, act like one!"

"I'm sorry," Mac whispered, as the breeze ruffled his hair. He wasn't even sure what he was sorry for. Sorry he was still alive. Sorry he had failed. Again. "I'll call Marrins."

"I'll call when I get to the airport." She hung up.

Mac looked at the phone. He wanted to run. Find some dark hole to hide in until the familiar panic ebbed away and left him empty again, but Agent Rose said act like a bureau agent. Act like her. He could do that. Even shaking and screaming inside, he could do that for an hour or two. Two pills, he promised himself. If he could just get through this, he'd take all the pills he could find and slip into quiet oblivion. One more lost cause dying in the shadow of heroes.

CHAPTER 11

> More good is done, more atrocities prevented, every day by the fine men and women of the Ministry of Defense than can ever be reported to the people of the Collective. Their actions ensure you live.

> ~ President Toinen I1–2074

Saturday June 8, 2069
Alabama District 3
Commonwealth of North America

Mac was the first person to see Detective Altin pull into the drive with his lights flashing. While the kitchen was crawling with bureau personnel borrowed from District 4, Marrins had posted him in front of the door to the living room and told him to keep the dog out after Hoss tried to bite Marrins's hand off—at least, that's what Marrins claimed. Mac was pretty sure Hoss was just trying to lick him. Either way, he wasn't surprised by Marrins's sending him out.

His orders were to stand there and stay out of trouble. It wasn't a hard order. Anybody could stand. You didn't need to be a hero, or even have a processing, sentient brain: even trees could stand. Which made trees better bureau agents than him because Mac was about to pass out.

"What's going on?" Altin demanded as he stalked past Mac without even a nod and stormed into the kitchen. "The whole radio's buzzing with bureau chatter, and I don't even get a courtesy call? What kind of bull pucky you throwing out, Marrins?"

Mac caught the door as he held Hoss back.

Agent Marrins glared at the detective. "It's an internal matter."

"Sounds like a police matter," Altin said, glowering at the bureau techs loading the late Mordicai Robbins on a stretcher and photographing the scene.

"Rose's house isn't in the city, so it's out of your jurisdiction. It's in mine." Marrins waved to Mac. "Get him out of here."

He wants me to get rid of Altin? Mac glanced at the much taller man skeptically but made his way toward the detective.

"You've got a dead body tied to my case, and you think you can lock me out?" Altin demanded, shoving Mac away.

Mac's phone buzzed. He slunk into the empty living room, breathing in the scent of dust and perfume like an elixir. "MacKenzie."

"It's Sam—what's going on?" She sounded calmer.

"Marrins is working the scene. Altin just showed

up." The yelling in the next room escalated. "They're fighting over jurisdiction."

"Tell them there's a ruler in the top drawer by the fridge. They can whip it out and measure. When they're done dicking around, they can get back to work."

Mac laughed in spite of himself. "Sure, I'll tell them that." *Right after I retire.* He rubbed his eyes. "Do you have a coffeemaker here? It would make everyone a lot happier."

"I can't stand the stuff. Marrins can run to town if he wants some," Sam said. "How's Hoss?"

"Not happy." Mac petted the massive beast in question. Hoss leaned his head on Mac's thigh, trying to knock him over. It was the beast's new favorite game. "I don't think he likes intruders."

"Probably not. Look, the earliest flight I can get is four this afternoon. Can you ask Marrins what he will do with my dog?"

"Sure, gimme a sec." Mac poked his head into the kitchen. "Sir?" Both Altin and Marrins whipped toward him, looking ready to kill. "Agent Rose wants to know what we're doing with the dog."

"Drop him at the pound," Marrins said.

"Sure." Mac closed the door again. "He said the pound," he told Agent Rose.

"No! That's doggy prison!"

"Um . . ." Mac cleared his throat. No more ums. "I could . . . could take him to my place. Like we planned."

Agent Rose sighed. "Sure, that works. I'll come get

him when my flight lands. It'll probably be late. Oh . . ." she hesitated. "Does Marrins want me to report to the precinct for questioning first?"

Mac nudged the door open with his foot. "Sir, Agent Rose is catching a red-eye flight back to the state. Do you want her to come in for questioning or do you want someone to pick her up at the airport?"

Marrins glared at him. "It's three in the morning. I want her to find a hotel room and promise not to ruin any more of my weekend. My schedule didn't have 'homicide' on it."

"Right." The door swung closed. Marrins wants you to put yourself under house arrest at a hotel until Monday."

Even over the phone, he could hear the heavy sigh that always accompanied Rose's disappointed eye rolls. "Fine. I'll pick up Hoss as soon as I get to town."

"Okay." He hung up and tugged Hoss's collar. "Want to go for a walk?" The nubbin wagged.

The dashboard clock read half past ten when Sam parked her car in front of an apartment with a peeling facade. At a gas station across the street, two police cruisers huddled around the remnants of a drug deal gone wrong. An ambulance siren wailed through the night.

MacKenzie's place was all 2020 architecture: a strong, boxy design that fit the mood of a failing country, painted in scorched-earth tones. It needed renovation, possibly done by a local arsonist in colors of gasoline and fire. He rented a ground-level hovel in a back corner of the complex between a broken streetlamp and an overgrown, empty lot that seemed to double as the local landfill. In the humid June night, the smell of ripe and rotted garbage was gagworthy.

Hoss barked wildly when she knocked. Sam winced, wondering for the first time if she should have just left the dog alone and found a hotel for the night.

The sound of chain locks being undone jolted her out of her daze. MacKenzie tugged the door open with a yawn and ran a hand through sleep-styled hair. "Agent Rose?"

She managed a weak smile and pulled her purse over the ketchup stain on the hem of her dress in embarrassment. "Hi."

"Come on in." He switched off whatever late-night chatter was showing on the TV and collapsed into a dark green sofa.

She petted Hoss, taking comfort in his familiar warm bristle. "I'll grab his stuff, and we'll go find someplace up by the highway. There's a No-tell Motel they haven't condemned yet."

"You . . . you could stay here," MacKenzie offered hesitantly.

"Here?"

MacKenzie stood, awkwardly brushing debris from his sofa. "On the couch? I don't . . . don't mind."

"Thanks." The memory of Jane Doe's tortured body flashed through her head. "It wouldn't look right."

"Neither would your car wrapped around a tree." He held out a crocheted afghan. "You're falling over, and there's nowhere else to go."

Thunder rolled outside, and the heavy beat of rain hammered the roof. She fell into the couch beside the ME and bit her lip. *Saint Jude, protect me.* "Right. Do you have a bathroom where I can get washed up?"

"Right by the kitchen."

Sam went back to the car for her overnight bag and gave herself a quick tour. Living room, narrow hall with one door that led to a closet, and another that smelled of unwashed clothes and despair—that was probably MacKenzie's bedroom. Kitchen, folding card table, empty cupboards, and a small door to a smaller bathroom, the ceiling and linoleum both cracked. A sink with rusting pipes practically sat in the lap of anyone using the toilet, and the weak yellow light overhead showed a dingy ring around the shower stall.

Outside, the storm was rumbling and rolling, settling in for a good night's soaking. Sam locked the door and showered, leaving her perfumed shower gel next to a sliver of green soap that looked as welcoming as a military basic training unit. How did MacKenzie live like this? Simply being here filled her with shame. All the work society had done to rebuild. All the laws and man-hours put into revitalizing a broken nation, and this is what they achieved?

The bedroom door was shut tight when she slunk out of the bathroom, red-eyed and wearing sweats with the word ATLANTA stretched across the chest.

Hoss wagged his nubbin before stretching out on the floor beside the couch, happy to have his human back. She patted his side. "Good puppy." She picked up the pillow MacKenzie had left for her and gave it an experimental sniff. Much to her surprise, it didn't smell of mildew, sweat, or Smelly Boy—just a hint of eucalyptus laundry wash and dust. The blanket smelled the same.

She pulled it over her head, listening to the much-needed rain until she fell into a restless sleep.

CHAPTER 12

You might exist in every world of quantum possibility. Who knows? Who cares? Unless an individual is einselected to become a Node, they are nothing more than background static.

~ Excerpt from a private journal found
at the Odde Street house I1–2076

Sunday June 9, 2069
Alabama District 3
Commonwealth of North America

At five, the phone rang. Mac hit it with his fist, sending it clattering to the floor to be lost in a pile of dirty clothes. Falling after it, he managed to unlock the phone and answer. "Eh?"

"Get to the morgue. Now. We've got bodies." Harley hung up.

Mac sighed. The withdrawal headache had already started. This was going to be a bad day. His palm itched to reach for the bottle, to drown the memories in chemical oblivion.

Rain pounded on the roof, trying to repair a six-month drought in one go. He paused in the living room long enough to pull on his rain jacket, and not, he assured himself, to watch Agent Rose sleep. Black curls and an aquiline nose—he realized with a start that with a few extra pounds to round out her lean features, Rose would be a dead match for the computer-generated image of Jane Doe.

That was an avenue of delusion he didn't feel like exploring. He had enough problems with this case to begin with. In his more lucid moments, he was willing to admit that Jane was becoming an unhealthy obsession. Any free time not spent working Harley's cases was spent staring at the images of Jane's autopsy, trying to find that vital clue he was missing. Trying to give her a name. Trying to return her to her family.

Hoss's whining woke Sam up. She uncurled and stretched on the creaking couch. There was something horribly wrong about waking up in a strange apartment alone. "Hush, Hoss." Sam checked her phone: one call from Marrins, thirteen messages from Detective Altin. Nothing from her host.

"MacKenzie?" Her voice echoed through the house. "Mac, you here?" A quick check of the apartment showed he was gone.

Hoss bumped her knee. "I hear you. I hear you." She grabbed the leash and shuffled out onto MacKenzie's patio in her slept-in clothes to let Hoss relieve himself on a patch of brown grass and mud. "I need food. What about you?"

The dog barked.

"Let's see what we have." Sam dialed Marrins's number as she started searching MacKenzie's cupboards. As the phone rang, she found a stack of paper plates, some plastic forks, a brown ceramic bowl, and a box of opened Charmy Flakes with an expiration date of December 2067.

"Marrins," said the clipped voice in her ear.

"Hey, it's Rose, how's my house?"

"Still standing. We moved the body out. Altin's people were looking the house over. Monday morning, when you get in, there are going to be people here with questions. I'm going to need answers, good ones, or you're getting dinner Monday night courtesy of the county lockup."

"Sir, you know the only reason I would ever go to county lockup is to visit someone I sent there. I'm innocent."

"It doesn't look good: your house, your case, your only suspect. I sent an order down to the ME to figure out cause and time of death. We should know by tomorrow, but there's no way to make this look good."

"I didn't—I wouldn't—kill anyone, sir. I have no motive." She tried to sound calm even though her hands were shaking. "Sir . . ."

"Monday," he said in a warning tone. "I'm doing everything I can to give you the vacation you wanted. If I played this by the book, I would have had someone pull you out of D.C. as soon as MacKenzie called in the body."

"I know, sir, and I'm grateful that you have enough faith in me that you haven't—"

"Faith?" Marrins snorted. "Evidence is what I don't have. Being on a plane at the presumed time of death is a pretty handy alibi. Harley's going to do a full autopsy on Monday, but until then I don't have enough to lock anybody up. Consider that your holiday bonus for the year. If you stay out of the clink, I'll have a new case for you to work Tuesday. Something low-profile. I want you out of the way."

"Sir, this the first decent lead we've had in this case. We can finally prove there was more to the break-in than college high jinks. Put one of the morgue denizens on this, find the weapon, find some clues, and I can wrap this case. If nothing else, the time of death is going to prove I'm innocent."

Marrins clicked his tongue over the phone. "Can't do it, Rose. I can't have you on the case." Marrins hung up.

She dropped the phone into her purse on the counter. Off the case? No, there had to be a way around that. "I'll be back soon," she promised Hoss as she headed for her car. The only thing Marrins would hate more than getting off his fat behind would be working with Detective Altin.

Ten minutes of breaking the speed limit, and she was in a cozy suburb with rosebushes and backyard swing sets.

"Morning, Rose," Detective Altin said as he answered the door. He was bare-chested, a line of wiry gray curls peeking above his pajama pants with the local university mascot printed on them. "Rough weekend?"

"Are you free?"

"We're just getting up for church." He nodded at her sweats. "Lacey's going to make you change if you're coming with."

"No. I needed to talk to you before—"

"Before I talk to Marrins?" Altin motioned for her to step inside.

Sam paused. "You've been talking to Marrins?"

"Not cordially, but we've been talking." Altin gestured for her to come all the way in. His wife was already dressed for Sunday service in a lime-green dress with matching pillbox hat and a string of pink pearls. "Lacey, Agent Sam Rose from the bureau. Rose, this is my wife."

"How do you, ma'am? I'm sorry to interrupt your morning."

Lacey Altin sniffed. "Shouldn't be about any business but the Lord's on a Sunday." She gave Sam a disapproving once-over. "Breakfast is hot. Come on in." She put a steaming plate of cinnamon rolls on the table. "I'm making eggs. You gonna eat like a good Christian woman, or are you one of those devil Northern heathens who thinks food is bad?"

"She'll eat," the detective said. He winked at Sam. "She's just pulling your leg. Married to a police officer all these years, she knows how it goes. Eat the eggs, though. She's got a thing against starving-model types."

"Starving models are heathens?"

"When you worship at the church of Southern fried food they are." He held a chair out and found Sam a plate from the sideboard. "Now, about the case."

"I need to be in."

"No, you *want* to be in, but you're out."

"I can help."

Altin poured orange juice out of a pitcher as Lacey brought in the scrambled eggs. "No."

"Case is over," Lacey said. She dumped three heaping spoonfuls of egg on Sam's plate. "Eat up. You're never gonna catch a man if you don't put some meat on you."

Sam took a bite. If eating eggs could help her catch killers, she was going to eat a dozen a day.

The detective shrugged. "Melody Chimes called yesterday afternoon from Paris, France. Marrins sat in on the phone conversation with her family. He's convinced she's not under duress, she just wanted to be a kid. No harm done."

"And the lab?" Sam took a bite of egg, to be polite. They weren't half-bad. *Better than stale Charmy Flakes.*

"There's nothing missing. I've been there several hours a day since the vandalism, I've seen the inventory. Emir is paranoid and delusional."

"And Mordicai Robbins?"

Altin patted her hand. "Well, that's what I wanted to ask you about, but I thought it would be better if there were a lawyer present. Don't you?"

"I didn't do anything, Altin. You know that."

"I know there was a dead man in your house, and I should have dragged you in for questioning the moment your plane landed."

Sam raised an eyebrow. "Why didn't you?"

"That body was days old, and dumped. Marrins may not believe it, but this isn't my first rodeo. First time I've seen a body dumped in an investigator's house, though." Altin tapped his fork on the side of the plate. "That bothers me."

Lacey Altin looked up from her meal. "No work at the table, dearest."

Altin winked at his wife. "Do you have someone you could stay with until we find out what happened to Robbins?" he asked Sam.

"Not really. Why?"

"You stepped on some toes somewhere. Someone thinks you're a threat."

"An empty house on a nearly deserted road?" Sam said in a wheedling voice. "Why don't we call this a coincidence?. The house looks abandoned."

Altin gave her a flat, unamused look.

"I'm pretty sure I can convince Marrins it was co-incidence."

"With that giant dog there? And a security code? There's no love lost there, but even your senior agent isn't that stupid."

"I was counting on him being too lazy to care," Sam said. "Pretending this wasn't a threat will help me sleep better tonight."

"I wouldn't count on him being that lazy—not with this case, not anymore. Besides, where do lies leave you? They won't keep you safe." Altin glared at her. "Did the security company call you?"

"No." She folded her arms and leaned back in her chair.

"Whoever dumped the body knew your code, or knew how to turn the security off. Someone knows where you live, knows you're tied to this case, and they're willing to kill. Think about that, Sam. Who knows your code?"

"My best friend Bri. My mom probably has it on file because she has my next-of-kin packet." She thought about it for a second. "Oh . . . and MacKenzie does because he picked up my dog."

"He was first on scene, too."

"The security was on when MacKenzie arrived," she said, shaking her head. "Whoever dumped Robbins had come and gone when MacKenzie arrived."

"Says who?"

Sam took offense at that. "Agent MacKenzie is CBI. Not a killer. Not a suspect."

"You're CBI," Lacey Altin put in between dainty bites of breakfast. "You're a suspect."

Sam shook her head. "Agent MacKenzie has trouble with bleeding clone corpses. He wouldn't kill someone, then drag the body to my house."

Lacey Altin tapped her fork on the side of her plate. "Did he say why he was at your house?"

"He was picking up my dog," Sam snapped back at her.

"Really?" Altin asked, looking skeptical. "I didn't realize you two were that close."

"We aren't. The trip to D.C. came up suddenly. Marrins had the interview and ticket lined up, but I didn't have a kennel reservation. MacKenzie offered to dog sit for me. It's not a friend thing. He was being helpful."

"He had means and opportunity," Altin said.

"But not motive," Sam pointed out. "If MacKenzie wanted to kill someone, he wouldn't need a dump site—he has the morgue. If he wanted to threaten me, he had no reason to call Marrins about the body." Her stomach twisted. She'd spent the night at his house. He hadn't tried to hurt her. He couldn't . . . Sam shook her head. "This is pointless. Have Harley identify the time of death. I'll give you my timeline. You can see if they sync. Have MacKenzie give you one, too."

Lacey Altin added another cinnamon roll to Sam's plate. "Eat up, honey. You're spending so many calories thinking, you're going to fade away at my kitchen table."

Altin took the last roll. "We'll figure it out, Sam. I'm not going to write you off as dead and buried yet."

Sam escaped the local superstore several hours later with some new clothes, a toothbrush, and food. She was standing in the fine drizzle, a couple of steaks cooking over a new minigrill on the back porch when the front door slammed open. "MacKenzie?" She wiped her hands on her jeans and went looking for the ME. "Hey, MacKenzie, I'm making dinner."

Agent MacKenzie huddled in the shadowy corner behind the front door, slowly rocking.

Hoss bumped him, and the ME reached up to touch the dog, hands shaking.

"Are you hurt?"

He murmured something that sounded like, "Pills."

"You need pills?" Sam put her hands on her hips. "You don't need pills. You need food. Maybe some sleep."

He kept rocking.

Sam went back to the kitchen and grabbed a crispy potato wedge still hot from the oven, spiced with chili powder and salt. It smelled heavenly. "Look." She waved the wedge in front of MacKenzie. "Food."

Hoss licked the potato wedge out of her hand. "Dumb mutt, you're not helping." She ran back outside to flip the steak and grab more wedges. "Here."

With a shaking hand, MacKenzie reached for the potato wedge. He gripped it violently, squashing the potato into mush. "Hot."

"Yes, hot, I just pulled it from the oven. You want more?" she asked, as he stared at his hand. Sam tugged him to his feet. "Let's get some food."

"Marcellus is dead," he whispered.

"Sure he is," Sam agreed, running through a short list of morgue personnel in her head. There was no Marcellus in the office.

"I didn't bring the baby home."

Sam helped him sit in a cracked plastic chair. "You don't have a baby."

"I told her I'd bring . . ." MacKenzie sucked in his breath, eye twitching. "I told her I'd bring her baby home. Baby home." He pulled his knees to his chest and started rocking in the chair. "Couldn't save him. Couldn't save him. Couldn't. Couldn't."

Sam rescued the steak from the grill, set it on the counter, and called the morgue.

"This is Henry," said the cheerful voice on the other end after the prerecorded greeting finally cycled to a living person.

"Hi, this is Agent Rose from the bureau. Do you know what case Agent MacKenzie was working on today?"

There was a brief moment of static. "Harley pulled him in this morning to handle the three-car pileup from last night."

"Who was working with him?"

"Ma'am?"

"Who was helping Agent MacKenzie?"

"Why would he need help?"

That answered all her questions. "Thank you." Sam hung up and looked at the broken agent. "Mac, where are your pills?" He was bound to have a stash lying around. All addicts did.

"Pills? No pills. Agent Perfect said no pills."

Her thumb hovered over the dial button for the bureau emergency line. MacKenzie was a lost cause.

He needed professional help, and a long stay at a medical house where he could get therapy.

Still, she hesitated.

Her father had gone to one of the medical halfway houses. They'd kicked him out into the Toronto winter one bright New Year's Day with nothing on but a pair of khakis, a T-shirt, and red-felt slippers. At least she'd been there to help him recover from the therapy and the drugs. From what she could tell, MacKenzie had no one to catch him when the system kicked him out.

"They give me pills. Pills." He shook. "I don't want more pills." He seemed to shrink in his seat, almost slipping under the table.

"Getting yourself off the pills is a great idea. I fully support kicking the addiction, but unless you address the root cause, you'll find another."

He stared ahead silently.

She piled green beans next to his steak. "Fine. Skip that. How long have you been like this?"

"Five years," he said in a low monotone.

Saints and angels. Her father had abused the prescription painkillers for less than six months when her mother caught on and took him for therapy.

"You have the pills for depression?" Sam brought over two glasses of water.

A nod.

"What triggers your depression?" Silence. She fancied she could hear a cricket chirping in the background through the patter of rain on the window. "Rejection? Failure at work? What?"

"Blood," MacKenzie whispered in the same monotone. He reached for his glass. "Violent death."

She looked at him, appalled. "What are you doing in the morgue, then?"

"Contract."

"How many years do you have left?"

"Eight."

That couldn't be right. Contract bureau workers were former government employees of the United States who had switched jobs and were guaranteed work when the US joined the Commonwealth. Eight years left, five already done. That sounded insanely long. Almost like . . .

Military.

"Which branch?" Sam asked.

MacKenzie looked at her, frozen in place, then he slouched back down.

"You're a military holdover, aren't you?"

The barest nod.

"Is that what you have nightmares about? Did you . . . Did you see someone die?"

The glass in MacKenzie's hand shattered, making Sam jump back. His head twitched side to side as he shook violently.

"MacKenzie?" Sam stood slowly, placing her napkin on the table with exaggerated care. "What's wrong? Are you having a seizure?"

He jerked away from her reaching hand.

She focused on the glass. He was still clutching

it, grinding the glass into his palm. *Mother Mary have mercy*. "You need a hospital."

"No. More. Pills!" MacKenzie stood and threw the glass at the sink; shards of glass jutted out of the padded flesh of his thumb.

"MacKenzie. Agent MacKenzie?"

"Linsey?"

He jumped visibly when she used his first name, like a whipped man.

He licked his lips, eyes wide and dilated, panicked. "Mac."

"Mac?" Grabbing his napkin as she passed the table. She held out the clean napkin. "Your hand is bleeding."

He stood in front of her, shaking. Fear rose in his red-rimmed eyes. "I didn't . . ." He licked his lips again. "I didn't . . ."

"You didn't do it?"

His head jerked side to side. "Couldn't. Couldn't save him. I tried. I tried. ItriedItriedItriedItriedI . . ." He fell down, curling into a ball chanting, "I tried."

Sam moved down with him, trying to capture his hand. "You tried what?"

"Tried to, tried to, tried to save him. Her baby boy. Baby. Just a baby. Baby-faced butter bar. I tried . . ." He held out his hand, gasping for air. "Blood, blood, blood, blood. Couldn't, couldn't find a, find a pulse. Couldn't make him breathe. Couldn't. Couldn't. Couldn't. Couldn't find a head."

Sam rocked back on her heels. "Couldn't find a head?"

"A head. Explosion. Shrapnel." He sprung to his feet, looking around, twitching, shaking. "Can't. Can't."

God have mercy on his soul. He's reliving it. He needed so much more help than she could give. More than a doctor could give, probably. She looked around, helpless, when she saw her purse sitting on the counter. An idea started to form. Ignoring MacKenzie's stuttered reenactment of his private nightmare, she dug in her purse and tipped two orange breath mints into her hand. "MacKenzie? Mac!"

Her shout drew his attention.

"Pills?"

He let out a sob, grabbed the pills, and swallowed them whole. For a minute, he sat there shaking, with his eyes closed, tears streaming down his face.

Sam breathed a sigh of relief as he wiped away tears. "Let me see your hand."

Mac stared at her as if he didn't recognize her. Maybe he didn't. Whatever nightmare world he was remembering, she wasn't a part of it. She tried to look perky, wholesome, and safe.

He held out his bleeding hand.

Using a napkin, she wiped away the blood. "Just a surface cut. I'll put some liquid bandage on, and everything will be fine by morning."

He slumped back.

"Do you want to talk?"

He shook his head. Back to the beginning. No wonder therapists didn't work. This was a constant loop of crazy. *So stop thinking about this like a therapist.*

Mac was past that, he was . . . what? A dog, she decided. A bad dog brought home from death row at the pound. You couldn't undo a dog's past, but you could retrain the dog. Give it a new name. Set new rules.

MacKenzie wasn't a hopeless case. He wasn't violent. He'd broken the glass and thrown it across the room, but he hadn't thrown it at her. That was a good sign. "Mac?" He looked up from the floor. "What do you want to be?"

His eyes went wide. "I . . . I want to be . . . to be me." He sighed, turning to look out the window into the dark night. "Dependable," he whispered. "Highspeed. Gets things done. Go-to guy. Trust him. He gets it done.

"Superman."

CHAPTER 13

> By careful observation of einselected nodes in other iterations, we are able to predict the event horizons where decoherence—the collapse of all possible histories but the prime state—will occur with over 80 percent accuracy. At this time our calculations suggest that humanity will reach the next event horizon before the decade is out.
>
> ~ Excerpt from Lectures on the Movement of Time by Dr. Abdul Emir I1–20740413

Monday June 10, 2069
Alabama District 3
Commonwealth of North America

Hurricane Jessica stormed into town on Monday, a bitter woman with a grudge against humanity. She shredded the Gulf Coast, leaving the resort towns of Florida's panhandle in retreat. She tore through lower Alabama, swelling the rivers and spawning tornadoes. In record time, District 3 went from concerns over summer wildfires to sandbagging sidewalks.

In the short sprint from Sam's car to the bureau's

front door, the rain drenched her, and mud from the flooded sidewalk splattered her pants. She leaned against the glass doors, managing a half smile for Theresa. "Rough weather."

Theresa pursed her lips. "Senior Agent Marrins is upstairs with Detective Altin. They've been waiting for ten minutes."

"Wonderful." Sam grimaced as she pushed away from the door.

Altin stood in the hall outside the conference room, thumbs hooked on his belt. Behind him, the horse-faced Officer Holt glared at her, hand resting on her cuffs. "Agent Rose."

Sam smiled. "Good morning, Altin. Loving the weather?"

The old detective sighed. "Hardly."

Marrins sat at the head of the conference table, swilling his off-brand coffee. "So glad you could join us." He made a show of checking his watch. "Running a little late, aren't we?"

"No, sir, technically my pass is good until noon today. I showed up three hours early just for you."

He narrowed his eyes. "Keep it professional, or Officer Holt there is going to have you in cuffs." The senior agent smirked at some private joke.

Sam tried not to visualize the horse-faced Holt and Marrins enjoying some unprofessional kink together. It was repulsive at an awe-inspiring level. "I'm not at fault here."

Altin sat. "That's what we're here to determine, isn't it?"

"Shouldn't I have a lawyer and a judge?" Sam asked.

Marrins shook his head. "This is a friendly little inquiry, Rose. Altin is going to ask a few teensy-tiny questions because this ties to his case. Then I'm going to ask some rather serious questions because violent crime leading to death is a bureau problem, and—if you answer the way we want—everyone will break for lunch without major changes to anyone's living arrangements."

Sam took her seat at the back of the room with a tight smile. "Ask away, Detective Altin."

Altin sat. Deputy Holt stayed near the door, artfully blocking Sam's only means of escape. Altin pulled out his notepad and an old-fashioned pen. "All right. You are Samantha Lynn Rose, junior agent of the Commonwealth of North America Bureau of Investigation?"

"Yes."

"You were assigned to Case 516-29-5698 involving the property damage, and assumed break-in, at N-V Nova Laboratories?"

"Yes."

"Prior to the order to join the case, did you, or anyone you are in close contact with, have knowledge of, communicate with, or work for N-V Nova Labs?" Altin asked.

"No."

Altin made a note. "Did you, or anyone you are in close contact with, have dealings, contracts, knowledge of, or a friendship, with the deceased security guard Mordicai Robbins?"

"No."

"Had you ever seen Mordicai Robbins before he was found at your house?"

Sam raised an eyebrow. "I never saw Mordicai Robbins at all. I have his file photo in my case files, but I haven't ever seen him in person, dead or alive."

Altin frowned and made a note. "Is there any reason why Mordicai Robbins might have been at your house at the time of death?"

"Was he at my house at the time of death?" Sam turned to Marrins. "I thought he was dumped there. No one said he was killed there. Did the forensics team find blood? A murder weapon? Anything?"

"Ah." Marrins coughed. "Actually, we're still waiting on the report."

Altin gave Marrins a tired look. "You said this morning Robbins died at the house."

"I said he might have," Marrins protested.

"Do you have evidence?" Altin asked.

"We're working on it." Marrins crossed his arms.

There was a knock at the door, and Coroner Harley waddled in. "Sorry I'm late. Rain." He took his donut and dry coat to the other side of the table and sat. "I miss anything?"

Marrins held out his hand, snapping his fingers as if he was calling a dog. "Harley! Where's that autopsy report?"

"Which one?"

"The traitor who got his throat shot out gang-style. They found him in Rose's freezer. That one."

Harley leaned back in his chair. "Don't know, that's bureau business. Where's your boy, the scraggly one? I told him to do it."

"Agent MacKenzie?" Sam asked through gritted teeth.

"Yeah, him."

"As the agent who found the body, he isn't supposed to work on the case," Sam said. "And yesterday, MacKenzie worked for fourteen hours on autopsies for the city. I know. I called to ask about Robbins."

"Shouldn't have done that," Harley said with a belch and a smile. "It looks bad."

Sam looked to Marrins for help.

The senior agent rubbed his temples. "Harley, I told you to take care of the body. You promised me you would handle this."

"Right, it'll be handled. What's the rush? We know the cause of death. He choked to death on his own blood because his throat was cut out by a bullet."

"We're trying to determine if there is enough evidence to arrest Agent Rose on suspicion of murder," Altin said patiently.

Harley frowned. "Rose?" He looked over at her in confusion. "Did you kill that guy?"

"No, but the law demands proof." She glanced at Altin. "I still don't have a motive—isn't that enough?"

"It was your freezer, Sam. At least give me an alibi," Altin said.

"How can I give you an alibi when I don't know

time of death? I wasn't there when he died. It's not like I have 'Make up alibi for 3:15 Friday' penciled in my planner."

"Wasn't dead on Friday," Harley said.

"What?" Altin demanded.

The ME shrugged. "Body bloated like that? He was probably dead Wednesday or Thursday, maybe early Friday if he was left in the sun a bit."

"That's not good enough," Altin said as he leaned back in his chair. "Honest to goodness, Marrins, what kind of circus are you running here? I've got half the force tied up waiting for the dams to break upstream, and instead of doing something useful this morning, I'm jumping in your clown car. Please tell me you have something I can work with."

Marrins thumped the conference table, making everyone's drinks jump. "Fine, I'm not making any arrest. Rose, I want you to document your every waking moment of the last week." She'd already done that after speaking with Altin on Sunday but decided it wasn't worth bringing up again. Marrins continued, "When Harley is done with the autopsy, we'll see where you were at the time of death. In the meantime, you're on office duty. Stay in your office, go straight home at the end of the day, and no leaving the district until you're cleared."

Sam forced herself to sit still even though she wanted to yell.

"Altin, the bureau will collect the case files and look

them over. If Robbins's death can be tied to the break-in, we'll take over. Otherwise, we'll cut that loss and call it funny timing."

That did it. "You honestly think it was a coincidence?" Sam demanded.

"I honestly don't think we're going to get the timing to become admissible court evidence! There are no prints, no murder weapon, nothing that ties Robbins to anyone. We still don't have any evidence that something was stolen from the lab, but no, Rose, I don't think it's coincidence. I think someone is doing a damn fine job of covering their tracks."

She crossed her arms and slammed back in her seat.

"The death of Mordicai Robbins will be treated as a separate investigation until we find evidence I can take to court. Harley will do the autopsy. I'll handle the investigation."

Reluctantly, Sam nodded agreement.

"Anything else?" Marrins asked. "Good. Now y'all get out. Except you, Harley; we need to talk. Close the door on your way out, Rose."

Sam stormed out of her seat but waited to slam the door behind Altin.

Holt sneered. "It's nice to see the old man protecting you. How many lap dances did that cost? Was it more or less than it took to buy you a job?"

"Out of line," Altin said. Holt rolled her eyes. Altin frowned. "I'll meet you at the car." He waited until the Holt moved away before turning back to Sam. "You better get used to that."

"Being insulted? Please," she said, rolling her eyes. "It would take more than Officer Holt to get me upset."

Altin gave her a small smile for the nickname. "Seriously, though—there are rumors floating around the district, basically since you got here. Marrins was pretty free about telling people you called in a favor to get this position." He shrugged.

"I did: my friend called around to some senior agents. That was it."

Guess it takes being a murder suspect for others in law enforcement to show what they really feel about you.

"I'm just letting you know it's out there," Altin said.

"Appreciate it."

"Where's your office?"

"This way." She trudged to the end of the hall and motioned for Altin to make himself comfortable.

"Do you have the paperwork I asked for?"

"Yes," she said. She looked at him critically. "Why didn't you ask for it in there? We went over this yesterday."

Altin gave her a pitying look. "This has setup written all over it. You don't like your morgue geek for this, but I do, and if he's in on it, then I'm willing to bet my next paycheck either Marrins or Harley gave the go-ahead."

"No." Sam shook her head. "No bureau agent would do this. I'd bet *my* paycheck on that. MacKenzie might be . . ." she scrambled for the word, "he's plenty of things, but not a killer. Senior Agent Marrins has a solid career with over twenty years in service. I can't even wrap my mind around the idea of him breaking the law."

Altin shrugged. "Give it another ten years. I've seen officers go bad."

"He's not police. He's CBI." She could barely conceal the insult. She had always considered Altin a . . . maybe not a friend, but a colleague who shared mutual respect with her. Now, though, with his revelation about the rumors of her and Marrins, and this weird conspiracy, she wasn't so sure.

"Papers?"

"Yes." Grabbing her purse and files, she handed over her work from Sunday afternoon. "I listed everyone I talked to, everything I remember saying to them. Nothing screamed 'guilty' to me."

Altin took the file. "I meant what I said. Keep your head down. Get a roommate if you can. Stay where there are security cameras. I don't want you off grid."

She couldn't help it this time: the bitterness came through as she said, "Because it'd help a lot of careers if you could close this case quick, and I look guilty as Eve?"

"Because I don't want to pull *your* body out of the next freezer. Get it through your head: someone wants you dead. Play it safe."

"I'll do what I can."

"Do you have the standard GPS and call recorder on your phone?"

A wet strand of hair dropped past her eye as she nodded.

"Turn it on."

Marrins's door slammed, and voices filtered through the hall.

Altin put on his stern face and walked out of her office. "Yes, you will. Stay away from my case. I don't want you tainting it," he said, just a little louder than necessary.

The lights flickered, and Marrins cursed. "Rose! I need to go kick the generators. Keep an eye on things!"

Sam dropped her head to her desk, gently banging it against the synthetic wood as the first winds of Hurricane Jessica whipped the building. She should have taken Bri's offer to hide out with her at the lake in the Georgia mountains until this blew over. Of course, then she'd look even *more* like a suspect, this time fleeing the crime.

There was a soft tapping on the doorframe, barely audible over the thundering rain outside. Lightning stretched across the sky and illuminated MacKenzie, dripping-wet, dark brown hair hanging limp over his face. "Hi," she said.

"Hi." He rubbed his neck. "Do you still work here?"

"I guess." She snorted in laughter and sat up. "I file paperwork. It's like being a secretary, except I'm still on call for all major emergencies."

"Are you going home tonight?"

"Yeah, I have a green light to go back to my house. The freezer was taken as evidence, and the back door.

Someone from the security company is coming out to assess the damage today. It should all be covered." Thunder rumbled. "I'm waiting for the call saying they have to cancel because of the storm, but the forensic team took pictures, and I have some plastic sheeting to cover the hole. I'm not worried," she lied.

MacKenzie nodded. "I'll . . . um, I'll drop Hoss off if you want. Harley is sending everyone home in the next hour. We . . . we're just boarding up the building."

"Have fun," Sam said. She looked around her office and tried to sync his comment with his presence. It didn't work. "Why are you here?"

"Um . . . a-a couple of things. The Melody Doe blood test results, do you still want them?"

Sam raised an eyebrow. "I'm off the case. I can't discuss it with you."

"So, do you still want me to run them?"

"I have no opinion," Sam said through gritted teeth.

"So, if I couldn't find a clone marker on Melody Doe just like I couldn't with Jane, you don't want to know about them? No report on the similarities?"

She pursed her lips. "You need to wait for Agent Marrins to request that information before you do anything with it. I have no opinion."

"Right."

"What else do you need?"

He grimaced. "A favor?"

"What kind of favor?"

He dug in his back pocket and unfolded a square of soggy orange paper. "My landlord is redoing the floors. I need to move my couch. Could I . . . can it stay at your place? Since you aren't being kicked out?"

She took the paper from him as the lights turned back on with an annoying buzz. The paper was bright orange and rain-soaked, but it did say that all tenants needed to move bulky furniture out so that the floors could be redone. She shrugged. "If you can move it, you can drop it at my place with Hoss." She handed the paper back.

"Thanks."

"You watched my dog," Sam said. "I can babysit your couch." MacKenzie hovered on the other side of her desk. "Anything else?"

He licked his lips. "About . . . about last night. I'm sorry." His cheeks flushed pink. "I . . . I haven't been that bad in years. The flashbacks, the pills make me a walking zombie, I know I'm not functioning like I should, but the pills keep me from being . . . there again. I'm sorry if I said anything I shouldn't, or hurt you. I didn't mean to hurt you."

Sam sat back in her chair. "You didn't hurt me. You didn't even try. Do you have enough medicine for now?"

"I . . . yeah." His shoulders sagged. "I took two of the new pills this morning."

"And those worked?" she asked, incredulous. If breath mints could solve PTSD, she would win a Nobel Prize for medicine.

"I remember things. Too many things. But I'm thinking. I can get out of bed without wanting to kill myself. I guess that means they're doing something."

The door to the main office slammed shut. "Rose! Hurry up and shut down the computers. That generator isn't going to last much longer!" Marrins shouted from down the hall before launching into his rant against secondhand, outdated equipment.

"Yes, sir," Sam shouted back. The door slammed again. "Back to work I guess. Marrins believes putting in a full day will be good for my soul."

Mac leaned on the morgue door to close it against the wind.

Harley stepped out from the side hall. "Pack up. Get everything off your floor. If this turns into another Hurricane Derek like we saw back in '57, we're going to need waders just to find our desks for a week."

"Boss! I can't lift this!" one of the interns shouted from the back.

"Get going," Harley ordered, going to help the intern.

Mac nodded and moved, nearly slipping on the smooth, concrete floors. He slid into his office as he stifled a yawn. The previous night was a jumble of memories, the smell of oranges mixed with the sound of mortar fire and a woman's voice. Sitting, he started saving his files so he could shut everything down. Agent Rose smiled up at him from the file.

He blinked. Right. He was cyberstalking Agent Rose through the CBI system to find her line number for the Melody Doe report. A few minutes of digging through the piles on his desk, and he found the file lying on the floor. He checked the files and line number. Everything good to go.

A flashing red light on his monitor called his attention. "Search Completed—Match Found for Jane Doe 756581530263." Search for more pills was what he needed. He saw the orange bottle out of the corner of his eye, wallowing under a mess of unfilled reports. Grasping for it like a dying man Mac reached out. No familiar rattle greeted him. *Empty.* His stomach knotted in terror.

Dry-mouthed and shaking, Mac jerked back to the computer monitor and away from half-buried memories. He clicked the search button, and Agent Perfect's file reappeared.

He hadn't closed out of it. Figured.

Mac closed Rose's file, cleared his electronic desktop, and reopened the search results. Jane Doe 756581530263—Match—Agent Samantha Lynn Rose . . .

It wasn't possible. There was . . . He licked his lips. All right. Yes, there was a way. Jane didn't have a clone marker. Melody Doe didn't have a clone marker. Both were dead. Both were seen after their deaths.

The simple math made perfect sense.

A rich daughter missing, now running loose in Europe financed by a trust fund. The other a CBI agent, the daughter of an ambassador. Not as wealthy as a business magnate like Mr. Chimes but still worth the trouble for a terrorist group.

Shaking, he sagged in his worn office chair, staring

at the screen. Agent Rose, he wouldn't have guessed. She was so . . . perfect. Too perfect, maybe.

"Mackenzie, we're shutting the generator down!" Harley yelled.

"Aye, sir." His hand hovered over the keyboard. Eighty percent accuracy, damning even on a bad day. Mac hit the SAVE button and shut off his computer. With a quick yank, the cord snapped out of the wall socket, and he rolled it up. Scooping up the scattered texts and papers on his floor, he made a hasty pile that leaned dangerously.

The light shut off. "Let's go, MacKenzie. I'm locking up!"

"Coming." He grabbed his jacket and hurried to the door.

"Keep your phone on you," Harley said. "If the dams break, we'll all get called in, police and bureau." He hesitated, then clapped Mac on the back. "You okay? You look a little peaked."

Mac jerked a nod. "Yeah. I'm fine. Just fine. Tired."

"Uh-huh, well, get some sleep this afternoon. It's not like you have anything else to do."

Nothing else at all, Mac thought as he stepped into the driving rain. Except return one slobbering dog and drop the couch off with Agent Rose.

The clone.

By three o'clock that afternoon, the skies were pitch-black, and thick curtains of rain hid the parking lot from view. The lights flickered off again. Marrins knocked on her doorframe. "Go home. Grab something to eat and plan on a late night. The district just called: we're going to lose Harris Dam up the river."

Her heart sank. "Are they sure? We're already getting reports of flooding downtown. If we get any more . . ."

"The National Guard is bringing in sandbags, and we'll be out there to help." Running a hand over his balding head, Marrins sighed. "Decades of neglect. They knew the dam was falling to pieces," he muttered. "But do we get the funds? No." He drawled the word sardonically. "The Commonwealth is an improvement for everybody on top, but the little guys, the working stiffs at the bottom? We just have to suck it up and make do." He growled, then jumped, as if he had forgotten Sam was there. "Get home. Drive careful. I don't need any more paperwork because of you."

"Yes, sir." Sam gathered her things and walked through the eerily silent bureau building. Wind howled outside, lashing waves of water across the sidewalk to slap the front door. Taking a deep breath, Sam muscled the door open against the wind and slogged through the rain to her car. The little Alexian Virgo gurgled as it started and whined as she drove out of the parking lot. "St. Christopher, holy patron of travelers, protect me. Amen." If the saints were inclined to listen to one lax Catholic, this would be a perfect opportunity to step in and keep the hurricane from drowning her.

There was no traffic on the roads. Everyone who

could had already left town, and those who remained were hunkered down somewhere safe. She crossed herself again. The nuns always said thunder was God talking, but that had never helped.

She drove at a crawl as gusts of wind buffeted the car. Once she'd turned onto the farm road for the house, she punched MacKenzie's number into her phone. It went straight to voice mail. "MacKenzie, just keep Hoss for me. I'll pick him up after the storm."

An hour later, hands shaking, she finally pulled her car to a stop in front of her house. Another burst of wind whipped past, forcing the ancient oak trees to bend until the branches brushed the ground. *This is how horror movies started*. The menacing creak of branches and shoes sticking in the mud. It didn't matter if she ran for the door or waltzed, she would be soaked to the bone and quite possibly twist an ankle.

The car door groaned in protest as she pushed it open. Her heels sank into the ground. She ran for it, fighting the storm and leaning against the wind to reach the house. Her front door fell open as she reached for it, and Sam landed sprawled on the floor.

"Hello?" Her voice echoed in the dark living room as the security light flashed a merry green, disarmed and docile. Hoss barked from the kitchen. Sam scrambled to her feet. "Hold on, Hoss."

Grumbling under her breath, she walked into the kitchen, and stopped. A glass hurricane lamp filled with blue oil sat on her ancient table illuminating Miss Azalea with gun in hand standing at the back entrance watching MacKenzie kneel on the floor with his hands behind his head.

The elderly woman nodded to Sam. "Fine storm tonight," her landlady said as the wind stretched the heavy plastic tarp Sam had taped over the empty doorframe.

"Yes." Sam slowly set her purse on the table. "Is everything all right, Miss Azalea?"

"I found this young coot breakin' in," her landlady said. "He didn' think anyone was home."

Hoss bumped Sam's knee, and she stroked his head in a daze.

"Sam . . . Rose." Mackenzie's eyes were wide with fright.

Miss Azalea bumped his shoulder with her Smith & Wesson as Sam's phone rang.

"I thought you were in Florida, Miss Azalea. And, Mac, what are you doing out here?" She checked her phone, and they both started to talk at once. Not to be outdone, Hoss started barking. "Yes?"

"Rose, where on the green Earth are you?" Marrins demanded. "I've been calling for the past hour! We lost the dam five minutes after you left, and they're calling in everyone. Get down here."

"Shut up!" Sam yelled at the dog, her landlady, and her landlady's hostage. She shoved a finger in her free ear and squeezed her eyes shut. "Sir, I just got home. There's a bit of a situation here." She peeked over her shoulder.

MacKenzie mouthed the words *Help me*.

"It's not another body, is it?" Marrins asked.

"No, it's my landlady."

"What's she need?"

"I honestly have no idea."

"Well, sort it out," Marrins snapped. "We need help out here." He hung up with a grumble.

She stared at the floor for a long moment before turning back to the strange tableau. "Miss Azalea, weren't you in Florida?"

"Was," her landlady agreed affably, "but the storm done sent me home. The crick's rising so fast, it's crawling out of its bed into mine. I come up here to see you. I'm gonna stay up here, or I can go to Widow Carnegie's place if that's a problem. She's got the guest room done up real nice."

Sam shook her head. "No, it's okay. I'm renting one room, not the whole house." She frowned at MacKenzie. "What are *you* doing here? Didn't you get my message? Why would you try moving furniture in this weather?"

He grimaced. "There was a break in the rain."

"Those are called rain bands. You should have used it to buy groceries." Sam grabbed the barrel of Miss Azalea's gun and pushed it toward the door. "You can let him up. He's harmless."

"Harmless?" The old lady humphed. "He broke my back door!"

"The door was broken over the weekend," Sam corrected. "I just hadn't fixed it yet." Miss Azalea tugged at the gun, but Sam tugged back harder. "Please tell me you loaded this with some liquid bullets before threatening a CBI agent."

Miss Azalea sniffed and folded her arms. "If I shoots someone, I aims to kill 'em, not let 'em have a light nap."

Mac was starting to shake. A few more minutes of this, and she was going to have an incident.

"Miss Azalea, these things are illegal." Flipping the safety on, Sam laid the gun on the counter. "You can't go waving a gun at everyone who drives up. Especially not Commonwealth agents." She moved between her landlady and the man kneeling on her floor.

Mac stood up slowly and backed away. "Um . . ." He rubbed his arm. "I should . . . I should be going."

"Do you have a truck?" Sam asked.

"Yes." His focus was elsewhere, probably lost in the past remembering whatever tragedy had driven him down this road.

"Can you give me a ride to the staging area?" Away from Miss Azalea. "I barely survived the drive home—my car isn't heavy enough to handle the wind." And her nerves weren't up to fighting the steering wheel. If Mac was driving, she could shut her eyes and pretend she wasn't living through a nightmare.

He bit his lip, blinked, then nodded. "Sure. I guess." One deep breath later, and he seemed as close to normal as he ever was.

"Great, let me get changed real quick. Is there anything you need before we leave, Miss Azalea?"

Her landlady was still frowning at MacKenzie. "You sure you can trust a city boy?"

"Farm boy," MacKenzie said. "I was born in Idaho on a farm. I'm a farm boy."

"Right, Idaho," Sam said, as if she'd known that all along."

"Fine. But he best be fixin' that door once this storm blows through."

Sam nodded, knowing it wasn't worth repeating that it hadn't been Mac who had broken the door to begin with. "It'll be a top priority as soon as the back porch is dry." She rushed upstairs, stripped off her soggy work clothes, and found a pair of old jeans suitable for drowning in. From the depths of her closet, she pulled out a neon yellow raincoat that she'd bought on a whim when she'd moved to Alabama but never worn. She tied on her oldest sneakers and went back downstairs, where MacKenzie was cowering behind Hoss as Miss Azalea glared. "Come on, Mac."

He patted the dog and stood.

"I'll have my phone in case you need anything, Miss Azalea." Sam pulled her hood on. She turned to MacKenzie. "Are you parked around back?"

He nodded again.

She crossed herself and followed him into the storm. MacKenzie pulled the passenger-side door open for her and slammed it shut once she'd climbed onto the high seat. The truck smelled comfortingly worn: the scent of leather and sweat and man. She settled back in the seat, dropping her wet jacket on the floorboards as MacKenzie pulled out onto the road. Wind buffeted the truck, but it didn't budge.

"You won't have trouble driving in this, will you?" Sam asked, trying to keep her nervousness from showing.

"I've driven in worse," he said, as they accelerated. MacKenzie kept glancing at her.

"Is there a problem?"

He jerked his head side to side. "No."

"Then keep your eyes on the road." Sam drew her knees to her chest and shut her eyes so she wouldn't see the waves of water cresting on the highway. They turned onto the main thoroughfare, where concrete barriers blocked the worst of the wind, and she felt MacKenzie watching her again. "What *is* it?"

"Hmm, nothing. I just . . . it's nothing." He refocused on the road. "It's about the Jane Doe case."

"Can it wait?" Sam asked. The truck hydroplaned, and she screamed.

MacKenzie chuckled as he brought the truck back under control.

"We're about to die, and you're laughing?"

"This isn't bad. I've driven while it's mudding."

"Mudding?"

"It's what you get when a sandstorm and a rainstorm collide. It muds." He grinned. "This is so much better."

"No it's not!" Her voice climbed an octave as the truck's traction light flashed on and off. "Please slow down."

"Play it chill, Rose. It's just a storm."

"I don't like storms." She squeezed her eyes shut.

The truck slowed. "I'm sorry. I'll be more careful."

"Thank you."

Now if I could only get God to promise the same thing.

CHAPTER 14

People cower behind facts. When life becomes a
storm of emotion, they cling to their rationales
and statistics like a mother holds the dying child.

~ Excerpt from *The Heart of Fear*
by Liedjie Slaan I1–2071

Tuesday June 11, 2069
Alabama District 3
Commonwealth of North America

Cold rain dripped off Mac's nose as he loaded the last
sandbag onto the truck. Thunder rumbled overhead,
but at least the wind had dropped in the last hour. The
shopping district was evacuated, the river was flooding
downtown parking garages, and the local community
college was under a foot of water. He shuffled back to
the line and reached for a canvas bag that wasn't there.

"We're out." Agent Rose trudged through the mud
to the table where the bags had sat. "We used the last
one already. And we're not going to get another truck-
load tonight."

Mac looked over at the beat-up Natura Amazon truck piled high with filled sandbags. "That's not going to hold the river back."

"It's all we have until we get more supplies in."

He rubbed tired eyes, not willing to fight the inevitable. "What time is it?"

"A little after four in the morning."

Someone shouted at the edge of the hill. Rose moved first, but Mac followed right behind her. From the safety of the loading site, they watched the line of sandbags bulge, slip, and fall in slow motion. The rescue workers ran from the break. The line collapsed, and a floodlight fell with an echoing crash.

Behind him, Holt swore. Agent Rose kicked at the mud.

"It could be worse," a volunteer said, as mud-thickened water tore across the pothole-studded streets toward vacant buildings. "This could be the good end of town."

Agent Rose looked back over her shoulder at him, her face pale and wraithlike in the floodlights' glow. "Mac, isn't that your apartment?"

"Yeah." Mac bit his lip as the water engulfed his apartment. He tried to conjure some sorrow for the loss, but all he could think of was how his unwashed socks were now polluting the public waterways. A twinge of guilt nudged him, and he ignored it.

The volunteer swore. "Sorry."

"Not your fault," Mac said.

Mac froze as Agent Rose made eye contact. "Are you all right?"

"Why wouldn't I be?" He couldn't be sure in this light, with the hood of her rain slicker pulled up, but he thought she was glaring at him.

"Do you have some friends you can stay with?"

"Friends?" He almost laughed.

"Someone who will understand if this"—she gestured at the mud and rain—"adds to your stress."

What a tactful way to ask if he was about to have a major breakdown. "I was in a desert, not trench warfare. Rain doesn't do anything but get me wet."

"Right." She started to move away, and he reached for her arm before he knew what he was doing. Agent Rose stiffened under his touch, and Mac snapped his hand back.

"Um . . ." The words deserted him. It was a simple question, on the tip of his tongue, he just needed to ask . . .

"Rose!" Marrins's voice pulled her away.

Mac followed. Maybe it was the fatigue, or subliminal suggestion, or maybe just her. Every time Agent Rose moved, it seemed like he forgot how to breathe. He couldn't remember the last time a woman's opinion had mattered. No one else's censure made a noticeable difference, but one frown from her, and he was trying to fix his life.

She's a plant. She's already killed once, Mac reminded himself. Pursuing her would get him buried right next to the real Samantha Rose.

Marrins nodded as Mac caught up with the other agents. "We need to account for everyone in the shelters tomorrow. When the current slows down, we'll start a house-by-house search for survivors and corpses. MacKenzie, did I hear right, that was your place?"

"Yes, sir."

Marrins hmmphed from the depths of his raincoat. "Most of the shelters are full, but you should be able to find someplace to bunk."

"Yes, sir."

"Everyone reports in by ten. I want us out and working at full light."

"Yes, sir," Mac heard Agent Rose's echoing answer. She turned back to him. "You good to drive?"

"Sure. I can drop you off and go sleep in my office."

"You'll do no such thing," Agent Rose said as she walked to the waiting line of vehicles. "You can crash at my place with Miss Azalea." She blinked and shook her head. "I meant like her, not with her. There's a room downstairs by the kitchen that's free."

"That wouldn't look right."

"We already had this argument," Rose reminded him. "At your place, when the storm started? I lost that time. I'm not losing this round. Besides, Miss Azalea is there."

"Very reassuring."

"I'll go in first and hide guns."

"Thank you."

Sam's lips twitched into a grin. "Aren't you glad we aren't her real kids? Imagine what she was like when her girls started dating?"

"Bet you ten bucks someone's horny prom date got buried in the backyard."

He almost smiled . . . but then remembered that Sam was a murderer.

Mac sighed as the truck pulled to a stop behind Agent Rose's house. A gust of wind howled past them, making it impossible to open the door for a minute. Agent Rose started to fall out of the car as her door snapped open, catching herself at the last moment. "We never had weather like this in Toronto."

"Home?" Mac didn't bother locking the truck. He'd bought the black Adveni Trust back in 2063, when the company was still a going concern and the Trust was *the* truck on the roads. Six years of permanent neglect had left their mark. Red mud dripped from the sides like thick blood. He patted the hood.

"Are you coming?" Agent Rose demanded from the safety of her back porch.

A crude comment tickled the tip of his tongue, but he bit it back.

"MacKenzie!"

"Coming." The waterlogged grass squelched under his feet as he followed Agent Rose inside. "Clone," he muttered to himself. "Terrorist plant. Dangerous."

Hoss lifted his massive head as Mac stepped inside. By the time Mac had his muddy boots off, the dog was snoring. Apparently, Mac wasn't a threat worth waking up for.

"There's a grandmother suite through the mud-room," Agent Rose said. She left her dirty shoes on the back porch and dropped soaked socks in the washing machine. On the far side of the mudroom was a little green door with a lock. Rose pushed it open to reveal a small room complete with brass bed, a plastic-wrapped mattress that looked older than he was, and a beautiful wooden armoire.

"No closet. I tried to get the armoire out, but I think it was built in the room. I can't get it through the door, so you can use it." She sounded a little annoyed that she couldn't drag the thing upstairs to her picture-perfect room.

Mac smirked, imagining the tiny agent trying to move the armoire up the stairs. The thing probably outweighed her by a good thirty kilos.

"I'll bring down some sheets. There are some clothes Miss Azalea left in the mudroom. Some of them are men's clothes. I don't know if any of them will fit." She looked at him. "Well? Come in here. I can't get out with you blocking the doorway."

He considered mentioning he liked to sleep naked. If he went that route, he'd probably offer to let her sleep naked with him, then he'd screw her brains out, and . . .

Agent Rose moved around him and started lifting her shirt.

Mac froze, then pivoted away. "Did I say that out loud?" Where the hell did that come from? He hadn't thought about sex since he'd gotten back from Afghanistan.

"Say what out loud?" Rose demanded.

He peeked over his shoulder to see Rose dropping her outer shirt in the wash. A second, tighter shirt was still covering her body. "Nothing. Sorry. The fatigue is talking." Or the hormones. He needed to check his pill bottle. The antidepressants usually killed libido faster than a nun as a chaperone, but right now, he was feeling perfectly happy. And perfectly willing. Danger had never been such a turn-on.

Mac rubbed a hand over his face and realized Agent Rose was standing in the door, waiting for an answer to something. "Sorry. What?"

"I said you can shower first. There's a little bathroom through there." She pointed at an even smaller white door that looked like it led to a broom closet.

"Um. Sure, thanks."

"There's no bathtub, so don't thank me yet. I'll bring down the soap with the sheets." Agent Rose hesitated on the far side of the mudroom. "Can I leave the house unlocked tonight?"

"Why couldn't you?"

"You aren't going to do anything, are you?" Her eyes narrowed. "Stuff me in the freezer after slitting my throat? Attack my landlady?"

"That hadn't crossed my mind as an option," Mac said honestly. "Living is a top priority for me at the moment. I'll stay downstairs, making no noise and pretending I don't exist."

"That was a movie quote."

"I like the classics."

She was watching him with those perfect, soul-melting brown eyes. "Do you want anything?"

His libido wondered if she might need a one-night stand, but he kicked his hindbrain out of the discussion. "I'm good."

"I'll set the alarm for eight. It's hardly worth going to sleep, but a hot shower and a nap would be nice."

"Eight." Mac agreed. "Sounds good."

"Great." She left.

Mac dug through a pile of neatly folded clothes. There were two pairs of jeans and a couple of tees that looked like they would fit. He stripped off his shirt and pulled on a green tee as Agent Rose walked in. She frowned at him.

"What?"

"That's not a bad color on you."

"Thanks?"

She set a pile of white linens and a bar of soap on the drying rack. "Here. I'm turning on the upstairs shower in fifteen minutes."

Mac watched her walk away, reminding himself that her statement was not an invitation.

Eight came too early.

It always came too early, but usually Sam had a six-hour buffer of sleep to keep her from wanting to take someone by the throat and shove them through a meat grinder. Without that buffer, Marrins's caffeinated humor left her fists balled. She kept her mouth shut and kept away from the main rescue group. Hurricane Jessica hung around, lazily churning overhead, whipping the area with rain bands as the humidity level soared to something like 110 percent.

The heavy jeans Sam wore dragged in the foot of standing water left by the swollen river. She tipped forward carefully and reached underwater with her gloved hand, trying to guess what she'd hit. If she was lucky, it was another tire. If she was unlucky, it was another drowned street cat. Some of the cleanup crew made a game of it, awarding points and laughing at the most interesting finds.

Sam rubbed her cheek against her shoulder. Wishing everything was over wouldn't help. Pulling dead things out of the water, so they didn't fester and spread disease, would. She pulled the lump out, a ripped sandbag filled with trash from the gutters. She stuffed it in her bag and moved on.

"Agent Rose."

Saints and angels! Was there no escaping that man? Sam took a deep breath before twisting to look at MacKenzie. "Yes?"

"Are you ready to go back?" MacKenzie asked.

For someone running on three hours of sleep, he looked just fine to her. Better than the day she met him. Although not having the drugs in his system probably helped. "Go back?"

"The shifts are trading out. Marrins said he hadn't seen you come in yet, and I . . ." He'd been wading closer, but something stopped him an arm's length away. "Did you hurt yourself?"

"No." Sam shook her head. It hurt, but just from dehydration and the sweltering heat.

"Your eyes are all red."

She tried putting on a stern face. "Agent MacKenzie, I'm wading in a river of filth. The fumes are enough to make your eyes water. Yes, my eyes are red."

"Oh." He didn't look like he was buying what she was selling.

"It's the heat, and the smell, and the dead cats."

He grimaced. "Sorry. Marrins would give you a different detail if you asked. You could . . . could do something else."

"I could sort refugee and insurance claims, count heads, or wade in the river. The first person who complained about spending eight hours on a cold gym floor would lose their head. I'm not civil with less than six hours of sleep."

"Oh."

"Exactly."

"You should still break for lunch. Being in the water too long isn't healthy."

Sam rolled her eyes. "Thanks for that news flash." She shuffled to turn around and tried to follow a slightly different path back to dry ground. "Do we have a head count yet?"

"Not an official one, but no one is officially missing either."

"Any bodies in the apartments?" She hadn't worked

up the courage to go with that group. Some of firefighters and EMTs had volunteered, saving her the
heartache.

"No. Most of the tenants were in hotels the next
town over because of the remodel this week."

"Lucky timing."

Mac made a noncommittal sound.

"What'd I miss?"

"There was a strong gasoline smell. Like ah . . . ac-
celerants?"

"Arson?"

Mac nodded, and Sam laughed. "The owner would
burn the apartments down?"

He shrugged. "That's one theory."

"Unreal!"

"Jessica hit it first, though."

"Saves him the price of matches and a trip to jail.
Isn't that sweet of her."

Mac grimaced. "South of here, things aren't so good."

"So I heard." *As if things are great up here.*

"Apartments are filling up fast."

Sam tried to get a good look at his face. "Did you
get a place?"

He shook his head.

"I'll ask Miss Azalea if she'd give you a contract for
that back room."

"Really?" MacKenzie sounded surprised, and re-
lieved.

Sam shrugged his gratitude away. "It's the law, Mac.
'Any persons owning a domicile that can harbor more

than the current residency must, in times of emergency, give shelter to those in distress.' We're legally in a state of emergency. She can't refuse you."

"No one would notice if she didn't offer, though."

"I would."

"You . . ." He stared at her for an uncomfortably long time as if trying to decipher something from a long-dead language. "You don't mind having me there?"

"Living in the same area? Right now, I don't want to be in the same district, region, state, or country as any other living creature. I want to be on a deserted island, swinging in a hammock under the shade of a palm tree and drinking ice-cold water. I want to have complete and utter silence for a week straight. I'll settle for a shower, twelve hours of sleep, and never, ever seeing whatever lovers come over."

It took a minute before she realized he wasn't keeping up with her. "You stuck?" Sam asked, squinting to see Mac's expression with the sun at his back.

"I don't have a . . ." He choked on the word "lover."

"Fine. Whatever. If I go to breakfast and find someone other than you in the house, I'm calling the cops."

MacKenzie started slogging again. "You won't find anyone else."

"Good." She took a deep breath and regretted it immediately. The face mask kept the insects out of her nose but didn't filter out the smell of rot as they waded to shore.

MacKenzie climbed out first and held out a hand to help her out of the water.

She hesitated. "And the freezer thing. Neither of us goes in the freezer."

"There is no freezer."

"The hypothetical freezer that is going to arrive as soon as I purchase one. That freezer. No more dead bodies in the freezer. Agreed?"

"Agreed."

She took Mac's hand and let him haul her onto the muddy bank.

"Rose!" Marrins waved to her from his seat on the sidelines. He was sitting in a camp chair with a box of donuts on his lap. "Haven't seen you since we started. You decide to take time for a manicure?"

"Yeah, boss." Sam pulled off her gloves, rolling one into the other, and pulled her face mask down. "I got a facial while I was out, too. You should have come, they had a two-for-one deal."

Marrins scowled, looked her up and down, and grunted. "You're joking."

"Yes, sir. I was over that way." Sam pointed to the shallower end of the river. "I figured getting caught in the undertow would make people cranky."

"You never know," muttered Marrins into his donut.

"Think of the paperwork, sir." One of the Red Cross volunteers came over with a bottle of water and a bag for Sam's trash. She accepted the water gratefully and collapsed onto the soggy grass. "Holy Mary, can it get any hotter?"

"We're due for another lash of rain," Marrins said. "The weather people say the storm is still turning."

"How much longer do they think she'll stick around?"

"Another day, maybe two." Marrins shrugged as he picked up another donut.

MacKenzie sat beside Sam. Watching him eye the box of donuts was amusing until she realized how hungry she was. "What time is it?"

"Pushing five," Marrins said. He burped into his fisted hand.

"Is anyone serving lunch?"

"The Red Cross had hot dogs around eleven, but I think they're out."

Sam stared at the senior agent, waiting for him to get a clue. When it became obvious Marrins had no intention of offering to let her leave, she gave in. "Sir, can I be released to get lunch, and some sleep? I've been here since ten. A couple of more hours in this heat, and I'll be in the first-aid tent."

"Sure." Marrins waved her away. "Get some food, take a nap. Send me the files on the lab and Chimes case, will ya? I still need to get on that."

"Yes, sir."

MacKenzie stood when she did.

Marrins frowned at him. "You going back out already?"

"I was going to go home," MacKenzie said.

"What?" Marrins looked confused. "Harley could

use some help down in the morgue if you want to get out of the heat."

Sam saw Mac's eyes glaze over. "Sir?"

"What?"

"Agent MacKenzie needs to drive me home, sir. My car is stuck in the mud until a tow truck can come rescue me." It was only a little lie, and Marrins wasn't likely to check. "I gave him gas money to pick me up this morning and drive me home. He's been out here as long as I have."

The senior agent said something under his breath that Sam knew was crude, but he nodded. "Whatever. MacKenzie?"

"Sir?"

"Get in early tomorrow. Harley doesn't like doing all the work himself. If I don't have an agent down there, I'm never going to get results. We're getting overflow from the morgues down south, but we still have our own work to do."

"Understood, sir." MacKenzie gave her an inscrutable look and followed her up the hill to the cars. "You lied to him."

"You weren't going to stand up for yourself."

"I would have been fine."

"And I could have been Miss United if I were a foot taller and got some implants." She ran wrinkled fingers through sweat-tangled hair. "Give it a rest. Marrins is a mouth-breathing oxygen thief. Everyone knows it." When he unlocked the car, she opened the door and climbed into the broiling truck. The scent of old synthetic leather and MacKenzie's soap drowned out the smell of mud. It wasn't fresh like her car, but it was a miracle elixir after hours wading in the river. She tipped her head back with a sigh of relief as the engine turned over, and cool air filled the cab.

"Home?" Mac asked, as they pulled onto the highway.

"Home."

CHAPTER 15

You cannot cross to another reality with any
doubt. Do that, and you will die.

You cannot look into the eyes of your Possible Self
and pull the trigger if you harbor any desire to be
that person.

~ Private conversation with Agent 5 of
the Ministry of Defense I1–2070

Wednesday June 12, 2069
Alabama District 3
Commonwealth of North America

It would have been satisfying to drop twenty tons of
dead tree onto Marrins's desk. Electronic data files just
weren't as fun as antiques.

The senior agent raised an eyebrow and looked at
the data pad. "What's that?"

"The files from the Chimes case and the N-V Nova
Labs break-in. I sent you a copy Monday, but you told
me to hand over all my work. I annotated everything.
Most of it is cross-filed with Altin's report."

"Why isn't it all cross-filed?"

"Because I am off the case and suspected of murder until Harley finishes his autopsy and establishes a time of death."

Marrins looked a little lost.

"Mordicai Robbins? The security guard in my freezer?"

"Oh. That." Marrins waved a beefy hand. "You weren't a suspect for me. Can't see you shooting a man through the throat. It's a messy death, you need balls for that."

Closing her eyes, Sam let his ire wash over her.

"You could have at least done the paperwork."

"I'm locked out of the case files, sir. So I don't tamper with them," she added in case the idea couldn't penetrate his thick skull.

"You should have said something. I would have let you back in. I hate cross-filing data."

Sam hid her smile. "I'll take the case back if you don't want it, sir. I've got nothing better to do." There was still cleanup in the city, and the shelters needed volunteers, and in terms of charity toward her fellow-man, there was quite a lot of good to do. But in the current heat wave, she was certain that staying in the air-conditioned office was all that kept her from decking the next idiot who asked for the shirt off her back.

Firefighters and pickup lines.

She'd considered stopping at the local department store to look at costume jewelry. Maybe if she stuck a big enough rock on her left hand, everybody would back off.

Marrins gave her a patronizing smile. "There's plenty of work for a girl like you, Rose. Maybe not at the bureau, but there are plenty of places for a girl who knows how to keep her mouth shut. Now, get back to your office while it's still yours."

The door closed quietly behind her. Sam wanted to slam it shut, preferably on Marrins's fat head. Storming back to her office in a quiet fashion was out of the question, so she walked, letting the rage simmer.

Her phone rang, interrupting her pity party. "Agent Rose speaking."

"Rose, it's Altin, get me Marrins."

"Why don't you try calling Marrins's phone number?" Sam sniped.

"Marrins isn't answering." Altin made it sound as if it were all her fault.

"So leave a message!"

"I can't. Dr. Emir is having fits over here and demanding the bureau's attention."

Sam puckered her lips as she leaned against the wall. "You know that's not my problem."

"Get off your rear and walk it down to Marrins's office."

"He's just going to tell me to leave," she said.

"Hand him the phone."

"I'll get the door slammed in my face." Again.

"Then put on the speaker and slide the phone under the door! Tarnation, Sam! Get me Marrins.'"

"Fine!" Sam walked back to Marrins's office with a

little extra stomp in her step. "Sir? Detective Altin is on the phone. It's urgent."

Marrins scowled up at her from the game of cards he was playing on his phone. "What's he need?"

"Emir is throwing tantrums again."

"I don't want to deal with Emir right now. Tell him to shut his mouth and get back to work." With a flick of his finger, he moved a card and grunted in approval.

Sam relayed the information to Altin.

"He doesn't care?" Altin fumed. "It's his job to care. He gets paid to care."

"I don't think he cares about that either," Sam told Altin. Marrins glowered at her. "Sir, what do you want done?"

Marrins waved her away. "Handle it, Rose, it's not my problem."

"Rose," Altin growled over the phone. "If someone from the bureau isn't down here in twenty minutes—"

"I got it covered," Sam said. She scooped her purse from her desk. "I'll be there in fifteen."

"You shouldn't be on this case," Altin said. "You've already been threatened once."

"Your choices are me or Agent MacKenzie from the morgue."

Altin swore away from the phone. Sam couldn't hear everything, but there were a couple of creative insults about Marrins's parentage that she tucked away for future use.

"If it helps any, Agent Marrins is satisfied with my alibi. I was on a plane when Mr. Robbins was shot."

"Your alibi isn't near as troubling as the death threats."

"Threat, singular," Sam said. "It was a message for the bureau, not me in particular, and there have been no further incidents."

"Fine," Altin said at last. "Come here. Talk Emir off his pedestal, and I'll deal with the fallout."

"I can go to an early lunch instead," Sam offered as she climbed into her car. "That wouldn't bother me at all."

"You're enjoying this," Altin grumbled.

"Getting my case back? Why, yes, thank you ever so much, I am. I got run off because of your overprotective Good Guy instinct, and now I'm getting asked back in. Why shouldn't I be happy?"

"I still don't have an ME report on Robbins," Altin's voice held a note of warning.

"You will have it as soon as Harley finishes it. And we both know it's going to show I couldn't have possibly killed Robbins."

"Doesn't clear your boy MacKenzie."

"MacKenzie jumps at his own shadow. Can you honestly picture him shooting anyone? At all?"

Altin grumbled.

"We'll find the killer, but we're wasting time looking in the bureau for the murder weapon."

"We'll see." Altin didn't sound convinced. "Now, get over here before I take a swing at the doctor. That man makes my fists itch like I'm eighteen again."

She pulled out of the parking lot. "See you in fifteen."

THE DAY BEFORE 185

She didn't bother hanging up the handset, just dialed MacKenzie when she hit the first stop sign.

"Agent MacKenzie."

"Hi, Mac, it's Sam."

"Can I help you?" he sounded baffled—par for the course with MacKenzie.

"I need the autopsy results on Mordicai Robbins."

"By when?"

"Yesterday."

"I thought you were off the case. For that matter, I thought *I* was off the case. I know I don't always track these things well, but I'm pretty sure we aren't supposed to be involved." He sounded annoyed, which beat drugged any day of the week. Eventually, she'd tell him he was using breath mints as medical treatment, but that little factoid could wait until her transfer to anywhere else came through.

"Dr. Emir is demanding someone from the bureau speak with him. Marrins sent me," Sam told him. "So I guess that means I'm back on the case. And Altin is demanding the autopsy results ASAP."

"Really?" Mac sounded skeptical.

She turned onto the highway headed out of town. "Marrins told me to handle it. Those were his exact words."

There was a pointed silence.

"What?" she asked with all the innocence fourteen years of Catholic schooling had taught her.

"'Handle it' does not mean get involved in the case again," MacKenzie said.

"It's very nearly the same thing," Sam argued.

"No, it really isn't."

"Just finish the autopsy."

There was a low rumble of objection from Mac, then another sigh. "Anything in particular I'm looking for?"

"Time of death, motive, anything that can tell me who killed him. There's a murderer loose. Maybe we have a polite killer who left us a note tucked in Robbins's pocket."

"What about the Melody Doe autopsy?"

"What about it?"

"They tagged it last night. Harley had it down in his locker, but Robbins is in there, too. If I'm going body snatching, I might as well make the most of it."

She raised an eyebrow. "Would anyone notice?"

"All I need is twenty minutes per body to run the scan. If I can program the cold chambers to connect with my workstation instead of Harley's, I can run secondary scans later."

"How long would that take?"

"Maybe an hour for both."

"Oh." So much for that idea.

"Don't worry: Harley likes long lunches." She thought there was a hint of a smile in Mac's voice. "You want it done?"

Maybe she wouldn't mention the breath mints after all. It was nice to have a mentally able coconspirator. "Yes."

"Who gets the results?"

She hesitated. Marrins should get the results, but . . . *But indeed.* She bit her lip.

"Sam?"

"Altin and Marrins. Altin, me, and Marrins."

"Marrins?" The tone of Mackenzie's voice said he didn't agree.

"Marrins is in charge of the case."

"If you say so. I'll do the autopsy, and we'll go from there. MacKenzie out."

She knew his reservations, but she also knew that protocol said Marrins needed to know. What MacKenzie didn't seem to get was that any information that landed on Marrins's desk was lost in a black hole; he'd never read it. She pulled into the N-V Nova Labs parking lot just as Altin headed for his car. "Where are you going?" Sam asked as she locked her door.

"Domestic situation just went critical at one of the shelters," Altin said. "I've got to get down there. Emir is inside. Talk to him. Calm him down. For the love of all that is holy, do not promise him anything. The man is delusional. I'll see if I can get the department shrink down here next week." His radio screamed with static. "I've got to go."

Sam waved as he peeled out of the parking lot, hit his lights, and gunned the engine down the road. So much for the idea of backup.

"Thanks."

The atrium had been repaired. All the cracked windows and lights were once again in place. A small cleaning bot buffed the floors to a mirror finish. Three burly guards sat at the main desk. Another pair were split, one at each entrance. Sam showed the first guard her ID, then walked over to the desk to sign in.

"Hi." She flashed the guards a bright smile. "I'm Agent Rose with the CBI. Where is Dr. Emir?"

A flat-eyed guard with the name SMITH pinned to his chest picked up the in-house phone. "We'll page him. Go sit down."

She would have tried looking impressed, but it would have been faked. It didn't matter since Dr. Emir was racing out of the door toward her when she turned. "Agent Rose! Agent Rose! Yes. Yes, of course, the paladin rushing to the rescue. It makes perfect sense. You will help me." He grabbed her hand with sweaty palms.

The little man who looked like a skinny Santa was thinner than she remembered, disheveled, shaking. "Dr. Emir, are you hurt?"

"No. No. Not yet. I haven't been hurt yet." His eyes darted left and right, as if he expected someone to grab him at any moment. With a startled jump, he dragged her back to his lab. "Not safe. Not safe out there. Some-one might see me."

"That's what security guards are for." Sam tugged her hand, ineffectually trying to break free. "Don't you like the security guards, Dr. Emir? They keep you safe. Keep your work safe."

Dr. Emir let out a manic sound. After a minute, Sam realized he was laughing. "They don't protect me. They *watch* me. For him. This is my prison." He rubbed a gnarled brown hand along the door lintel. "This is my prison of my own making," he said sadly, almost as if he were speaking to himself. "I will die here."

Sam frowned in worry. "Dr. Emir, are you not feeling well? Were you threatened?"

"Threatened?" His head snapped up. For a moment, his eyes were distant and disoriented, then he shook himself back to the present. "Threatened, dear me, no. Why would you ask, Agent Rose?"

"You just said this was a prison, and you were going to die here." *And because I want to kill you, so I'm just assuming others do, too.*

"Oh." He gave a light laugh, and it sounded forced. The smile on his lips never touched his eyes. "A figure of speech. I was being metaphorical. I meant I devoted my life to this work. Everything I do must be done. I must go forward with it. I have gone forward with it." Mania gripped his expression again, then slipped away.

Sam waited cautiously by the door. If he lunged, she was running, high heels or no.

Dr. Emir gave her a tight smile. "Why are you here, Agent Rose?"

"You wanted to see someone from the bureau."

"Yes, but why *you*? Agent Marrins is handling this case. I am well aware of this fact. He has impressed that on me several times."

Really? When? "Agent Marrins was busy, so he sent me."

"To speak for him?"

Sam shrugged. "I suppose. We work for the same people."

"Oh." For some reason, that seemed to disappoint Emir. His shoulders drooped, and he looked at the floor. "Very well. I will explain. Marrins understands the importance of my work better than you, I expect."

"I'm sure," Sam murmured, keeping the sarcasm out of her voice.

Dr. Emir wrung his hands in worry. "It is critical, what I do. It will save lives. I don't agree with what your senior agent thinks. I don't think the machine can be made to bend the way he suggests. But it will save lives."

"That's the important thing." Stating platitudes sounded good right now.

Emir nodded. "That is the most important thing. But, here." He pointed at the strange black box he'd shown her on the previous visit. "You see what is wrong, obviously."

Sam raised her eyebrows. "Oh. Golly. You're right. Look at that." She looked over at Emir for a clue.

Strutting like a gamecock, the doctor pointed at a dial on his bulky machine. "You see this? You see? Right here?" A scowl etched itself on his face.

She inspected the little dial, green on a field of black. "Yes."

"What color is it?" Emir demanded, as if the color weren't blindingly obvious.

"Green."

"Yes!" he yelled.

"Is it not supposed to be green?"

"Ah." Emir rocked back on his heels, thumbs hooked through his red suspenders. "So good to meet a halfway-intelligent bureau agent. So very pleasing. So very rare. No. This dial is meant to be blue. I *made* it blue. My mother's favorite color. It was blue three days ago. Now, it is green." He laid the information out with solemn dignity.

Sam shook her head. "Is the dial important? Rare? Expensive? I don't understand why the color change matters, Doctor."

"Someone has touched my research!" he shrieked.

"Did you talk to the graduate students? Perhaps one of them knocked the dial loose and replaced it with a new one. Maybe they painted it. A practical joke, perhaps?"

Emir pursed his lips, fuming. "This is no joke. I have told the detective time and time again. I am being threatened. This is a subtle and diabolical reminder that I am being pursued. The dial should be blue!"

"Fine." Sam stepped away from the machine before whatever leaking radiation from the box that had permeated Dr. Emir's brain cells affected her. "Change the dial. It shouldn't be that hard."

"It's evidence!"

"Yes—of a green dial. To be anything more, I need records, proof the original dial was blue, video from security." She didn't really, but she hoped he'd think that to be too much and drop this ridiculousness. *Who cares about a stupid dial?*

Emir stared up at the video monitor as if he'd never seen it before. "Video, of course. I had not thought of that."

Sam nodded. "If security will release the video—"

"No, no," Emir said abruptly. He waved her request away. His face suddenly took on a paternal smile full of goodwill. "My mind, it's not what it was. The dreams become reality, the reality becomes dreams. I forget myself. So sorry to take your time. May I show you out? Buy you lunch? A T-shirt from the gift shop?"

"There isn't a gift shop, Dr. Emir."

"No? That must have been my dream then. Silly me. Perhaps we should build one, then I can buy you a T-shirt."

"That's too kind." Sam danced out of his reach before he could infect her with the crazy virus. "Is your intern around? I'd like to have a word with him if he's free."

"Henry?" Emir frowned. "Yes, he should be arriving at the lab shortly."

"Great, I'll just wait then. Have the security guards tell Henry I'm looking for him as soon as he checks in."

Sam waited in an empty conference room for Henry Troom to arrive. Her gut instinct said there was something wrong here. Not the color of the dial per se, but the whole feel of the lab. Something was ever so subtly wrong.

There was a knock on the door, and Henry walked in, hair mussed and tie askew. "Agent Rose? The security guard said you needed me for something urgent."

"Not urgent, just a few questions to clarify what's happening." She took a seat and smiled sweetly. "Dr. Emir called me in this morning because he was worried that something had been tampered with in his lab."

"I didn't do anything," Henry said. "I told him the balloons weren't my fault. Nate did that."

"Dr. Emir didn't mention balloons. He was concerned because the dial on his machine was a different color. You helped construct the machine, didn't you?"

"Oh." Henry pulled a chair out and sat down. "No, I didn't work on the original prototype. The one we have in the lab is a fourth working model that Dr. Emir has made."

"Do you know what color the dial on the machine is?"

"Green."

"Has it always been green?"

"Ever since I started working here. Green for go." Henry shrugged. "Why?"

"Dr. Emir insists the dial was blue three days ago."

Henry sighed and rubbed the bridge of his nose. "Was he talking really fast? Did he mention dreams or anything bizarre?"

"As a matter of fact, yes. He offered to buy me a T-shirt from a nonexistent gift shop."

"Are you taking notes on this?" Henry asked.

"Not yet, should I be?"

"It's just . . . I don't want to get Dr. Emir in trouble. Government grants are hard to get, and . . ." He frowned and looked away.

"You don't want my report to strip Dr. Emir of his grants or you of your education funding. I got it. Is Dr. Emir doing anything that would make him lose his grants?"

"No!" Henry squirmed in his seat, obviously uncomfortable with sharing his information.

Sam sighed. "I'm good at keeping secrets, Henry."

He rested his elbows on the table and leaned forward. "Have you ever been to Dr. Emir's house?"

"No."

"It's covered in surreal paintings."

"Like, Picasso? His big secret is he collects stolen art?"

"Nothing like that, he paints them. Huge canvases filled with the most otherworldly spaztastic stuff you've ever seen. Cities straight out of a bad B-movie. Science-fiction stuff I can't even explain. It's unreal. And it's all in the wrong colors."

"How do you mean *wrong*?"

He shrugged. "Green skies. Blue grass. Yellow buildings with silver lights. Dr. Emir is color-blind. He has to be."

"Okay." Sam tilted her head. "Why is this a deep, dark secret no one should share?"

"The color-blind thing isn't an issue. It's the manic rages that worry me. Dr. Emir is a genius, but he is truly one of the great tortured geniuses of our age. He'll go for days, sometimes weeks without sleep. I've seen him take a catnap at the lab, then run home and lock himself in there for three days because he had a dream and couldn't rest until he'd put it on canvas."

Sam connected the dots and relaxed. "So he called me during one of these manic phases?"

"We try to keep him calm and make sure he gets the downtime he needs, but with everything that's happened . . ." He held his hands up in a gesture of futility. "I'm sorry he bothered you."

"Don't apologize. This is my job. I just needed to know what help Dr. Emir needed."

"He needs some melatonin and a good night's rest without any of his weird dreams. He talks about them a lot, and they're very vivid. It's one of the signs of high intelligence, vivid, nearly lucid dreams. After everything's settled, you should come to one of our lab parties when he gets talking. It's mind-blowing some of the stuff he comes up with."

Sam chuckled. "I'll take your word for it." She stood up. "Thank you for talking with me, Mr. Troom. If you do see any anomalies in the lab, please call me. And please assure Dr. Emir that the bureau is doing everything it can to keep him safe."

Putting all the pieces in place painted a better picture of the lab. Dr. Emir was a distracted genius who couldn't tell reality from dreams. It happened. Some of the world's best inventions had come from similar minds. She walked to the car, trying to shake off the unsettled feeling. The shadows of the lab followed her home.

CHAPTER 16

When an iteration of reality collapses what happens? Some would imagine that the people populating the alternate timeline die. That theory defies the basic laws of the conservation of energy. Recall what I have said about the wave: everything must come back to the prime iteration when we hit the event horizon. During past decoherence events, everyone has experienced the dissonance of two realities colliding. A dying node briefly inherits the conscience of the dominant iteration, recalling things that are to come. The memories of our shadow selves become dreams and nothing more.

~ Student notes from the class
Physics and Space-Time I1–2071

Thursday June 13, 2069
Alabama District 3
Commonwealth of North America

Mac chewed his nails as his chair swiveled back and forth in front of the dim computer screen. Damn her for putting him in this situation. He looked plaintively at the ceiling. "God—if there is a God—I could use some help here. A sign. Something to tell me that helping her isn't the worst thing I could do."

No choir of angels or neon flashing sign manifested a divine will of any kind.

Sighing, he picked up the efile with the report on Jane Doe . . . aka, Samantha Lynn Rose the second. A clone working for the bureau was an even bigger security threat than a clone working for N-V Nova Labs.

Sam needed to be dealt with.

A rapid clone test would work if she were an age-advanced clone, but a good black-market-clone operation would have ways around that. Getting the lab in Atlanta to do a test for Verville traces meant getting a second signature. If Rose was a clone, getting her signature was the next best thing to committing suicide. If he went to Marrins, the test would never happen. The senior agent would accept the computer search and turn Sam over to bureau.

They'd would kill her.

He dropped the efile on his desk again and went back to chewing his nails. The bureau would euthanize Agent Rose after interrogating her with techniques that would make old Guantanamo look like a spa in comparison. She wasn't human, but she looked human. She sounded human.

The memory of her stripping off a wet shirt made him feel all too human. She was nice to him, but nice wasn't an excuse. He swore again.

There had to be another way.

"MacKenzie?" Harley leaned around the corner, a cloud of cheap cologne following him. "I'm going to lunch, you want anything?"

"No, thanks." Mac shook his head and avoided eye contact with the older man.

"Okay. I'm going to the grill. Be back in an hour or so, cover for me if someone calls. You know what traffic is like on that end of town."

"Yes, sir," Mac said, as the senior coroner shuffled off to the Bon Temps Grill . . . and golf course. The morgue doors slammed shut with a leaden thud. With one final curse for God, the universe, and everything else that had conspired to bring him to this point, he grabbed his dissection equipment and went to find Melody Doe.

There were two interns sitting in the small break room between his office and the bodies he wanted to inspect. He shoved his efile into his lab-coat pocket and faked a smile. "Hey, what are you guys doing?" Keeping to his normal pattern of behavior and ignoring them would have been safer, but Mac doubted they'd had enough experience with espionage to be concerned.

They still looked at him bug-eyed, as if they couldn't believe Mac could form full sentences. One said, "Eating lunch."

"Coroner Harley just left," he said in a casual, hinting tone that would have worked on any military recruit. The interns just stared. "We're getting another busload of bodies from the coast tonight. Since we're going to work after hours, why don't you boys go take a long lunch?"

That did it. Their eyes lit up at the promise of sunshine. "Can we?"

"Just be back before three. Harley keeps a one o'clock tee time on Thursdays."

"Right," one of the interns said. "But he'll be back once he realizes the course is flooded."

"There's a TV and alcohol. He'll be gone for at least two hours."

The interns looked at each other and shrugged. "This is real chill of you." The younger man patted Mac on the back as he hustled out.

Mac leaned his head against the cold walls of the morgue as the interns ran off. He was going to get court-martialed for this. Lose his citizenship. All for a pretty pair of brown eyes.

And amazing legs. Truly stellar stems. Can't forget those.

"I'm hopeless," he muttered, walking into the cold room. The smell of chilled antiseptic wash hid the odor of delayed decay as he rolled out the remains of Mordicai Robbins and plugged his data pad into the scanner to download. Then he went searching for Melody Doe and found her in the walk-in freezer with a dozen bodies that had washed out of their graves during the storm.

Melody had been pretty in life, he knew that from the pictures, but looking at her now . . . He shivered and reached for a pill bottle that wasn't there. His hand clenched into a fist.

He should have just handed Marrins the evidence. Called it a day. Gone home, or gone house hunting. Anything but this. Memories of the desert, heat, and blood blurred into reality as he looked at Melody Doe's fractured skull. With shaking hands, he wheeled her gurney into the scanner box, hit the right buttons, and hurried down the hall to dry heave in the comfort of his office.

Eyes watering, throat burning, he frantically pushed aside piles of junk to find his pills. There had to be one somewhere.

The morgue door slammed. A belch echoed through the halls. Harley couldn't be back already, could he? Maybe the golf course was flooded.

Pushing unsteadily to his feet, Mac dropped the search for pills and stumbled toward the cold room. He'd have to make do with incomplete scans or call the whole thing off.

Harley's footsteps echoed behind him.

Mac sped up, barreling into the cold room with a controlled skid.

Mordicai Robbins was unhooked and halfway to his storage spot when the heavy doors swung open. Warm air from the hall swept into the room, with the scent of Harley's cheap cologne.

Mac slammed Mordicai into place and wrenched open the walk-in freezer. Grabbing hold of the nearest gurney, he pushed it in front of him as if he were merely checking the graveyard rejects and not digging into a case that wasn't his.

Harley stood by the door, arms crossed. "Whatcha doing?"

"Ah, just making sure we send the right bodies back. I thought you, um, wanted them checked?" His tongue deserted him as memories of Afghanistan assailed him. There was blood. So. Much. Blood.

Harley eyed Mordicai's locker for a moment, then grunted. "Right. You get lunch yet?"

"Um, n-not yet." He slid the gurney he'd grabbed into the scanner next to Melody Doe and took the efile from its dock. Scan complete. "I, um, sent the interns to lunch just now," he added. Mac hesitated in front of Melody's body, unsure if he should pull her out of the machine for the coroner to see.

"You okay?" Harley asked.

Mac jerked his head in a nod. "It's just, I'm waiting on my refill. All these bodies . . ." Weren't bothering him nearly as much as they had a month ago.

A heavy hand landed on his shoulder. With a painful squeeze, the coroner shook him. "Lemme handle it. You go sit in your office. I can clean this up."

His hand slipped to the efile; he had what he needed. "Sure. Sure. Thanks."

"Not a problem."

Retreating to his office, Mac turned off the light and rested his head on a pile of old forms. Sunlight streamed in through the ground-level window. He could see the parking lot, Agent Rose's office window . . . and Agent Rose, stepping out of her car, wearing a perfect navy skirt on her perfect tan body. For a moment, his ghosts fell silent. There had to be a mistake.

There was no point to planting a clone in the bureau unless they were primed to do something, to feed information to someone. But there was nothing in District 3 anyone could possibly want.

Except for the lab. And a CBI senior agent who would rather write Jane Does off as clones than open murder investigations. No wonder Sam wound up as a target. Young and eager to please, she was just the kind of person they didn't want. Whoever *they* were.

And with a cushy promotion, the clone-Sam could do even more. Muddle more investigations. Destroy evidence when a politician was replaced. A whole conspiracy to destroy the country was blooming in front of him, and he didn't want to stop it because the little soldier had finally woken up from a five-year nap.

"MacKenzie?" The office door opened with a squeal of protest. Harley squatted beside his chair. "You doing all right, son? I saw that girl—she was in a powerful bad way. Not a pretty sight. Why don't you take off early?"

Mac sat up. "I'd like that."

"I'm sure you would." Harley picked up a pill bottle from Mac's desk. It rattled with toxic relief. "Take a couple of these on the way out. You'll sleep better."

He took the bottle gratefully and dumped a pill in his hand even as Harley walked away. The bitter aftertaste made him gag. The taste was off, and he idly wondered what the expiration date was on these meds. Rolling the second pill between thumb and forefinger like a worry bead, he pulled up Agent Rose's file again, his mind wandering down the tunnel of depression. Too many people had died because of his mistakes already. He couldn't let Sam be a victim. But she was dead already. He spun in his chair.

Agent Rose was dead . . . maybe. The woman he knew as Sam was a clone . . . maybe. The answers were there dancing just outside his reach. If he could shake the fog. Ghosts of dead men stared at him from the darkness of his own mind. Fallen friends waiting for him to make that last, fatal mistake. And he was running out of time.

Mac shook his head. He had to buy time. Had to get sober.

Had to . . .

Had to . . .

He frowned in confusion at the pills. Had to get off the pills. Five years of living with his head in a fog so he could forget one cold morning in February of '64. Five years of twelve pills a day. Five years of barely remembering his own name, forgetting to eat, losing everything. He bit his lip, tasted blood.

He couldn't think like this. Couldn't think with his head in the fog. Couldn't remember what he was supposed to do. Trembling, he walked out of the morgue, dumping the pills onto the lawn.

Agent Rose looked across the parking lot at him.

Mac swore under his breath. Wiping a cold hand across his mouth, he flicked the pill bottle into the grass. Her eyes followed the fall of the bottle.

If looks could kill. "Agent Rose, hi." Mac tried for cheerful and wound up sounding desperate.

"I was looking for you." She crossed her arms and glared at him. "MacKenzie?"

Mac shook his head. "Sorry. I'm . . . I'm not feeling well."

She glowered at the pills in the grass. "Where did you find those?"

"Harley had some extras."

"I see." Agent Perfect was not happy.

He was shaking. Mac rubbed a hand over the back of his neck. "I had one. Just the one. And I feel . . . I feel nauseous." Exceptionally nauseous, he realized. Burning-in-the-heat-ready-to-pass-out nauseated.

"You look it," she said, sounding disgusted. *So judgmental . . . but who is she to judge? At least he was real.*

Then again, what's "real . . ."

"Why don't you let me drive?"

Mac nodded. The world was spinning around him, but he could focus. And focusing on Agent Rose was no hardship. He giggled.

"What?" She pulled him up and helped him steer his unruly feet toward her car.

"The world revolves around you." He laughed and fell into the backseat.

"Does it now?" She tilted her sunglasses down so he could see her eyes.

He sighed. "God, you're beautiful."

"Save your prayers for later, Mac. Where'd you get those pills?"

"From . . . from my office." He frowned. "Harley helped me find them. I left . . . left the bottle there, because of the prescription number."

"Just the bottle?"

Mac battled his memory. He remembered the empty bottle, he'd left it on the edge of his desk so he could call in the refill. "It was empty. But it's not."

Agent Rose patted his knee. "Stay right here." She walked off and came back with the bottle, a couple of pills, and grass clippings on her knee. "Pull your legs in."

He groaned when the car started. Agent Rose's hand came into view with two small orange pills, just like the ones he'd been taking over the weekend. He gulped the fruit-flavored medicine down. "Feel worse," he groaned. "Mixed . . . shouldn't mix."

"I know. Just don't die on me before we get to the house. I think you're in for a bad night."

Mac heartily agreed.

Sam barely managed to get MacKenzie into his room. He was feverish to the touch and shaking, but still somewhat responsive. Time for phone calls.

"Altin here."

"Altin, it's Rose. I have some pills of suspicious origin, and I need to get them tested."

"Is this a bureau thing?"

"I don't know. I asked MacKenzie to do some autopsies for me. At lunchtime, he was fine, this afternoon he's—" She heard MacKenzie throwing up in his bathroom. "It looks like the flu—fever and vomiting— but I don't know a virus that hits this fast. He found some pills in his office, thought they were his, and took them."

"What sort of pills does Agent MacKenzie do?" Altin's asked with polite menace.

"*Do,*" she thought. *Not "take." That seems about right.*

"He's currently addicted to Orange Sun breath mints."

"Say that again?"

She smiled in spite of herself. "It's a long story. Anyway, he takes five to six breath mints a day from a regular medicine bottle. It's all placebo. I knew there would be some withdrawal symptoms, but that's not what this is. Mac said he remembered emptying this bottle. Then Harley handed him a bottle. And now he's delirious."

"Where are you?"

"My house. MacKenzie's apartment was caught in the flood, so he's renting the back room."

"I didn't see a back room."

"No one sees the back room. It's on the other side of the mudroom, and everyone thinks it's a closet."

"Give me thirty minutes. If he gets worse, head for the emergency room."

"I will." Sam set the bottle on the kitchen counter and went to check on Mac. He lay on the floor outside the bathroom, curled in a fetal position. "Any blood?"

There was a faint whisper, "No."

She sat on the floor beside him. Training had never

covered this situation. *"Do you get poisoned often?"* sounded like a pickup line from a cheesy goth sitcom. *"How do you feel?"* was too trite. He shivered, and she rubbed his back gently, trying to think of something to distract him from the agony. "Did you get the autopsies done?" *Brilliant, Samantha, absolutely brilliant. You are never going to win a Partner of the Year award.*

"Yes. Harley . . . Harley came." Mac coughed and groaned. "Told him I was working on the graveyard bodies."

"Did he believe you?"

"I don't . . ." He unrolled and rushed to the bathroom again. Sam went to fetch a towel and a fresh bar of soap. MacKenzie gave her a weak smile when he came back. "Thanks."

"Go shower. I have Altin coming over with one of his lab monkeys. We'll see what he says about the pills."

Sam was waiting at the door when Altin's patrol car pulled up with a younger man in the passenger seat. "Sorry about the after-hours call," she said, holding the screen door open. "I locked Hoss upstairs. Mac is in the back room."

Altin nodded, not looking convinced. "This is Vik Zhoundroff, one of our EMT boys."

Sam couldn't tell if Vik was eighteen or thirty-eight; he had blond hair, blue eyes, and the high cheekbones she'd learned to associate with Slavic ancestry. He would probably look like a teenager until he was ninety. "Nice to meet you, Vik." She held out a hand.

"Agent Sam Rose, CBI." She nodded to the kitchen. "I'll show you the pills. He's still alertish, so I didn't want to make a hospital run."

"'Ish'?" Altin asked.

"He's talking, but I think he's hallucinating. But then again, it's Mac. So I can't tell."

Vik picked up the orange prescription bottle from the table. "What's he taking pills for?"

"If I had to guess, PTSD," Sam said, crossing her arms. It wasn't her story to tell, but Altin was scowling, so she went on. "He was USA army, before they joined the Commonwealth. From what Mac says, he saw some rough stuff overseas."

Altin raised an eyebrow. "Army?"

"Yeah."

"I never would have picked that out. He's so quiet."

Sam shrugged. "Well, he *has* been on heavy antidepressants for about five years."

Vik fished out one of the pills. "This is fluphenazine. One of the older antipsychotics. We use them at the hospital as a bridge drug when we have to change medications. It's not something you can take long-term." He dropped the pill back in the bottle. "I actually don't think they prescribe these anymore."

"So how'd it wind up in Mac's office?" asked Sam.

"Never mind *how*—*why* is a better question." Altin looked at Vik.

The EMT shook his head. "A fatal dose is over twenty milligrams. The pills are ten each."

"He said he took one, but he usually takes two pills

in a pop." Sam said. "I saw him dumping pills in the grass and went over to ask what was going on. He was having trouble walking and looked feverish."

"You can give him a small dose of antihistamine," Vik said, "but only if he starts scratching at his skin. Otherwise, it should wear off in a day or so."

"Does he still have the other drugs in his system?" Altin asked Sam.

"I don't know. They were antidepressants—how long do those stay after you stop taking the drugs?"

"Days to weeks, depending," Vik said. "The drugs could interact. Maybe. I wouldn't suggest mixing them." Sam looked at him, and he must have noticed the I-could-have-came-up-with-that look she was giving him. He shrugged. "That's the best I can do, considering the lack of info."

"Can we take these?" Altin shook the bottle.

"Be my guest," Sam said.

The detective put the pills in his pocket, but then frowned. "Are you reporting this?"

"I'm doing that right now."

"But he's bureau, so I'm not the one to report to.

Sam shook her head. "Mac works for the coroner's office more than the bureau, so it *does* fall under your jurisdiction. I believe him that the bottle was empty. Someone planted the fluphena-whatever in his office. I don't see how this could be a mistake."

Altin nodded. "What was MacKenzie working on?"

"This morning I asked him to do those autopsies you asked about. I'm not sure what else Harley had him doing, probably grunt work, identifying bodies found after the hurricane."

"The cases this morning could stir up trouble," Altin said, picking his words with care.

"Trouble enough to kill an ME over? There are a lot of things I'll believe, Altin, but telepathic serial killers isn't one of them. There's no way anyone outside the coroner's office knew which case Mac was working on today."

Altin gave her a pointed look.

Sam shook her head. "No. There's no one like that in the bureau."

"Like what?" Vik asked in confusion.

She pressed her lips together, uncertain of how much of Sunday's conversation about MacKenzie she wanted the EMT to know about.

Altin waved her off. "I know what you think, Rose. But every day this looks more and more like an inside job. Dead bodies do not dump themselves. And strange pills don't appear in bottles without help."

In Mac's room, the shower turned on. At least he was still alive. Sam turned to the detective. "If you think this is an inside job, you better start watching your back, Altin. I'm not the only one on this case."

"That a threat, Rose?"

"You know it's not. Out of everyone, I'm the only one with an alibi for today. But if you think someone at the bureau is doing this, take a good look in the mirror. You're the lead on this case. If anyone should be worried, it'd be you and Marrins. I'm small potatoes."

Altin nodded. "I'm going to talk to Marrins in the morning, just in case. I've known him for years, and his heart's not that good—he's pretty discreet about it, but he takes pills all the time, too." This was news to Sam—Marrins definitely didn't eat like he had a heart condition. "You and MacKenzie can handle these sudden shocks," Altin continued, "but if this same joker dropped these pills in Marrins's desk we'd have a dead senior agent in this district."

Sam nodded with grim understanding. "Tell him to turn on his home security, too. He lives alone. Whoever murdered Robbins will see Marrins as an easy target." She walked them out, then double-checked the lock on her new back door. Somehow, she didn't think she'd sleep easy.

CHAPTER 17

We are each the sum of our choices.

~ Excerpt from *The Oneness of Being*
by Oaza Moun Il–2070

Friday June 14, 2069
Alabama District 3
Commonwealth of North America

Shadow and light fell on the still form of Agent Rose standing in the doorway, hands on her hips. An amused smile made sensuous lips curve in invitation. "Most of my dreams start like this," Mac said. The previous night was a blur. If the taste in his mouth was any indication, he'd spent half the night riotously drunk, and the other half violently ill. The way Rose smiled at him, maybe they'd both been happily drunk, and he'd only been disgracefully ill.

"You start most your dreams alive and healthy?" she asked.

"Something like that." He rubbed his face against the pillow as memories from the day before teased his brain.

"Get up." She tossed something on the foot of his bed. "Get dressed."

He hitched the blanket up over his shoulders. "I'm good, thanks." She smiled, and for a moment the world was right. In the back of his mind, he knew it was only in his private fantasy. Even if Agent Rose wasn't a murderous clone bent on killing him, she wasn't interested. He knew the symptoms. He was falling in lust at a terminal velocity, and she was giving him a look reserved for the last puppy in the shelter.

"Up, Mac. We're going running."

"Beg your pardon?" He rolled on his back and lifted his head. She wasn't laughing. She was smiling, and it wasn't a nice smile. "Running?"

"Yes."

"I hate running!"

"The EMT who came by last night said that a light workout this morning would help you feel better."

"The EMT lied. Running will make me feel miserable."

Her predatory smile widened. "Exercise is good for depression."

"I'm not depressed, I have flashbacks. The two are not the same."

"You'll have fewer bad memories if you make some good memories."

Then get naked. Mac stared at the ceiling. The commentary came from a part of his brain that insisted Agent Rose was everything he wanted. The rest of him was a little more interested in self-preservation.

He lifted his head again, watching her. "Why are you doing this to me?"

"For your own good." She probably meant it too. Everything about her said PROTECTOR in all-capital letters. Agent Rose was a crusader, a guardian. It didn't matter what she thought about him, she was going to keep him safe. Which killed his murderous-clone theory and blew away his defenses.

"It's not worth it."

"What's not worth what?"

"Saving me. I'm not worth it."

"What?" She frowned in confusion.

"I'm not worth anything." The ceiling fan turned, creaking in the vacuum of his statement. Angry footsteps signaled Agent Rose's approach. He pulled the blanket higher.

She leaned over him, dark eyes narrowed. "Ten minutes, Agent MacKenzie. And then we are running until you puke."

He closed his eyes. "That shouldn't take all that long."

She left, slamming the door behind her.

Mac rolled on his side, shutting his eyes tight. He wasn't running. He did not want to run. She could not make him run. He had to be at least a foot taller than her. Thin as he was, he still had to outweigh her by a hundred pounds or more. She couldn't physically force him to run.

Five minutes later, she poked her head into the room again while wearing tiny black running shorts and a running bra that did nothing to flatten her chest. "Let's go, Mac."

"Yes, ma'am." He sat straight up.

Her head reappeared. "Did you just 'Yes, ma'am' me?"

"Yes, ma'am." He rolled into a sitting position and stripped his shirt off with a weak grin. He was sick, not dead, and he'd have to be dead to ignore a body like that flouncing in front of him.

Agent Rose's eyes narrowed. "I'm going to make you pay for that."

"You can't kill me," he pointed out. "They'd miss me at work."

"Not until tomorrow."

He dressed quickly and chased after Rose. "What do you mean not until tomorrow?"

"You have today off, and tomorrow you don't go back until you've had a physical."

"I get a sick day for a hangover?"

Rose tied her hair back in a ponytail. "You think you're hungover?"

"It sure feels like a hangover. My head aches, my stomach is in knots, my tongue tastes like I spent an hour licking the alley behind the bar."

"Ewww! I don't even want to know how you could possibly know what that tastes like." Her nose scrunched in the cute way only pretty girls could manage.

"What happened to me?"

"Medicine mix-up. You weren't looking so good, but the EMT Altin brought over said you'd survive."

He tied his shoes and tried to piece together facts with the flashes of memory from the night before. "Why did Altin come over?"

"Because I asked him to."

"Why not just take me to the ER?"

She whistled for her dog and put a harness on him. "Because the nearest after-hours clinic is an hour away, and Altin isn't. I wasn't sure what an hour's drive would do. And if you needed to go to the hospital, you were going in a patrol car, not mine."

"Gee. Thanks."

She handed the leash to him. "Ready to go?"

"Um . . ."

Rose opened the door. Warm morning air swirled around his feet. "Let's go running. Come on, Hoss!"

Before he could get a handle on what was happening, Agent Rose was sprinting down the gravel drive, and Hoss the monster dog was dragging him behind. They jogged half a mile before Rose stopped for stretching and push-ups. Standing on one foot as she pulled the other back, she smiled at him like a maniac. "Race you to the lake, MacKenzie?"

He shook his head. It was already over seventy outside, steamy warm and smelling of magnolia blooms. "Let's go take a shower."

"If you're hot, you can jump in the lake."

"No . . ."

She leaned over to look him in the eye while he stretched. "Come on, MacKenzie, you're not going to let a girl beat you?" And then she was running again. "Are you?" she shouted over her shoulder.

Hoss barked once before trying to run after her. They went another mile before Mac let go of the leash so he could stop and empty his stomach again.

Rose caught the dog and kept running. He trudged back to the house in defeat. He was out of the shower and staring at the cupboards trying to find food when she came home, glowing like the Greek Goddess of Running.

She beamed at him. "Good job this morning! You made almost two miles. I thought you'd be dead by one."

The tension in his shoulders eased. "Really?"

"In this heat? The first time I tried running in an Alabama, I made it less than a mile. Give it a month or two, and you'll be able to race me to the lake." She grabbed an apple from the counter. "Not beat me, but race me."

He smiled. "Maybe."

She winked. "There's the positive mental attitude you need. Call in sick and enjoy your day off."

Mac called the office as soon as Rose left for the day.

"Coroner Harley, it's MacKenzie."

"How you feeling?"

"Terrible," he said honestly. "Those pills you found weren't my regular meds."

"So I heard," the older man said. "Agent Rose was kind enough to call in and let us know what happened. The interns have been playing pranks all month, but this one went too far. I don't think they meant anything by it, but I don't find this kind of thing funny."

"Neither do I," Mac said as he collapsed onto his worn green couch. It was still damp, but it smelled cleaner than before.

"I'm writing them both up. I'd have 'em both in county lockup if I could. But Daddy's got money and threatened to lawyer up unless I could provide evidence they'd done it."

"And the security cameras still aren't working?" Mac guessed.

"You know it. Good news though, I had them clean your office," Harley said. "I realized you didn't get a new computer when we upgraded the rest of the labs."

"Don't worry about it, the one I have runs fine."

"No, no," insisted Harley. "You need an upgrade. Since you were out today, I'm having the tech people set up your new computer."

Mac groaned quietly. "You don't need to, sir."

"No trouble at all."

Except for all the files he was losing. "Did you have them make a backup file?"

"We're using the one from Friday, just like always."

"What about the work I did yesterday?"

"I have the autopsy for the bridge case."

Mac bit his lip—he couldn't remember if he'd saved

any of the autopsy data Rose had wanted or not. "That's good. Do you know what the interns gave me?"

"Both of them are denying everything, but I think someone said it was a dose of fluphenazine hydrochloride. Nasty stuff."

"An emetic?"

"No, an antipsychotic. Overdoses usually end in cardiac arrest. Saw it once when I was in college. The nurse overdosed a patient by accident, didn't realize he'd been given his evening meds already. It makes people drowsy sometimes. If we'd released him on schedule, he would have wrecked his car, and we'd never have known. As it was, he fell asleep and had a heart attack. If we hadn't been testing his blood levels for something else, we never would have caught it. Honest mix-up, but deadly."

"Remind me to thank the interns when I get back." His stomach flipped with delayed fear.

"Now, now, Agent, play nice. They're just kids. They don't know what this stuff can do."

"I'm surprised they found the pills at all."

"The city gave me a full kit of medicine when I went out with the rescue workers. I'm guessing they grabbed the pills out of it when I wasn't looking."

Mac wondered if that was a subtle dig at him for looking at the bodies Thursday. The interns weren't the only ones sneaking around without Harley's permission.

"Take it easy," the coroner advised. "By the time you get back, I'll have everything under control."

Mac swore as he hung up the phone. The last few hours in the lab were a blur. He remembered reaching for a pill out of habit, but they weren't there. A breeze bent the oak tree outside as he searched for a recollection of what had happened next. There had been the empty pill bottle, then Harley coming in, and he'd stammered through a lame excuse so he could run off with the data pad. Then Harley had given him some pills. Big, fat, bitter pills—a drug the old coroner seemed all too familiar with.

It was the perfect setup for murder. Harley slipped him the pills, Rose took him home and quietly let him die. Except she hadn't . . . so whose game was she playing? He needed his lab and to find out if the files linking Jane Doe to Agent Rose had vanished without a trace, along with the autopsies of Melody Doe and Mordicai Robbins. That would at least let him make an educated guess about who was doing what.

Mac reached for his shoes. Screw sick days. He could sleep in when he was dead. *I expect that could be any day now. . .*

CHAPTER 18

Our very existence is threatened by these dissidents. They would have you believe we are at war. We are not the warmongers, we are the guardians. We are the ones defending our world from the annihilation of free agency.

~ Press brief from Colonel Aina's I1-2073

Wednesday June 19, 2069
Alabama District 3
Commonwealth of North America

Sam pushed away from her desk, rubbing her neck and wishing for an insane gunman to drop through the ceiling and take her hostage. Anything to distract her from checking insurance claims against the district records. There was a tap on the wall.

She jerked her head up. "Agent MacKenzie? Are you all right? You look . . . deflated." There were corpses in the morgue who looked better. His pale skin was flaccid, but his eyes weren't bloodshot. *Mother Mary have mercy,* she thought, *he looked bad high.*

Who knew sober could be worse?

"Where have you been? Did you go to the hospital?" His truck was missing when she returned from work on Thursday, and Marrins had kept her buried with busywork for the past week. Hunting down her erstwhile roommate hadn't been a priority. "You should have called if they were going to admit you."

"Can . . . Can we talk?" he asked in a hushed voice. His hands trembled.

"What about?"

"The . . . Jane. Jane Doe."

Sam nodded. "Sure. I'm going to lunch. We can talk there. Let me close my files up real quick."

Marrins's door opened, and Charlie the Plastic Skull bounced off the wall in front of a startled MacKenzie. "Give that to the coroner on your way down!" Marrins shouted.

Rolling her eyes, she closed the computer down. "A real winning personality," she told MacKenzie, faking a smile. "He's been throwing it at people all week. If you accidentally lost it in the Dumpster on the way to Harley, I'd consider it a national service."

MacKenzie didn't crack a smile.

She dropped Charlie on the secretary's desk as they walked past. "This is for the coroner, courtesy of Agent Marrins." She ignored the dirty look Theresa gave her and kept walking. "Mac, seriously, are you all right? You look like you haven't slept in a week."

He shook his head. "I haven't."

"Were you at the hospital?"

"No. Office."

She gave him a stern look. Whatever the reasons, he looked ready to collapse. "How about we walk over to the café?" He nodded and plodded after her, a reluctant puppy on a leash. "Talk, MacKenzie. What were you working on?"

"The autopsies. Mordicai Robbins and the . . . the Jane Does."

They stepped out into the swamp of June in Alabama. "Weather control, is that too much to ask for?" she muttered. "Lower the humidity here about 20 percent, that's all I'm asking." Her suit jacket, so perfect for staying warm in the air-conditioned office, was suddenly three times too thick for comfort. She took it off, catching MacKenzie's stare as she did. "What?"

He shook his head, turning to look at the hibiscus blooming along the sidewalk. "Sorry."

"Focus. Tell me about the autopsies."

"Harley took my computer Thursday morning." Mac sounded angry. "All the work I'd done on Melody Doe and Mordicai Robbins was erased. Both bodies were cremated."

She whistled softly. "That was fast."

"Too fast, but I had a backup copy on my data pad. I'm not sure if Harley knew that or not when he ordered the hard drive wiped."

Sam took a deep breath. At least the outside smelled better than her overchilled office. "I don't think he would have erased the data if he didn't—it's too valuable to lose." When Mac didn't respond, she switched topics. "Did you hear about the arrest yesterday? Altin wasn't happy, I heard all about it because Marrins was dodging his calls again. Someone said they saw the guy's car out by the labs the night of the break-in. It's not much to go on, but I guess it's a start."

"They let the kid go an hour ago." Mac sighed and sat.

Sam waved to a waitress as she took her usual seat on the patio outside the Peach Blossom Café. The self-serve screen popped up in the center of the table, and Sam entered her order from memory. "How'd you find that out?

"Harley told me. We got into a fight. I told him the evidence didn't back up the arrest. The kid's nineteen, works a night shift at the cinema, and was at work when the lab was broken into. Same alibi for the time of death. The only reason they took him in was that Officer Holt has tried to arrest him twice for breaking the noise ordinance in her neighborhood—he likes to turn the radio up when he drives home—but the charges never stuck."

Sam rolled her eyes. "Sometimes I think Altin is the only competent person on the force." A flower petal drifted across the menu screen, and she flicked it away. "I hate to ask, but do I have an alibi?"

Mac nodded. "About the time someone shot Mordicai Robbins's throat out, Detective Altin was at your house getting a signature to exhume Melody Doe."

"That's nice." She relaxed a little. "Do you know what you want?" MacKenzie shook his head, so she doubled the order: two thick turkey sandwiches with fruit salads on the side. Mac sat with his hands clasped, leaning on his knees and avoiding her gaze. Sam leaned back. "So. I guess you didn't want to see me about the Melody Doe case. What did you want to talk about?"

He looked across the street at the small grove of trees that were optimistically dubbed the city park. "This is a mess."

"The city? The case? The state of the nation? I need more to go on if we're going to have a conversation." A waitress brought out two glasses of pink lemonade. Sam sipped hers, and waited for Mac to come around to the conversation.

Mac sighed. "Melody Doe is an exact DNA match for Melody Chimes. No clone marker. Everything matches the latest DNA record of Melody Chimes."

"Which was when?"

"Wannervan Security did a full DNA scan when she signed on in October of last year."

"But in October 2068, Melody Doe was decomposing in peace in a mass grave."

"That's the first problem."

"What's the second?"

Mac kicked a chair at their table, glaring at the park like he held a personal grudge against trees and ground his teeth.

"Mac?" Sam prompted, trying not to sound amused.

"I pulled up Jane Doe's files while I was running some scans on Melody Doe."

"So?"

"The trauma patterns to the bones match."

Sam set her cup down with exaggerated care. "What are you suggesting?"

"Both women were killed by the same thing. I think Jane was hit harder, but I don't know what hit her." He pulled out an efile on his small computer. "This . . ." Mac shook his head, obviously arguing something with himself. "This is Jane." The suicide from May popped up on the screen.

The waitress stepped out with their lunches. "Thank you, Autumn," Sam said, reading the girl's name tag. She took a bite of her sandwich, swallowed, and nodded at the screen. "Let's see Melody." Mac hit a few buttons, and Melody Doe appeared, the fracture pattern on the skull was highlighted. "Okay, I see what you're saying, but it still doesn't work."

He frowned at her.

"All this says is that both women were hit in a similar way. That's not enough of a connection. Melody wasn't—" She caught the word "tortured." This was a public place, after all. "Melody wasn't treated the same way as Jane. They weren't the same age. They don't show the same abuse. You need more of a connection if you want to tie them together. The same weapon doesn't make this a serial-killer case."

MacKenzie held his sandwich with reverence, venerating but not eating. "What about both being dead women with identical genetic matches to living people? No clone markers."

Sam raised her eyebrows. "That could do it. You found a name for Jane?"

He nodded. "Eighty percent accuracy. There are a few differences, but there's also a five-year age gap between the two."

"That takes care of the other 20 percent." She took another bite. "Okay. Give me the name."

MacKenzie put his sandwich down and tapped at the screen. Another window opened next to the body, a file.

Sam turned the screen to read . . . Her name. Her file.

All the little things she'd noticed the first day and dismissed as quirks of genetic drift were there. Physical similarities listed next to those of Jane Doe's with little blue tick marks.

Check.

Check.

Check.

Sam smoothed her hands over her skirt. "Why . . . why don't we walk? Grab your sandwich." She dumped MacKenzie's lunch into his hands, grabbed her own sandwich, and dropped their plates off at the cleaning station tucked behind an oleander bush. She didn't wait for him but knew he was following. "This way." Her high heels clicked on the hot sidewalk as they crossed the empty street to the small park surrounding city hall in the center. MacKenzie was right behind her, juggling food and computers.

She took a deep breath. "If this is a joke, MacKenzie, it's not funny. Not at all."

MacKenzie set his computer on a stone bench. "It's

not a joke." His breath was ragged. "I . . . I . . . stopped. Everything. No pills. No nothing. I'm sober. You wanted to know where I've been the past six days? This is where. When the search results came up, I thought I was hallucinating. I've rerun the data."

"I'm not questioning your sobriety, you bastard," she hissed. "I'm questioning your conclusion. Are you honestly suggesting that this woman was my clone?" She glared at him, nails digging into the stone bench.

"No."

"Good."

"Jane is five years older."

Her heart stopped. "Older?"

He nodded.

That means. . .

"You think . . ." She didn't want to say it. It was too ludicrous. She looked at Mac's eyes. She had once thought, if they'd been sober, they'd actually be rather nice-looking eyes. Now, all she saw was determination. He really believed it. "You think *I'm* a clone?"

MacKenzie didn't answer.

"I am Catholic. My parents are Catholic. My mother goes to Mass seven days a week. There is no way in this world, or the next, that I am a shadow." She waved her hand at him. It was pointless. *Saints have mercy.* Maybe Father Mark at the local church could give her a prayer.

Dear God, I'm a clone, please don't hate me.

She tossed her limp sandwich at the bench, where it bounced and fell to the ground. "I'm not a clone."

"There . . . there are other explanations."

"Eighty percent accuracy? I'm too good a genetic match. My career is going to hell because of 80 percent accuracy. What were you thinking, MacKenzie? I'm alive! Maybe that should have been your first clue that I'm not the dead Jane Doe!" Sam sucked in air. Hands on her hips, she walked back and forth in front of the bench. "This isn't happening."

"I have two victims, with evidence they were killed by the same weapon, who are both genetic matches for living people. I'm not saying that Jane Doe is you—obviously that's impossible. But what do you want me to say? You're a robot?"

"You think I'm a robot?" She couldn't believe what she was hearing. She wasn't sure she'd stay around to hear that much more anyway.

"No," he said, meeting Sam's eyes. They didn't flinch. "No, I don't think you're a robot. But I don't . . . I don't have an answer." He returned to staring at the ground. "Sam, I can't make the facts make sense. I can't. I need to run tests. On you. On Melody Chimes."

"Testing for what?"

"A DNA sample to start. Melody's DNA sample was too perfect. Either Melody Doe is Melody Chimes, or the woman who signed as Melody Chimes somehow used Melody Doe's DNA for the security firm's genetic testing."

"She was dead nine months before Melody Chimes even got the job, remember! Since I don't believe in vampires or zombies, I think we can eliminate that possibility." Sam snapped. Tears burned her eyes. *God in heaven and Holy Mary, full of grace.*

"Sam"—it was the second time she'd heard him use her name—"I need to test you for clone markers."

Cleansing breath in, bad energy out. Just like yoga class. She tugged at her blouse, trying to pull herself together. *Cleansing breath in. Cleansing breath out.* "You won't find any."

"You wouldn't know if you were a clone," Mac said quietly. "Your parents might not even know. There are cases where ransomed children were replaced with clones. One hospital in Monterrey was replacing high-risk infants with clones and selling the real children."

"That doesn't sound like a good moneymaking venture," Sam growled.

"When the parents were already paying for a shadow? The hospital charged a little extra, gave them the clones, and sold the children who would live past fifteen into slavery."

Sam glared at him. "Let me repeat: my parents are devout Catholics. Cloning is a sin. I have *never* had a shadow. It's *never* been an option."

"Did you ever travel out of the country as a child?"

"Yes, my mother was the Spanish ambassador to Canada. We held dual citizenship until Canada joined the Commonwealth." Europe hadn't welcomed the Commonwealth with open arms—far from it, in fact. People who held dual citizenships were required to pick a country. Her mother picked Spain. Some days Sam thought the only reason her parents were still married was because her mother enjoyed the convenience of having a Commonwealth spouse. It made getting a visa so much easier. Regardless, they had definitely traveled a lot when she was younger.

Sam looked up at the sky through the lacy veil of leaves. There was no way her parents were involved with cloning of any kind. Which meant this wasn't happening. Any minute, she would wake up from this nightmare. Maybe.

I'm not a clone. She wasn't sure how she was so sure, but every fiber of her being—everything about her upbringing and life so far—told her that it wasn't possible. *I'll prove it if I have to.*

"How do we do your test?"

"I send a blood sample to the lab in Birmingham."

"Why not use one of the test kits we have in the office? They used one on Melody Chime's shadow."

Mac coughed. His cheeks flushed red. "You're too old. The clone marker wasn't introduced until 2048. You were born in 2047."

Her cheeks warmed with a blush. That was a first. Most the time people said she was too young. "Won't they question why a CBI agent's blood is being tested?"

"We send in known samples to make sure the lab is testing correctly on a routine basis. No one will question the test as long as it has two agents' signatures."

Sam pressed her lips together. "And then what?"

"When we get a negative result back, we start looking at the absolutely impossible options."

She glanced sideways. Hazel eyes were studying

her intently. Mac looked drawn and angry, but she realized with a little shock that the anger wasn't directed at her. "You think the results will be negative?"

"I think it's almost impossible to fake a gene test with a major security firm, but it takes twenty minutes to hack the CBI database and falsify data if you're an agent with a clearance code."

She raised an eyebrow. "How do you know that?"

"I did it this morning when I couldn't sleep. Marrins spent six minutes as an Indian woman, or at least his genetic profile did. I changed it back!" he said hastily when he saw her expression of disapproval.

"Okay. Fine. Why would anyone do that? Crimes of intent have motives."

"For Melody Chimes? I think that's identity theft. Someone wanted her life, and they took it. Melody is dead. Melody Doe is Melody Chimes. The thief had to hack a known system, put in her DNA, and list it as Melody's. Difficult, but not impossible."

"And me?"

"Career assassination. Clones are owned things," he said with disgust. "If you were a clone, wrapping the Jane Doe case as a suicide would be ruled a confession of murder. You'd have stolen an identity, impersonated a federal agent, and killed her in pursuit of your clone agenda. The media would tear you apart."

Literally. . .

Still, she held out. "If I don't know I'm a clone—"

"It doesn't matter," he said, cutting her off. "A clone has no rights. With the political climate right now?"

He shook his head. "You don't stand a chance. With a suggestion of being a clone on your record, your career is over. Even being a clone sympathizer is career suicide right now."

Sam stared at him. "Who? Who would do that to me?"

He looked pointedly at her bare left hand. "Who hates you enough to ruin your career?"

Only one name came to mind. "Ramirez? My ex? No." She shook her head. "He might not have loved me, but he doesn't hate me." Sam paced some more. The clock over the local church chimed one. "I need to get back to the office. What did Marrins say about all this?"

"Marrins?"

"Yes, Marrins, the fat senior agent in charge of my career. What did he say about this?"

"I haven't told him."

"Why not?"

"Because it would be even easier for him to change your data than your ex-boyfriend in Toronto. Marrins is a misogynistic bigot with a chip on his shoulder, and you're everything he hates."

Sam stared, startled by Mac's convictions. Finally, she said, "My, what a paranoid imagination you have, Agent MacKenzie."

He tipped an imaginary hat. "I blame you."

"How is any of this my fault?"

"If you hadn't come down to the lab to argue about the case, I never would have gotten mad enough to go digging." A crooked smile split his tired face. "Initiative is not something I've used in the past few years."

She smiled back. "Are you going to use that new-found initiative to get some sleep?"

"I'll come home tonight. Right now, I need to bury my tracks in the system and pull up everything I can on Melody Chimes."

"Altin is going to want a report on that. Can you give him what you have without suggesting I'm Jane Doe's clone?" She managed to say it without her voice breaking.

"There's enough evidence. Her address was wrong. Her DNA match is too perfect."

"You said that, I still don't understand. Shouldn't a match be perfect?"

"Only if the sample was recent. Over the years, you mutate, that's why you age. Your body is changing. The two-year difference between specimens should be evident between the Melody Doe sample and the Melody Chimes sample we have on file. It isn't there."

"Which means the person posing as Melody Chimes kept a DNA sample."

"Or altered the file to match." Mac nodded. "Unless someone discovered a way to travel back in time to dump bodies that I don't know about." He smiled.

She faked a laugh. "Yeah. Let's not put that option in the report. I don't need to have a psych eval on my record."

"I'll have something for you and Altin by tomorrow. I can do the blood sampling at the house if you're comfortable with that."

She wasn't, but she nodded anyway.

"I'm sorry."

She shrugged. "It's not your fault. You're not the one trying to ruin my life. If anything," she admitted, "you seem to be helping me." *And why that is, I'm still not sure.* The clock chimed again, and she began moving back to her office. "I'll see you tonight."

For better or worse.

Sam was too tense to eat dinner. She left the office early and hid at the gym for three hours, working herself into exhaustion. Bri didn't show. After a six-mile run, her body demanded calories, so, admitting defeat, she drove home. Mac's truck was parked in the back.

She heard the shower running when she stepped inside. Unless she wanted to hop in and share the hot water, she'd have to stay sweaty.

Sweaty it is.

Grabbing her phone along with some spaghetti noodles, she dialed Brileigh. "Hey, Bri? It's Sam. Where were you today? I missed you at the gym."

"Gym?" Brileigh laughed. "Sammie, I'm not hitting the gym for another six weeks."

"Why?" Sam looked in her little freezer for vegetarian spaghetti sauce.

"I broke my leg at the lake," Bri said, as Sam put the pasta sauce in the microwave to heat. "We went up Monday to get away while the AC got replaced, the canoe fell off the car and snapped my leg in two."

"Ouch!"

"Tell me about it. Hubby had panic attacks. Ruined the whole vacation for us." Bri bit into something crunchy, and said around sounds of chewing, "Any word yet from D.C.?"

"No, I don't think I'll hear anything. I botched the interview and sounded like a schoolgirl on a field trip."

"Oh, sweetie, I'm sorry."

MacKenzie walked in, towel-dried brown hair sticking up in wet spikes and wearing some gray sweats that were too short for him. Sam nodded hello. "Sit down. Dinner in a minute."

"What?" Bri demanded. "Who are you eating with?"

"Someone from work. His apartment got flooded out by Jessica, and there are two other rooms for rent here. He's staying here until he finds other digs. The kitchen is communal."

"Uh-huh," Bri said, not sounding convinced. "Is he hot?"

"Excuse me?"

"Hot. Attractive. Filled with pulchritude. Swervable. Curvy. Solar. Single?"

Sam blinked at MacKenzie. Then turned back to the stove before her eyes started wandering. "No."

"Then why are you making him dinner? Girl, you need to go find someone so solar you get wet when he smiles."

Sam laughed. "No, thanks. I don't need any right now."

"How long is that going to last? When is the last time you had sex?"

"That's classified information."

"That long, huh?"

Sam dropped the noodles into boiling water and put garlic bread in the oven to heat. "It's no big deal. I'm too busy for all of that right now." She blushed when she saw MacKenzie watching her. He blushed, too, and looked away. "Listen, Bri, this is a bad time to have this conversation. Can't you come to the gym later this week? Do some weights or something?"

"I can't drive."

"How are you getting to work?"

"Bus for at least six weeks. I can barely move my hip. And there's no way I'm going to the gym in sweats. I can do arms at home."

"Bri! I need girl talk."

"So come over Friday, we'll stay in and watch movies. Hubby can take the kids camping or something."

"I'll try. Talk to you later. Bye." Sam hung up the phone in frustration.

"Sorry," Mackenzie whispered.

"Why?"

"You're unhappy?"

"It's not your fault. Bri broke her leg." She sighed. "I guess I'll keep hitting the gym alone. I can ignore creepers. Or I could drag you with me."

"Like the run Friday?" He looked up at her with a lopsided smile, and her stomach flipped. Cleaned up and human . . .

Curse Bri for putting ideas in her head. So far she'd

done her best to ignore what was between them. Not an attraction, but an awareness of the strength and intelligence Mac had to offer. Sam turned around before Mac could see her turn red. "Spaghetti for dinner," she said just a little too brightly. "And then you can stick me with your thing."

There was a spluttering sound behind her. "Excuse me?"

Sam stirred the sauce with an innocent air. "The blood test? Needle?"

"Sorry, that's not . . . my mind was elsewhere."

Yours and mine both. "Why don't you go put on a shirt? You don't want to drip sauce on your, ah"—she glanced back and turned around quickly—"self." *Abs.* When did Agent MacKenzie get abs?

He came back dressed in jeans and a green T-shirt. Dinner was fast and silent. MacKenzie brought out a needle after he cleared his plate.

"Do you know how to take a blood sample from a living patient?"

With a ghost of a smile he nodded. "Yes."

Sam held out her arm with bad grace, looking away as he washed a fingertip. His hand was warm and sure.

"Just a little prick."

"That's what they all say." She scrunched her eyes closed, only to realize he'd frozen. "Mac?"

"Do you always joke around like this?"

"When I'm stressed, scared, and tired beyond all belief? Yes. I can go back to yelling if you like. I used to just yell. Bri's a bad influence on me. She puts crazy thoughts in my head."

"I see." His voice was a little too quiet.

Sam licked her lips. "Sorry. That was unprofessional. I'm not used to being around a coworker after hours."

He cleaned her finger. There was a pinch, and he squeezed gently. "I'll send the sample out in the morning."

She looked down at the blood welling on her fingertip. "When will the results be in?"

"In a week or two."

"Okay. Good." Standing up, she tried to put some distance between them. This was strange, nervewracking, wrong on so many levels. "Good." She wiped her hands on her pants, wincing when she saw the bloody streak.

MacKenzie tucked the sample into his kit without a word.

"If . . . if it comes back positive, what are you going to do?"

"What do you want me to do?" he asked without turning around.

She studied her hand. "If I am?" She took a deep breath. "If I am, I want to turn myself in."

"That won't buy you any leniency."

"I know. But, if it comes to that, I want to make the choice. It'll be the last thing I do as a free human being. I want to make it mine."

MacKenzie tensed. "It won't come to that."

"It might."

She retreated upstairs to recover. The day had been too surreal. A hot shower behind a locked door, then to bed, with the door locked again. Hoss snored on the floor. She dropped an arm over the side and rubbed his belly . . .

She didn't remember falling asleep, but the ringing of her phone woke her before her alarm went off. Wind whipped the oak trees outside.

Two in the morning.

"Agent Rose here," she said groggily.

"Agent Rose! You must come down here at once!"

"Dr. Emir?" Sam sat up in bed, resting her feet on Hoss. "Dr. Emir, why are you calling me? At all? Senior Agent Marrins is handling your case."

"Agent Marrins can't help me. Can't help me at all. He doesn't understand. This work is too important."

Sam rubbed her eyes. "Right." She yawned. "You realize that it's two in the morning, Doc? Shouldn't you be asleep?"

"This is the only time I could come to the lab knowing he would not be here."

"He? Agent Marrins?"

"No! The other iteration. He comes to my lab. He is stealing my work. Changing my formulas. He sneaks in here when I'm not looking."

Hoss whimpered. Sam scratched his ear in commiseration. "He, who, Dr. Emir? One of your colleagues? One of your interns?"

"Not he," the doctor screeched, "me! I have come here. I change things. He and I."

Sam checked her phone. It looked like her phone, but this was obviously a dream.

"Agent Rose, I implore you. You must save me."

"From yourself?" she guessed.

"There are others who would kill me for this research."

"Like the ones who broke your bots and killed the security guard? Except, wait, nothing was stolen during the lab break-in."

Dr. Emir was quiet for a minute. "Yes. There might have been—" He coughed. "I think there is a better explanation for that. Although the evidence does not fit observed facts."

"Dr. Emir, have you considered going to a doctor?"

"My cough is not that bad."

"I was thinking someone with a doctorate in psychology. You should consider professional treatment." Hoss's head thumped on the floor as he went back to sleep. Sam wished she could do the same.

"I am in danger, Agent Rose. Very serious danger. Why do you not believe me? How can you not comprehend this? Do you not see how important my research is? Do you not know who you are talking to? I received the Misakat Award for Speculative Science two years in a row. Two years! I am brilliant! And you suggest I have problems?"

"Dr. Emir," Sam said, abandoning all tact. "I'm not suggesting anything. I'm stating a fact. You are not right in the head. It's two in the morning, and you're calling me to rant about, what? I don't even know. All I know is that I'm awake when I should be asleep."

"I called you to tell you that I am in imminent physical danger, Agent Rose," Emir said, loading his pronouncement with scorn. "Another iteration of myself is tampering with my work and coming to kill me. A real CBI agent would have wasted no time in coming to see to my safety."

"I'm not the agent covering your case. Before I can do anything, I would need permission from Agent Marrins. Don't you think calling him first would make more sense?"

"Marrins does not want to help!" Emir screamed. "Marrins is a hindrance."

Sam closed her eyes. "You've already called Marrins?"

"Yes."

"And what did Agent Marrins say?"

"He used some very foul and abusive language that insulted both my ancestry and my intelligence."

Sam hit her head on the pillow. It didn't help. "I think Agent Marrins has a point, Emir."

"He does not understand the gravity of my situation."

"I'm not sure anyone can."

"Exactly! This is why I'm telling you. I know others, like yourself, who are not possessed of my intelligence see only random chaos. To my superior intellect, that chaos is an obvious pattern."

"Really?" Sam lay back in bed, almost enjoying the raving madman. He was delusional, but he was worth a laugh next time she went to dinner with . . . whom-ever. Maybe she should let Bri set her up on a blind date.

"You are not taking this seriously, Agent Rose."

"You called me to tell me that you broke into your lab?"

"Yes! Now you understand!"

"No. Now I hang up." Sam shut the phone off and looked at Hoss. "That man is insane, and he will drive me crazy." Hoss snored. The phone buzzed in her hand. She shut it off, and, for good measure, slid it under her stack of gym clothes. Emir was Marrins's problem.

CHAPTER 19

What did I think the first time I saw another version of myself? I thought she was a coward. She was weak. I am not.

~ Private conversation with Agent 5 of
the Ministry of Defense I1–2074

*Thursday June 20, 2069
Alabama District 3
Commonwealth of North America*

Mac dropped his bowl in the sink as soon as Sam peeled out of the driveway. He'd slept enough the night before to function, even if human conversation wasn't possible until he found where Agent Perfect kept her coffeemaker. She'd been joking about not having one, right? So far, a thorough search revealed a lot of scary-looking health food, enough dog food to bury a body, and zero performance-enhancing substances like the caffeine he desperately needed to stay awake.

Hoss lumbered down the stairs, sounding like a herd of poorly coordinated elephants. The dog gave him an intelligent look.

"I saw her feed you," Mac warned.

Hoss dropped his head in Mac's lap and looked up with caramel-colored eyes.

"Do I look like I have food?"

The nubbin of a tail wagged.

"I don't have food," Mac clarified. "I'm not food."

Hoss licked Mac's hand.

"Fine, let me get my keys. I'm sure there's someplace that sells artery-hardening poisons between here and work." There was a donut shop; they sold cider, smoothies, fruit juice, and milk from a local dairy, but no coffee. It sounded oddly unpatriotic to him. Wasn't coffee one of those rights granted in the new constitution? Or maybe it was the old one. He bought milk instead and fed a donut to Hoss.

They pulled up to work, and the first thing Mac noticed was that Agent Rose was missing. Her gray Alexian Virgo was in the same spot every day, rain or shine. Hurricane and burning summer weather never stopped her from parking opposite his window, where he could admire her tan legs getting in her car. If she knew he liked her parking there, so he could watch her legs, she'd probably start parking across the street and running for cover. Or gouge his eyes out. Either was possible.

Hoss hopped out of the car and followed him.

Mac wasn't sure why he'd let the dog come with him. Pity, maybe. No, he decided as he walked into the morgue, he'd brought the dog out of a latent self-preservation instinct. If Agent Rose saw him today, she was far less likely to kill him if the sad-eyed dog was watching. Without the canine backup, she'd leave pieces of him scattered across half of lower Alabama for threatening her career.

Hoss growled at something in the dark.

"What in the Sam Hill is that?" demanded Marrins.

Mac's eye twitched. "Um . . . a d-dog, sir."

"I see it's a dog. What's it doing here?"

"You sure it's a dog?" Harley asked. "It looks like a pony to me. You could ride that thing, Rob."

Rob? Oh, Marrins. Mac shook himself. "It's, um, one of the search dogs. I was going to go out with the . . . the clean-up teams. I just, um, stopped to grab something from my office." He closed his eyes so he couldn't see the senior agent turn beet red with anger. The stutter was back. He didn't think it was permanent. He'd managed full conversations with Rose, after all. But she didn't scare him to death.

Well, she kind of does . . . but not in a bad way.

"Get that thing out of here," Marrins ordered angrily.

Hoss snarled, crouching like he was ready to pounce. Mac grabbed the dog's ruff. "Sorry, sir. I'll put him back in the car."

"What'd you need from the office?" Ol' Harley asked. "I can grab it for you."

"Just. . . ." *Just what, you gez?* "Just a water bottle, and, uh, his leash. I think I left it . . . left it there last night."

The morgue door slammed open. "Senior Agent Marrins?"

All three men stopped to savor the sight of Agent Rose framed against the sunlight. He'd have to write the director of CBI and ask that all female agents be required to wear sheer white blouses as their formal uniform. It would perk up morale to no end.

"Marrins?" Rose demanded again. "I've been trying to call for the past hour. Altin has a major FUBAR situation down at the labs, and Emir is screaming for bureau attention again."

The senior agent sighed. "I hate this guy."

"Join the club," Rose said through clenched teeth. "You're not the only one he called at two in the morning."

"I told him *not* to call you," Marrins muttered as he brushed past Mac.

Hoss growled and snapped at the senior agent.

"Your rescue dog needs retraining," Marrins said.

Mac tried to make eye contact with Rose. Her gaze passed over him, as if deleting him from the scene entirely. "Yes, sir."

"Feeling better?" Harley asked, as the other two agents left.

In the dim hall light of the morgue, Mac couldn't glare the way he wanted to. "Fine, thanks. How are your interns?"

"Contrite and still proclaiming their innocence. The young do that sort of thing." He reached for Mac's shoulder, and Mac dodged, pulling Hoss between them.

Hoss grumbled quietly but didn't try to disembowel the coroner.

The desk in his office looked far too clean for comfort. Mac shut the door and checked his computer. In a few keystrokes, he pulled up the station log. Someone with little skill and less intuition had been looking through his files. They hadn't found anything incriminating although they'd checked his e-mail accounts and entertainment viewing files.

People liked to think that using a keyboard from infancy meant they could work their way through any computer system. It didn't. It just meant they could point and click their way through life. He'd left the point-n-click mob about the time he'd started looking at computer code as just another language to learn. It wasn't hard when he knew the basics. But the basics could kick most people through the stratosphere.

Agent Rose's profile was still on his computer desktop, just as he'd left it. He skimmed the contents of her file one more time, then closed out, shutting down the computer cold. Someone knocked on his door. "Yes?"

"Agent MacKenzie?" One of the interns opened the door. "I'm supposed to make a specimen run up to Birmingham."

Mac frowned. "I thought you had classes on Thursdays?"

"I do, but . . ." He mumbled something out of hearing range.

Mac could guess. "Did you mean to poison me?"

"I didn't poison you at all!" the intern protested. "I don't know where you'd get drugs like that, and I'd never mess around with someone's medicine. I took this internship because I want to get into the bureau. Do you think I'd screw that up for a prank?"

Mac shook his head. "It's chill."

"Arthur didn't do it either."

"Arthur?"

"Arthur Frenzi? The other intern."

"Oh. Sorry, I'm not good with names." What an understatement. "It's chill, really. I believe you." He took a deep breath. "Tell you what, take the afternoon off, go to class, I'll drive the specimens up to the lab. I didn't want to . . ." What had he told Marrins he was doing? Hoss bumped his hand. "I didn't want to walk with the salvage teams today."

"You sure?" the intern asked.

"Positive." Letting anyone else see Rose's sample in the specimen lineup would only lead to trouble. Someone might do something intelligent, like ask a direct question. If Harley weren't such a sloppy good-for-nothing, Mac wouldn't have coasted under the radar for so long.

He massaged his temples. The world was coming back into sharp clarity. Pills didn't seem an option anymore. After the weekend's bout of near death, he had choked on his regular pills. Drinking his way into an alcoholic haze sounded promising, but his stomach churned at the thought of the massive hangover. Staying sober meant dealing with life like a responsible adult, yet that sounded too impossible for words. "Tell me, pup," he said, scratching Hoss's ear. "How do you kill all thought without drugs or alcohol?"

He looked out the window at where the gray Alexia Virgo wasn't. Suicide by physical exertion? Rose would happily run him to death if he asked. An unbidden image of other ways she could exhaust him flirted with his imagination. He licked his lips. Maybe in his next life.

Wait, no, wrong religion. Whichever faith handed out beautiful women after death, he was pretty sure atheists didn't qualify for benefits.

Hoss barked.

"I hear you. Let's get going."

Mac tripped over his own feet coming through the back door. The kitchen was dark, the house silent. Hoss barked happily and bounded up the stairs. Shaking, Mac stumbled into his room. A three-hour commute to Birmingham wasn't exactly physical torture, and his head was still churning. On the way back he'd stopped for a light lunch although he couldn't remember eating much. Halfway to the lab, the shaking had started. By the time he reached the lab, he couldn't see straight.

Just the smell of the morgue was enough to make him throw up. He'd run out without telling anyone he was back. Passing the cemetery behind the Baptist church on the way to the house brought back memories. There was a monument somewhere with every name but his etched in stone for eternity.

In the dark, he lay shaking and dry heaving. He dragged his hand across the dry skin of his arm, trying to rub away the constant itch. His arms burned. The shaking in his legs became a rhythmic tattoo. Squeezing his eyes shut, he tried to hum a song, sing something, think of anything but the pain.

He rolled in the darkness to check his arms. The metal was there, just under his skin, he was sure of it. He could feel the shrapnel and sand cutting him.

Someone was standing in the dark.

Lieutenant Dan Marcellus watched him, weapon slung across his chest. Mac could smell the dust and sweat of the twenty-mile trek into enemy territory. The soldiers smelled of anger. The baby-faced butter-bar lieutenant smelled of fear.

Alina Marcellus's baby boy, her only son. She'd brought cookies and hand-knit scarves for the whole unit. Cornered him at the farewell dinner. Begged him to watch her little boy.

Mac rubbed his arm, trying to peel skin off. No, the sand was peeling his skin off. The sandstorm wouldn't quit, but they had to get out of there.

He stood in the desert. Sand beat against his face, beating his safety goggles and stripping skin from his body whenever it sneaked past the layers of protective clothing. The temperature was over 120 Fahrenheit. They'd been hiking through mountains and deserts for days. Another four miles, and they'd be at the safety perimeter. Three days, four max, he'd be in a cold shower smelling like Old Spice and Axe. After a week of sleeping, he'd spend two weeks in the chow hall eating everything in sight.

The LT signaled from the top the hill. A whole valley stretched beneath them like Shangri-La in the Middle East. Yellowed grass grew in clumps under the shadows of rocks.

A dusty road wound through the rocky terrain. It was nothing, just another valley. There was no sign that anything but wild goats had moved through here in years. Still, his gut clenched. He grabbed the LT's arm and frowned at the scene. Something was wrong.

Top Sergeant Abel moved beside them. "We're good to go, sir."

The LT nodded. "Let's move out. I want a shower."

He looked at the valley floor again. All was quiet. Mac moved down the hill and hefted his gear on his back. Team medic meant last in line for almost everything. He was at the back, so he could fix anyone who did something stupid up front.

The team crawled over the hill and started working their way down to the valley floor. He slipped on loose dirt and slid into a rock, bumping hard enough to make his pack rattle. The noise sounded like gunfire. He rolled his shoulders, moved with a smile, and screamed.

There was blood everywhere. Dust. Explosions. Sand. Someone screamed. He screamed. Marcellus was down, he had to get to him, had to get him home.

Mac grabbed the body of his friend and felt heat. . .

The smell of lavender overwhelmed him.

It was dark, he was shaking, and his hand was on something wonderfully warm and soft. He leaned forward, gasping for breath, and rested his head on bare skin. Trembling hands tightened on human flesh. Warm, human.

"Shhh," a quiet voice whispered. A hand ran through his hair. "You're all right."

A steady heart beat a quieting cadence. He fought

for control of his breath and lost it again as his hands slid higher and touched cool satin with a lace trim. There, in the dark, heart beating wildly, what was he to do? He turned, brushing his face against her lavender-scented skin. All he had to do was pull her down into the bed with him. Lose himself in her soft curves. Bury the memories of war in erotic exhaustion.

His arms trembled as he fought to remember why he shouldn't. Shaking, he pushed her away. Breathing was hard with her still in his hands, the scent of her filling the room. Mac focused on the woman in front of him, silhouetted by a light from the mudroom. She had to leave. Now. "What the hell do you think you're doing here?"

Rose dropped her hands to her hips. "You were screaming. I thought you were in trouble, so I came down to help. Why are you yelling at me?"

"You came to help?" He stared at her as his eyes adjusted to the light spilling in from the laundry room. Heaven help him, there was so much to stare at. Sun-kissed skin with skimpy black shorts and a barely-there see-through shirt. "Where's your gun?"

"My gun?"

"You heard me scream, so you ran down here, unarmed, dressed like that?" Anger was the only refuge. "Are you trying to be a statistic?"

She frowned. "I came down to help."

"No. You came down to scream like a girl. I'm twice your size. If someone were attacking me, they would have no trouble taking you down. You don't have a gun, you don't have a phone, you don't even have clothes on!"

"I'm dressed."

Mac's breath hitched as he did another once-over. There was no safe place to focus. If she moved an inch forward, he was going to lose control and tackle her. Run his tongue all over that bare flesh. Spend an hour or two kissing her breathless, so her heart raced like his. Looking in her eyes—too dangerous—he'd lose himself there. Promise her anything. "That is not dressed."

"Whatever," she said, her voice annoyed. "Sorry for interrupting your horror show. Next time, I'll just put in earplugs and let you die."

Mac shook his head as she stormed out. Then followed, watching her strut through the kitchen and living room. Those hips. He really was brainless. He should have kissed her.

CHAPTER 20

Love is a destructive force.

~ Excerpt from *The Heart of Fear*
by Liedjie Slaan I1–2071

Friday June 21, 2069
Alabama District 3
Commonwealth of North America

A shadow fell across Sam's desk. Glancing up, she saw Senior Agent Marrins frowning down at her. "Yes, sir?"

He kicked the spare chair away from her desk and dropped into it with a heaving sigh. "How did you ever become an agent, Rose?"

"Sir?"

"A little slip of a thing like you? Born in Canada?" He shook his head. "Yet here you are, in the States, running around and getting lucky."

"I don't understand, sir. Why would it matter what part of the Territories I was born in?" *Never mind that: "getting lucky?"*

"We weren't born in the same country, you know.

The vote to join the Commonwealth was the narrowest in the history of the United States. One little change, a handful of people thinking differently, and you never would have sat in this office," Marrins told her as if she'd slept through modern history class. He held up an efile. "I wrote up your quarterly eval, looked over your record. It's not stupendous. I'm sure you know you aren't the best agent in the bureau. Good agents spend their junior-staff time in big cities getting trained for the real work."

And if I hadn't had to take care of my father, that's exactly where I'd be. Not this dungheap you call Alabama.

"Has my work been unacceptable, sir?" Under her desk, her fists clenched.

Marrins sneered. "It's not bad. Working the hard crime cases would do you good. I put that recommendation in your file. You're not fully trained, and they need to know that before you transfer."

Sam gritted her teeth at the implication. He seemed indifferent and continued on.

"You're also cleared of the charges of murder and conspiracy to murder Mordicai Robbins. The time of death isn't exact, but we have Detective Altin's eyewitness report that you were home alone during the time frame. He pushed it through against my better judgment."

Sam cocked her head to the side. "I'm a bit surprised it's official, myself. I could think of a few ways around those alibis."

"Are you trying to talk yourself into a murder conviction?" Marrins asked.

"No, sir. I just wish I had a solid alibi that would stand up in court."

"Don't worry about it," Marrins said. "This isn't going to court."

"Sir?"

He shook his head. "How Robbins became a security guard I'll never know. He had a criminal record, drug charges. I've seen kills like that before. A shot across the neck at close range? That's gang-execution style. I saw it when I worked as a junior in Laredo."

"But why my house?"

Marrins looked out the window. "I guess that'll be the great mystery of our time."

"Not reassuring, sir. Someone broke into my house and got past my dog."

The senior agent nodded. "Robbins was a drug dealer. Connect the dots, Agent Rose."

"Sir?"

Marrins sighed. "This is what I mean, Rose. No experience. Can you name the local druggie? Who was he dealing with? Who had access to your property?

"Means. Motive. Opportunity . . ."

Sam gasped. "MacKenzie?"

"You're a sweet girl, Rose. I hate to destroy your innocent view of the world, but drug addicts do strange things. Agent MacKenzie has been a wreck since we inherited him from the old United States DoD. No one wanted to see him waste his life on the pills, but some people can't change."

"I don't think that's quite the case, sir." She licked her lips, weighing how much to tell Marrins.

The senior agent rapped his knuckles on her desk as he stood. "Stay in your weight class. Keep away from MacKenzie. I'll make sure he doesn't give anyone else trouble."

"Yes, sir." She wanted to dive for her phone as Marrins walked out, but she didn't want anyone overhearing. Flipping the efile into her computer, she read over what Marrins had to say. Damning with faint praise was a hitherto unexplored talent she hadn't known Marrins possessed.

By his account, she was an uninspired, plodding junior agent who sought out direction rather than taking initiative. The words "woman" and "girl" were liberally sprinkled throughout, as if gender was any indicator of work ethic. Twice he mentioned her ties to Canada—he used the old country name—and he attributed some of her failings to homesickness.

Misogynistic, prejudiced bastard. Was he trying to say she was useless because she was born in Toronto, or get her transferred home because he thought it would help her career? There was no way to tell.

The bell at the church downtown chimed noon. Sam dropped her phone and files in her purse. She needed out of the office before she did something fatal to her career.

Like stick my stilettos up the senior agent's rear end.

Outside, the heat was extreme, but a light breeze and the shade in the city park looked inviting. She hesitated before sitting on the stone bench. This was where she'd sat when Mackenzie accused her of being a clone.

She was a clone.

He was a murderer.

Next, Detective Altin would pull up and announce he was moving to Key West to work as a drag queen. She needed a break in this case before Jane Doe broke her.

She sat on the bench, in defiance of all the drama, and checked her to-do list. Oh, naturally. It was her mother's birthday. Grinding her teeth, Sam dialed the number. "Samantha." Her mother managed to turn her name into a full-scale dressing-down.

"Happy birthday, Mom."

"Happy birthday? You haven't called home in nearly a month, and you think you can get away with a quick happy birthday? Talk, young lady. What have you been doing?"

That was the plan. "Working."

"On what?" her mother demanded.

"On work. I can't talk about it. The cases are classified until they've reached the court system, and unless I'm called to testify, I never know when that is." *You know—like I've told you every time you ask about work.*

"That's all fine, darling. I know work is important. I even forgive you for not calling after the hurricane to let me know you were alive. It's not as if I sat watching the Weather Channel for three days straight."

She winced. "Sorry."

"I'm sure you are. Now, tell me you got me what I really wanted for my birthday."

"Name it, and I'll have it in the mail this afternoon." There was probably a special hell for daughters like her.

"Wedding invitations."

Oh, dear holy Mary and all the saints, no. "Ah . . ."

"Samantha Lynn?"

"No, Mother."

"I can't reserve the chapel and Father John until I have a date. If you don't hurry, you'll have a winter wedding. Winter weddings are atrocious. The garden will be in complete disarray. Everything will look gothic, all black and white. I won't have it."

Sam cringed in the face of her mother's enthusiasm. "Mom, I'm not seeing anyone."

"What? Why? Didn't you get my e-mail about that nice young Nieto boy? He'll be a member of the Madrid Assembly in a few years, and he goes to Mass every week."

"He also lives in Spain, and I'm a member of the CBI in Alabama. I don't think the long-distance relationship would work out." *And I won't marry someone I've never met, either, but that's beside the point.*

"I don't believe there is no one in that awful country who isn't at least somewhat suitable."

"There's a fabulous girl at my gym—"

"Samantha Lynn Rose!"

"What? I'm not Orthodox Catholic, and neither

is she." *Of course she's married, but that's* also *beside the point.*

Her mother's exasperated huff made her smile. "I'm going to light a candle for you. Why would God give me such a wayward child?"

"I don't know." Maybe God hadn't. Her shoulders slumped. Maybe the cloning industry had given her mother a wayward child.

The phone buzzed as Mac stepped out of the morgue into the afternoon heat. "MacKenzie here."

"Agent MacKenzie, this is Dalton Kim over at the Birmingham lab. How are you?"

Mac patted his pocket for his car keys. "Doing just fine. Shouldn't you guys be knocking off for the day?"

"I'm the weekend lab manager," Kim said. "Your test results came in. They're marked as priority. Do you want the rundown over the phone?"

"Yes, please, and the results sent to my files." Unlocking the truck, he hopped in and turned on the AC.

"Copies to anyone else?"

"Not at this time." Whatever fallout there was, he wanted control of it. "What do you have for me?"

Dalton Kim laughed. "These were some fun tests. We had people working late just so they could see how everything turned out."

"Yeah?" That didn't sound promising.

"Yeah. I won dinner off my supervisor over the results from the third sample," the lab tech bragged.

"Nice job." His palms were sweating.

"The first sample, M-1, that came back clone negative, disease negative. You asked us to compare the samples with those in the public database for extant individuals."

"Yes."

"We came back with college student Melody Chimes. The sample is a pure match for her current DNA record held by Wannervan Security, where she is currently employed."

"Good work," Mac said.

"Thank you. M-2, our second sample, came back clone negative, disease negative. It is also a match for Melody Chimes. You asked us to do a full records check. The last DNA data holder for Miss Chimes was Auburn University in Alabama. She gave them a DNA sample when she enrolled two years ago."

"And?"

"The DNA match is within the limits of time progression, but not a pure match. M-1 and M-2 are a match. From the state of cell decay I would say M-1 came from an older sample."

Which meant Melody Doe was older than the known DNA sample for Melody Chimes.

"What time span does the test say there is between when the two samples were taken?"

"No more than six months. M-1 is the most recent sample. M-2 was taken and left out. Did you have an incubator break?"

"No. It was just a test. One of the agents thought a decayed sample might give us different results."

"If I hadn't done a background check, I wouldn't have been able to date them. We compared the similarities between the two samples with the college DNA data. M-1 had more points in common, making it the most recent sample."

"Right. What about J-1 and J-2?" His heart pounded, and it wasn't even his life on the line. The scene blurred. Panic made it hard to breathe, and he was on the verge of slipping into a flashback. His hand clenched, wanting pills and escape.

"J-2 was sample three. Clone negative, disease negative. This one was tricky, it's not a good match for anyone in the database."

"Mmmhmmm," Mac said noncommittally. His eye twitched.

"We ran J-1, clone negative—"

Mac breathed a sigh of relief.

"—disease negative. J-1 is a conclusive match for Agent Samantha Lynn Rose. That took digging, she's a government employee so she didn't show up in our initial search, but we found her."

The panic ebbed. "How positive are you that the search was accurate?"

"Since you'd asked us to look at data tampering for the M-1 sample, we ran it on all the specimens. That's a smart trick, by the way. I'd never thought to compare progression between current samples and older archived data. There are cases I'd like to revisit with that trick on my free time."

"What did you find for J-1?" Mac insisted.

"Agent Rose is a well-documented lady," Kim said. "Her first DNA test was at ten weeks gestational age. There have been regular DNA recordings within a year interval or less through until college. All the progression lines up perfectly. The only thing I don't know is why her? Did she lose a bet?"

"I couldn't get anyone in the morgue to volunteer."

"It's always like that," Kim commiserated.

"Did you match J-2?"

"Once we had a clue what we were looking for, we tracked her down. It was an imperfect match for Agent Rose. Looking at the current sample, and taking into account the history of progression, I'd say this is a sample from Agent Rose that's been aged. How you aged it is another question."

"We all have our secrets," Mac said. Right now, he'd kill to know what the secret was. "Do you have a theory?"

"Yeah. We figured you were cloning an organ or growing a skin graft and left the sample in for too long."

"It didn't have a clone marker," Mac reminded him.

"Small organs never do. The clone marker is part of the final brain-development process. If you take a clone from its vat too early, the clone won't have the marker either."

Mac nodded. Kim's theory didn't fit the evidence,

but there was a clue there. "Thanks for getting back to me. Can you send the written report by Monday?"

"Sure thing. Have a good weekend."

"I will." There were questions, too many for him to articulate, but it didn't matter. All he could think of was telling Sam and seeing her breathe easy again. Her eyes would light up, the weight would slide off her shoulders . . . Who knew, maybe this would be enough to win one of her rare smiles, and for that moment he'd be a hero again.

Her roommate's truck pulled up as Sam tossed another squirt of lighter fluid on the coals. Flames roared skyward, searing the tears on her face dry.

"Let me guess, your phone broke so you're sending up smoke signals?" MacKenzie asked.

"Go away."

He made a show of sniffing the air. "Why does it smell like the industrial revolution?"

"Because I wanted steak cooked over a fire. I bought charcoal."

"Solar grilling works just as well."

"It doesn't taste the same," Sam said. She crossed her arms, refusing to be drawn into the conversation.

Mac leaned against his truck with a smile. "Can we talk?"

"No. I want to cook, not talk. Go away." She reached for the lighter fluid.

"Do you need help?"

"Your cooking expertise begins and ends with pouring things in bowls."

"I wash dishes, too," he said cheerfully.

She glared at him. "Go away."

"Yes, ma'am."

"Don't 'Yes, ma'am' me. I am off work. I don't need to deal with that at home."

"Yes, Samantha Lynn."

She pivoted, shaking her tongs in his face. "Leave. Me. Alone. I am having a bad day."

He put his hands up in defeat and walked inside, smirking. Idiot. A few minutes later, he reappeared. "What was the name of your friend from the gym?"

"Brileigh. Why?"

"No reason." Ten minutes later, the back door slammed shut with a creaking thunk as Mac walked out, white china platter in one hand and her phone in the other. "Turn right there, not left," he told the person on the other end of the phone. He held the platter out to you. "You left this on the counter."

"Intentionally." Sam snatched it away and glared at the fire, pretending not to listen.

"Sure. That will be fine," Mac told the person on the other end of the phone genially. "Bring both," he told the phone. "Yeah. See you then. My pleasure." He hung up, still smiling. "Bri is coming over."

"Why? I told you I wanted to be left alone." It was smoke from the grill making her eyes water, nothing else.

"You need to talk to someone."

"And what gives you the right to tell me that? Is it because you're a man? Or older? Or, what, do tell me, Agent MacKenzie, what gives you the right to run my life as if I were some doll?"

"I don't have any right. I just don't want you burning the house down." He walked away.

She glared at him and went back to cooking dinner.

Food was so simple. Every single time you did the same thing. Every single time you found the same result on your plate. There were no variables. Cake never failed to rise because it was having a bad day. Steak didn't refuse to cook because you wore the wrong dress. Food didn't judge you. Food didn't play games with you. No one told you to avoid food for the good of your career.

No one sane or worth listening to, at any rate.

Blue and orange flames rolled across the black charcoal, a tiny shimmering sea of plasma. The briquettes charred, turning gray. Pockets of orange-white hid beneath the coals. She basted the steaks and flipped them. Eager tongues of fire jumped upward to lick the dripping marinade and kiss the meat.

She dropped the corn on the grill and took the steaks off to rest. The corn blushed deep gold as the smell of browning butter and chili tickled her nose. It was so perfect. Churned cream, a touch of chili powder, farm-fresh corn: three ingredients. No drama.

If weddings were that easy, she would have married Joseph years ago. Man, woman, preacher; it sounded simple, but it wasn't. There were decorations, flower girls, dresses, colors. Who needed colors at a wedding? The bride wore white, the groom wore a tuxedo. The person who introduced the idea of ribbons and knickknacks should have been beaten to death with a cheap plastic cake topper.

She pulled the corn off the grill and took the food to the house. There were fresh peaches sitting by the apples. Delicious. Leaving the steak and corn in the oven on warm, she took the peaches outside to the grill. Brushed with a little butter, drizzled with a little honey and a pinch of cinnamon, there was dessert perfection in under five minutes. Black grill marks added visual contrast any professional chef would have been proud of. Sam smiled. The door swung open as she walked back to the house.

"Feeling better?" Mac asked with a knowing smile.

She glowered at him. "I don't need an intervention."

He looked away rather than answering. "Are you going to share any of this with me?"

She looked at her feast. There was more than enough for her, Mac, Hoss, and everyone else in the county. "I was planning on eating alone."

"All right." He headed for the dishwasher, pulled out a bowl, and went straight to the cereal cupboard.

Sam groaned. "Fine. I'll share. Anything to save you from another bowl of chemicals."

"There are grains."

"Gen-engineered rice as the fortieth ingredient does not count as a serving of grains."

He read the box with theatrical slowness. "It's not the fortieth."

"I stand corrected," she said dryly.

"It's thirty-ninth."

Sam rolled her eyes. "Put it away, and I'll share."

"Thank you."

She snarled at him, but he didn't seem to mind. Loading her plate with steak, salad, corn, and peaches, she sat. Where to start? With the peaches, obviously. Hot, grilled peaches. She closed her eyes, savoring a bite. Juice dribbled down her chin, and she licked it away. "Perfect."

"Indeed."

She shot MacKenzie a sharp look, but he was cutting another bite of steak.

"What marinade is this? I've never tasted it before."

Sam took a bite of steak before answering. "It's blueberry teriyaki."

He paused midbite. "Blueberry?"

"Is there a problem?" She raised an eyebrow, daring him to fight.

He swallowed. "We might run out of steak. Can we talk now? I have news."

"I don't care if you're the new Pope. I'm eating dinner. Unless you need the ER right now, it can wait."

Mac shrugged. "Sure. It can wait."

The doorbell rang when she was finishing her second helping. Hoss went wild, jumping and barking like a fiend. "That's probably Bri," Mac said, wiping his mouth on his napkin. "I can take care of the dishes."

A healthy meal was enough to take the edge off her temper. Sam smiled. "Thank you."

Bri stood on the porch, supported by her husband, a short, plain man only made attractive by stunning aquamarine eyes.

"You didn't have to come," Sam said by way of apology.

"Nonsense." Bri balanced a hand on Sam's shoulder.

"She needed to get out of the house," Jake said. "The kids and the mess are driving her crazy. If you can keep her entertained for a couple of hours, I can get everything cleaned up, and maybe tomorrow she won't threaten to bulldoze the house and build a new one."

"I think it's a fabulous idea," Bri grumbled. "Jake, baby, carry me over to the couch, would you?"

Jake set Bri on the couch, with her leg set on the new coffee table. "When'd you get this?" Bri asked, running a hand along the couch. "It's comfy."

"It's Mac's. One of the few things he managed to rescue from the flooding."

"And where is Mac?" Brileigh craned her neck, looking purposefully at the stairs.

"In the kitchen. We just finished eating."

"Oh?" Bri patted the couch. "Come sit, Sammie."

"What time do you need your coach, pumpkin?" Jake asked.

"Give me four hours," Bri said, and she blew her husband a kiss. "Love you!"

He winked and waved good-bye. "Love you, too." He blew Bri a kiss and left.

THE DAY BEFORE 271

"He's sweet," Sam said.

"He's amazing." Bri smiled. "And you, I hear, are having a miserable week. Why did your roommate call me?"

"Because he's a meddlesome fool?"

"Sammie," she said reprovingly. "He seems sweet." She craned her neck again, looking at the door this time. "Will I get to meet him?"

"No. Bri, please, don't. I should have called you back and told you to stay home. I'm not good company today."

"What happened?"

"I called my mother."

Brileigh curled her lip in disgust. "Why? I only call my mother if someone dies, and even then, it has to be someone I like."

"It's her birthday."

"That's what e-cards are for. Why waste phone time? Think of the poor starving birthday-card artists who will go without pay this week because you didn't buy your mother a card. What did she do, try to set you up with a new boyfriend?"

"Some politician's son in Madrid. She said she wants wedding invitations for her birthday. I should have stayed with Joseph."

The temperature in the room dropped twenty degrees. "Excuse me?"

Sam pulled her knees up, curling into a ball at the end of the couch. "If we'd stayed together, we could have had a fall wedding."

"Not just no, sweetie, but never. Dumping him was a good thing, I promise. You can't let your mother bully you like this. It's your life, you don't need to live it to please her."

Sam sniffed. Tears blurred the already-dim room.

"Listen," Bri said, "you don't really feel this way about Joseph. He was a cheating scumbag, someone you once called—and I quote—'a tiny-dicked douche bag' that you hoped 'caught syphilis from his own mother.' Sound familiar?"

Sam rubbed her hand over her eyes. "I never called him 'tiny-dicked.'"

"I assumed." Bri grinned. Sam couldn't help it: she grinned back.

"That's settled, then. No more talk of weddings unless it's about your having met a wealthy, handsome man who brought you to multiple orgasms and you're flying off to Vegas tomorrow. No?" Sam shook her head, and secretly thanked Mac for calling her best friend over. Bri shifted and reached for the table. "Good. I brought some movies for you. How about we watch assassins, soul-stealing fiends, and an epic battle in the maze of glass?"

"The higher the body count, the better." Sam sat up, wiping her face on her arm.

Bri handed her the movie. "Here." Sam put it in the player. "Is the TV new? I thought you didn't have one."

"Mac bought it yesterday. His insurance money came in, or part of it, at least; I didn't get all the details."

"And he put it out here?" Brileigh raised an eyebrow. She leaned forward. "You're sharing electronics? Sam, what aren't you telling me? Was I close about Vegas?" She smiled slyly. "The orgasms?"

She studied the remote intently. "Mary have mercy, Bri, drop the roommate thing. Mac shares a kitchen with me, that's it." Sam wasn't sure why she felt like she was blushing. *Probably because I am.*

But now she wasn't sure *why* she was.

"You call him Mac."

"And I call you Bri, and myself Sam. I don't like long names." She sat back, arms crossed across her chest. They were not having this conversation. Ever.

"Fine, forget him. But it's only healthy, Sam. Find some guy you won't mind spending an evening with, go to dinner, and have some wild sex. Or skip the dinner. Just get it out of your system," Brileigh advised. Her eyes went wide. "That's not why you have the roommate, is it? No, I'm sorry, I promised I wouldn't ask. Wait, no I didn't. So is it? You're going to have an office romance with him, aren't you? Clandestine meetings in the break room maybe?"

"No!" Sam pulled her knees closer. "I'm not dating Mac. We have nothing in common."

"Well, you work and—apparently—live together." Bri raised an expressive eyebrow. "I think she doth protest too much."

"You're wrong. There's nothing there. No attraction. No interest. We tolerate each other; and then only when we have to. I'm not going to have anything with Mac except maybe a discussion on how to load the dishwasher correctly," she said hotly.

The kitchen door creaked shut, and Mac cleared his throat. "Um, sorry. I brought popcorn and walked in on the wrong part of the conversation."

"Mac!" Bri gushed. "I'd jump up and give you a hug, but I'm not jumping much at the moment. It's so nice to meet you. Sam's been telling me all about you."

"Really?" Mac sounded dubious. He approached the couch slowly, popcorn held between him and them like a shield.

"Sorry," Sam whispered, miserable.

Mac gave her a lopsided grin. "You don't need to apologize."

Bri smiled up at him. "You have gorgeous eyes. Sam, why didn't you tell me he had nice eyes?"

"Because you're married."

"I could start a collection. MacKenzie, have you ever considered the benefits of living in a reverse harem?" Brileigh asked.

Mac coughed. "Um, no. Thanks though. I'll, uh, um."

"Mac isn't interested," Sam translated. "Not every breathing male on the planet falls flat on their face for you. Mac, how do you make this remote work? I want to watch the movie."

He reached down and hit three buttons. Light flared on the television.

"Thank you." Sam stared hard at the TV.

"Anytime. I like to pretend I'm useful," Mac whispered by her ear, and her cheeks grew hot.

"You can cook," Bri said cheerfully.

"I can pour things in bowls."

"Sometimes that's all that needs doing—it's never a bad thing for a guy to know where to put things." Bri took a handful of popcorn and smiled; Mac blushed. Sam wondered if there was room to crawl under the couch. "You could have far creepier roommates, Sam," Bri said. "I approve."

Mac laughed. "You didn't tell her about the screaming."

Sam leaned her head back to look at him. Bri was right, he did have amazing eyes. She narrowed her gaze to a glare. "I'm still not talking to you, tattletale." He blinked, looking a little hurt. "Besides, what you scream in bed when I'm in your room is none of Bri's business." She hit the PLAY button while Bri squeaked a wordless demand for information. Mac left laughing, and Sam remained stubbornly silent on the whole subject of nocturnal activities while they watched the movie.

CHAPTER 21

> There is always a price for war. When the war is
> within our own being, the cost is either a loss of
> weakness, or a loss of strength.
>
> ~ Excerpt from *The Oneness of Being*
> by Oaza Moun Il–2070

Saturday June 22, 2069
Alabama District 3
Commonwealth of North America

Wiping sweat off his face, Mac put the lawn mower away. He was secretly hoping the drought would last all summer and kill the grass. So far, the weather was against his master plan. It was helping the nightmares though. He worked himself to physical exhaustion every day, and the dreams seemed to stay away. And there was an added benefit to trading pills for exercise: he was in better shape than he had been in five years.

A dark blue Jabon Savanna sparkled in the sunlight as it pulled up to the house. Mac smiled. "Good morning, Miss Azalea. Sam's still sleeping, but the rent checks are in the kitchen."

"I was just heading to town." The old woman toddled over to him. "And how is my favorite boy?"

He blushed. "Don't say that too loud—Mr. Cummins will get mad at me."

"Pff! The old man's been dead twelve years now."

Mac held the door as they walked inside. "Here's the rent. I mowed the lawn again, but I haven't put the weed killer down yet."

"That needs to be done. We wait too much longer, and you going to be mowing weeds. They grow faster than grass. You be mowing twice a week if the weeds win."

"I'll take care of it tomorrow," he promised.

"That's my good boy." Hoss walked in, and Miss Azalea let out a delighted squeal. "There's my handsome man! There's my beautiful one. Are they feedin' you right? Are they feedin' my babykins?" She wiggled the dog's jowls. "Sweet thing. Let me check my purse. Do I have a treat for you? Do I have a treat for ma puppykins? Yes I do! Right here! Who's a good boy? Sit!"

Hoss's rump hit the ground like a bowling ball.

"Good boy! Isn't he adorable?"

"A charming, slobbery mutt," Mac agreed.

"And a purebred mutt at that. Well." She sighed and shook her head at Hoss. "Slobbery is right. I need to wash my hands if you don' mind."

"It's your sink," Mac said, stepping out of the way. "I just rent it."

She washed her hands and turned back. Hoss lay down, then rolled over, trying to earn another treat.

Miss Azalea reached for her purse, and Hoss jumped up hopefully. "Nothing more for you, ungrateful greedy gut." She looked at Mac. "I got something for you and Miss Rose, a little card. I wanted to thank you for cleaning my car after you borrowed it. And, here"—she pulled some coins from her purse—"these were in the car. You must have dropped 'em. I couldn't keep them, it would be stealin'."

Mac took the pennies in stunned silence. "Miss Azalea? Did you say we borrowed your car?"

"Yes, dear. Just the other day. And returned all nice and clean and shiny. I thought it was sweet of you. I never wax my car when I wash it, but it does shine now, doesn't it." She smiled fondly out at her Jabon Savanna.

He nodded. "Beautiful." With a few more words for Hoss, Miss Azalea left. Mac dropped the pennies in his pocket, frowning. It was disturbing to have that much of his life missing—and he thought he was doing so well off the pills. He couldn't remember borrowing a car at all.

The sound of stairs creaking made him turn to the living room with a half smile. Sam was up. Hoss bounded forward, all four feet leaving the ground at once. Mac followed after, opening the door so the mutt could enthusiastically greet his favorite human.

Sam pushed the dog away and yawned. Sleep bedraggled, she was still beautiful.

"Miss Azalea brought you your change."

She tilted her head to one side. Sam looked blankly at the pennies. "My change from what?"

"You left it in Miss Azalea's car when you borrowed it."

Sam frowned at him. "When did I borrow her car?"

"I don't know, but she dropped by to pick up the rent and say thank you for washing the car."

"She said I took the car?" Sam looked at him with worry written on her face.

"She said we did." Mac looked at her pleadingly. "I don't remember going anywhere with you."

"We didn't go anywhere."

"That makes me feel better."

"It makes me feel worse. Who would Miss Azalea think was us?"

"I don't know, but they washed her car and left her three cents in change."

Sam's hands clenched. "Remind me to talk to her on Sunday. I can give one of her daughters a call, too. They can take her to the doctor." She glanced at the pennies in his hand. "Keep the change."

He followed her into the kitchen. "I wanted to tell you last night, but . . ."

"What?"

"Birmingham called."

Her knuckles went white as she opened the fridge. "And?"

"No clone markers. For any of the samples."

"Accuracy?" her voice was shaky.

"As close to one hundred percent as possible."

Tears swam in her eyes, and Mac wished he could take the pain away. "That makes no sense."

"Both of the matches we sent in for Melody Chimes came back confirmed."

"But one is Melody Doe?"

"Right. Melody Doe is the most recent sample. A statistically perfect match for our missing security guard."

"Who is in Paris."

"According to Agent Marrins . . ." He let that thought dangle.

"What are you saying?"

"I'm saying I'd really like a DNA sample from the Melody Chimes in Paris. It's a niggling thought I had last night. Probably nothing, but it gets better."

"Go ahead."

"Jane's DNA is a match for you, but the mutations match an advanced age of five years, which fits the age range of the body."

"We already knew that. Physically, Jane is older than I am."

"With more breaks, too." He nodded. "I had them run your DNA against archived data. You are Samantha Lynn Rose. Jane is you . . . in five years."

She frowned. "How do you explain that?"

"Illegal cloning, maybe. Someone here is running a lab, probably not far from the field where we found both bodies. They're making clones without markers."

"But why me? And which one do you think I am?" She sat at the table. "I'm confused. How can anyone make clones without markers?"

"At a guess, you're Samantha Rose. Jane was an

overmatured clone. If you pull the clone out of the vat early, the clone marker won't show up, but you can't control the rate of growth, either. As to why: ease of DNA access. Do you ever go out to clubs, bars, anything like that?"

Her lips twisted in a frown. "Regularly enough. Bri and I usually hit the clubs on Wednesday. Fewer crowds, and it's nice to know you can have a minivacation midweek."

"Melody Chimes had pictures of her out with groups of friends at clubs. Getting a DNA sample wouldn't be hard. Depending on the tech, it could be something as simple as grabbing a strand of hair."

"Or leaving a drop of blood?"

"Um, I've never been to that kind of club, but blood would make it that much easier."

"There's a chair at one of my favorite places that has a nick in it. I've sliced my ankle on it more than once. Someone complained after they did, and the chair is supposed to be gone."

Mac shrugged. "If I wanted to collect DNA for illegal clones, I can't think of a better opportunity to grab free samples. Take the blood, grow a clone with no marker at an accelerated rate, and you have an adult sex slave in under eight months. Sure, the clone won't last more than a few years without the clone marker, but that doesn't matter."

She groaned. "Marrins isn't going to like this. It's the little house of horrors all over again."

Mac made a noncommittal noise.

"What?"

"Agent Marrins has been here for a long time. How many Jane Does has he ignored, do you think?"

He could see her thinking about it before she shook her head. "No. Marrins is a bureau agent. He might have passed over some Janes as suicides, but that would be the end of the matter. If he had any idea there was a clone lab operating in his district, he would shut it down faster than you can say sting operation. He has no motive for allowing illegal clones."

"Probably," Mac said.

"It must be a man thing," she murmured. "Altin thinks Marrins is twisted. Marrins thinks you're a killer."

What? "Me?"

Sam ignored him. "You think Marrins is hiding something. What is it that makes men so paranoid?"

"Experience," he said with authority.

"We need more. We need to find a connection."

"Dump site?"

"Not enough."

"Murder weapon."

"Still not enough, unless we find the weapon and can prove it's unique."

Mac shook his head. "If I had some possible weapons, or an idea of how the weapon was used, I could probably narrow down the details. Right now, I have skull fractures from some form of impact."

"What about other Jane Does in the area?"

"What about them?" he asked.

"We need to find a connection between them if you want to push a serial-killer case."

"That's stretching the hypothesis to say that all Jane Does dropped in this area are illegal clones," Mac argued.

"Fine. Where would *you* start?"

"With material and funding, follow the money trail. The person doing this needs technical know-how and money for supplies. Around here, that's a short list."

Sam leaned against the doorjamb. "District 3 is rural. Just because a lab is here doesn't mean the operation is based here."

"There'll still be a record of some kind. Land sales and taxes if nothing else."

"Any thoughts on motive?"

"Not without knowing who is behind the means. So far, our two suspected victims are both young females. Using a technique without a clone marker means that there is no long-term prospect for the clones. Sex slaves, snuff porn, something like that could be the motive."

Sam wrinkled her nose.

"Or someone angling in on the money aspect and trying to clone replacements. Both you and Melody come from wealthy families."

She shook her head. "I'm not buying that theory."

Mac shrugged. "It makes sense. Both you and Melody Chimes were in positions that could bring wealth and influence. If someone cloned you and could control the clone, they could be set for life."

"But it doesn't fit the evidence. Both victims were

brutally beaten, killed by an impact of some kind, and Jane was tortured. You don't kill the clone if you want to use it as a replacement."

"You do if you want to threaten another clone," Mac said. "Or we come back to the fetish clubs. Clones are used for bondage and dark-fantasy sex play. I could see a club owner buying clones of local women just so they could sell the fantasy better."

"That's disgusting."

"Doesn't mean someone won't pay for it." They shared a look.

Sam shivered at the thought of someone paying for the pleasure of beating her to death. "I can see it, but it doesn't feel right to me. We'd have heard rumors by now. Or found more bodies."

"There aren't a whole lot of other scenarios that fit the evidence," Mac said. "Assassin training yard, serial killer with his own clone-at-home set, time travel."

"We need evidence, not soap-opera plot lines."

"And I hadn't even gotten to the fun ones yet."

She rolled her eyes. "What's the connection between Melody and Jane? Why them?"

"Age, social status, wealth, neither of them are white, there's a good chance you went to the same clubs. Maybe it was a fetish. Or maybe it was an attack of opportunity. Maybe the cloner picked up DNA samples at random and cloned them for fun."

She shook her head. "There's more. There has to be more. I'm going to go through Melody's file again. We're missing something."

CHAPTER 22

> There is no such thing as impossible, there is only
> a place where that possibility is not yet available.
>
> ~ Dr. M. Vensula, head of the National Center
> for Time Fluctuation Studies I4- 2070

Monday July 1, 2069
Alabama District 3
Commonwealth of North America

The phone rang, another interruption during an already-busy day. Sam picked it up. "Agent—"

"If someone doesn't have a clone marker, are they clone or human?" Mac asked without wasting any breath.

"Is this an existential question?"

"No. What is the legal designation?"

"Human. Without a clone marker, there is no way to prove someone is a clone. The marker stabilizes an adult clone, and all clones predating the marker law will have their genes on the Verville list," Sam said, reciting the legal definition from memory.

"Neither Jane or Melody Doe has Verville traces of any kind. The full report just arrived. I thought the original test of Jane missed something, but Birmingham retested, and there is nothing that matches the Verville list. Legally, both Jane and Melody Doe are human."

"What . . ." Her voice trailed off, and her eyes went wide. "Holy Mary."

"We have a serial killer. Officially. One we can take to Marrins."

"No. No, we still have only two deaths."

"Three."

"Another Jane Doe?"

"John Doe. When the body was found just before I moved here, they weren't able to identify him in the system. John was listed as an illegal immigrant and buried three plots down from Melody Doe. He's a perfect match for Matthew Vensula, a biology student who finished his internship at N-V Nova Labs before going missing. He was last seen at the lab talking with Dr. Emir. He has the same fracture pattern and was found in the same field. Same dump site. Same weapon."

"Same doctor." Sam slammed her fist on the desk. "I'm really starting to hate that man. Emir is linked to all these Matthew, Melody, and Mordicai."

"Dr. Emir is listed as the last person to see both Melody Chimes and Mordicai Robbins alive, in case you were wondering."

"Naturally. Maybe he really hates people whose names start with M." A shiver of apprehension ran up her spine. "Just so we're clear, I never want to be left alone with Dr. Emir."

"I wouldn't recommend it unless we use the M theory, then I'm the one at risk."

Sam looked at the district tax records on her screen. "Problem: he has no motive. People don't haul off and murder their interns and security guards for no reason."

"Maybe they saw something they shouldn't have."

"Like what?"

"Like the clone of a bureau agent? I don't know, but get me to that lab, and maybe I can find out."

"You know I can't tie Jane to the case without bringing up questions I won't answer. For that matter, I can't bring up Melody Doe. The official word from the Chimes's lawyers is that Melody is touring France with her new boyfriend. That leaves us one body."

"If Marrins brings it up, you can say Jane and Melody Doe were possibly cloned in an identity-theft scam. The Melody clone worked: Melody Chimes was killed and replaced by her clone, who fled the scene of a crime when the lab was attacked because she was scared she would be caught. You were the next victim, possibly because of your ties to the bureau but more likely because you come from the same wealthy background as Melody. Your clone overcooked, and they sold it to a fetish shop before dumping it."

"That's going to be a hard sell."

"Tell Marrins we might catch a clone ring in the act of cloning a bureau agent. Not that it matters, without the clone marker and Verville traces, all three of the Does are legally human, but you know how Marrins thinks."

She sighed in resignation. "Fine, the logic is still spotty but I'll take it to Marrins and get a warrant. When I get to the lab, what am I looking for?"

"Blood? A signed confession? Emir to have a nervous breakdown when you show him the warrant? I don't know, what do you want?"

"Mac," Sam said in a dry tone, "I meant, what should I look for as a possible weapon?"

"Um . . ."

"Don't say 'um.'"

"No sharp edges. Nothing that flakes. I almost want to say something soft."

"Soft?"

"Have you ever seen a body hit by a sonic blast?"

"I've never had the opportunity."

"Sound waves can shatter a body. It reminds me of that, but the blast isn't hitting the organs and liquefying them, it's striking the bones. The fractures radiate out from the point of impact like ripples. Whatever it is, don't look for a conventional weapon. It will look benign."

Sam rubbed her temples. "That's going to be fun to look for, but I'll try to find something."

"It would help if I could come."

"No it wouldn't—you're not field trained. Some days, I don't even think you're housebroken."

"It would satisfy my curiosity."

"Mmm, that I believe." She started pulling files up on her computer. "Do you think you could tie Robbins to this at all?"

"Probably not. I can look over the autopsy again, but he was killed by a bullet to the throat. He choked to death on his own blood."

"Lovely." She rubbed her own throat in sympathy.

"Premeditated, execution style. Marrins was right about that, I looked it up, and it's a common method of dispatching gang members who turn traitor in some areas of the country. Serial killers don't get creative with their killing styles. They find something they're comfortable with, and they use it again and again."

"I'd still like to talk to Melody Chimes, or whoever is using her name, and get her account. Marrins won't give me the recording, though."

"Is it in the database?"

She blinked, gaze falling down on the morgue windows in the building below. "MacKenzie, that's a loaded question. Marrins is the only one in this office with authorization to access those files. As the lead agent on this case, I can't authorize you to break the law or go against a direct order from our senior agent."

"I wasn't asking you to authorize any such thing."

She thought she saw a flash of white lab coat in Mac's window as he swiveled in his chair. "Let's not give Marrins an excuse to fire us both. Okay?"

"Do you need the recording?"

She only hesitated for a moment. "Yes."

"See you at dinner."

It took her an hour to write up the report for Marrins. The senior agent was resting at his desk when she knocked. "What can I do you for, Rose?"

"Sir, hypothetically, if I had three individuals all killed by the same weapon and dumped in the same area, would we classify it as the work of a serial killer?"

"Not if they're clones."

"No clone markers, sir."

Marrins raised bushy white eyebrows. "Sounds like a good working hypothesis. What'd you find?"

"When we dug up that mass grave—"

"Waste of time." Marrins sneered.

"I know, sir, but you did order me to identify everyone before we reburied them."

"That grave's made us the busiest district in the state for the past month," he grumbled. "Even with Hurricane Jessica. I've never filed so much paperwork in my life!"

Ignoring him, she pressed on. "Three of them died under unresolved circumstances. All of them unidentified victims. All killed with the same weapon. All dumped in the same field. All close to the same age."

Marrins pulled the file closer with a frown. She'd left just the autopsies and the Doe names, he didn't need the faces or links. "Go on."

"We have a positive ID on the John Doe: he was a biology student who worked as an intern at N-V Nova Labs. He's been missing for almost three years."

"Emir," Marrins breathed.

"Yes, sir. He was the last person to see Mr. Vensula alive."

Marrins drummed his fingers on the desktop. "Emir. He's been yanking my chain way too hard this past while. I think it would be good to put the fear of the bureau back into him."

"Agreed, sir. Will you request the warrant, so I can search the labs?"

Marrins grinned like a shark. "I will indeed."

"I'd like to take the coroner with me, sir," Sam said. It was a gamble, but she needed Marrins on her side.

"Our bureau one?"

"No, sir, Coroner Harley. He handled the original John Doe case, and he has more experience than anyone else at our disposal. I'd like to request the city loan him to my case for the duration of the investigation. If he can come with me to the lab, he might be able to tell me what caused the fracturing that killed our Does."

"Assuming they were all killed there."

"I'll admit it's a stretch, sir. We can definitely tie one body to the lab. I'm running a computer search now to see if we can tie the other two to the lab as well. If I can get positive ID matches to the bodies from former lab employees . . ." She spread her hands. "It would be a nearly perfect case."

Marrins nodded. "You'll have the warrant, but you're taking our morgue freak."

Guess you don't think he's a murderer anymore, do you?

"Sir?"

"This is not the city's case, Agent Rose. I don't want Harley near this."

"Yes, sir." She hid her smile until she was safely back in her office.

A late-evening breeze rustled the oak leaves and stirred night-blooming jasmine in the yard. The lazy ceiling fan creaked but did little else to alleviate the muggy heat of the evening. As the air-conditioning kicked in, moving the drapes, the temperature moved from sauna hot to sultry warm. It was a night made for tangos, swimming naked, or kissing someone under the stars.

She didn't miss anyone in particular, Sam told herself as she put away the last of the clean dishes. It was the idea that she craved. Right now, she wanted someone to hold her, to sweep her around the room, to kiss her senseless. Her brain was in overdrive worrying about what would happen in the morning. Would Emir run? Confess? Pull some crazy proof she was a clone out of his data file?

I just want something to happen, something wonderful for once, before the world is crazy again.

Hoss looked up a second before the back door swung open. Sam was already reaching for the butcher knife.

"Hi! Oh." MacKenzie held both hands up. "Sorry. Were you expecting trouble?"

She stepped away from the knife. "I'm on edge."

"I see that." He petted Hoss's giant head. "Did you get the warrant?"

"We'll have it by morning. Marrins assigned you to the case."

His eyebrows went up. "How did you swing that?"

"I asked for Harley. The senior agent delights in giving me what I don't want."

"Strange man." He pulled an efile from his back pocket. "I brought you a present." Sam held out her hand, and he held the efile up a little higher. Mac leaned close and whispered, "What do I get in return?"

"Dinner."

"Ooo, you wicked temptress you." Mac winked and laughed. Sam snorted and snatched the efile as he walked to the oven. "What am I eating?"

"Does it matter? You'll eat anything that holds still two times out of three."

"That doesn't mean it will taste good."

"Cajun chicken sandwiches." She slid the efile into her phone to play. "What did you bring me?"

"Audio of Melody Chimes pulled from her university record, her Wannervan Security record, and from the phone call from Paris to New York where her parents met with their lawyers and bureau agent Citavia." He made himself a plate and sat at the table opposite Sam. "Go ahead and listen."

She hit PLAY.

"Hi, I'm Melody Chimes," said a cheerful voice that was young but already turning smoky. There were good genes there and just a hint of Dulcet Chimes-Martin's upper-class accent. "I'm jixed as a pickle to be a student at Auburn. War Eagle!"

Sam bit her lip. "I want her to be in Paris."

The recording switched files. "My name is Melody Chimes, civilian registration number 78A-56-9A2B. My height is sixty-eight inches, my weight is 123 pounds. I am African-descent American, brown hair, brown eyes." On the audio, Melody Chimes sighed, and said away from the recorder, "Brown is so dull."

Mac didn't make eye contact.

Again, the recording switched. "Mum! How are you? I'm sooooooo sorry I haven't called," a syrupy thick voice gushed. There was no hint of smoke. The accent was thick, but false. "I love Par-ee! I just had to come with a friend. You understand."

Sam put her sandwich down as a man's voice asked where she was, if she was alone and safe.

"I'm with friends," the possible Melody said. "Quite happy. Perfectly happy. Everything is wonderful. I'll call you soon. Loves!"

She shut the recorder off. "That wasn't Melody Chimes."

"The recording is scratchy, bad for a trans-Atlantic call. Just listening once I caught what you did. I ran it through a voice-data match and"—he shook his head—"there's just no way."

"Her family believed this was Melody?"

He raised an eyebrow. "Their baby girl is missing. They'd rather believe that's Melody, than admit she's dead. People are like that when they grieve. They'll grasp at straws. Carry headless bodies miles on end because they think something can be done. With a bureau agent sitting there, it must have seemed possible."

"Why would Marrins lie?"

"Why does Marrins do anything?"

Crossing her arms, Sam sat back in her chair. "I don't like this."

"Mmm." Mac finished his sandwich. "You have a gun?"

"The bureau issued a splat gun we have for emergencies. Why?"

"You need to start keeping it on you. Call it a hunch, but I think things are going to get worse before they get better."

CHAPTER 23

What keeps our society stable is not our religions,
our charitable institutions, or our educational systems. Those are all lovely things but, mathematically speaking, what keeps our society stable is
the fact that we have more einselected nodes than
other iterations. If we ever lost that, we would lose
our primacy.

~ **Student notes from the class**
Physics and Space-Time I1–2071

Tuesday July 2, 2069
Alabama District 3
Commonwealth of North America

Pulling away from the donut shop, Sam handed MacK-
enzie his bagel and smoothie. She'd found him asleep
on the couch this morning in his running gear. "Ready
to play Agent Bad?"

He took a bite of his bagel. "Sure. What am I supposed to do? Run in and start shooting?"

"We go in, show the lab our warrant, and ask a
few questions. I'll start with Matthew Vensula, see if
anyone remembers him."

"It's been three years."

"I don't care. I'm going to ask about Melody Chimes, too. Maybe she had a roommate, or a boyfriend."

"Or a stalker," Mac said.

"A stalker?"

"Someone who wanted to steal her life even more than a clone shadow."

Sam shook her head with a laugh. "You watch too many movies."

"You don't watch enough."

"Novikov-Veltman Nova Laboratory?" Mac read as they pulled up to the lab. "That's an interesting choice of names."

Sam glanced up. "It's Russian." She shrugged. "Not very patriotic, but there's no law saying your heroes have to be American." She parked her car near the exit just in case they wound up chasing a deranged scientist. She was half hoping it would be that easy. Mac climbed out of the car, towering over her. She squinted against the sunlight, then brushed a crumb from his mouth. "Let me do the talking. Your job is to stand around looking intelligent and mean."

"Mean?" He looked bewildered.

I'm actually skeptical on the "intelligent," too. . .

"Never mind. Can you do cold?" His lip curled a little. "That looks like a bad Sarah Teel impersonation. Try detached." His hazel eyes went flat and distant. "Perfect."

She walked into the lab, showing her ID to the security guards, and sauntered over to the main desk. "Are any of the doctors in yet?"

The security guard scanned her badge and pulled up the log-in screen. "Dr. Emir is the only one in, Agent Rose. He has an experiment in progress and left orders that he's not to be disturbed."

"That's fine, I can start with the guards."

"The guards, ma'am?"

She pulled out the warrant. "We have a few questions. We'll need to speak with Dr. Emir, but I can start interviewing the guards if he's too busy."

The guard's eyes went wide. Forced to choose between protecting the lab from a marauding CBI agent and bothering the deranged doctor, Sam wasn't sure what she would have chosen. Lucky for her, it wasn't a choice she had to make. "Agent MacKenzie, start walking the perimeter, see if you can identify what we were looking for the other day."

He did a once-over of the room and gave her a bare shake of his head. The weapon wasn't likely to be here anyway, but it never hurt to look.

"See if you can find where the security circuits connect. The lab never gave us a reason why all the windows were shattered."

MacKenzie nodded, leaving her to deal with the security guards. She barely had time to ask them how long they'd all worked for the security firm, and had just begun asking if they knew Melody Chimes, when a harried intern came rushing out.

He was a round-faced, thin man with an already-receding hairline and near-black hair. "Agent Rose?" he wheezed. "We weren't expecting you."

Handing the warrant over for inspection she waved the guards away.

"Murder weapon?" the intern squeaked.

"Murder weapon?" Sam asked innocently. She looked at the warrant with false interest. "That's there for later searches. I'm here retracing the steps of an intern from a few years ago. When did you start working at the lab? It's Henry, isn't it?"

"Troom," he volunteered. "Henry Troom. I've been here twenty months next week."

She remembered him now. He'd tried to explain Emir's machine the first time she came with Altin. "You're counting?"

He smiled sheepishly. "I have four months left of my internship, then a semester left before I graduate."

"In what?"

"Physics and advanced biological sciences," Troom replied with a bright smile.

"Did you ever meet Matthew Vensula?"

"Matt? No, I never met him, but I've heard about him. I'd got here after he went missing. Everyone was in shock. Dr. Emir said he would go far."

"Mmmhmm." *What was it? Less than ten miles to the dump site, wasn't it? Maybe Matt didn't go as far as the doctor anticipated.*

Mac circled up to them. The corner of his mouth curved in a smile; he suspected something, but he wasn't going to give it away.

Sam turned back to the intern. "Mr. Troom, is Dr. Emir ready to see us? We need to talk with someone who knew Matt well enough to answer some questions about his recreational activities."

"Sure." Troom led them to the right door and to Emir's lab. "Do you think you've found Matt? I know it hit the lab hard when he went missing, I can only imagine how his family felt."

"We have a possible lead," Sam said without committing to anything. There was a new set of thick, heavy, armor-plated double doors. "A new safety feature?"

"Sound-wave dampeners. Dr. Emir's experiments are reaching a very complex stage."

"I see."

Mac cleared his throat. "What is Dr. Emir working on?"

"Ah," Troom pushed open the door, and Sam was hit by an unseen force.

It felt like a giant pillow had pushed against her body and knocked her back a foot. A warm hand on the small of her back steadied her. She twisted just enough to see Mac frowning, his back pressed to the wall and his hand on her.

"Henry!" Emir shrieked from the far side of the room. "What have I told you about opening those doors? Never open the double doors when the machine is in operation. Someone could be hurt." He crossed the room in six quick strides, leaving a black china teacup on the edge of one of the desks. The machine sat in the middle of a bare circle with concentric rings marked out in yellow tape.

Sam regained her balance. "Hello, Dr. Emir."

"Agent Rose." He pursed his lips.

"I need a few minutes of your time to ask you about one of the interns who worked here in 2066."

"Bah," Emir began.

"She has a warrant, Doctor," Troom warned him.

Emir rolled his eyes. "Very well. For the ever-insistent Agent Rose, I will make the time. Step into the safety zone, Detective." He motioned them toward an area behind a green line of tape, where several desks were shoved together at odd angles and piled with the detritus of the lab.

"We are still calibrating the device," Emir explained. "If you are within the inner radius, there is no effect. I am working to close the wave zone outside that to a minimal level." He turned. "Run the system again, seven-A this time." Emir made a circling motion over his head. The lab workers punched in numbers on a computer behind a heavy metal wall with a glass peephole.

"It looks dangerous," Mackenzie said.

"Only to the unwary," Emir assured him. "Now, Agent Rose, what questions did you have that could not wait until later?"

"Do you remember Matthew Vensula?"

"Matthew? Of course, he was one of my best students." Emir turned around with a frown as if he could conjure the missing intern.

"He did his internship here three years ago," Sam prompted. "You may remember him leaving?"

"Leaving?" Emir frowned. "Yes, yes, I recall. Such a promising—" Glass shattered.

Sam spun, dropping to her knees as she pulled a dart-loaded gun.

Dr. Emir's black teacup lay on the floor, shattered in a circular pattern. "Commendable reflexes, Agent Rose." Emir patted her shoulder. "Gentleman! Calculate when the next wave will hit. Then try four-A. We are not making significant progress."

Mac was studying the cup intently, not moving. She gave him a questioning look, unsure what would trigger another panic attack, but he only returned a slight shrug.

She holstered her weapon and tried to continue with the same nonchalance the men seemed to have acquired. "Do you remember if Matthew Vensula had any friends in the area? A significant other of any kind?"

"Dr. Emir," Mac interrupted, "what is it that your machine does?" Sam glared at him, but he shifted is eyes enough to show he was serious. She nodded slightly; *Okay—it's your show for now.*

"Are you familiar with the work of Novikov, Agent?"

"Only a little," Mac admitted in a distant tone. "He was a Russian science-fiction writer."

"Yes, indeed." Emir beamed at his new star pupil. "Novikov hypothesized that mass could be moved in all four dimensions."

"Time travel?" Mac asked. "But, surely, you have the paradox that nothing can be in two places at once. That's why time travel doesn't work."

"Nonsense!" Emir declared. "Are you who you were yesterday?"

Mac considered this, then nodded. "Yes."

"Exactly?" Emir persisted. "Down to your molecular structure? Down to the chemical base? Of course not. Humans are the very embodiment of the chaos theory. Every thought changes us. A smell can trigger a cascade of hormones and chemicals drenching our system. We change constantly. For my work, humans are useless. What I endeavor to do is much more worthwhile, much more reasonable."

Sam bit her tongue. It was all nonsense to her, and if Emir started rambling about otherselves and iterations again, she'd shoot him with a dart and call it a day.

Emir waved a hand at his contraption. "This machine does not move living particles back in time but simple wave patterns of molecules."

"Like Morse code?" Mac raised an eyebrow. "To what purpose?"

"To send information, of course. My predecessors were all grand men of vision. They thought they could change the world by moving themselves back in time, little realizing that time only moves one direction. Time will always move forward. Even if I could send a living thing back in time, which can't be done, you would not have two identical copies with the same history; you would have split history and had two copies of one person. Two separate lives. One of them living in the wrong timeline. The wrong iteration, if you will."

"Of which, logically, there must be an infinite number," Mac said.

"No! No, no, no! Think!" Emir yelled. The machine in the center of the room rattled, and fell still. "Four-A!" Emir called out.

He turned back to them. "This is what everyone believes. This is why they never achieve anything. Think! If I sent Agent Rose back in time, what would happen?"

Mac looked at her. "She'd be angry?"

"Also, dead. Living tissue cannot survive the transfer. But aside from deceased and angry, Agent Rose would be in a separate world. I tried to explain this to your Agent Marrins, but he didn't understand. That man dreams of changing his own past."

Sam perked up at that but didn't interrupt as Mac continued his interrogation.

"Are we talking about parallel dimensions?" Mac asked.

"Eh, something similar." Emir waggled a hand in a seesaw motion. "There are only a finite number of universes where there is enough connection for a person to survive. There must be a positive probability of the person's living in that universe for a connection to be made. That was my great discovery."

Sam fought to roll her eyes. Still, with Mac here, she found she could understand what the pompous Dr. Emir was saying.

"The elements I use to power my machine have an extended half-life," Emir said. "When we run power to the core, it creates a ripple. We can control the ripple, and move it backward along the space-time matrix. In time, perhaps I, or another genius"—his tone indicated that he did not believe such a person existed—"will discover a way to turn that ripple into a portal so that larger objects could move along the wave. Now, perhaps I could send something a few atoms thick. Such objects exist, but they are of little use to me."

Sam raised her hand. "What does that have to do with parallel dimensions?"

"Ah! Excellent! Not many students understand. What we realized in the very earliest of my experiments is that the premise that you could go back and change your own history was wrong. A complete fallacy. The idea of an infinite number of dimensions is mathematically sound but does not hold with the laws of entropy and physics. When you apply the laws of physics to this problem, you see that all iterations of time, all possibilities, must collapse like a wave form. There must be a ground state. Every action you take either moves your timeline closer to the ground state and stability, or to chaos and collapse."

"I'm confused," Sam said. Emir looked offended, as if Sam had offered him the deadliest of insults.

Luckily, MacKenzie stepped in at that moment, quickly saying, "He means that even though there is a mathematical possibility that dinosaurs and humans coexist, that possible reality would collapse because the likelihood is so astronomically small."

"This is true," Emir agreed, seemingly forgetting

Sam's "gaffe." "Our current available molecules would be too different from those in a theoretical Dinosaur Universe. The probability of your existence there is too low to make a connection. My machine can only connect to universes where there is a high probability of another such machine existing."

"So the messages you send can only be sent to an iteration where the messages would be sent, or could be sent, at some time?" Mac guessed.

Emir nodded again. "Yes. And the key is," he said, excited, "that it will save lives. Perhaps not our own, but I think we will benefit in the end when the timelines come back together. This is a means of achieving a greater good for the species. Just think: a terrorist could attack tomorrow, and I could send a message to myself, today. I would know in advance. Think of the military good this could do! It brings our ground state further from extinction and closer to peace. One day, who knows: maybe our iteration will be the one that finds world peace. But"—he chuckled in a self-deprecating way—"this is all speculation until the machine is finished."

Sam thought about it—and the manic man standing before her—and all she could see was chaos.

CHAPTER 24

Every action has an equal and opposite reaction.
Time must obey the laws of physics. Even I am not
immune to this.

~ Excerpt from Lectures on the Movement
of Time by Dr. Abdul Emir I1–20740413

Wednesday July 3, 2069
Alabama District 3
Commonwealth of North America

For the first time since she'd called the meeting, she
wished MacKenzie was here for backup rather than
down in the morgue helping Harley sort bodies sent
up from the coast for identification. But it was probably
better this way.

Dr. Emir had said it was impossible to move bodies
back in time. Mac liked the idea of time-traveling
crime, and even she was willing to admit that theory
fit the evidence better than the clone theory she was
about to present to Marrins. But Emir's machine evi-
dently didn't work, and there was still no motive link-

ing Emir to Melody. On the other hand, Emir did have a background in cloning, access to everything needed to create a clone, and a disciplinary record from his previous employer showing that he was reprimanded for "having unnatural relations with clones." She wasn't sure what counted as unnatural, but she was fairly certain she'd sleep better not knowing.

Locking Emir up was the solution to a lot of her problems.

Not that it hasn't created other problems. . .

"I told you to stay away, Rose." Altin walked in, his hand unconsciously coming to rest on his gun as he scowled at her.

Sam leaned back, eyes wide. "I stayed away from the case."

He glanced at the mess on the conference table, where she had spread out her the evidence of the case. "It sure doesn't look like it."

"That was a lab break-in with the possibility of stolen goods," she said defensively. "I'm looking into a serial-killer case. If the two are related, I'm sorry, but the killer takes precedence over some broken glass."

Marrins came in with a mug of cheap office coffee. "Rose. Altin." He nodded cordially, oblivious to the tension in the room. "Where's our skinny boy?"

"Harley needed him," Sam said.

"Good for him." Marrins nodded and sat. "All right." He took a sip of his drink. "What'd you find?"

Sam gestured for Detective Altin to sit down. He scowled again while doing it. *For good measure, I sup-*

pose. Standing up straight, she said, "While going through the mass grave to make identifications, we came across three unidentified bodies with similar skeletal trauma. All three were dropped at the same dump site. We identified the first as a former intern of N-V Nova Labs. Another, I believe, is Melody Chimes."

"She's in Paris," Marrins said. "Talked to her myself."

Sam pushed the readouts of the voice comparisons toward him. "I pulled these this morning to listen to them. Even a bad connection doesn't account for the change in vocal patterns. I believe that the woman you talked to killed Melody two years ago and stole her identity."

Altin took the paperwork while Marrins looked at the voice printout. It was his turn to scowl.

Marrins set his coffee cup down. "All right, let's hear this theory you've cooked up."

Sam cleared her throat. "John Doe is a biology student. Both Jane Does were found dead before any similar person was reported missing, which is why I suspect identity theft might have been a motive."

"You have an ID for the second Jane?" Marrins asked.

She took a deep breath. "A possible match, yes, sir," Sam answered, hoping they wouldn't press for names.

"Clone markers?" Altin asked.

"None, which supports my theory that these individuals were victims of extreme identity theft. Agent MacKenzie has suggested it could also support the theory that these were all quick clones, rapid aging and short-lived, but without the Verville traces." Altin began to protest, but Sam cut him off. "*Until* we can confirm they are clones, we're legally required to treat this as a homicide case."

The detective whistled.

"Regardless of their technical status, the fact is there is no clone marker on either victim, Detective," Sam pressed on. "The second Jane was tortured, and the suggestion has been put forward that someone might be fast-cloning women for a fetish club. If you pull a clone out of the vat early enough, they won't have a clone marker. They also age faster and have limited mental capabilities. The evidence suggests that something similar might be happening in this case."

"How does this tie to the lab, besides that two victims worked there?" Altin asked.

Here comes the leap of faith. "All three bodies have a strange radiating trauma pattern. Dr. Emir is working on an energy-pulse machine that produces the same results. He doesn't intend for it to be a weapon, but I think he could kill someone with it. And I think the first death was accidental."

Altin looked dubious. "You're suggesting Emir takes cloned whores back to his lab, gets his kicks, then offs the hookers?"

"Or that Emir was using the lab to create quick clones, and they got caught in his experiment's cross fire. Or, worst-case scenario, Emir was killing his employees and selling their identities on the black market," Sam said. "I'll admit we're still a little light on motive. But means and opportunity are definitely there, and all the evidence is pointing to that lab.

"Now, the warrant I had allowed me to go to the lab and question everyone, but I need special permission to take the equipment and the purchasing records. I need to see if Emir bought cloning equipment or stole it. We'll need to inventory the entire lab. Tracking down the woman who traveled to Paris as Melody Chimes will be crucial, too." She looked at Altin. "That's why we need your help, Detective."

Altin just sat there, face composed in thought.

Marrins wiped a hand across his face. "*Gez*, Rose. That's a mess and a half. That's a government-funded lab."

"Would it explain the break-in?" Altin asked, breaking his silence.

Sam nodded. "When I was in the lab during testing, a teacup was cut in half and shattered by a pulse from Emir's machine. It matches the pattern of glass we found after the break-in. A large pulse from Emir's machine could account for all the damage we saw. He wasn't supposed to be in the lab, but Mordicai Robbins left, and if Emir knew that the Melody Chimes working in the lab wasn't the real Miss Chimes—if he had a hand in cloning her, which is a possibility—what would stop him? She was a small woman. It wouldn't have been hard for him to overpower her or lure her back to the lab."

Altin nodded. "Not all the pieces are there," he warned.

"No, Detective," she agreed. She turned to Marrins. "I'd like permission to bring Emir in for questioning, sir, and I'd like a full team to go out to the lab and look for trace residue from these three deaths and that of Mordicai Robbins. If Emir killed other people in his lab, that's where he would have been most comfortable killing the security guard."

"Why kill Robbins?" Altin asked.

"To cover his rear," Marrins said. "It all fits. I hate it, but it fits. Robbins probably came back, walked in on something he shouldn't have. Emir would try to buy his silence first. I'm guessing Robbins wanted more money, told him he'd tell everybody. Emir tells him the cash is ready and shoots Robbins when he comes in." The senior agent mimed shooting a gun. "Emir is plenty old enough to have a war-era gun, something with real bullets."

"And by then, he'd already met Agent Rose," Altin said. "Dumping the body at your house." He sucked his breath between his teeth. "I told you it was a warning."

"You were right," Sam said.

Marrins finished his coffee and crumpled the cup. "I can't get a team in there fast, bureau red tape will slow us down." He paused to do some mental calculations. "Friday will be the soonest. You did good work, Rose. Real good work, but you don't have the pull to make this case stick."

"I understand, sir." The lab was hallowed ground. Government-funded, politically backed, the scientists working there did so with the full sanction of the local government. Getting in there would mean removing Emir's immunity from prosecution. The weapon he'd used was perfect. It was experimental, so he could claim all three deaths were tragic accidents. The best they could hope for—politically—was to pin Robbins's death on Emir, and even that would be hard.

But we have to do it. Even if only to give Melody's family closure.

"I'll handle Emir," Marrins said. "Rose, you work on the cloning. Check all the unidentified bodies. See if we have any more matches. And when I'm done with Emir, I'll see what I need to do with you."

"Yes, sir."

Altin rapped the table with his knuckles. "Call if you need local backup. I know this is bureau territory, but the last thing this town needs is a killer on the loose. Do you want my people to check the clubs?"

"Do it," Sam said, ignoring Marrins's scowl as she invited Altin to tramp through their turf.

Sam ate leftovers for dinner, then locked herself upstairs as she tried to sort the evidence. With a sigh, she shoved everything off her bed. No matter how she looked at it, the evidence didn't support the idea of a clone lab doing quick, aged clones. Nothing lined up.

Downstairs, the back door shut, and she heard Mac's truck start up. They hadn't eaten dinner together. At work, it was easy to fall into the role of friendly coworkers. Once back home, back in her safe haven, things turned awkward.

With a sigh, she shut the lights off. Sitting up reading wasn't going to get anything done—she was too tired to make any progress on the case tonight. She needed twelve hours of sleep and an epiphany.

The emergency ring on her phone woke her four hours later. "Agent Rose, this is Emir. You must come to the lab. Now! You must come now!"

Sam yawned. "What's wrong?"

"Agent Rose, you must come to the lab," Emir repeated.

"I'm sure you think so."

"You owe me that much," he pleaded.

"Emir, I don't get out of bed in the middle of the night for anyone, but I'll be happy to meet you tomorrow morning. How does ten sound?"

"My life is in danger. They are coming for me. If I don't give them what they want, they will kill me. They know it works now. I can't stall any longer."

She rubbed her eyes. "What do they want?"

"My machine! You told them it works. You showed them it works."

"*I* told them?" She scratched her nose. "I told Senior Agent Marrins about my visit. Detective Altin was there, too, and yes, the senior agent wants to talk to you. He has questions about some missing person cases. And, yes, this might destroy your career. But that's something you need to talk to a lawyer about."

"Agent Rose!" Emir's voice rose in a panicked wail.

"Please, I beg of you. Come to the lab tonight. Bring your partner, bring Altin, bring anyone, but come. Save me!"

"See you first thing tomorrow." She wasn't sure, but she thought Emir was crying when she hung up the phone. Dropping a hand over the side of the bed, she petted Hoss's ear.

Would it really hurt to drive out there tonight? Mac was downstairs, with enough cold water, she could wake him up so he could do his best impression of a human before noon . . . No, he was at work.

Her fingers dug into Hoss's ruff in sudden terror. She was alone.

If she went now, she'd have to face Emir alone.

Melody Chimes probably did the same thing. She'd go alone tonight to answer his frantic terror-driven call and be nothing more than a body in the ditch by morning. Locking the door and propping her desk chair under the handle, she went back to nightmare-filled dreams. Dr. Emir could wait until daylight, and backup, arrived.

CHAPTER 25

> Old age is a rare gift in our profession. All I hope
> for is a quick death.
>
> ~ Agent 5 I1–2074

Thursday July 4, 2069
Alabama District 3
Commonwealth of North America

An ambulance sat idle in front of the labs. Sam parked behind it. One of the EMTs gave her a nod she returned with a tight-lipped smile. It wasn't even seven in the morning, and her day was already heading downhill.

"Agent Rose?" Altin stood in the middle of Nova Lab's atrium. "How'd you get here so fast?"

She raised an eyebrow. "I drove the speed limit and left at six thirty so I could talk to Dr. Emir before I went into work this morning. He called last night babbling about being threatened. Why?"

"Holt was supposed to call you. Emir is dead."

"What?" Sam fumbled for her phone. "I talked to him a couple of hours ago." She pulled up the recent calls list and shoved the phone at Altin. "I talked to him less than five hours ago. He's alive. He has to be alive. I have questions for him."

Altin sighed as he read the number. "Emir was shot sometime last night. Mr. Troom called us when he showed up this morning and found the lab unlocked, but the doctor wasn't there. We found the body ten minutes ago back along the tree line behind the lab."

"Can I see him?"

"Sure, it's bureau jurisdiction." He led her through the back atrium doors and past the stone picnic tables up the little hill to the pine trees, where Emir lay face-down on the ground, turned away from her.

"His throat's shot out." All she saw were the ragged edges of the wound, but it was enough.

"Yup. Same as Robbins." Altin tapped his fingers on the butt of his gun. He studied her for a long, silent minute.

"What?"

"He called you?"

"Yes."

"Because he was threatened?"

Her jaw clenched. "Yes." *Go on. Ask it.*

"Why didn't you come down?"

"Because I didn't think it was safe. He's a primary suspect in a homicide case." *Because I didn't believe he was in danger.* Damn, that stung. She should have found some body armor and gone anyway.

Altin said nothing but tossed the phone up and down. "You had your GPS turned on last night, all of that?"

"I've recorded every conversation with Emir since you asked me to turn the recorder on. He calls constantly, two or three times a day, at odd hours of the night sometimes. He's not . . ." The words trailed off as a sob caught in her throat. "God, forgive me. I thought it was just another crazy ramble." She crossed herself.

"The boy who cried wolf," Altin said. "You going to be okay?"

Like there were any choices. "I'll be fine. Let me get my stuff from the car, and I'll start talking to people. Maybe we'll get lucky, and the security guards will have seen something."

The copper penny spun in the fading sunlight, knocked into the efile of Melody Doe, and rattled to the tabletop. Mac picked it up and spun it again. This was the massacre at the valley all over again. He felt it in his bones. Something was missing. If he just looked hard enough, he would find the link and avert disaster.

Apply a little gray matter, MacKenzie. If you're all jizzing smart, why can't you see the obvious?

He flicked the penny up and caught it on his hand, flipping it over to see if it landed heads or tails. *Heads.* Lincoln and Eva Perez smiled at each other from the one-cent piece. Mrs. Perez looked like she'd had her hair updated, too. He flipped the coin again. *Tails—* 2074.

He flipped the coin again. *Tails.*

Wait. . .

Mac looked at the date—2074.

Impossible. That was five years in the future. The mints might be efficient, but no one would . . .

The efiles dragged his attention. Three people, all dead before they went missing. Three cases of identical trauma. Mac dragged his hand across his mouth as he started sweating. This was madness. But that was the obvious answer, wasn't it?

Time travel.

Emir had knocked three people back in time.

Even the fracture patterns could support that. Jane Doe's ripples were nearly continuous. She'd been the closest to the blast and traveled the farthest back. Melody Doe, Melody Chimes . . . she'd never left the office. The explosion in Emir's lab killed her, and knocked her two years into the past to when Emir was first beginning his experiments. Matthew? The radial pattern was barely discernible, how far was he knocked back? A day, perhaps? A week at the most. Not enough to cause notice.

Mac flipped the coin again: 2074.

Mrs. Azalea said Sam borrowed her car. That Sam left the coin in the car . . . but Sam hadn't. She *would*, though. Some future Sam would leave the penny in the car after borrowing it from Mrs. Azalea.

The front door slammed open and shut. Mac shut the files down and looked up expectantly. Sam walked in, perfection in a straight-laced bureau uniform. Everything from her starched white shirt to her navy blue pumps were in place. His eyes rested for just a moment below her neckline, wondering if she was still wearing the lacy black bra from the first day they'd met.

She tossed her purse on the counter and went to the fridge to pour water. "Tell me you have good news."

"Rough day?"

"Twelve hours of interrogations, reviewing security video, and listening to hours of Emir's phone calls. He's dead, by the way, I don't know if you got the memo down in the morgue. Someone shot him execution style. So, please, tell me you've cured cancer or something."

"I solved the Doe case. The killer, an explanation for the bodies, an explanation for the ripple pattern of the Janes, a location for Melody Chimes, and I can even tell you where to look for the clone lab."

"Not quite cancer . . ." Sam deadpanned, but he could tell she was eager. "You've been busy."

He flipped the penny again. "I got lucky."

"A lucky penny? Cute." They looked at each other for a second, until Sam said, "Do you need an invitation? Tell me what you have!"

Mac tossed her the coin. "Read the date." He waited until her confusion turned to a furious frown.

"Is this . . . ?"

Mac nodded. "Emir's machine works, perhaps a little too well. Matthew, Melody, Jane . . . all three were bounced back in time by the machine. He said each iteration, the parallel dimensions, would produce a duplicate person. It's cloning without clone markers or test tubes. I'm willing to bet that Matthew and Melody were accidents."

Sam touched the Jane Doe efile lightly. She turned it around. "But I wasn't?"

"I don't know, yet. You're still alive."

Sam's brow furrowed. "How does Emir send me back in time if he's dead?"

"Maybe he doesn't. Jane is a *possible* you."

"A *probable* me. "That's what Emir was saying about ground states. No matter how many variables you plug in, the majority of iterations come back to one ground state. A similar path of history. All timelines become one timeline. Isn't that what he said?" Sam asked.

"Yes."

"So Jane is me in five years."

Mac took the file away from her. "No. That won't be you." He said it so firmly that Sam's head snapped up. His eyes caught hers, and he made it clear how confident he was. *I won't let it be you. Ever.* He watched as she swallowed, her eyes softening.

"Tell me what happened to Emir," he said quietly.

Composed, Sam said, "He was tied up behind the lab. Shot through the throat like Robbins. His intern called the police first thing this morning." She licked her lips. "He called me last night."

Mac frowned. "The intern?"

"Emir . . . He called, begging me to come to the lab. He said they knew it worked, and they were going to kill him. He couldn't stall them."

"They who?"

"He didn't say." Her hands clenched. "I didn't go. I could have saved him, and I didn't."

"How were you going to save him?"

Sam looked up sharply. "What?"

"You were going to rush in alone? Again? For what? They—whoever they are—would have tied you up, and you'd be dead with Emir."

Her eyes narrowed.

"Why didn't you go?" Mac asked, knowing the answer before she said it.

She looked out the window with a hundred-mile stare. "I thought it was a trap."

"You were right."

Sam crossed her arms. "It doesn't help. If I'd called Altin—"

"He wouldn't have believed it any more than you did."

"I know. Altin said the same thing when he listened to the phone call this afternoon." She sighed. "I hate failing."

"No kidding?"

Sam smiled before shaking her head. "We need to tell someone about this."

"Who?" He raised an eyebrow. "It's time travel, Sam. The first thing anyone is going to do is lock us up for a psych eval. After we've spent three months in padded rooms, we'll come out with our careers shot to find out they've classified this into a black hole. This is dangerous information."

"Are we crazy? *Should* we go in for a psych eval? I mean, time travel?"

"It fits all the evidence we have. The DNA, the patterns on the skeletons, the penny." He held up his lucky coin. "It all lines up."

She laughed. "It lines up?"

"Occam's razor—the simplest answer is usually the correct one."

"And you consider time travel simple?"

"I consider it the only explanation that fits with the evidence we have."

"Why didn't Emir know the machine worked, though? He said it only sent waves. If it could do more, why wouldn't he publish that information?"

"Even if he could only send small things back in time, think of the damage. Next year, someone sends back an advanced phone prototype. The research labs tinker with it, and we make a huge advance, but then someone sends back a phone from ten years in the future. It's too advanced, so we just re-create it without developing the science. What happens from there? When do we hit a point where we are dependent on the future?"

Sam slipped the penny from his fingers. "What happens when someone travels too far back and introduces a new virus, or a new weapon?"

He took the penny back, letting his hands linger on hers. "What happens when we send people back, and we have iterations instead of clones? If your husband's duplicate comes back in time, who are you married to?

Does the duplicate have a right to your bank account? Your health care? Your children? Genetically, aren't they his? And that doesn't even address the nonliving things—books, art, music—that could be sent back in time. Buy a famous painting, send it back, sell it as your own."

"If all iterations reach a ground state where they are the same . . ."

"Emir said this was based on wave forms. All the waves cancel each other out. Every time you split history, it creates a wave, and the wave crashes back to the ground state. Sam"—he took her hand—"anyone who has this information is going to want to use it."

"I don't!" She looked panicked. "Do you?"

Glad he was holding her hand, Mac nodded. "If I could go back and warn my platoon what would happen . . . if I could prevent the massacre from happening? I would."

"It would be a way to test the machine," she offered carefully.

"No. Luckily for me, the temptation is more of a pipe dream."

"What do you mean?"

"The machine wasn't invented then, so I couldn't go that far back. At least I think that's how it works. Because if I could, I don't know if I could stop myself. The idea of undoing all that pain . . ." He looked past her, seeing the sand and sun and blood and fire . . .

"Mac?"

She said it so softly, at first he wasn't sure he heard.

But then he swallowed, finally saying, "Anyone who knows this machine works will use it."

Sam frowned. "Someone killed Emir because the machine worked."

"Yes."

"Did they kill him to stop the machine or because he wouldn't use it the way they wanted?"

"I don't know."

"I really, really hate not having any answers."

Mac flipped the penny. "Then let's find some."

CHAPTER 26

Today you have elected stability. Today you have
elected temperance. Today you have elected peace.

~ Excerpt from President Toinen's
inaugural speech I1–2072

Friday July 5, 2069
Alabama District 3
Commonwealth of North America

When Sam came back, Mac dished up two bowls of
fiery hot chili topped with cheese, sour cream, and
chives. He slid her bowl across the table and smiled.
"Thank you for making dinner."

She smiled back and took a bite. "How was your day?"

"Ballistic. I spent the morning playing with guns in
the lab until I found a match for the injuries on Robbins and Emir. I don't have a bullet for either, but they
were killed the same way. The shot across the throat is
distinctive. From the amount of damage, I think they
were killed by the same weapon, or similar weapons.
I'm guessing same for the sake of simplicity."

"Why the throat?"

"Execution style for a traitor or liar."

"I know, but that's a regional thing. As a rule, gang members don't travel far. We don't have the right population for that kind of gang violence here. And I've been reading up," she said, "and none of the outfits in the cities near here do that. So why do it this way? Think like the killer for a minute. Whoever did this could have killed Emir and Robbins any way they wanted. Emir was tied up. It could have looked like a suicide. It could have looked like a drive-by."

"The killer wanted attention." Mac ate for a few minutes and shook his head. "No. It's more than attention, isn't it?"

Sam finished her chili. "The killer is making a statement. He wants us to know that these men were traitors. He wants us to know they were killed because of what they did. Emir was killed because he called me, because the killer thought he was a traitor."

"Our guy thinks he's safe," Mac said. "Two violent deaths, and he's flaunting it. The killer has a god complex. Thinks he's untouchable."

She tapped her spoon on the empty bowl. "I wish it weren't true."

"You'll find him. Or her," he added as an afterthought.

"Before another body turns up? I'm getting paranoid, Mac. Everybody looks like a suspect right now. I'm ready to canvass the town and ask everyone what they did last night. I have nightmares where the whole city is in on the murders. I was home alone, sleeping. Where was everyone else?"

"I was at work," he offered.

Sam gave him an odd look. "Were you? Or are you lying? I can't even tell anymore. I've started twitching at the office. If someone steps into the hall, I reach for my gun. A bird flew past my window this morning, and I jumped out of my seat." She started rubbing her neck. "I can't live like this."

"Welcome to my world." Depression had seeped in as the nightmares became less vivid. It seemed like he was hovering over the abyss, ready to fall. Sam was the only reason he crawled out of bed in the morning.

"Are you always like this?"

He could see the despair and darkness cocooning her, trapping her the way they had him. He forced a smile and lied. "After a couple of years, you trade twitchy and paranoid for sleepless nights and depression. It's not an improvement, but it's a change. More chili?" he asked as he stood.

"Yes, please."

He served up more food. "The case is going to break soon. He's killed two people, and there are CBI agents crawling all over the lab. Someone is going to find something. There are no perfect crimes. People see things. People remember things. Little things stick out in the mind."

"I hope you're right."

Sam's phone rang as she fed Hoss. She picked it up as Mac finished the last of the chili. It wasn't a number she knew. "Agent Rose, how can I help you?"

"Rose, it's Marrins. We've got a situation down at the office."

She groaned. Across the room, Mac frowned at her. "What do you need, sir?"

"Get down to the bureau building ASAP, and don't tell that idiot from the coroner's office what's happening. This is an almighty mess, and his fingerprints are all over this. You be careful." Her gaze slipped to where Mac was sitting, arms crossed and frown in place. "That won't be a problem, sir." She turned off her phone and set it down with a casual nonchalance. Panic slithered down her spine, a living terror. Where had he been last night?

Mac raised an eyebrow. "What's all that about?"

Those ballistics tests were a handy alibi if anyone accused him of handling a gun. "Hmm? Oh, Marrins is having computer issues at the office. He wants me to fix it for him." She shrugged and reached for her purse. "You want me to pick up anything while I'm in town?"

"All the stores are closed."

"Oh, right." She fiddled nervously with her keys. "Right. Well. Good night."

With a frown Mac stood up. "Why don't I come with you?"

"You don't need to," Sam slurred her words as she stepped backward.

"I'm good with computers, and we can talk about the case while we drive."

She shook her head. "No. No, that's not a good plan. You worked late last night. Get some sleep. Take a break."

His eyes narrowed.

"Stop looking at me like that! Really." She lifted her chin. "There are limits we need to respect here. We work together. That doesn't mean you need to follow me everywhere I go. Okay?"

He nodded. "Sure."

"Good. Good-bye." She practically ran from the house, worrying the entire way about what Marrins had found.

Mac slammed his fist into the door, leaving a small dent. That woman got under his skin. They weren't friends? Going on runs together in their free time, and working on the case, even eating meals together. Okay, so it wasn't a lot of free time, but it wasn't nothing. He thought they were building a rapport.

A phone buzzed behind him.

Stupid woman, she'd left her phone. He picked it up with shaking hands and saw Bri's face next to the phone number. "Hello?"

"MacKenzie? I thought I called Sam."

"She just left to run some errands."

"Without her phone?" Bri sounded concerned. "She was supposed to call me tonight. She's not mad at me, is she?"

No, apparently she's mad at me about something.

"No, there was something with work." Which made less sense the more he thought about it. "I'll have her call you when she gets back." Sam was a creature of habit, and the image of her running off to work without her work clothes on or her phone in hand didn't compute.

The phone weighed heavy in his hand. After a long moment, he trudged out to his truck. He knew where she was going. If he hurried, he could catch her at the bureau building, hand over the phone. The pills were gone, but there were other ways to flirt with oblivion. And there were at least ten liquor stores between here and morgue. By the time she got home, he could be so soused, he wouldn't be able to tell dawn from damnation.

The Alabama back highway was empty as a church during Carnival. A full moon hung low over the trees. He tried a few of his preprogrammed radio stations, but none were playing what he needed. There probably weren't songs for this anyway. No one wrote sound tracks for abandoned, unwanted people sliding into the depths of depression. A passing graveyard beckoned. He could go there to drink. Sit with the dead and drink until he joined them.

He turned into the city and pulled into the square to park in front of the bureau building. Mac took the phone and walked across the low-cut grass. A light flared upstairs in Marrins's office. Angry voices filtered down through the thick glass.

Stepping back, he craned his neck, trying to see who it was. The light went out. He looked around the parking lot, finding Sam's Alexia Virgo parked in the usual place and a red DLD Zibann he didn't recognize parked by the main entrance. The building door swung open, and two people walked out, carrying a third between them. They tossed the body in the backseat, and drove off in the Zibann.

Terror held him by the throat.

The car pulled out and slowly circled the main square. Knees trembling, Mac ran to his car. Bile filled his mouth.

Lieutenant Marcellus knelt beside him, his uniform torn and bloody. It was an ambush. All around him, the ghosts rose from his memory, watching him, condemning him...

With a white-knuckled hand, he punched redial on Sam's phone. The phone rang while he started the car, pulled into traffic, and watched the Zibann weave through the streets ahead of him.

He held the phone up and dialed Marrins's number. A warning light on the dashboard reminded him to plug his phone in for safe driving. He ignored the light and hit the accelerator.

The Zibann pulled onto County Road 10, heading west across the bridge, when the yellow phone light lit up, and the car swerved as it slowed.

"Marrins," the senior agent answered with a growl.

"Um . . ." Mac slowed too. "Um, sorry. I was trying to find Agent Rose."

"You're using her phone, *gez*."

"Right. Sorry. I was, um, trying to call her friend. Um . . ." He was sweating, stomach cramping in fear. "Sorry." He dropped the phone and watched the Zibann's phone light turn off as the car sped up. Coincidence was a nasty thing.

Pulling to the shoulder, he flicked the lights off. The road ahead was flat for miles, and it was easy to see the Zibann's lights flickering between the low scrub on either side. He pulled his own phone out and dialed Marrins's number again.

"Who the *gez* is this?" Marrins demanded as the Zibann's phone lights turned on again.

Mac hung up without answering.

He barely managed to pull the car to a stop and open the door before he threw up. Sam was in trouble.

He found her phone and dialed Altin's line. Mac knew he himself was useless, but Altin would go in.

"Detective Altin's line, this is Officer Holt," a female voice said.

"Holt? This is MacKenzie from CBI. I need Altin. Now." His stomach clenched as bile crawled up this throat.

"Detective Altin is handling an interrogation right now."

"This is more important. Agent Rose is missing."

"Good for her. Check the strip clubs. You understand, dontchya, peach?" said Holt, in the same syrupy accent as the fake Melody Chimes.

He dropped the phone to the pavement. Mac cowered in the bushes. *Marcellus yelled for everyone to get down. Hiking into dangerous territory to rescue the POW . . . he couldn't remember what arrogance drove him to believe he could do that. He'd walked in, calm and sure. He'd gotten Marcellus's team out and left the fort in flames.*

Almost home, they'd been ambushed. Everything he'd done meant nothing. He'd almost had Marcellus's team home.

Almost been safe.

Almost was failure.

Bile and nausea swamped him as his eyes watered, blurring his vision of the weeds on the roadside. A dandelion, sadly muted by the moonlight, seemed to nod in understanding.

Sam would die.

A sweet, astringent smell tickled Sam's nose. Squeezing her eyes shut, she tried to turn from the smell and scraped her face on cold leather.

"Drunken *gez*," muttered Marrins.

Marrins? She lifted her head, peering into the darkness. Green and yellow lights floated and coalesced into buttons on a car.

"We should take care of him," a woman said a little too fast to inspire confidence. "Shouldn't we? What if he tells someone?"

Sam tried to brush hair out of her face but was hampered by a pair of handcuffs.

"Him? He's a drunken pill addict who can barely string a sentence together. Harley nearly had him in the ground last week. Clueless *gez* never asked a question," Marrins said.

"What if he calls Altin again? I can't intercept every call."

Sam lifted her head, trying to get a good look at the second speaker. Moonlight reflected off a police badge. *Officer Holt.*

Marrins chuckled. "This won't take long. In a couple of hours, it will all be over. With Emir's machine, we can go back in time, back to the good ol' US of A. I won't have no black man telling me what to do, or some little Mexican whore showing me up in my own district."

The car hit a pothole, and Sam groaned. Her head was ready to burst from the pressure, and the smell wouldn't go away. All she could remember was pulling up to the bureau and seeing a light upstairs. She'd gone up to see what had upset Marrins, and now she was here.

Marrins slowed the car as it bounced across train tracks, and again. Double train tracks. There was a set on the west side of town going toward the lab. She'd been stuck watching the fast trains from Birmingham race down to the Gold Coast in a sleek white blur.

Slowly, she wiggled so she could see the door. Unlocked. She lifted her hands above her head, freezing when Holt moved. "Can we turn on the radio? I'm sick of listening to you breathe."

"Whatever."

Holt punched on the radio to a country station.

The car slowed again, preparing to take a sharp turn. Sam took a breath and opened the car door. As Marrins turned, she slid out, kicking herself free. Holt yelled. The car swerved, and the heavy door slammed on her ankle.

Screaming in pain, she pushed herself to her feet and started to run. Two steps later, her ankle collapsed under her. She hit the ground hard, rolled, and pushed back up, trying to reach the tree line. It wasn't a good idea, or even decent cover, but it was a goal, at least.

Someone tackled her from behind, and she hit the ground again, head bouncing off the asphalt. "Stupid bitch," Marrins snapped, kicking her leg.

She yelped, and curled tight.

Holt pulled her to her feet. "You never were too bright." Her cheek burned where she'd scraped it on the ground. Blood, turned black in the moonlight, dripped onto her hands. She tried to brush her hair off the injury and Holt shook her. "We ought to kill her now."

"Not here." Marrins snapped. "We still need her. Someone's got to take the blame for all those bodies Emir's machine is dumping here. I'm not having my name blackened. She'll take the rap and pay us all back."

Sam growled. She tried putting weight on her sore ankle. Pain shot up her leg, making her wince.

Marrins slapped her, then smiled as he rubbed his hand. "Do you know how long I've wanted to do that? Every day since you showed up you smiling at me with your rich-girl pearly whites, all superior and smug because Daddy bought you a job."

Sam tried to shake Holt off. "I earned my position in the bureau."

Marrins hit her again, splitting her lip. "I used to shoot wetback whores like you for target practice. You should have stayed on your back with your legs up. That's all you'll ever be good for. Get her to the car."

Holt supported her, dragging her forward as she hopped to the car. Running on a broken ankle wasn't an option, but neither was getting back in the car. She looked at the dark tree line, licking her bleeding lips.

Holt pushed her into the backseat. "Run again, and I shoot your kneecaps off."

Sam sat still the rest of the ride, hoping against all reason someone would find her.

Marrins parked near the back of the laboratory, pulling alongside a propped-open door. A Wannervan security guard stood in the rectangle of yellow light. "Get her inside and lock her down somewhere," Marrins ordered

"Got it." Holt grabbed her arm hard enough to leave bruises.

The guard nodded. "Evening, sir."

"Any problems?" Marrins asked.

"Not yet." The guard held up a gun with the safety off. "But I'm ready."

"Good man. You do your country proud." Marrins threw him an odd salute. The guard led them into a back hall Sam wasn't familiar with. Holt pulled her down a small walkway, pushing her when metal shelving made the passage too narrow for him to walk beside her.

Holt pushed her into a small room with a drain at the bottom and a flickering bare yellow bulb hanging ten feet overhead. "In." The officer pulled out a set of heavy manacles used for transporting dangerous criminals.

Sam twisted away from her with a scowl. "You realize what you're doing is illegal, don't you? Kidnapping a CBI agent? I don't care what Marrins told you, there's no place on Earth you can hide."

Holt scowled at her as she secured the manacles to the wall. "A CBI agent? When we're done, there won't be a CBI. There won't be a Commonwealth at all. We'll get back everything that was stolen from us."

"With Emir's machine?" Sam guessed as she played for time. "It doesn't work. He killed people trying to make it work. All you're doing is staging a very elaborate suicide."

"The backlash? We already know about that. It's why you get to stay, and we don't." Holt gave her a nasty smile.

"You can't even go back that far in time," Sam argued desperately. "Even if you did make it work, you can't go back any farther than when Emir originally invented the machine."

"Emir babbled all about the iterations and alternate timelines. All we have to do is go find the one where the unification doesn't happen. Marrins gets his promotion. I get the job I want. Everyone is happy, except you. You'll be dead."

Sam glowered at her captor. "No one will listen to you if you go back in time. You'll wind up locked in a mental-health ward for the clinically unstable."

"We'll have proof. Technology and papers. We will make people understand how bad this choice is."

"Technology that can be stolen from high-tech labs and reports that you could forge? You had some brains, or you wouldn't be an officer, Holt. Try using them. This is futile. Call Detective Altin. Get some help. Get Marrins some help. This is insane." Sam shut her eyes and tried to find a thread of reason. "No job is worth this."

Holt leaned in close. "You know the way you speak your mind? I always hated that about you." The door slammed behind Holt as she walked out, leaving Sam alone in the darkness.

Wiggling her leg, Sam managed to get the running shoe off her swollen foot with a gasp of pain. There was no doubt her ankle was broken. It throbbed in time with her heartbeat. Heavy footsteps sounded in the hall outside, and she hauled herself to her feet. Pain shot up her left leg. Wincing, she put her weight on her right foot and struggled to stay upright.

The door creaked open.

"Hope this is the one," Marrins said. Yellow light from the back hall of the lab turned his florid face a hideous mask. He grimaced at her. "Can't imagine what you want with her."

"No," said a cultured voice. "I don't imagine you do." Sam gasped.

Dr. Emir walked into the room . . . or someone who looked like Dr. Emir. He wore a crisp, starched white lab coat, and there were fewer lines on his face, and no glasses. "Detective Rose, I'm so pleased to have finally caught up with you."

She leaned back against the cold wall.

Marrins shrugged and stepped outside. "We'll be waiting for you, Doctor. Ten minutes, then we need to get this show on the road."

Emir gave her a chill smile as he closed the door. The bare bulb overhead swayed in the breeze from the air-conditioning vent. "Detective Rose, you cannot begin to imagine the inconvenience you have caused me by running through this iteration."

Sam cleared her throat. "It's agent, not detective."

The doctor raised an eyebrow. "Your cover has been blown, Detective. Mr. Marrins was kind enough to show me the autopsy records. The aging trick was risky. I wouldn't have done it." He chuckled. "But I appreciate the artistry that went into killing your doppelganger. Tell me, did you enjoy watching yourself die? I admit, I have no stomach for that sort of thing. Marrins proved useful there. I promised to show him how to reverse time, and he's bent over backward to please me. Shooting my other self from this iteration was too unpleasant a task to undertake myself."

"I am CBI Agent Samantha Rose, everything you say can and will be used against you in a court of law." The words came out in choked gasps.

Dr. Emir stepped closer, dark eyes boring into her as his smile turned cruel. "Really, Samantha? Aren't you done playacting? Bad enough that you had to play the part of a junior agent, but do you truly wish to stay lost in this third-rate, self-destructing time loop? You've proved your point. The machine needs better security, better controls. I will recommend you to Director Matthews." His hand fluttered like a priest granting a blessing. "The promotion is yours, Detective."

Sam drew herself to her full height. "I am Agent Sam Rose, of the Commonwealth of North America. I don't know who you are, but I will not go anywhere with you willingly."

"Childish, Detective." Emir pulled the key to her cuffs out of his jacket pocket. "Try not to be more tiresome than you already are. The agent I'm using insists that the Samantha Rose from this iteration is dead, so we're no longer in danger of collapsing into this history. All will be well. Shall we go home?"

She held her breath as he leaned in. The handcuffs fell off with an echoing click. "I saw you dead," she said

"The Emir of this iteration, yes, of course. He had to be removed to destabilize this iteration. The doctor, the soldier, the paladin—all the local einselected nodes near the machine have been deactivated. Ideally, the other nodes would be closer, and we could deactivate them as well, but I feel confident that we have reduced this iteration to yet another bad dream. Horrid little place, isn't it? Come along."

Obviously, the drugs Marrins used to incapacitate her hadn't worn off. That explained the fuzzy feeling in her head, the somewhat muffled sound, and the dead doctor politely offering her his shoulder so she could hobble down the corridor. It was like having her wisdom teeth removed all over again. Any moment now, imps and goblins would jump out of the walls to play in fairyland until the sedatives wore off. What a shame the drugs didn't do anything for her throbbing ankle.

Emir unlocked a side door that opened to his office. Police tape still wrapped around his desk. "Give me a moment. Let me collect the dial." He opened the bottom drawer and pulled out the original blue dial for his machine. "A little present for my other self. It was cruel, I know, but I couldn't resist giving him a chance to escape. It's not in my nature to run, though. Abandoning my work is unthinkable in any iteration."

"The other iteration. He comes to my lab. He is stealing my work. Changing my formulas. He sneaks in here when I'm not looking. Not he, me!" Emir's lunatic rants echoed through her mind.

Another iteration.

A working machine.

A way to travel through time.

What would Marrins . . . the nationhood vote? Marrins wanted to go back and prevent the Common-wealth from forming, that's what Holt was going on about. Marrins would remain an FBI agent, with guaranteed promotions every few years.

He's willing to destroy this world to change jobs.

"Quickly now," Emir said. "That fat native who calls himself an agent will come poking along any moment now. That is one pseudohuman being I will not regret losing in any iteration."

He punched in a series of numbers.

"Philistine, the fool thought he could only travel back in time. Marrins is a complete cretin." The machine trembled. A deep purple light shot out of the front, spinning like a vortex. As the rotation speed increased, the color melted from purple to blue to a vibrant white. "Time to go." Emir grabbed her arm as the machine shook sideways.

Burning cold embraced her, stealing her breath, then she was falling onto a flat gray surface. Sam gulped down air and looked around. *Damn. Mother Mary, forgive me. Saint Samantha, Saint Jude, help. I am in so much trouble.*

Against all reason, her ears buzzed. It would have been nice if drugs could explain this rather than the more logical conclusion that she had a minor concussion and had just stepped through time.

No one took notice of her as Emir sauntered toward a computer screen, happily regaling his people with tales from his latest trip. Names appeared on the screen in front as the lights dimmed: DR.—Emir, PALADIN—Rose, SOLDIER—MacKenzie . . .

"Who are you?" a querulous but all-too-familiar voice demanded.

Sam pivoted and looked into her own face. Different, yes, but still recognizable, even with an ugly bob of black hair framing sharply angled cheekbones. Whenever *here* was, they apparently had a famine going on. Healthy people had more flesh on their bones. Beside her, Emir's machine beeped as the vortex slowed, and the white light gradually dulled to a dark blue.

"Rose?" Emir stepped onto the platform and stared at them in horror. "What is the meaning of this?"

"It means you missed," the other woman said. "You brought one of their nodes home with you." She drew a weapon in one fluid motion.

Sam threw her head forward, slamming her face into her doppelganger's. She staggered and fell to the ground, the gun dropping to Sam's feet.

Emir reached out as Sam fell. She rebounded, using all her weight to throw Emir back as she stood with the new gun. His eyes rolled back as he flailed in pain. The other-Sam scrambled to her feet, grabbed at her shoulder, and pulled her away. The strange gun dropped from her hand. Sam rolled into the vortex as it chimed again.

This time the cold was a heat that seared her to her bones. *Almighty and merciful—*

The floor slammed into her. Or she slammed into the floor. Sam wasn't sure—she thought she'd been holding still. Gasping for breath, she lay on the floor, looking at the line of grungy yellow tape. She was back in Emir's lab, safe inside his tidily taped circle . . .

Safe beside a machine that let killers wander between worlds.

And away from two people who wanted her dead but closer to two others who wanted her dead. Good job, Sam.

Lights flickered, and someone shouted.

Shaking, she scrambled to her feet, limping toward the door as fast she could move. No one was in the hall outside. She limped down the long hallway to the laboratory atrium. Empty. Marrins's muffled voice came from the rear of the building, where he had dragged her inside; shadows moved in Emir's lab, but the atrium was dark.

She ground her teeth, took a deep breath, and ran for the darkness.

Pain like cold fire shot up her leg. Hot tears burned the cut on her cheek where she'd skidded on the gravel earlier, but she made it, collapsing in a shaking heap next to the empty security guard's desk as lights swept the atrium.

A muted shout came from the depths of the lab. Sam pushed the chair away and pulled herself into the space under the paneled desk. Silently, she rolled the chair back into position.

Heavy footsteps ran down the hall with a confusion of shouts. A gun fired. The lights turned on.

Sam hugged her knees to her chest.

"What's going on?" asked the security guard who'd greeted them at the back entrance, close but not near the desk.

"Someone drove up to the lab," said Holt, her voice tight with anger.

Sam smiled in her dark hidey-hole. Backup had arrived. She took a quiet breath and debated getting out to cover the back entrance so no one could escape. Her ankle throbbed, and she decided it probably wasn't an option.

Leaning her head back against the cool wood of the desk, she waited. The front doors squeaked as they opened. Sam leaned forward, trying to peek through the crack between the desk panel and the floor to see what was happening.

"Get him inside," Marrins growled.

Sam jerked back upright, her hand hit something that rolled with a clatter.

"What's he doing here?" Holt asked.

"What are *you* doing here?" an angry voice demanded. It was familiar, but Sam couldn't put it with a face. "I work here."

"Work's over for the day," Marrins said. "You should've stayed home."

Sam's fingers brushed the floor, searching for the object that had rolled. She touched something cylindrical, smooth, heavy, and slightly thicker than an umbrella handle. Heavy was good. Her fingers curled around the potential weapon as the group beyond the desk moved.

"Get inside," Marrins ordered. "We'll figure this out."

The chair rolled away with a squeak, but no one looked.

Sam gazed at the object in her hand. It was a security guard's truncheon, the kind that extended when you pushed a button, with an Auburn sticker. Melody's truncheon, undoubtedly dropped the evening Emir's machine killed her, and rolled where no one thought to look. Her grip tightened around the handle. It wouldn't be useful against Marrins's gun, but it was better than nothing.

"Holt," Marrins said, "come with me while I figure out where the doc went."

"You, Krenstien!" Marrins barked at the security guard. "Watch this guy. You think you can do that?" Sam heard Marrins shuffle out, followed by Holt. The lights flickered.

"Stop!" Marrins shouted, his voice had an edge of panic.

The lights went out, and the security lighting turned on, a dull green glow. She peeked around the edge of the desk as Krenstien charged down the hall after Marrins. On the other side of the doorway Henry Troom sat tied to the rolling chair with a length of twine

The weight of the guard's baton steadied her. She crawled out from under the desk, checked around the hall corner, and hurried as best she could to Henry. "I'm going to get you out," Sam whispered as she knelt beside him, left leg stretched out so she didn't put weight on her broken ankle. He looked dazed, pupils dilated. The gun she'd heard must have been Marrins's bureau-issue splat gun with drugs.

Sam patted his pockets and found his keys. She used them to loosen the twine around his wrists. "Let's go."

Henry didn't move fast, but neither did she. A door slammed down the long hall. There was an indistinct shout, then Holt yelled, "Where did he go?"

Sam pushed Henry out the door. A red car was pulled up to the front of the lab. Henry stumbled toward it of his own volition and she followed, sliding into the driver's seat.

Behind her, someone cursed. Water gurgled as the old engine warmed up.

"Marrins!" Holt shouted, her voice echoing in the atrium and spilling out into the darkness.

Sam tried the ignition again. The engine turned, and the car sputtered to life. She stepped on the accelerator and the little car rolled forward with a clink. Henry coughed, choked, and opened his door to throw up.

"No, stop!" Sam grabbed his shoulder and pulled him backward as a shot rang out. Metal hit the plastic door of the car, and she smelled ozone. "Get in." Sam reached across Henry to slam the door shut. She barely sat up in time to twist the steering wheel and avoid a tree. They escaped the parking lot, and Sam gunned the asthmatic engine on the only road back to the main highway.

Marrins fired two more shots, missing her and hitting the road like flint strikes with little bursts of sparks.

His third shot hit home.

The car spun out of control as the tire exploded. She steered into the swerve as best she could, wrestling with the wheel. Her seat belt dug into her throat as the velocity threw her forward. She lost control, and all she saw were the air bags popping into her face as the car hit a tree.

CHAPTER 27

We are reborn moment by moment. The darkness awakens within us an awareness of truth. In that instant of greatest fear, we realize who we truly are.

~ Excerpt from *The Heart of Fear*
by Liedjie Slaan I1–2071

Saturday July 6, 2069
Alabama District 3
Commonwealth of North America

A full moon shone on Mac with all the gentleness of a searchlight. The breeze that stirred the grass was no longer the lightly perfumed breath of spring but the hot, bone-dry promise of summer. His mind was playing tricks. He kept waiting for screams, looking around for the bodies.

An owl was silhouetted against the moon for a moment as it silently drifted overhead. They had owls in Idaho. One summer, the forestry service had paid for proof of owls in the area, and he'd spent every night sitting outside with his dad's old camera. He'd been thirteen.

Mac sat up, shaking his head and trying to remember the last time he'd thought of the summer of owls. Years, at the very least. Sam made his thoughts turn to home more often. He caught himself comparing her food to his mom's, and picturing his mother and Sam trying to share the kitchen as they cooked a holiday meal.

Sam . . .

He looked across the bridge and the road that led to N-V Nova Labs. Occam's razor was dangerous, here. Marrins could have gone anywhere. But the lab was the center of everything, Mac was sure of it. All the bodies could be tied to the lab. Mac had followed the senior agent down this road, it only made sense Marrins would be there. Which meant Sam would be there.

And that meant he needed to be there.

Soon. Not yet.

With a sigh, he looked up at the cold moon. Marrins had a gun, Mac had seen it around the office more than once, and Robbins and Emir hadn't shot themselves. If he wanted to get Sam back, he needed weapons.

The weight of a phantom gun filled his hand. He flinched at the memory of the sound of gunfire. Ghosts whispered in his ears, shouting orders, telling him to get down, take cover. Lieutenant Marcellus stood in front of him, looking to him for directions.

Mac turned away, looked at the grass, and waited for the phantoms to recede into the dark recesses of his mind. One more mission. Then he would join the dead.

The bureau building was dark when he parked beside Sam's car in the otherwise-empty lot. He pulled on the door—locked. With a grunt, he kicked the glass door in and took the stairs two at a time as the alarms blared. Red lights blinked in every corner.

A monotone voice announced, "You have unlawfully entered a secured government building. Please wait for the police to arrive."

"Not likely," Mac muttered. Where did Marrins keep the guns? There was something about protocols and safeties. He rubbed his aching head and tried to remember. There was an old gun cabinet in Marrins's office. They kept the splat bullets there. Marrins's door splintered under his weight. The safe was open and empty. The old American flag had been torn down to expose a hidden wall safe with a discarded box of Starfire ammunition. Marrins had more than his bureau-issued weapon.

Mac looked out the window, a line of police cars screamed toward the bureau from the far end of town. Well, at least Altin was coming. But more likely they'd arrest him for disorderly conduct than believe him.

Too bad.

He ran down the stairs and pulled out of the parking lot before the cops arrived. They'd have fun running around. Maybe call Marrins and ask for help. That would be an interesting conversation.

Giving the truck's steering wheel a savage twist, he turned into the bank parking lot. Bankers' hours once meant banks closed at five, a ridiculous time considering the majority of their clients worked until six. Now, at least one bank in town ran a twenty-four-hour office. His did.

The bank clerk behind the front desk was a neatly scrubbed young man with a green pin-striped suit and brown bow tie. "Can I help you, sir?"

"Safety deposit box 203, I need to get into it. Tonight."

To his credit, the bank clerk only blinked once. "Of course, sir." He pulled out a black panel. "If you'll just give me a palm scan for confirmation, and then sign here, sir. And here. And, a reason for the rapid withdrawal, sir? I need something for our records."

"I'm going to kill someone."

The clerk hesitated. "I think I might need the manager's approval before I could use that reason, sir. Our insurance frowns on murder."

Mac tried a friendly smile, but from the way the clerk tripped backward, he guessed it didn't work. "I'm proposing to a girl tonight. Her present's in there."

"A much better reason, if I may say so. Go right on in, sir."

The doors weren't halfway open before Mac pushed his way in and typed in the code. Box was a misnomer: it was a small storage locker, just large enough to hold an old duffel bag and a few very important mementos.

He pulled out the pieces to the HK416 Marcellus had dropped in Afghanistan. Then the pieces to his own gun. The pistol he'd worn as a sidearm. And last, and certainly least, the bureau-issued splat gun he hated. Like Miss Azalea, if he shot someone, it wasn't going to be so he could have a nice chat with them later.

After a quick check to make sure there was enough ammunition, he stuffed everything back in the bag and pulled the duffel out.

The clerk stood in the doorway watching, slack-jawed.

"Is there a problem?" Mac asked.

"Uh . . ." The clerk shook his head.

"It's for a girl. She likes this sort of thing."

"Uh-huh. Um . . . congratulations?" the clerk said in a shaky voice.

As Mac walked out, he watched the clerk reach for the phone in the window's reflection. He might not get to Sam on time, but the police would have to be deaf and dumb to miss the trail he was leaving.

He got as far as the car before the shaking started. The memory of Alina Marcellus sat beside him. "Will you bring my baby home?"

"Yes. This time I will," he whispered.

Sirens sounded in the distance. He put the truck into drive and headed for the lab.

His ghosts came along for the ride.

Red-hot, an all-enveloping with-you-to-death sort of pain that Sam never imagined possible burned her leg. She went to rub her eyes, but metal handcuffs hampered her movement.

Marrins stood by Dr. Emir's machine wearing a black shirt that read AMERICAN HERO in blood-red letters. Harley was standing next to him in a matching shirt. Krenstien limped in, and there was Holt . . . Sam craned her neck trying to get a head count as her headache receded. One of the lab people, she couldn't remember his name, and three other security guards. That made eight.

Bureau training hadn't included classes on how to rescue yourself—an oversight, in retrospect. Even the survival and evasion tactics weekend course she'd taken had assumed that an agent would never be dumb enough to get caught.

And no one had ever considered a situation where an agent was being held captive by other agents.

Holt walked over to Marrins to whisper something.

Marrins scowled and turned to Sam. "Still alive? What does it take to kill you?"

"What did you expect me to do?" she asked, as he stalked over.

His heavy hand smacked her cheek. "What lazy Mexican wetbacks always do, hold still and squeal."

"I'm Spanish, you bloody idiot."

He smacked her, harder this time. *Racial pride not a key to self-preservation when captured: check.* Her whole head thrummed. "You"—he pointed an accusatory finger at Krenstien—"keep her in line."

"Yes, sir." Krenstien glared at her and sat out of reach. Sam turned to study the paint on the wall.

Marrins stomped his foot. "I know what the man said, Harley! I'm old, not senile. You, intern, what's your name? Get over here!" She turned to see Henry dragged toward the machine by a grim-faced Holt. "What's your name?" the senior agent demanded again.

"Troom," the student whispered.

Marrins grunted. "What's wrong with the machine?"

Troom looked down at the abomination with loathing. "Nothing. It's just a prototype. Dr. Emir never made it do anything more than break teacups."

"It can do more," Marrins shouted. "We've all seen the proof! I've got a stack of corpses that prove this machine can move people around in time. It can save us."

Sam shivered. One of those corpses was hers, some future her, maybe even the ugly version with a gun.

"No," Troom argued. "It doesn't. You can't . . ." He sighed and rubbed his head. "Dr. Emir is dead. So is his machine."

Marrins said, "We need the one timeline that steers all the others so we can keep the United States from selling herself and letting filth in. Emir said there were iterations, variations, something like that. The machine can make the United States come back." He scowled in Sam's direction. "Dr. Emir promised his machine could do that. He said he knew how to make everything fall in place." An edge of desperation bit into Marrins's words.

"I can't make that happen!" Troom said, with a shrug. In his drugged state, he seemed indifferent to the danger he was in. "The machine doesn't work like that. If it did, I'd go back and save Dr. Emir."

"He's useless," Marrins said in disgust. He jerked his head toward the corner Sam was in, and Holt threw Henry hard into the floor by her.

Sam was about to talk to the intern when she saw the lights flicker off again as the machine whined to life. The lights were flickering because the machine must be drawing more power than anyone expected. The night Melody Chimes had died, the lights had gone out entirely because of the machine. She laughed.

"Shut up." Marrins shouted. "Somebody shut her up."

"Emir lied," Sam said. "And then he left you." Laughing hurt, but she laughed anyway. "He lied, and he left you here with a mess. You're a murderer, Marrins, and you can't get away."

"SHUT UP!" Marrins roared.

He stalked over to Sam and pulled out a gun. Not the standard-issue bureau weapon with purple liquid bullets that knocked a victim out, but the old-fashioned lead-bullet kind. "Go ahead. Keep talking," he said. "I'll leave your brains spread all over the floor."

Sam just glared, but it must have satisfied Marrins since he turned back to look at the machine. Lying on the floor, she counted ceiling tiles until Krenstien's attention drifted, and he moved toward the machine. Marrins seemed to think that beating the machine would make it work, but she doubted it. Keeping one eye on her ex-boss, she whispered to Troom, "Are you okay?"

Troom cleared his throat and snuffled.

She risked a glance. His eyes were puffy. "Are you hurt?"

He shook his head.

"Do you think you can run?" she whispered.

"He'll shoot me!" Troom hissed, a little too loud. Krenstien scowled over his shoulder, and Sam went back to counting ceiling tiles.

When Krenstien turned away, Sam said, "I can distract them, but if I do, you need to run. Call someone."

"They turned on the priority security system. No phone reception. No live-feed camera going off-site.

We're only supposed to use it during certain tests." Troom sniffled again. "None of the guards that like me are here. I think . . . I think they're dead."

So he's not going to be much help. Sam cursed under her breath. *I'm an idiot.* Marrins had told her who the killer was—not tonight, but days ago. He'd told her exactly what the shot across the throat meant and why. He'd started out as a police officer in Texas working violent crimes. The casework was in his public record, and she'd ignored it because he was a bureau agent.

Holt turned, pacing in their direction. Sam lay still and stared ahead blankly as Holt passed by, black shoes reflecting the overhead lights. She moved away, and Sam stretched to look at the machine. *No time to worry about missed opportunities—have to take advantage of this one. And if this twerp won't make a break for it, then he might still be able to help.*

"How do I break it?" she asked Troom.

"Break it?" he asked in anguish. "Why?"

She turned to glare at him. "Do you want to live?"

"They'll kill you."

"Some things are worth dying for." Some deaths were better than others, and she'd rather go out with a bullet to her throat than slowly tortured to death in whatever parallel timeline Marrins might drag her to. Troom was silent as Krenstien made another circuit. In the center of the room, Marrins and Harley seemed to reach some agreement, and the lab lights dimmed as the machine powered up again.

"Besides—they'll probably kill us anyway. Might as well *try* living." Sam looked at Troom, his eyes wild. "How do I break it?"

"Y-you could smash it, or remove the core. Or . . . or push it into the anomaly." He squeezed his eyes shut as tears appeared. "Smash it. Break the power coil off, and it will shut down. We had to bolt the casing to the floor because the linkages were so fragile. The slightest bump means you need to recalibrate. A solid hit would probably destroy it beyond repair."

She took a deep breath. "Okay." Even without a broken ankle, it wasn't a perfect scenario. Marrins had lead bullets, Holt probably had her gun, and goodness only knew what everyone else was carrying. She patted her pocket and pulled out the small truncheon. She felt the Auburn University sticker on the handle. It was fitting, really: Melody Chimes had lost everything, and now part of her would be there for the final payback.

I hope.

Sam nudged Henry Troom. "When I move, crawl for the door, get outside, and run. Don't stop for anything. Call Detective Altin. Tell him everything."

"He won't believe me."

"I know." She sighed. "But you have to try, you know?" He nodded. "Good. Have . . . have someone tell my parents I was doing my job. They'll understand. And tell MacKenzie it wasn't his fault. He couldn't have done anything. Tell him to take my dog." Poor Mac. She wished she had the time to say good-bye. At least she hadn't taken him to meet Marrins and an unwelcome end.

The machine's whining grew louder. Krenstien cut his circuit short and moved into the safety zone marked by yellow tape. Sam couldn't help but notice that she and Troom were both lying in the death zone, the riptide of time was just waiting to suck them down and smash them to brittle bits.

Fun.

Nodding to Troom, she army-crawled forward. Sam stopped and pushed herself to a crouch when Marrins started hitting buttons. Her ankle burned. Her arm ached. *It's just for a moment,* she promised herself. She glanced back. Henry was crouched near the door, watching with a terrified expression. She nodded, and he opened the door. As light from the hall stabbed the dark lab, she erupted into motion, lifting the baton and hurling it at the machine like a spear.

It missed, bouncing off Marrins's arm instead, but she was already twisting away. He yelled out, drawing his sidearm. Sam ducked, rolling forward in the confusion of light and darkness, and came up with the truncheon in her hand again, slamming it into the machine as someone tried to pull her away.

The machine fizzled, blue-green light washed in kaleidoscope ripples around the room and fell dark.

"Sam! Down!"

She hit the floor before she realized what was going on. Lights were turning on as the machine died. There was a gunshot. She recoiled on involuntary reflex, waiting for the burn.

It didn't come.

Agent Marrins dropped beside her, a stunned expression on his face.

Blood dripped on the tile floor as another gunshot sounded. She flinched, shutting her eyes. There was a burst of noise, more gunshots, the sound of bodies dropping, then an eerie silence.

Someone touched her leg, and she screamed.

The light flickered off as the machine behind her coughed a death rattle. There was pain, and the soft sound of liquid hitting the tile. Sam forced herself to open her eyes and turn. Light from the hallway silhouetted a bulky figure in exo-armor kneeling beside her. "Captain United, I presume?" she joked with a tear-filled laugh.

"Close, but not quite," the man said, his voice calm, deep, and familiar.

"Mac?" Tears stung her ripped cheek.

Strong hands helped her sit up. "Captain United was busy, beautiful. Will a US Army Ranger do?" She started crying in relief. He slung his gun over his back. "How bad are you hurt?"

"Facial contusions and some bruises. I might have a concussion, I was feeling pretty light-headed for a bit. Oh, and my ankle is definitely broken."

"The left one?" Mac guessed as he unrolled something from his pack.

"How did you know?"

"Jane's autopsy. She had a fractured left ankle that had healed over." Tenderly, he lifted her leg as she winced. "Consider me your doctor for the evening." She gasped as his warm fingers probed gentle flesh. "Broken. Can you hold a flashlight?" he asked as he pulled one out of his bag.

"Sure." She eased back against the bulk of the dead machine. It was surprisingly cold for something that had sucked up so much energy.

Mac flicked the flashlight on, illuminating a smile. "Do you have that black-lace bra on, because if you do, I have this fantasy about—"

She kicked him with her good foot.

"What? I've always wanted to rescue a girl wearing a black-lace bra. Can't a man dream?"

"Unlock me, MacKenzie."

He dangled a set of keys in front of her. "Standard bureau-issue-cuff master key. I picked it up earlier this evening."

"When?" She twisted her head to watch him unlock her arm.

Mac grimaced. "On my second trip to the office. Did you know the bureau armory doesn't have any serious bullets? All we have are those rubber ones. I miss the States, it was easier to find weapons there."

She glanced sideways, where the bulk of Agent Marrins lay still, and shuddered. *He missed the States, too . . .* "It looks like you found something effective."

"Hmmm," Mac said noncommittally as he finished wrapping her ankle. "Yeah. I'm not sure if any of the toys I brought are legal." He moved around her and unlocked the cuffs.

She rubbed her wrists. "Thank you for coming for me. I know . . ." She took a ragged breath. Her heart was racing, and the tears were coming back. "How'd you even find me?"

"Bri called. *Your* phone. I was coming to give it to you and saw Marrins dragging you to his car."

"My hero. Thank goodness you have that combat training . . ." Her face went ashen. "Oh, Mac, I'm so sorry . . ."

A weary smile spread across his face as he slid her other shoe off. "It's okay. I almost didn't come. I thought I couldn't."

"But you did."

"Tomorrow, I'll have nightmares about not getting here in time. When I start screaming, you can come tell me everything is fine."

"Even in my pajamas?"

He chuckled. "I'd love that." Strong arms scooped her up. He was warm, solid, comforting, Sam rested her head on his chest and took comfort from the quiet beat of his heart. "Stay just like that, beautiful." Cool air from the hall brushed over her skin, and she shivered. "Keep your eyes shut," Mac said. "You don't want to see this."

She squirmed, wanting to see what he wanted to hide. A hand covered her eyes. "Don't look. You don't need to see this," he repeated. "Trust me."

I do.

He didn't move his hand until the door clanged shut behind them. Police sirens screamed in the distance. "There's the cavalry."

"How are you going to explain this?" Sam asked.

Mac's truck beeped as he unlocked it. "What do I need to explain? I'm a bureau agent who put down a group of home-grown terrorists and exposed a weakness in the local police force."

"With no orders?"

"The senior agent for the district was incapacitated. As the only other level four in the district, I made a command decision."

Sam gasped, tilting her head back to look up at him. "You're serious? You outrank me?"

"Probably not for long." Mac chuckled. "If they don't promote you after tonight, I'll be surprised."

"You outrank me! Why didn't you ever say so?" She slapped his arm in mock outrage.

"I'm a doctor, too, and you never use that title," he pointed out, as police cars flooded the parking lot.

"You were a medic," Sam said.

He grinned. "Before I went to the army med school. I'm not a brain surgeon, but I'm a pretty good for a field surgeon."

She put her head back down. "I like a man who's full of surprises." Mac sat in the car, holding her tight until the EMTs took her away.

In the ambulance, she missed the feel of his arms around her.

CHAPTER 28

One person can change the world. One person can tip the favor of balance against us. If this is so, then I say: Kill that person. No single person should have that kind of power.

~ Colonel Aina—Commandant of the Ministry of Defense War Colleges I1- 2072

Monday July 8, 2069
Alabama District 3
Commonwealth of North America

Agent Benjamin Anan stood by Sam's hospital bed, frowning. "Listen, Rose, I'm not trying to belittle you. I know you've been through a traumatic experience, and I am trying to help you. Now, once more, who unlocked the handcuffs and helped you get out of the building?" The setting sun glinted off his gold pen as he waited for answers.

"Once again, I repeat, Dr. Emir unlocked the hand-cuffs the first time."

"The Dr. Emir who died last week?"

"No, the Dr. Emir who killed that Emir last week."

"His twin?"

Sam rolled her eyes. They'd been stuck on the same question since Anan showed up with breakfast, and even she was beginning to question what she'd seen.

"Come on, throw me a bone. I'm on your side."

"Maybe it was his clone," Sam finally said.

Anan snapped his notebook shut. "Thank you! That, at least, is something I can use in court. Time machines? Agents who are also serial killers? Do you know what a mess this is? And I've got to go to court to cover all of this as the bureau's representative down here." He looked longingly at the chair beside her bed.

"I was there for all of it, and if you'd sign the release paperwork, I'd handle this in court."

"You know that can't happen. If you represented the bureau's case, it would become a game of he said she said. It's already embarrassing enough."

"I haven't done anything wrong."

A nurse pushed aside the curtain. To Sam's surprise, Lacey Altin scowled back at the two of them. "Officer, visiting hours were over ten minutes ago."

"My apologies, Nurse, I just have a few more questions."

"So does her doctor," Lacey said, pushing the curtain aside and wheeling in a tray with a cocktail of drugs. "Now you either get on out of here, or I'll put a shot of this painkiller in your butt and admit you for a concussion when you hit your head on the ground."

Sam swallowed a giggle.

"Get!" Lacey Altin drew herself up to her full Valkyrian height and pointed at the door, chin trembling with fierce pride.

Anan held his hands up in surrender. "I'm going. Sorry. I didn't realize things were that strict around here. Rose?" He slapped the door lintel. "If you think of anything, give me a call."

"Bless his heart," Lacey muttered. "How you doing?"

Sam shrugged. "I ache everywhere. Nothing makes sense. I want to go home, but I think I'm going to go to jail." Tears welled up in her eyes.

"Do you think you can handle one more visitor?"

"Yeah. I won't promise I'll answer their questions, but they can come in."

On cue, Detective Altin turned the corner holding a picnic basket. "Hey, Rose." The distinct aroma of Miss Azalea's fried chicken filled the room.

"Hi." Her stomach grumbled. If he wasn't planning on sharing that chicken, he was going to wind up in the bed next door with a broken arm.

Altin kissed his wife on the cheek. "Thank you, honey."

"Ten minutes," Lacey warned, "and then you have to be out of here."

Sam motioned to the empty chair beside her. "Have a seat. Are you allowed to tell me anything?"

"Officially? No. That's why I'm here after hours." He propped the basket on his knee. "I swung by your place, had a quiet chat with your ME, and brought you some real food. Your landlady threatened to report police abuse if I didn't see you were fed."

Sam clapped her hands. "I'll tell you everything, just feed me! Tofu burgers do not live up to the hype."

With a chuckle, Altin set the basket on her bedside table. "All right, I think I got most of the story from MacKenzie. The machine you broke killed Melody. Marrins killed Robbins and Emir. It took a bit of doing, but we found the bullets, and they match the ones from the gun he had on him at the lab." He sighed. "I was going to tell you on Monday. I've got the warrant and everything. I think Robbins was going to back out, tell someone what happened, and Marrins had a golden opportunity to silence Robbins and get you off the case." He leaned back in his chair shaking his head.

"Marrins arranged the interview in D.C., so he could dump the body at my house?" She couldn't keep the disbelief out of her voice.

"I'm sorry, Sam. I really am. I should have let you know as soon as I suspected anything. After Emir's death, the phone call you had . . . things started to click. I knew someone was trying to get you, but I didn't figure Marrins would ever go that far. I feel guilty as hell."

Lacey cleared her throat. After a stern warning look for her husband, she went back to silently counting out Sam's pain pills.

Sam shrugged. "You told me it could be someone in the bureau. You warned me, and I didn't want to believe you. Even if you had warned me about Marrins, I wouldn't have believed you. There was no way I would have believed a bureau agent was involved."

Altin crossed his arms with a frown.

It wasn't worth arguing over. "When's the trial start?" Sam opened the basket and pulled out a piece of greasy chicken. Heaven. Artery-clogging, horrible-for-your-hips heaven.

"Friday. Closed court. No jury. Since everyone involved was a government employee, they've decided to do a judges' panel. I don't think five of them is enough, but I'm old-fashioned like that. And they couldn't find any other judges with the security clearance to see all the information. I don't have clearance, but I will by Thursday."

Sam was confused. "Mordicai Robbins wasn't a government employee: he was a civilian contractor. So was Melody."

"The murder cases won't go to court. The guilty party is dead, case closed, justice done."

There was a long silence. She knew what the next question had to be, the tension was gnawing at her, but still . . ." What about me? Do you know what's happening to me?"

"Psych testing, physical therapy, and weekly mental-health meetings is my guess. I'm not entirely sure what Agent Anan is going to recommend. Except for the psych eval—I saw the paperwork on that. Kinkarri is a good doctor. You'll like her."

"What about Mac?"

"What about him?"

"Is he in trouble?"

Altin shook his head. "The bureau's using him as the example of a national hero, swooping in to save the day at the last possible moment. No mention of the PD assist. We never get credit."

"And neither do I? What the hell? I had things under control!" Sam protested. "Mostly." *Except for the fact I was probably about to be executed after I broke the machine.* "I was trying at least. Why am I the victim?"

"You don't want the answer to that," Altin said.

"Of course she doesn't," Lacey cut in sarcastically. "That's why she was asking. Here, honey, take these. That's a good girl." She patted Sam on the back as she swallowed the pills with a glass of lukewarm water.

Altin patted her good knee. "No one likes a self-rescuing damsel in distress, but you'll survive. No one gets to the top of their field without getting some bad press."

"Top of my field? Altin, all I want at the end of the trial is to still have a job!" Sam collapsed back onto her pillows.

CHAPTER 29

The Paladin: she whose faith in humanity has the
power to save humanity from itself.

~ **Writings of The Student 13–2073**

Tuesday August 6, 2069
Alabama District 3
Commonwealth of North America

"**C**an you really call her a federal agent?" a bubbly
redhead asked her television cohost. "I mean, if she's a
fully trained agent, I'm a lawn chair!" The studio audi-
ence laughed on cue as Sam watched, detached from
her public humiliation.

"You should turn that off," Bri said over the crowd's
roar of approval. "The lot of them are going to rot in
prison for the next forty years, that's all you need to
know. It doesn't matter what anyone else thinks. It's
over, and you're free and moving on with your career."

Sam hit the button on the hotel remote and stood
up. "There was nothing else on." She picked up the
sweatshirt Brileigh had dropped off the first week.

The hospital stay had been the worst weeks of her life. Therapy, isolation for psychological evaluation that she was certain she'd only passed by lying, and more interviews with various bureau officials who were all certain she'd done something wrong. In between, there were phone calls from her parents. Well, her mother at any rate. Her father's therapist had called to say he was in an emotionally delicate place right now, and something as drama-filled as this wasn't what he needed.

If only her mother had been in a similar frame of mind. Somehow, through everything, her mother had latched on to the idea that she was quitting. When news of Sam's several failed escape attempts became a matter of public record, her mother started pushing her to resign. She was tarnishing her family name, ruining the reputation of the CBI, the only decent thing to do was to admit the whole law-enforcement idea was a horrible fit for her and step away. Her mother even offered her a flat in Madrid, all expenses paid. But Sam couldn't bring Hoss. More importantly, she didn't want to quit.

Her mother had seemed more swayed by her loyalty to the dog than Sam's desire to stay with the CBI, but she'd still been disappointed.

"Do you want to pick up dinner on the way home? Jake said he didn't mind if we stayed out late. Celebrate Wednesday Lady's Night a little early since we're both on our feet again."

Bri had been a lifesaver. And between her visits, Lacey Altin had stopped by to bring Sam updates the bureau wasn't willing to let her have. No one had been willing to let her testify for the public trial—she'd given her version of events to the judges in private—and to the world at large, she was nothing more than a junior agent who had become a victim.

The media feeding frenzy left her feeling isolated, and more than a little worthless. Even Marrins had more support. He'd been laid to rest surrounded by crowds of protestors, only some of them there to decry his crimes. There was no family left to bury him, but he'd found like-minded souls in death.

"Sam?" Bri touched her elbow. "Are you okay?"

"I'm fine. Just . . . a little tired. I didn't sleep well last night." It was hard to sleep when all she did was relive the nightmare again, and again, and again. Repeatedly during the night, she woke up in cold sweats with a throbbing headache where an imaginary bullet had hit her. Marrins had never pulled his trigger, but her psyche didn't seem to accept that fact.

The only good thing to come out of the debacle was that Emir's machine was broken. No one was going to go back in time to prevent North America from unifying. No more bodies would be showing up from Emir's other iterations. With luck, and some heavy-duty sleeping pills, she'd forget about the other-Sam she'd seen and get back to normal.

"Let's go," Bri said, picking up Sam's suitcase. "We'll pick up some steaks and cheesecake at the Fonteyn on our way home. It's never crowded on a weeknight."

"Cheesecake is good." Sam looked around the

room. "Home . . . home is good." She picked up a long purple envelope from the bureau that lay on the table. Tears welled up in her eyes. Home sounded empty. "I miss Hoss," she said through a forced smile.

"MacKenzie will be there, too," Bri promised as she held the door open.

"Maybe," Sam said. Her ankle ached as she limped forward. "He said he was looking into finding a new place." *It doesn't matter,* she promised herself. The envelope from the bureau rough in her hand. *It doesn't matter.*

Mac looked up as the door swung open, bringing the sound of crickets and the scent of Sam's perfume. He lowered his bowl to the table, so he could watch her. A white purse hung off her arm, matching her white skirt and jacket. "You're home early." Could he say anything stupider? Home early? Why not, *I love you, Sam?* "I . . . I wasn't expecting you until tomorrow."

She froze, startled face pale in the moonlight. "I didn't see you there."

"Sorry." Mac muted the television. "I was eating." Since that night at the lab, she'd been gone, and he'd fallen into the habit of watching TV with dinner since Agent Anan had ordered him away from the hospital.

Sam nodded, closing the door and locking it. "It's over."

"I saw it on the news this morning. They threw the book at them It'll still be a few decades before any of them see daylight outside a barbed-wire fence. I would have lined them all against a wall with a firing squad out front."

She ran a hand across her face. Her lips pressed together as tears appeared in her eyes. "Emir . . . Emir wasn't there. They never found his body. The psychologists grilled me for a week, and now I'm not even sure what I saw. I thought he was there, but maybe it was a nightmare. Maybe all of this was a nightmare."

Mac sighed. "No one else saw Dr. Emir that night. I sat in on the interrogations with Altin."

"Everyone keeps telling me that. Marrins saw him. Maybe he kept the doctor secret from the rest of his team. Maybe they're lying."

"And you don't believe them?"

She shrugged. "I saw what I saw. What did they tell the court?"

"Marrins was part of an end-of-the-world sort of think group. Like preppers getting ready for zombies, but they never acted on it, just drank beer and talked about what they'd change. Some of the people were true anarchists, some just disgruntled and wanting a change, like Holt and Marrins.

"Late last year, Emir approached them and said he had a machine that could revolutionize the world. Holt said that originally, Emir promised them money, enough to buy back the Union from—and I quote— 'dirty foreign investors.'"

"That's not how constitutions work," Sam said.

"No, and Marrins was at least smart enough to figure that out. Emir told him about the device. For a long time, they thought it was only good for communicating. Marrins wrote an anti-Commonwealth manifesto in morose code to send back to the first machine."

She smiled bitterly. "And then we realized that the machine did more than that."

"Yeah." Mac sighed. "Holt was his second-in-command, along with Harley. I'm not sure why, but the others just took orders and didn't ask questions. Holt said they questioned Emir intensely about the machine before Marrins shot him—"

"But she didn't see Emir after that," Sam finished for him.

"Sam . . . I'm sorry." He gave her an apologetic grimace. There was nothing he could do to fix the situation. "For what it's worth, Agent Anan took my testimony, and the penny. He looked over our reports, all the autopsies. He believes us."

She shook her head. "One way or another, it's over. The machine's broken. There are not going to be any more extra people wandering around. I'm over it. I'm good." Another breathy sigh, and she forced a smile. "I need to go upstairs and pack, I have a flight leaving tomorrow at noon." She waved a purple envelope at him.

"Flight?" His heart raced. "Are you going to visit your parents?" The silence in the house was killing him. He missed her, wanted her back in his life. He'd been waiting for her to come home, to be with him, so they could have time to talk.

I love you, Sam.

"Not likely. My parents and I are no longer on speaking terms. But the bureau loves me. I've been transferred. The paperwork came in last week." She hiccuped, swallowing a cry. "I'm sorry. I meant to tell you. I just didn't know how."

She was leaving him. "Chicago?" Mac tried to keep the tone of hope out of his voice.

"Canaveral District in Florida. I'm reporting there to-morrow afternoon." Sam leaned against the door, look-ing at the stairs. Tears sparkled on her cheek. "I'm sorry."

"For what?"

"Dragging you into this?" Her voice was shaky. There was a laugh, soft and weepy. "I'm so sorry. Thank you. Just thinking about what he was going to do . . . I haven't slept well in weeks." She looked at the floor. "I'm the butt of every talk-show joke. People across the country are analyzing my life. I get letters, actual handwritten letters, telling me what a horrible person I am. A titty-show Web site sent me an invita-tion to pose for them. I feel so dirty."

"You aren't, Sam. Marrins was a manipulative bas-tard." And Mac wished he could shoot him again.

"I feel like I need a gun for a teddy bear."

He didn't know what to say. Mac rubbed his foot on Hoss's stomach. "You have us. I'm not much, but Hoss is good for security."

"And you do amazing rescues." Her laugh was brittle, but it was better than tears.

"Something like that." The tension eased from her shoulders. "But I have a once-a-year rule. You aren't allowed to get kidnapped for another twelve months, or you void my warranty."

The tears dried as a smile warmed her face. Sam licked her lips, distracting him. "Why Chicago?"

"What?"

"Why did you guess I was going to Chicago?"

"Oh, I have orders. I leave in three weeks. I was hoping I'd know someone there." He shrugged nonchalantly and reached for his bowl of chili.

Sam moved toward him. Her walk wasn't the confident, brisk stride that it had been. Her movements were tired, a little jerky, but she was smiling. "What are you going to do without me?" She ran a hand through his hair.

"I don't know." Mac leaned into her touch. "I love you." The words tumbled out without preamble.

She moved away. "No you don't."

"Sam." He stood up, following her to the stairs. "I love you."

"You love the idea of me." She wouldn't look him in the eyes. "You love that I'm there for you. You don't love me."

"I do."

She leaned across the banister, and her fingers tangled in his hair, the angel blessing the penitent. "You need to get away from me. Get out and meet people.

Eat dinner with someone other than me. When you get out there, you'll realize you don't. I wish you did, but I can't pretend you do."

Mac watched her go up the stairs and collapsed back into the couch. He ate mechanically, watching the TV and trying to bury the hundred and one emotions that fought for dominance. The stairs creaked under a light weight. Hoss raised his huge head and grunted. The dog's nubbin of a tail thrummed with excitement. Even in sweatpants and a faded T-shirt, she looked beautiful. It was his faded T-shirt, too, one from his army days.

"What are you watching?"

Mac twisted back to the TV, not quite sure. "Some old comedy. Slapstick, humorous confusion, and a happy ending. I have a weakness for happy endings."

Sam hugged herself. "I can't sleep. So . . . I . . . Can I watch with you?"

He nodded, and she sat down on the far side the couch, stopping to reach down and pat Hoss. Mac put his hand along the back of the couch, welcoming body language at its best.

Before the next commercial break, Sam was yawning, her head bobbing to her chest. "Go lie down," he said even though he didn't want her to go. Sam fell sideways, head finding his leg. His hand fell from the back of the couch to her stomach.

"Can I have a blanket?"

"Sure." Mac pulled the throw from the ottoman and draped it over her bare toes.

Sam caught his hand, pulling it back to her waist. "This is nice."

"Yeah. Nice." Long after she'd fallen asleep and he'd turned off the TV, Mac stayed awake. Guarding the only woman he'd ever loved from the darkness.

CHAPTER 30

> True love is this: to lift, to heal, to defend, to
> enable, to create. Love makes a person greater
> than the sum of their parts, and true love is ever
> unfailing.
>
> ~ Excerpt from *A Discourse of Broken Hearts*
> by Finne Mari 13–2071

Monday March 17, 2070
Florida District 8
Commonwealth of North America

Sam watched the EMT roll away the last of the lab-blast survivors. In her hand was the name tag of the last victim; Henry Troom wasn't walking out of this one. The police had pulled his plastic ID card out of the wall.

"Agent Rose?" The lab facilitator approached her cautiously. "I'm so sorry, why aren't they taking Troom out yet?"

"Because it's a crime scene, Dr. Morr, and because I can't allow anyone in there who doesn't have the proper security clearance. Someone will be here shortly," she lied.

Drenmann Labs was a major source of contention between Sam and her oversight agent at HQ in Orlando. Drenmann was a secure facility attached to NASA and sometimes used by the naval post and Patrick Air Force Base. All of which fell under the heading of Too Classified to Think About in Public and within the boundaries of Florida District 6.

Senior Agent Petrilli of District 6 had a full staff with ten full-time agents and two full medical examiners with class-four or higher security clearance.

Senior Agent Samantha Rose of Florida District 8—the Canaveral District—had one junior agent, an agreement with the local PD and coroner's office, and a bunch of retirees stretched along the space coast like beached albino whales. The crime rate here didn't justify keeping a larger CBI force. Drenmann Labs was the exception; it needed a full-time Marine Corps guard.

She stepped into a small conference room and locked the door behind her before calling the main office.

"Junior Agent Dan Edwin speaking, how may I direct your call, sir or ma'am?"

"Hi, Edwin, it's Rose."

"Agent Rose!" Her junior agent's voice cracked. He was an excitable puppy of a person. Sometimes it seemed like a miracle he didn't jump up and lick her face.

"Did you get in touch with Petrilli yet? I need that coroner."

"Petrilli has one out on vacation, and the other is elbow deep in something. I didn't get details."

"That's not what I want to hear, Edwin. What I need to hear you say is, 'Yes, ma'am. Your medical examiner will be there in twenty minutes.' Can you do that for me?"

"Yes, ma'am. I called around, and there was a conference in Orlando. One of the doctors has clearance, so I had him pulled off the plane. He should arrive shortly."

"Orlando is over an hour away," Sam said with a sigh. "Good try though."

"Not to worry, ma'am. The air force had a set of fighters doing a refuel at the airport, so I commissioned one of them to bring the ME to the local airfield, and there's a car waiting. They should be touching down now, ma'am."

Sam rubbed the bridge of her nose. "You scrambled a fighter jet?"

"You said it was urgent, ma'am."

"Tell me, Edwin, have you ever heard the term overkill?"

"Yes, ma'am."

Outside, Sam heard the whine of police sirens coming closer. "What kind of car did you have waiting for our kidnapped ME, Edwin?" She had a sinking suspicion that she already knew.

"I called the PD, ma'am. You did say fast."

"Thank you, Edwin. Remind me to note your diligence and willingness to think outside the box in your next performance review." Sam hung up the phone and shook her head. Excitable little pup. If he hadn't been a six-foot-ten Viking with curly red hair and an eager smile, she might have broken down and used her private nickname for him out loud.

Sam walked back into the main lobby as the ME walked in with police escort. Six-foot-something in shiny black dress shoes, dark hair, muscular, wrap-around sunglasses, and wearing a thick black trench coat over black slacks and a black shirt. Wherever he was flying to, it wasn't in the South, where early-spring temperatures were already making it shorts and skimpy dress weather.

"Dr. Morr," Sam called, motioning for the facilitator to come over. "Our ME has arrived. Do you want me to go back with him, or would you like to be there?"

"Um." Dr. Morr twisted a handkerchief in his hands. "Is it likely to be, uh, organic?"

"Most deaths are. But it would help us immensely if you could look over the scene and comment on the position of equipment, maybe tell us if anything is missing." The doctor paled. "If you'd like to wait until after the body is moved, however, that's fine."

ABOUT THE AUTHOR

LIANA BROOKS is a full-time mom and a part-time author who would rather slay dragons than balance the checkbook any day. Alas, Adventuring Hero is not a recognized course of study in American universities. She graduated from college with a bachelor's degree in marine biology, a husband, and no job prospects in her field. To fill the free time, she started writing. Now her books are read all over the world (she says she's big in Canada) and she's free to explore the universe one page at a time. You can find Liana on the Web at www.lianabrooks.com, on Twitter as @LianaBrooks, or on Facebook under the same name.

Discover great authors, exclusive offers, and more at hc.com.

Dr. Morr nodded.

"Agent Rose," a familiar voice said. "You are the only woman I know who would scramble a fighter jet just to see me."

"What can I say, Agent MacKenzie? I wanted to show you my corpse."

THE END